ADMISSION

Jean Hanff Korelitz was born and raised in New York City and graduated from Dartmouth College and Clare College, Cambridge. She is the author of the novels A JURY OF HER PEERS, THE SABBATHDAY RIVER, THE WHITE ROSE and ADMISSION, as well as INTERFERENCE POWDER, a novel for middle-grade readers, and THE PROPERTIES OF BREATH, a collection of poetry. A new novel, YOU SHOULD HAVE KNOWN, will be published early in 2014. A film version of ADMISSION starring Tina Fey, Paul Rudd and Lily Tomlin was released in 2013.

Praise for ADMISSION

"An intimate tale . . . [A book] you can't put down."

— *O, The Oprah Magazine*

"Challenges readers to grasp the importance of what we admit to ourselves."

— *Chicago Tribune*

"A skillfully subvers . . . nal universal by connecting her char . . . concern us all: how we will educate . . ."

— *Philadelphia Inquirer*

"An intelligently written, thoughtful novel . . . The realism is impressive . . . Korelitz has created a complicated heroine who is nonetheless easy to love, and readers . . . will be pulling for Portia just as powerfully as she roots for the applicants she falls in love with every year."

— *Christian Science Monitor*

"A great read . . . a reminder of what it's like to read a book by a writer whose style calls attention not to itself but to the story it tells."

— *Arizona Republic*

———————————

ALSO BY JEAN HANFF KORELITZ

The White Rose

The Sabbathday River

A Jury of Her Peers

ADMISSION

JEAN HANFF KORELITZ

faber and faber

For Ann and Burt Korelitz

First published in the USA in 2010 by
Grand Central Publishing
Hachette Book Group
237 Park Avenue
New York, NY 10017

First published in the UK in 2013 by
Faber and Faber Limited
Bloomsbury House
74–77 Great Russell Street
London WC1B 3DA

Printed and bound in the UK by CPI Group (UK) Ltd, Croydon CR0 4YY

A CIP record for this book is
available from the British Library

ISBN 978-0-571-30909-2

PART

I

TRAVEL SEASON

When I think of Princeton I think of many images:
ivy-covered buildings, students arguing philosophy in the dining hall,
shadows in the Yard. It is truly a great privilege to attend
a school like Princeton.

CHAPTER ONE

THE GOOD NEWS OF PRINCETON

The flight from Newark to Hartford took no more than fifty-eight minutes, but she still managed to get her heart broken three times. This was a feat at once pathetic and, bizarrely, something of an underachievement, Portia thought, making a painful note on the reader's card of an academically unadmittable Rhode Island girl and shoving the folder back into her bag. Any of her colleagues, she thought ruefully, might have had their hearts broken by twice as many applicants in the same amount of time.

In the real world, of course, Portia was no slower a reader than anyone else. She could fully scan *The New York Times* while waiting in line for her habitual (and necessary) Americano at Small World Coffee, half a block from the FitzRandolph Gate of Princeton University. She had even, once, completed Vikram Seth's *A Suitable Boy* during a weeklong visit to her mother in Vermont (when, admittedly, the whole point had been to evade Susannah, especially when she wanted to talk). Fifteen hundred pages in seven days—not too shabby. But she was well aware of her reputation as the slowest reader in Princeton's Office of Admission (singular, *nota bene*—not plural), and she probably deserved it. With an application open before her, Portia could almost feel herself decelerate, parsing the sentences and correcting the grammar, fixing the spelling, rereading to make sure she at least knew what they'd managed to say, if not what they'd meant to say, even as she took the temperature of her anxiety at falling behind, because she couldn't stop herself from lingering, lingering, lingering…on the kids.

She wasn't supposed to think of them as kids, she knew that. Few of them sounded like kids, they were trying so hard not to be young. They were ventriloquizing the attorneys they thought they wanted to be, or the neuroscientists, or the statesmen. They were trying to sound as though they already worked at Morgan Stanley, or toiled at a feeding station in Darfur, or were due in surgery. But so often the newness of them, the flux of their emerging selves, would poke through the essays or the recommendations, stray references to how Jimmy had grown since his difficult freshman year or Jimmy's own regrettable use of the word *awesome*. Their confidence was sometimes so hollow, it practically echoed off the page. They were all so young, even the ones who had already seen so much.

In this batch, on this brief flight, already there had been a wizened seventeen-year-old who lived with her younger brother in an apartment in South Boston, their parents back home in Taiwan. She wrote of the microwavable meals she prepared for her bisected family and the bureaucracy she had learned to manipulate for herself, the weekly phone calls from Mom, who had never been able to attend a parent-teacher conference, being unable to speak English and, incidentally, on the other side of the planet, but wasn't it worth it? Because she had six AP scores of 5 and four more exams still to be taken? Because she was first in her class of four hundred, with a very realistic chance of getting into a first-tier college and achieving her dream of becoming a doctor? And the boy from Holyoke whose mother had left her two oldest children to cross the border for her day job in a medical supply factory and her night job at Wendy's, whose father was described as "Unknown/No Information," who was a physics whiz and captain of the soccer team and All-State, who was applying not just for admission to Princeton, but for admission to America. And this last, from a girl in Greenwich, Connecticut, who was smart enough to know that she wasn't smart enough, only just very, very smart, and wrote with preemptive defeat about her hospital internship and the inspiration of her older brother, who had survived childhood cancer to attend law school. Smart enough to know about, or at least imagine, the ones she would be compared with, who had been handed so much less than she, and done so much more with what they had, while the children of privilege were penalized for having been fortunately born, comfortably raised, and excellent in all of the ordinary ways. Sometimes those were the ones who got to Portia most of all.

It was a sparsely occupied flight, of course; if it hadn't been, if there were, for example, a businessman or grandmother or—worst of all—high school–age kid within sight of her seat, she would never have extracted from her bag and opened, and then studied, the contents of these very private, very freighted files. Instinctively, Portia closed the folders whenever the single, tight-lipped attendant cruised the aisle, glancing at people's laps. She dropped her white plastic cup of tepid coffee into the attendant's proffered garbage bag or made the appropriate noises when he said they were ten minutes from Bradley, holding her place with a finger as she held the folders shut. This was the unwritten code of her profession and Portia's own inclination for secrecy, neither one more than the other, really, as if the numbers, letters, declarations, and aspirations within each file outweighed the secrets of governments or espionage cells—which, to the teenagers they represented, they surely did. Outside the window, beyond the ridge of the descending wing, the autumn trees of New England sharpened: electric red-and-yellow branches and spiky green pines divided by the highway. This trip, late in the season for its kind, would be her final airing before the approaching cataclysm of paperwork. In this post–Early Decision era, there were no longer any foothills in Princeton's admissions calendar; there was only flat land, then Everest, and the twenty orange folders in her bag were merely the first-from-the-gate forerunners of the onslaught to come. When that bell curve hit its apex in a month's time, she and her co-workers would simply disappear into their offices or their homes, emerging only sporadically until midwinter, before finally crawling out the other side, pale and gasping from beneath all that aspiration, all that desperation, in April.

But today, this brilliant New England day, would be calm seas before the storm. Today, Portia would preach the good news of Princeton to the preemptively converted, and with a glad heart, because at long last she was here in New England and shot of the West Coast, in whose intense, teeming schools she had toiled for the past five years. She had been waiting for the New England district to open up, waiting for her colleague Rand (actually Randolph) Cumming to vacate the helm, something he had shown no inclination to do. Rand had never once set foot beyond the charmed circle of venerated and wealthy educational institutions, not since the day his parents dropped him off at a certain tradition-draped boarding school (as, Portia liked to imagine, a howling babe, "untimely ripped" from his mother's breast). In due course, he had swanned off to Princeton (BA) and Yale (JD) and then, as if the whole notion of practicing law had been merely a whim, straight back to the (literally) ivy-covered walls of his alma mater's Office of Admission, where he spent the next two decades tending the very prep school garden from which he had sprung and becoming, more or less, the very personification of what most people imagined an Ivy League admissions officer to be: bow-tied, well groomed, class ringed, and always ready to be of service to an old classmate or a classmate's chum, whose fine young son was a rising senior with a letter in squash and a winning way with a sailboat.

Rand was, in fact, one of those boulders around which the waters of Ivy League admissions had parted, leaving him in a wake of soaring academic standards and dizzying diversity. He had bristled through every clank of progress, every painful adjustment in policy that aimed to transform the university from its dunderheaded Jazz Age uniformity to its rightful place as the best of all possible universities for the best of all possible students. The new Princeton, so wondrous and varied, so...multicolored, was not his Princeton, and his suffering was evident. He was an angry man, a furious man, beneath his veneer of irreproachable manners.

He had been waiting himself, Portia supposed, for the retirement of Martin Quilty, his chief antagonist in the struggle of tradition versus merit and the dean who had brought coeducation and surging minority enrollment, so that he could begin the slow but necessary work of turning back the clock; but when that blessed event finally arrived, Rand had found himself passed over in the most offensive way possible. He soldiered on for a year or two, making his opinion on just about everything known to the new dean whenever possible, and then, quite suddenly, the previous May, he had left—completing the circle of his unadventurous journey by taking the post of college counselor at his very own prep school.

And there, Portia knew, he was destined to prove as irritating a voice in her ear as when he'd occupied the office just down the hall from her.

But it was worth it to have New England. She had wanted New England for years, coveting the post as she'd watched Rand Cumming glad-hand his cronies at Groton and Concord and Taft. She had considered asking for it whenever there was a district reshuffle (Rand had seemed oddly immune to these.) And she had made sure she was the first one in Clarence Porter's office to ask for it—Clarence being the new dean in question—when the opportunity finally arose. Not *only* (she explained) because she herself was a product of Massachusetts, New Hampshire, and Vermont—in roughly that order—and not *only* because her mother, now a Vermonter, was getting on in years (hint, hint) and she would be personally grateful for the opportunity to drop in on her more often, but also because the New England district featured the kind of boarding school interaction she hadn't much experienced in the California-Oregon-Hawaii-Washington-Alaska applicant pool. That in particular was a deficit in her experience, a deficit unbecoming an admissions officer, and that embarrassed her. Serving Princeton to her utmost ability called for fluency with its traditional feeder schools: the Grotons and Choates and Andovers, whose top students the university had been cherry-picking for centuries. She had reminded Clarence of the miles she had logged for Princeton, not only along the coasts and valleys of California, but, before that, along the empty highways of the Midwest, plucking genius 4-H'ers and ambitious dreamers from the Great Plains. She had personally recruited the Inuit girl from Sitka, Alaska, who'd won Princeton's sole Rhodes scholarship last year. She had found Brian Jack, homeschooled (self-schooled) in some barely existent Oregon town, and made sure he chose them over Yale. (His senior thesis, a novel, had just been published by Knopf, showering Princeton with the fairy dust of reflected literary glory.) She'd been about to start in on the fact that her West Coast region had boasted the highest percentage of female engineer admits for all five years she'd had it when he stopped her and offered her the job. And a good thing, too. She couldn't have supported any claim of credit for those last admits, not really. There were simply more female engineers in the heavily immigrant population she'd overseen.

"I was going to give it to you anyway," Clarence had said, barely looking up from the call log on his desk. "I thought you needed a little shaking up."

A little shaking up. She hadn't quite engaged with that at the time—it had seemed more advisable not to snatch defeat from the jaws of victory. A hearty thank-you, a formally written letter of delighted acceptance later that day, and some unsolicited advice with regard to her replacement—she had done what was expected without ever returning to this nagging, vaguely shameful moment. The exchange had not been very satisfying, in any case. There was a kind of detachment to it, given that Clarence's mind had been more consumed by the call sheet on his desktop than by the very sincere and well-phrased request of his very present employee. His very competent employee, who had never asked for anything before or indicated in any way that she was in need of anything, required any concession or support, and was generally not in the habit of calling attention to herself. Portia had never, not ever, thought of herself as someone who needed shaking up, and it appalled her to realize that he, apparently, had.

Clarence had come from the Yale Admissions Office, a fact more than a few Princeton alumni were still—rather comically—grumbling about. Before he had been an admissions officer he had been a professor of African-American history at Yale, in fact the head of that fractious department, where he had taught the music, culture, literature, and lore of the Delta, an immaculate gentleman in full Savile Row regalia holding forth on Howlin' Wolf, Leadbelly, and Blind Willie McTell. He had an ever present silken handkerchief in the breast pocket of his beautifully cut jackets and a silken voice that rumbled an accent north of the islands and west of the United Kingdom. Before an audience he was magic, his beautiful voice equally calming to the jittery freshmen at orientation and the alternately fawning and preemptively furious parent groups he addressed. He could, better than any admissions officer Portia had ever worked with, soothe an irate alumni parent whose child Princeton had turned down, and unlike every other admissions officer Portia had ever known, he was never seen hauling around great sacks of folders but seemed to be able to retrieve an astounding range of data from memory. His office, too, was always serenely uncluttered, with a perennial vase of calla lilies on the corner of his desk and a rather nice Asher Durand on loan from the Princeton University Art Museum on the wall behind him. It was a far cry from the mixed-up-files cacophony the room had been when it belonged to Martin Quilty. (Back then, only Martin's assistant could guess in which pile or holding bin something might be stashed.) Portia, who was nothing if not supremely well organized herself, could only aspire to the minimalist mastery of her new boss. Theirs was not a warm relationship, obviously. But she did appreciate the calm. And she did appreciate that Asher Durand.

After they landed, Portia made her way into the terminal, pulling her small suitcase behind her. There was a real chill in the building, and she held the lapels of her tweed coat together at the throat. She wore one of the outfits she now rotated for these visits: a synchronicity of tweed and cashmere and brown leather boots, überschoolgirl, Sylvia Plath minus the pearls and plus the sunglasses, but comfortably of the world she was about to enter. The previous May, on her first visits to New England prep schools, she'd learned that they had rituals of their own, with more graces and ceremony than she'd been used to in, for example, a Bay Area public school. Typically, some sort of tea-and-cookies affair followed her presentation, which took place in a slightly shabby, generations-old salon, under the watchful portraits of (white, male) alumni. The first time she'd been ushered into one of these receptions—at Andover, as it happened—she'd experienced a discomforting moment, a kind of self-detected fraudulence—clad as she was in her basic black jeans and careless sweater. No one had ever discussed wardrobe with her or suggested she might be letting down the institution with her evident sartorial imperviousness, but the plain surprise in the eyes of the college adviser, the teachers, and even a couple of the students had sent the message home effectively enough. Later that day she'd dropped nearly a thousand dollars at an Ann Taylor outlet on the way to Milton Academy.

Portia picked up her car in the rental lot and took off directly, heading north on 91 to familiar lands. When she had learned to drive as a teenager, Bradley Airport had been at the outer edge of her home range, which extended this far south and as far as the Vermont border in the other direction. The highway was a spine supporting the breadth of New England. It was a part of the world that held firmly to its past, and how could it do otherwise? Indian attacks and iconic American furniture. Austere family portraits and most of the earliest groves of academe, Shakers and Quakers and colonial unrest, the place where the essential idea of American-ness was forged, its very filaments dug deep into the rocky earth. Growing up here, she had sometimes had the sense of walking over bones.

Portia pulled into the school parking lot and left her car. She reported first to the well-marked Admissions Office and was directed to college counseling in a brick building on the quadrangle. She had known many Deerfield students as an undergraduate at Dartmouth, where they had seemed to flow seamlessly into the culture of the college, retaining their friends, their rustic athleticism, even their prep school sweats (which were, handily, identical in color to Dartmouth's). Looking around at the fit and good-looking kids on the walkways, she was struck by the stasis of this vision, a self-replenishing gene pool bubbling up to fill these grand and lovely buildings. These kids were interchangeable with her own college classmates of two decades earlier: the same hale complexions and down jackets and laden backpacks, the same voices of greeting. They were sons of Deerfield, identical to the smooth-faced footballers in the sepia photographs she passed in the entryway of the administration building. Oddly, even the Asian or African-American faces did not overly thwart the general vision of blondness and fair skin.

At the college-counseling office, Portia introduced herself. The secretary, a pale woman with a noticeable blink, jolted to her feet. "Princeton! Mr. Roden's expecting you."

She had spoken with William Roden on the phone earlier in the week, mainly to assure him that she had directions, needed no overnight accommodation, had no special requirements — museum tickets? a room at the Deerfield Inn? — that might make her visit to Deerfield complete. He seemed surprised to learn that she had grown up not terribly far away, and almost distressed — as if her local status, her presumed education outside the prep school bubble, might predispose her, and by extension Princeton, against his kids; but he didn't quite articulate this. Now, bounding from his office, he looked entirely as she'd imagined him: a decade her senior, with a growing middle and fleeing hair, cheeks disarmingly pink.

"Ms. Nathan," he crowed, hand outstretched. "So glad to see you."

"It's so nice to be back," she told him, shaking his hand. "It all looks exactly the same."

"Yes," he said. "You grew up nearby."

"Northampton High School," she told him, anticipating his next question. "I used to play soccer here. I'm afraid we didn't stand a chance against Deerfield," she said indulgently, though her team — she remembered perfectly well — had in fact more than held its own.

"Yes, we're very proud of our athletics. Our students train very hard. And I don't know if we still used the old gym at that time." He was too polite to ask her age. "The new gym opened in '95. You should have a look while you're here."

She didn't need much, she told him as he took her back outside. They were going to a meeting room in the library, a modern building designed to harmonize with the older structures around the quadrangle. Inside, he led her into the librarians' lounge and brought her some coffee in a Styrofoam cup. "Starbucks hasn't come to Deerfield yet," he told her apologetically. "We do our best to carry on."

"I totally understand," she said, smiling. "I'd like to show a DVD, if I may. And I've brought some applications. If they're on the fence about applying, sometimes it makes a difference if we get the application into their hands."

"I don't think you'll have very many on the fence," Roden said. "You had, what, twenty-five? twenty-six? from us last year. I expect you'll get about the same this year."

"That's wonderful," said Portia. "We love Deerfield students."

"They are remarkable," he agreed. "Now, let's see about the DVD."

The DVD, in fact, was identical to the version on the Web site, but Portia had found that showing it to a group had an interesting effect. It made some students dreamy, others morose and uncomfortable, as if all those iron tigers and grand neo-Gothic buildings fringed by rippling ivy were a taunting Shangri-la. Kids got withdrawn or determined, she found, and while it nearly always came down to what was actually contained in the applications, there had also been times when a student had made such an impression, in just this kind of setting, that she had followed up and pushed things along. Just as Portia retained that little trill of excitement every time she opened a folder, so she still relished taking the temperature of a group like this. Undoubtedly, there were going to be future admits here. It was always intriguing to try to pick them out.

He took her DVD to the meeting room and left her with her terrible coffee, and Portia used the moment to review the numbers: in five years, 124 applications, 15 admits, 11 attends. Without doubt, Deerfield was a serious player in the construction of any Princeton class, and at a great school like this she wouldn't need to muster much of a sales pitch. On the contrary, she could walk into a room full of Deerfield seniors and tell them the university was a hole, the entire state of New Jersey sucked, and a Princeton degree was a poor return for the roughly $128,000 in tuition they'd have to come up with, and she probably wouldn't lose a single applicant (though she would undoubtedly lose her job).

"Is this a class period?" asked Portia when Roden came back for her.

"Yes, but we let seniors out. It's important."

Portia suppressed a smile and followed him into the meeting room: midcentury portraits of steely masters overlooking Williamsburg sofas and wing chairs. She didn't doubt that Princeton's admissions office was of vital importance to Deerfield. In spite of the laudable philosophy of the institution—the education of young minds or something of that nature—college placement was the raison d'être of every prep school, and the annual dispersal of students to the Ivy League and other selective colleges functioned like a stock market within their world; a prep school that found itself unable to place its students well would find itself unable to attract students in the first place. Indeed, these economically symbiotic relationships were so long-standing that they had attained the filmy gleam of tradition, Portia thought, allowing Roden to take her leather bag. But it was far, far more complicated now. And though there would undoubtedly always be Princeton students who hailed from Deerfield and Andover and Harvard-Westlake and Lawrenceville, it had also become harder and harder for those applicants to get in, a fact known to every single student waiting for her to begin her presentation.

The kids sat on the couches and on the floor, some perched on the window seats or leaning against the walls. They seemed to avoid the wing chairs, as if these were consecrated to adults. They smiled nervously at her or did not smile (in case it was a bad thing to smile, in case it made them seem too eager or insecure); then, thinking better of that, thinking that it might make more sense to seem friendly and affable, the ones who had resolutely not smiled began to grin. One bold boy in a green Deerfield Crew sweatshirt stepped into her path and introduced himself.

"I'm almost finished with my application," he said, squeezing her hand a little too tightly. "Just waiting on my physics teacher. I wish you still had Early Decision. I'm totally committed."

"This is Matt Boyce," Roden said helpfully. "Both his parents went to Princeton."

"Yeah, we're total Princeton," Matt Boyce said eagerly. "I was, like, wrapped in an orange blanket."

"I'll look forward to reading your application," said Portia with practiced warmth, noting the scowls of displeasure around the room as this exchange was observed.

Roden was deflecting other students who'd been emboldened by their classmate and held up his hand as they stood to catch her eye. "Later," she heard him say quietly. "Wait till later."

Later meant the inevitable reception, she thought. More bad coffee, but this time with Oreos. And full-throttle adolescent anxiety.

"Okay, settle down," Roden said. "Everyone..." He trailed off, eyeing a too-cool-to-care-about-college-admissions trio on one of the sofas. "Hunter, is there someplace else you need to be?"

"Absolutely no, Mr. Roden," the boy said, not giving an inch.

"Then let's please quiet down and give Ms. Nathan our attention. She's come a long way to be here with us today, so let's give her a warm Deerfield welcome."

Energetic applause. Portia stepped to the front of the room and gave her audience a swift appraisal. At least sixty of them. It was going to be a tough year for these kids.

"Hello," she told them. "I'm really pleased to be here, because I grew up nearby and I love coming back. Especially this time of year. Actually, any time of year except for mud season." This got a laugh. The tension slipped in the room, just slightly. "I'm a great believer in visual aids," she said, "so I'm going to show you a little film about Princeton. Takes about sixteen minutes. Some of you might already have seen it on our Web site, so you can just amuse yourselves. Work on your college essays or something."

Nervous laughter in the room, but they settled in. No one worked on their college essays. They watched, instead, the parade of bright kids through the bright courtyards and leafy glens of the campus and listened to the newly minted Princetonians on the screen speak about their freshman seminars, their adventures of the mind and spirit. "Each of you," intoned Clarence in an address to the freshman class, filmed a couple of years ago in Richardson Auditorium, "is the kind of person your classmates came here to meet." The students were admonished to play with their fancies, to step beyond their comfort zones and take the chance of learning something truly unsuspected about themselves. They were fantastic, articulate, adorable. And when it was over, Portia was not really surprised to see two girls wiping away tears.

"Okay," she said as the lights flicked on. "Lots of great schools out there. Lots of places to get a first-rate education. So why Princeton? What's so great about us?"

"You've got Toni Morrison," said a girl with a long red braid, seated on the floor in front of the foremost couch.

"Okay. And twelve other Nobel laureates. Thirteen, if you count Woodrow Wilson." She smiled. "But who's counting? We're not the only university with an outstanding faculty."

"What about Albert Einstein?"

"Alas," she said, "we no longer have Einstein."

"No," the boy said, chagrined, "I mean . . . he *was* there."

"Well, more or less. He was at the institute, not the university proper."
Due to the small matter of endemic academic anti-Semitism at the time.
But why rain on her own parade? "Here's my point," said Portia. "At Princeton, we're all about the undergraduate. Yes, we have graduate programs.
Graduate students are an important part of our community. But our professors are dedicated to the undergraduate. Now, you can go to a university with marquee-name faculty, and you can park yourself in a very large
lecture theater and have your mind blown by an hourlong talk on Milton
or Buñuel or fractals, or whatever it is you're into, but you may never get
closer to that lecturer than the first row of the lecture hall. And for many
students, that's just fine. But the ones we're looking for want more than
that. If you're the kind of student who wants more than that, we hope
you'll apply."

They laughed uncomfortably.

"Look, there is no mystery about this," she said bluntly. "There is no
secret formula or hidden agenda. I'm going to tell you right now what we're
looking for. We're looking for intellectual passion. What it's for—that's
secondary. We are looking for the student who is so jazzed about...*whatever*...that he or she can't wait to get to Princeton and find out everything
there is to know about it. And that's, by and large, not going to be the
student who's content to sit in the lecture theater and take her notes, and
take her exams, and collect her grade, and move on. We're looking for the
students who are looking for our faculty."

Now there were expressions of real dismay as well. She wondered if
she'd been too strong.

"Does this mean," she said, "that every Princeton undergraduate is a
genius? A prodigy? Absolutely not. But what makes Princeton such an
exciting place is that it's an environment where people care about ideas.
We have a faculty who are doing work they're passionate about, and every
fall, about twelve hundred bright and excited new students turn up to meet
them and argue with them and learn from them. And that makes them
happy." Portia shrugged. "Intellectuals...can be strange." She laughed.
"But sometimes that's what I think admissions really is: the care and feeding of the Princeton faculty. We procure fresh young minds to keep them
busy, and I have to tell you, we're very good at it."

She told them a story—true story—related to her some years before
at a History Department party. The man who'd told her this was a post-

colonialist in a limp suit, who'd had a student he was quite fond of, a sophomore from Pittsburgh. The student had a twin brother at another Ivy league school, which she naturally refrained from naming, who was also majoring in history. One day, the professor had been in his office at around ten in the morning when this student arrived, his identical brother in tow.

"This is Peter," said the student.

The Princeton student, whose name was Patrick, and Peter both took seats in the historian's office, and they talked. They talked about being twins and having twins (the professor had fraternal girls, so physically different that they barely looked like siblings). They talked about Peter's growing interest in cold war Europe and his recent class on the economic history of the Baltic states. They considered a couple of evolving ideas for Patrick's junior paper, compared and contrasted the schools' football teams, and discussed the relative merits of Bent Spoon and Thomas Sweet ice creams (the brothers had already embarked on a highly scientific study). They took a run at Pennsylvania Democratic politics and the failure of the Clinton health plan and the various repellent aspects of Karl Rove and the Blair scandal at *The New York Times*. They talked about the professor's daughters' obsession with Harry Potter and the twins' remembered literary obsessions from their own childhood, and they spent a good long while going over the paper the professor was readying for the AHA in two weeks, about the amateur photographs taken by British troops in the Boer War. And then finally, *finally*, the professor had looked at his watch, seen that it was nearly three o'clock, and announced that he had to go and pick up his children at school. Whereupon the twins burst into hysterical laughter, and Patrick turned to his brother and said, "See? I told you. I *told* you."

They had had a bet, the Princeton brother reported, when the two had at last stopped high-fiving each other. "Peter said I was always jerking him around when I talked about conversations I'd had with my professors. He said he never got past the TA in any of his classes, and he'd never be able to just knock on a professor's door and sit down and have a conversation. I said I did it all the time, so he bet me. Five hours! I have to say, you surpassed even my expectations. But don't worry." Patrick laughed. "I'll donate my winnings to charity."

"You ought to donate your winnings to *me*," said the history professor, but he wasn't really angry. In fact, there was definite pride in his face as he told this story, and Portia had happily purloined the tale.

"I'm telling you this," she said, "because I want you to think carefully about what you really want out of the next four years. Ivy League institutions may be wrapped up in one big ribbon, but these are very different institutions, offering very different experiences. Don't just apply to these eight schools because they created an athletic conference in 1954. You might be happiest in a huge university, or in a little college. You might want to see an entirely different part of the country when you go to university, or even a different part of the world. And let's not forget, some people just don't want to work that hard in college. They want to go, learn a little bit, play a little Frisbee, and get a halfway decent job when it's over. Not everyone is looking for the kind of intellectual environment Princeton is offering, and if you're not, I urge you to save yourself the effort involved in applying, not to mention the application fee. And I urge you to spare us the very distressing task of having to reject your application. Please be honest with yourselves, because this is about your well-being, and your goals, and your life."

She stopped there. They were all somber, of course. A few of them seemed actively engaged in some sort of internal catechism: *Because Mom wants me to? Because Dad wants me to? Because it never occurred to any of us that I wouldn't? Because I just want to get in, and I'll worry about all this Deep Thoughts crap in my own damn time.*

"Okay," said Portia. "I'm sure you have questions. I'm here to help. Is there something you'd like to know about the university? Or about admissions?"

It didn't take long. This was why she'd come, after all, not the promotional film or the save-us-all-the-trouble lecture or the cute story about the kid who'd never talked to a professor. They wanted in. They wanted the tricks, the secrets, the strategies. They wanted to maximize and package. They wanted to know what they should write their essays about, and if a 720 on the math SAT was good enough, and was it better to take six APs and get some 4's or three APs and get all 5's?

"Are the essays important?" said a girl with fearful eyes behind thick glass. "I mean, if you have good grades and good scores?"

"At Princeton, the essays are very important. I think perhaps more so than at other colleges. You should think carefully about them, and spend time on them."

"But," the girl said plaintively, "some people aren't that good writers. I mean, some people are good at other things."

"Oh, we understand that," Portia said. She nodded appreciatively at Roden, who was bringing her a chair. "We know that not everyone's equally gifted as a writer. We're not expecting every student to have the same fluency with language, and we know that people are intelligent in different ways. But as far as we're concerned, you've had about seventeen years to write your application essays." Predictably, the kids exchanged looks of horror. "Oh, you've been busy. Part of those seventeen years was probably spent, I don't know, spitting up and learning to ride a two-wheeler. You've been doing your homework and going to camp, or maybe working on your Facebook profile." There was a ripple of sheepish acknowledgment through the room. "But the fact is, you've had time to think about how you want to use these brief opportunities on the application, and that's how you should think of them: as opportunities. What are the most important things you need to tell us about yourself? *How* do you want to tell us those things? If you decide that you want to squander an essay declaring your undying devotion to the color blue, or your love for your childhood goldfish Fluffy, well, I'm going to wonder if you really have very much to say. On the other hand, there are so many things we want to know about you, and with the exception of your recommendations, this is just about the only way we're going to find out. We want to know what makes you tick, what gets you out of bed in the morning. If you love to play sports, we want to know why. If your favorite subject is math, we want to know why. If you can't stand biology, make a case for it. Tell us about it. We want to know about the people who have influenced you and the way you feel about our leaders and our national policies. We're interested in your thoughts on religion and even popular culture. Basically, we're interested in just about everything."

She turned to the fearful girl, who did not seem at all comforted. Portia sighed.

"And as far as the writing itself, again, not everyone has a natural, flowing, literary style. We understand this. But on the other hand, with seventeen years to write your essays, you've certainly had enough time to make sure you've made proper use of grammar, and that every single word is spelled correctly. Not because mistakes will tell us you're unintelligent. I freely admit that most of us in the adult world rely heavily on our computer spell-check programs! But a spelling or grammatical mistake in your application means that you haven't cared enough to make sure there aren't any mistakes. And that does mean something to us."

"You hear that?" Roden said. "Now you know why I'm always on your case about this."

"It isn't a timed exam, after all," Portia said. "You know, you might make an error in the middle of an SAT essay. It's not a disaster. Anyone can butcher the English language when the clock is ticking. But with your essays, you *have* time, so take the time to go over them. You might catch something, and be really glad you did."

"Any other dumb, avoidable mistakes?" Roden said. "Pay attention, everybody."

"Okay." She smiled. "A few. Please don't write us a long, rapturous essay about how much you want to attend Yale. You'd be surprised," she said when they laughed. "It happens quite a lot. The cut-and-paste function on your computer makes it easy to declare undying love for any number of colleges simultaneously. Unfortunately, it also makes it easy to slip up. I've read essays telling me why the applicant feels he is perfect for Stanford, Duke, Harvard, USC, you name it. You know, we get that you're applying to more than one college. We understand the kind of pressure you're under. But again, just take the time to make sure you're ready to seal that envelope. Or, in the case of the common application, or the online Princeton application, before you hit Send. Okay?"

They nodded. Some of them were scribbling notes.

"Another thing. Please don't mount a campaign. There's a reason we ask for two recommendations from teachers, plus an optional recommendation from someone who might shed light on another aspect of who you are. There's very little we can learn from four of your teachers that we couldn't have learned from two, and just multiply those extra letters by eighteen thousand and you can understand why we're going to get a bit annoyed if you ask everyone you've ever known to send along a testimonial. And think carefully about whom you want writing for you, and make sure they know you well enough to speak knowledgeably about who you are. And please, don't bombard us with extras. A recording of your instrumental work or some slides of your art, that's great. And as you probably know, we send these submissions to our departments for evaluation, so you don't have to worry about a tone-deaf person like me passing judgment on the quality of your Chopin. If you've written fiction or play the bassoon, by all means send it along. But hold off on the cookies. I won't deny that we eat them," she said, smiling. "But they don't help our waistlines and they won't help your applications."

They looked, she thought, oddly bereft, as if they had secretly taken comfort in the notion of baking cookies for the admissions officers, and now this option had been rudely stolen from them. It was an illusion, of course. These kids were far too sophisticated to try something so crass.

"But here's the main thing," Portia told them seriously. "The cardinal rule is: Tell the truth. You may say to yourself, They can't possibly check every single fact in every single application. And you know what? You're right. We can't. And we shouldn't have to. Because Princeton has an honor code, and we expect honor from the very first moment of your relationship with us. If you lie about your record, will we find out? Probably. And when we do, I can promise you that bad things will happen. Does anyone remember a little situation we had about ten years ago? This is probably too far back for them," she said, looking over at Roden.

"Johann something," he said immediately.

"Yes. Before my time, too, actually, but we admitted a student who wrote eloquently about his life as a shepherd out on the high prairie. How when the little sheep were asleep at night he took out his copy of *War and Peace* and read by the light of the stars, and how he wanted to study Freud as a philosopher, and write nonfiction with John McPhee. Only there was very little nonfiction about him. One day during his sophomore year, a student from Cornell recognized him at a football game. They were from the same hometown, it turned out. In Florida, which last time I checked didn't have much in the way of prairie." The kids laughed, but uncertainly. They were not quite certain whom the joke was on. Not that they really cared, as long as it wasn't them.

"He had a record for mail fraud, and an outstanding warrant, and he was thirty-something years old. So he had to drop out of Princeton and go straight to jail. Bad for him and certainly bad for us, but how could we have known? There is ample opportunity for fraud, as Johann discovered, because we have trust in this process, and the trust is mutual. You trust us to treat your application seriously, and with an open mind, and I can promise you that we will do that. You trust us to read it carefully—which, again, I assure you, we will do. We are going to give your request for admission very thoughtful, very respectful consideration. But in return, we trust you to tell us the truth. To write your own application. To take your own SATs. Any questions?"

No questions about that, at any rate.

Then, a hand in the back, from an Asian girl, her black hair secured tightly in a scrunchie. "Yes?"

"Yes?"

"Yes," said the girl. "I wanted to ask about how much it matters if your parents went to Princeton. It's easier for you to get in if they did, right?"

Portia considered. There was now palpable tension, almost hostility, in the room, which undoubtedly held more than the one Princeton legacy she had already met. In fact—and it would come as no surprise to anyone here—it did make a difference that an applicant's parent went to Princeton, even though the university bore little resemblance to the old boy network it had once almost exclusively been. Walking the tightrope between Princeton's sense of tradition and its outreach to the best available students from any and every background was one of her most serious charges, but it required calibration.

"Look," she finally said, studiously avoiding the gaze of her wrapped-in-an-orange-baby-blanket applicant, "our alumni are very important to us. They're part of our university culture. They *are* our tradition. Yes, it matters, and if you look at the statistics, you'll see that your chances of being admitted are higher within the legacy pool than they are in the nonlegacy pool. But don't for one minute think that having a parent who attended Princeton means you get to walk in. Again, the statistics for legacies show that most legacy applicants don't get in. And believe me, you don't want to be sitting in my boss's chair when the letters go out and that phone starts ringing. We could fill every class just with legacies, but we won't, because that's not our mission. In fact, we have exactly as many students who are the first in their families to attend college as we have students whose families have been attending Princeton for generations, and a whole lot of students who are neither of those things. Okay? Here's my advice: If you're not a Princeton legacy, don't waste your time worrying about it. And if you are, it's still a very, very competitive process." She looked at the girl in the scrunchie. "You don't look happy."

The girl seemed to remember herself. "No, that's okay."

"Joanne?" said Roden. "You had a question?"

Portia looked where he was looking. In the front row, a heavy African-

American girl sat cross-legged. Her Deerfield Lacrosse sweatshirt did not fully disguise something essential about her, a displacement. She lacked the sheen of money, the lean, muscular good health, good skin, good clothes. Prep for Prep, Portia thought right away, or one of the other programs that sponsored inner-city kids at some of the best high schools in the country.

"Yes?" Portia said. "Joanne?"

"Uh, well," Joanne faltered. "I was wondering about financial aid. Is it harder to get in if you can't pay the tuition?"

"Oh no." She smiled. "And I'm really glad you asked that question, because it gives me a chance to brag. Like most other selective colleges, Princeton is need-blind. We don't even look at your financial aid application until you've been admitted. Then we put together a package designed for you and your family that will enable you to cover your expenses. And over half of our students are on financial aid, so there's no stigma about it. Then in 2001 we eliminated the loan as part of our financial aid package. You know those student loans you hear so much about? The ones your parents are still paying off from when they went to college? We don't give them anymore. We give you a grant to make up the shortfall between what you can pay and what the tuition costs. We did that because we could. We could afford it, and we didn't think it was right to graduate our students already burdened by debt. Also, we trusted that our graduates would show their appreciation for our gesture, but later, when they could afford to do it. I'm being perfectly frank here. It's a little too soon to say whether we were right about that. Our first alumni to graduate since these changes were made are still at the start of their professional lives."

"So nobody's given you a building yet." It was Hunter, the smug kid on the sofa.

"Nope." She declined the bait. "Not yet. But we're not hurting for buildings."

She told them about the new student center, the new Neuroscience of Cognitive Control Laboratory, the new residential college to be named after the CEO of eBay, the $101 million arts initiative, Toni Morrison's Atelier, which brought performing artists to campus to create original artworks with undergraduates. Their eyes began to glaze. There was abundance fatigue, overstimulation. Even the eager ones were stupefied. The note takers had stopped taking notes. Some of them looked crestfallen, as if they could never hope to experience such a playground of riches. Some of them must have been thinking how nice it might be to go to a college where they could get loaded and play Frisbee, at least most of the time. Though selfishly, Portia wanted the Frisbee players to apply. The Frisbee players were the easiest to cut and set the intellectual kids in bolder relief. They made her job easier by providing contrast where the only typical contrast was far more subtle: wonderful student versus phenomenal student, terrific kid versus amazing kid, applicant upon applicant who could obviously come in, do the work, contribute to the community, and go on out into the world to project retroactive glory on Alma Mater. Her bag was full of them. Her desk back at the office was laden with them. And in six weeks' time, when the application deadline rolled around, the entire building would flood with them, and she, like all of her colleagues, would begin to swim with them, and struggle with them, and sink with them.

"So," she said brightly. "Any more questions?"

Miraculously, there were no more questions. They moved to a different room in the library: apple cider in waxy cups, cookies (chocolate chip, as it happened, not Oreos) on a paper doily. She spoke to a boy from Mumbai who wanted to be an electrical engineer, the girl with the long braid who wanted to take a class from Chang-Rae Lee, her favorite author, another girl who let Portia know that her father was a famous movie director.

"And what about you?" said Portia. "Are you interested in film? What are you thinking of doing?"

The girl looked up, notably shocked. Perhaps it had always been enough, having a famous director for a father. The thought of having to do something, having to be something, care about something, herself, seemed to have stunned her. Portia spotted Joanne, the girl who had asked about financial aid, near the cider and quickly went to pour her own refill. Joanne was a Brooklyn girl, and Prep for Prep. She was actually a year older than her classmates, she told Portia, having spent her ninth grade back home preparing for the SSAT and the academic challenges of a school like Deerfield.

"That isn't a problem," she asked. "Is it?"

"Not at all. Actually, it says a great deal about your determination that you were willing to step back and work that hard to get where you wanted to be."

Joanne nodded warily. More than likely, they had told her the same thing at Prep for Prep when they'd accepted her with this proviso.

"What are your thoughts about college?" Portia asked her.

"Well...ah...I'm kind of thinking about being a lawyer. But you know, I'm better at math."

"So you'll be a lawyer who's good at math. Maybe you can prosecute white-collar financial cases."

She frowned. "Or, like, accounting or something."

"Well, I'm actually one of those people who thinks it's better not to have too clear an idea when you go to college. Lightning strikes, you know."

"Yeah," Joanne said uncertainly, but her classmates were crowding her aside. The orange blanket baby wanted her to know that his lacrosse team made the regionals last year. Hunter from the couch wanted to give her a manila envelope containing, he said, his recent op-ed piece in the Deerfield student paper on the anti-intellectualism endemic at the school. Portia looked at her watch and noted gratefully that she was nearly out of time.

"Mr. Roden?" She looked around for him. He was standing with two ponytailed girls in front of the fireplace. She tapped her watch and he nodded, moving off instantly, probably leaving the girls in the middle of their angst-ridden declaration.

"Time to go?" he said, reaching her. "Listen, this was great."

"Oh, I love coming here," she said heartily. "The kids are so articulate."

"Yes, they certainly are. They're happy kids. It's a happy campus."

"Yes," she agreed, because it seemed like the appropriate response. She made eye contact with her orange blanket applicant, and Joanne, and told the director's daughter that she was looking forward to her application. Then they were outside in the bright midday sun.

"I remember this smell of burning leaves," she said as he walked her to the parking lot. "I think all of New England burns leaves the same week."

"It's a decree!" Roden said. Like her, he was killing time. "So where are you off to now?"

"Oh, Keene. I'm crossing the border."

"Public school?" he asked. There was an edge of hopefulness. It was bad enough that she should bestow her favors on any other school but Deerfield. He did not, in particular, wish to share her with his students' most direct competitors: applicants from Northfield Mount Hermon, Groton, St. Paul's.

"No. It's a new school, actually. I think they've only been going a couple of years. Outside of Keene. Wait a minute."

They were beside her rental car now. She opened up the passenger door and put her satchel on the seat. Then she leaned down and hunted out the downloaded directions. "Quest School. Do you know it?"

"Never heard of it," he said with notable relief. "Experimental? Sounds experimental."

"I actually don't know anything about it. It's a first visit for us. And we haven't had any applications so far."

"Ah." He seemed even more relieved to hear this. "Well, good to know what's out there."

"Absolutely." She put out her hand. "Thank you again, I think it was a very successful visit, and I can't wait to start reading the applications."

"Yes. And one or two I'll be writing to you about."

"I'll look forward to it."

He waited to wave as she drove away, a piece of arcane protocol about how the departing representative of the desirable college must be the one to break contact. Portia knew it had nothing at all to do with her. Their interaction had been thoroughly predictable, professional, impersonal. Only a couple of times, in fact, over sixteen years had Portia felt any real connection with the college advisers she'd dealt with, and both times the locale had been thoroughly remote, both in the geographic sense and in terms of Princeton's reach. The first was in the Central Valley of California, where the overwhelmed guidance counselor was herself newly graduated from community college and responsible for nearly six hundred seniors, many of them the kids of laborers or Hmong immigrants; the second took place in Sitka, Alaska, where she was the first Ivy League admissions officer ever to materialize, and the effusive guidance counselor had roused the entire PTA to throw a potluck in her honor, complete with dried bearded seal meat—an indelible culinary experience. (Portia could only imagine the potluck they must have thrown five years later, when the student she'd recruited on that trip had won her Rhodes scholarship.) Those two counselors had both moved on to other jobs, but Portia still thought of them. There had been time for human contact in their conversations, in their inelegant cinder-block offices, on rickety folding chairs, across laden

Formica desks. She still remembered their names and didn't doubt those women could produce her own. But William Roden would retain only one fact about her from this meeting: that she represented Princeton. She might have been lacquered in ivy and leading a tiger, Portia thought, driving west from Deerfield and winding north into the woods. He would not remember her face, or the fact that she had grown up nearby, or indeed anything personal about her. It was a good thing she had given him her business card. When it came time to get in touch on behalf of those "one or two" students he'd mentioned, he would undoubtedly need to reacquaint himself with her name.

I would have to say that I have been inspired the most by my older brother, Tim. Tim was diagnosed with a tumor in his lower leg when he was 14 years old. I remember when our parents explained to him that doctors would have to remove his leg. He was incredibly brave. He just said, "It's all right. I know it has to be done." After the amputation, Tim worked tirelessly to rebuild his strength and learn to use his new prosthesis. He eventually joined his high school lacrosse team and now plays lacrosse at UNH. His fortitude and perseverance have been the greatest inspiration to me, and I hope to follow in his footsteps at college and beyond.

CHAPTER TWO

INSPIRATION WAY

As borders went, Massachusetts/New Hampshire was not particularly dramatic. There were no long bridges to cross or welcome centers waiting just past the line, with placards declaring the name of the governor. There weren't even any highways in this part of the state, only the lacy network of smaller roads bound from wood to wood, some of them the descendants of far more primitive roads from a time before the borders themselves. Even so, this reddest of red states had always felt like a very foreign land to Portia, or so she had been taught to feel in the bluest of blue states she was about to leave. Vermont was Massachusetts's natural sibling, its cousin up north. One drove up to Vermont to visit friends, and friends of friends, and to attend music festivals and solar energy festivals and peace festivals. But nobody you knew lived in New Hampshire, land of Live Free or Die. Over there they were too busy incubating right-wing politicians and shooting their guns to take much of a look at solar energy or — God forbid — peace.

Many years before, it had come as something of a shock to Portia when she'd realized, crossing the Connecticut River en route to her Dartmouth interview, that she had never actually been to New Hampshire. So close and yet, to a girl raised in counterculture splendor by a mother who was gynocentric in all but her sexuality, an utterly foreign country. As in: *Why would anyone want to go there?*

"Why would you want to go there?" her mother would indeed demand six months later. (She was referring to Dartmouth in particular.) Cornell was pretty. It had gorges. Portia had also gotten into Barnard. Wellesley. There was always UMass just up the road. But Dartmouth was a school of louts and bullies in a state of louts and bullies. Who needed it?

I need it, Portia had thought. "It will be good for me," she had said. *If we're always surrounded by people like ourselves, how can we grow? How can we effect change?* She might not have actually said this part, but she was thinking it, or trying to be brave enough to think it. Because what she had really been thinking was unspeakable in the presence of her mother. She had been remembering how, on her college tour, skirting the lovely Green on which freshmen were building their towering stack of railroad ties for a traditional bonfire—one tie for each of the ninety-one years of their '91 class—she had had a powerful surge of feeling. There had been a sense of great order, great beauty, with tendrils of that elusive thing *Tradition* wafting around the handsome students, like the smoke that would itself unfurl from those railroad ties a few days hence. The Dartmouth girls were—to a one—skinny and graceful, some degree of blond. The Dartmouth boys were not like the boys in her high school, who had mottled complexions and, more likely than not, hair tied back. Instead, they were like the students she sometimes saw on the Amherst College campus, where the past year or so she had developed a nervous habit of walking, or masquerading, to see if she could pass. (Amherst, in fact, would be the only college to reject her: a bitter, bitter pill.) But here were the same boys, two hours north, with perhaps an extra layer of clothing against the cooler air. And so, when the decision had to be made, she drew on the full complement of rational ammunition for her mother—the stunning campus, the brilliant faculty, the Ivy League, for Christ's sake!—and hid the absolute truth. The truth was, she wanted to be one of those girls. And she wanted those boys.

Portia would spend most of the next decade in the state of New Hampshire, first as a student and later in her first admissions job, which was also at Dartmouth and where her first assigned territory was northern New

England. In those years, she would come to know every nook and cranny of the state, charged as she was not to miss a single promising native son (or daughter) who might not be with it enough to think of applying to Dartmouth. (The college had always looked out for its own backyard, an academic noblesse oblige that went back to its Daniel Webster days.) In those years she drove every road, paved or not, from the Presidentials to the shopping outlets along the Maine border, the blink-and-you'll-miss-it coastline, the prosperous little towns in the south. She might not remember the names of the roads, but she knew where they went, and she had been on this one before. There was, in fact, a distinct familiarity to the asphalt line coiling through forest, its spent foliage littering the roadsides, and the faint smell of burning leaves in the car.

MapQuest hadn't been entirely encouraging in its directions to the Quest School. There was something in the street address (One Inspiration Way) the Web site hadn't liked, and Portia had read with some resignation the usual admonition to do a "reality check" to confirm the existence of the roads and intersections. She hadn't done it, though. The town, North Plain, seemed likely to be small, and she figured the locals would know the way, if it came to that; but as she passed through Keene and north into deeper woods, she started to get a little concerned. It was nearly two, the time of her appointment, and she wasn't sure where she was headed or where she was.

When she found a gas station she pulled in, but her cell phone couldn't get a signal. The teenage boy tending the gas pumps had never heard of Quest School, or Inspiration Way, for that matter, but the man whose gas he was pumping said, "Wait, it's that hippie school, right?"

"I couldn't say," Portia said. "I'm afraid that's all the information I have."

"Oh," said the kid. "I know that place. It's up towards Gilsum, right? They took over that big dairy barn and fixed it up. I heard they, like, keep the cows."

"Yeah?" the man asked. "Why?"

The kid didn't know. Portia didn't know.

"Can you tell me how to get there?" she asked.

They told her. The drive wasn't long, but it was complex. The directions involved a red barn, a hex sign, and a new house with blue shutters. She listened with a sinking heart, calculating: twenty minutes late, at least; half an hour, more likely. Portia drove away. She found the red barn and then the hex sign, and made the appropriate turns. The road turned dirt. There were no new houses with blue shutters. There was no Inspiration Way.

But there was, to her great surprise, a large sign for the Quest School mounted on rustic logs at a crossroad in the woods. It looked handmade, like a student project. She turned down the lane indicated (an unmarked lane, but indeed—she supposed—Inspiration Way) and drove between sudden fields flooded with afternoon light. Cows grazed to the left. There was hay, baled and piled, on the other side. Ahead, she saw the white barn with cars parked around it. A group of teenagers played volleyball. Another group, seated beneath a tree, seemed to be having an open-air class. She drove past them, parked at the end of the row, and got out quickly, relieved to be only fifteen minutes late. No one seemed to notice her arrival.

Portia hunted in her satchel for the Quest School file. There wasn't much in it—a sheet with the name of her contact, Deborah Rosengarten, and the MapQuest directions. Also a printout that Abby, Clarence's secretary, had given her of the school's Web site, most of which was devoted to the mission statement. ("We believe that the purpose of education is to open doors, not close them. Recognizing that no one form of education will stretch to fit every unique individual, we cherish the beauty of each distinct mind.") She shut the door of the car and looked around.

The barn was massive and from the outside somewhat confusing. The great bay doors that had, presumably, once seen herds of cattle pass through were still in place, but they looked unused, possibly sealed. There was nothing else that looked like a door, let alone a front door. She walked to the end of the building and turned the corner, coming upon the outdoor class in their circle beneath a maple tree. The group regarded her with some curiosity, not least the evident teacher, a man roughly her own age in a white buttoned shirt and khakis.

"You look lost," he said affably enough.

"I'm here to meet Deborah Rosengarten."

"Deborah?" He looked at his students. "Anyone seen Deborah?"

"She went to Putney," said one boy. He had an open book on his lap and looked up only briefly. "She told me she was going to Putney."

"Oh," Portia stammered. "But . . . well, we had an appointment."

"I'm so sorry," the man said. He got to his feet. "Can I help? I'm John."

"Portia. I'm here from Princeton."

"Yes," he said, looking at her intently. "I remember you."

"Our appointment was for two. I'm a little late. I got lost. Perhaps she couldn't wait."

"Perhaps she simply forgot," he said, notably irritated. But at the missing Deborah, Portia thought. Not, she was fairly certain, at herself.

"I apologize," said John, confirming it. "This is terrible. Deborah… you know, she's a great educator, but prone to distraction. And you've come so far."

"From Deerfield, Massachusetts. Not that far," she said, loosening up a little. "So, what should we do? I'm happy to give my presentation if you'd like to round up your eleventh and twelfth graders."

He stood in the center of the circle and looked down at them. The kids were variously arrayed, supine, cross-legged, stretching. Some had put down their notebooks, but the boy who had spoken earlier read on, unruffled. He sat with his book unfurled across his lap, head tipped forward, thick black curls so shiny that they almost reflected back the sunlight. Curious, Portia tried to make out what he was reading and was just able to decipher the legend at the top of the page. *Edie: An American Girl.* The incongruity of that, here, beside a cow pasture in deepest New Hampshire, struck her as odd. Then sort of hilarious.

"What do you say, guys? Are you up for some college guidance?"

Portia looked at him. "Is this your eleventh and twelfth grade?"

"Not all. A few are doing other things. We'll ring the bell. Caleb? Would you ring the bell?"

A lanky kid got to his feet. He had an acne-spattered jaw and a blond ponytail. He walked off without a word.

"All of our sixteen- and seventeen-year-olds should attend, I think. We're trying to learn how to do this, actually. Our first students are just coming up to graduation this year. We've been focusing on other things."

"I see. Well, I expect you've had other colleges visit."

"Oh dear." He smiled ruefully. "Would it complete your already terrible first impression of us if I told you you were the first? I know we've put in a call to Hampshire. And Goddard."

"I think Goddard has closed, actually."

"Ah. Maybe that's why we haven't heard back."

"Maybe." She smiled. She was surprised to discover that she wasn't, actually, pissed off. She ought to be. But she wasn't. It had warmed up through the day, and the air smelled of hay and the best version of cow. At the very least, this was going to be interesting. "I've brought a short film. Can I use your television and DVD player?"

"Oh, I wish we had them. It's on our donation list. To tell you the truth, I think there's some resistance to the idea."

"Resistance? Do they think if they let in a TV, the students will all sit around watching *General Hospital*?"

"Essentially." He laughed. "You know, our parent base is part Luddite, part day trader. It's hard to get consensus on some things."

"Well, never mind. They can watch it on my laptop. They're a small enough group."

"That would be great," he said. "We'll go in."

Atop the barn, a bell creaked to life. The volleyball game stopped. Out in the fields there was movement as students slouched toward home. "That's a useful thing," Portia said.

"It's our original bell. It was once used to call the cows home for milking."

"Interesting metaphor for education." She smiled. "How long have you been here?"

"Me?" John asked. "Or the school? Well, it's moot. I was here at the birth. Six years. Eight if you count the time it took us to get set up. We were refurbishing inside and getting accredited. Some of us lived in trailers on the site. Thankfully, that's over."

"You must be very dedicated," Portia said, stepping carefully. Her leather boots, so understated that they virtually disappeared on the streets of Princeton, seemed absurdly urban in this setting. She felt as if she had left the familiar world, the world of Starbucks and cabs and *Vanity Fair,* and wandered through a hole in the backdrop, emerging in the dazzling light of 1967, or 1867, where the old bell rang to call in the cows and the farmers of both genders wore feather earrings. The students, save the still immersed reader, stirred and got languidly to their feet and began to amble across to the barn. She saw kids coming in from the fields and the volleyball court. There were a few adults now, looking curiously in her direction. Everyone wore jeans and had a sun-kissed, genially bedraggled air. Or almost everyone. The comparatively prepped-out John's white shirt seemed blindingly clean. It made him look as if he'd wandered seriously off course, somewhere between Groton and Brooks Brothers. *Mr. Chips Goes to Woodstock,* Portia thought, suppressing a smile. He had dark blond hair, thinning but oddly rakish. He wore a watch on a cracked plastic band. At least he wore a watch, she thought.

The barn was thoroughly renovated. They walked down a corridor flanked by classrooms, each fitted with a single long table. "One of our earliest decisions," John said, noting her attention. "We took ideas from everywhere, as long as they were good ideas. One of our board members went to Lawrenceville. Every classroom had a long oval table. No one gets lost at an oval table. We implemented that. We also borrowed our farming model from Putney and our all-school runs from Northfield."

"You've obviously thought long and hard about everything."

"Oh yes. We had a lot of time to think. And argue about things, it has to be said. After all, we were working on the school long before we had our first student. And we still learn something new every day. We're constantly tripping over places where rules ought to be, then we have to write the rules and implement them. That's a consensus process, so it takes time, but we get there in the end. I know we look like *Lord of the Flies*," he said apologetically, "but I can assure you, we're legit."

"I didn't doubt it," Portia said, though of course she had.

The corridor ended in a meeting room. A wall of new windows overlooked the cow meadow. The view was stunning, pristine. It was a jolt back into that other world: a room a millionaire might insist upon for his rustic New England retreat, though perhaps without the shabby, mismatched sofas that filled it.

"Our commons," said John.

"It's beautiful. Like something out of *Architectural Digest*."

"I'll let our designer know you said that," he said. "He'll be over the moon. Technically, he specializes in reclaimed spaces and green construction, but the truth is, he's a secret consumer of shelter mags. When you go to his house, there's a hidden stash of architectural porn in the cupboard next to the compost toilet. I swear I found it by accident," he said.

"I didn't ask!" said Portia, laughing.

The room was flooded with light, which made the challenge of showing a movie on a laptop all the more acute. She placed her computer on a table and inserted the DVD. Acceptable, but far less satisfying than the state-of-the-art equipment she'd been given at Deerfield. The room was filling with older students who drifted to the sofas and talked in loud, unself-conscious voices. No one here, it was obvious, was trying to impress the visitor from the Princeton Office of Admission. She saw the reader come in, a finger protectively inside his book, holding his place. John was talking to another teacher, a heavy woman in overalls with two fat, graying braids. The woman left the room without introducing herself and with—was it possible?—the faintest whiff of hostility.

"My colleague says that Deborah told her about this a couple of days ago," John said, returning. "I honestly don't know what happened. She's going to go take the younger students out to the field. Usually the older kids are in charge of afternoon milking, but we think this is more important."

"Oh," Portia said, both perturbed to be placed in the same category as a cow and relieved to have at least come out ahead. "Okay. Can we get started?"

He turned back to the kids and gravely raised his hand, palm front, as if he were a crossing guard. He said nothing, but as each student noticed him, he or she stopped talking and did the same. Gradually, a forest of hands were raised. The talk thinned to scattered voices, then one resistant pocket of girls in a corner, and then nothing. When there was silence, the hands came down, John's first.

"Thank you," he told them. "Now, we have a visitor. I'd like you to welcome her and give her your respectful attention. This is Portia Nathan."

He went directly to one of the couches, where the students compressed themselves and made room for him. Watching him, Portia found herself somewhat disconcerted, not so much by his quick departure from the stage—or the nondescript patch of floor that served as a stage—as by the fact that he had somehow remembered not only her first name, but her last. It took a further instant to decide that she could not remember having given her last name at all, though this was not a good enough reason to stand here, distracted, before the already dubious and unprepared students who were waiting for her. Of course, the elusive Ms. Rosengarten must have briefed her staff: Portia Nathan would be coming from Princeton. And now Portia Nathan was standing here, dumbstruck by the incongruity of social etiquette in a cow barn. *You're such a snob,* she just had time to tell herself. And there was no reason to feel so . . . bothered. But she was still bothered.

"Hello, I'm Portia," she finally managed. "I'm from Princeton. I've brought a film—"

"Isn't that a college?" said a muscle-bound kid in a Phish T-shirt.

"A university," she said. "Princeton University. It's in Princeton, New Jersey."

"How's that different from a college?" said a girl from the nearest couch.

"A college doesn't have graduate schools or graduate students. A university does. We have graduate students in many departments, so we're a university. Has anyone been to Princeton?"

None of them raised a hand.

"Have any of you begun looking at colleges?"

None of them raised their hands, but one boy said, "I'm going to UNH to study animal husbandry."

"UNH is great for that. It's not something we teach at Princeton. . . ."

With this, whatever authority she still retained seemed to dissipate. The mood in the room shifted.

"I'm not really convinced that college is necessary," one girl said from the back of the room. She was skinny as a stick, with a military haircut. Military for a guy.

"No?" Portia said, detecting the slightest of wobbles in her voice.

"No. Look, a college degree can cost a fortune. Why should we? It's like buying something you don't need, that happens to cost . . . What does it cost to go to Princeton?"

"Most of our students receive financial aid," Portia said tersely, deflecting the question.

"A lot of money, anyway. A ton. For a piece of paper and a couple of letters after your name."

"Well . . . ," Portia began. She found that she had let the thread of this surprising conversation escape her. Now, she was having a problem orienting herself. There was something about the cows outside, the intensely blue sky through the huge windows, and these kids, sorting out for themselves who she was and what she wanted, as if she were not standing here, ready to explain.

"Look," said the girl with the military haircut, "please explain to me why I should be applying to an elitist institution with a history of antiblack, antigay, and antifemale oppression." She got to her feet. She was tall, with narrow shoulders lost in an absurdly large lumberjack shirt. "I might concede that a college degree is necessary if you want to pursue the societally approved definition of success—you know, three-car garage and framed degree on the wall and a twenty-thousand-dollar watch. But what if that's not your goal? What if all you want is to lead a fulfilling life and make the world better? If you're not going to work for a corporation or run for office or be a lawyer, aren't you better off sitting in a room reading books for four years? That doesn't cost anything."

She looked at them with a certain growing unease. Nearly a decade at Princeton, and before that a six-year stint at Dartmouth, and she couldn't remember an encounter quite like the one this was shaping up to be. They were a little slovenly, of course, but you saw slovenly kids everywhere, even in the most rarefied of prep schools. She was used to piercings, tattoos, revealing clothing, even attitude, but the point was, even in the toughest high schools, the schools where educators were trying frantically to get their students out the door holding a diploma and not a baby or a gun, even there, the ones who bothered to turn up at her presentations were the very ones who wanted what she had to offer—or not just wanted, but yearned for, dreamed of. They knew the road to a different kind of life could be found weaving through Harvard Yard or Yale's Old Campus or under the Princeton archways. She didn't doubt that there were kids like this girl at every school she visited, but they tended to give her presentations a miss. They were not forward thinking. They did not have three-car garages on their minds, for better or ill. Or issues of elitism. Or ambitions of self-fulfillment that went beyond the immediate. She just never saw them. They were off smelling the roses or breathing deep the first joint of the day or plotting mayhem against their enemies. Or if they were in attendance—compelled by school requirements or ordered by parents—she supposed they just kept their mouths shut and amused themselves, watching their striving classmates try to impress the Princeton rep. Was it her responsibility to encourage them to apply to any college, let alone Princeton? Wasn't it hard enough to find the hungry kids, whose families were not educated, who lived without privilege, to let them know that there were still a few, a very few, magic portals in the world that led from one socioeconomic class to another, and she was standing next to one of them?

Looking at this group, variously reclined on the couches or cross-legged on the floor, every one of them alert to the strain in the room, she found that the language for this occasion simply eluded her. She knew how to speak to prep school students, to first-generation kids from all parts of the globe, to magnet school students in the inner cities. She knew how to speak to stressed-out kids in the affluent suburbs who looked at her with pleading, hopeless expressions: *Please let me in* and *I know you won't*, in woeful tandem. She had talked to groups of homeschooled kids, whose parents kept vigilant watch at the edges of the room, and foreign students, hurled from afar into American boarding schools or exchange programs, who hadn't seen their parents in years but understood that all of it had been for this. She knew when to be a salesman, a teacher, a counselor, or a motivational speaker. She knew how to hold hands and how to crack the whip. But these kids...she was having trouble making them out. What were they? Not hippies or Goths. Not scholars per se. They were fearless, that was clear. And rude. And curious, at least some of them. And not remotely hesitant to challenge her.

"It's an interesting question," Portia said uncertainly. "And your alternative, sitting in a room reading books all day, does sound very cost-effective. But it also strikes me as a little lonely. And not truly rigorous, if you think about it. After all, once you've read all those books, don't you want to talk to somebody else who's reading them, too? Or do you want to have the kind of education where your initial impressions are never challenged? Where you're never asked to refine your opinions or actually prove your theories? There's something very exciting about a community of scholars, you know."

"This is a community of scholars," the girl said a little petulantly. "We can go through our lives seeking out communities of scholars. What you're talking about is a corporation, no different than a bank or an oil company. Only your product is a piece of paper with some Latin on it. You let people pay you tuition and then you give them the piece of paper. Princeton graduates have a lot of status, don't they?"

"Define status," Portia said, idly wondering whether the charming John was ever going to come to her rescue.

"In the consumerist culture. In the corporate culture. They move into high-paying jobs where they shift numbers around on a piece of paper or a computer screen, and they live in privileged enclaves with guards at the gate, and they produce the next generation to go to places like Princeton. Or have I been reading too much John Cheever?"

Portia laughed despite herself. "Can one ever read too much John Cheever?"

"It's just I think we should be educating ourselves to be citizens of the world, you know? Not just citizens of the guarded, suburban enclave."

"Well, I happen to agree with that," Portia said tersely. "We, as a university, happen to agree with that. That's why we offer our students so many study abroad options, including our Princeton in Africa and Princeton in Asia programs. In fact, our university motto is 'Princeton in the Nation's Service and the Service of All Nations.' We're all about making citizens of the world."

"But you can't *make* citizens of the world," the girl said with annoying passion. "That's just my point. We have to *become* citizens. *Naturally.*"

"That's a very subtle distinction," Portia said. "Now, I'd like to—"

"No. I don't think so. I think the American university has become a sausage factory, turning out substandard product. That's what I love about this school. We follow our own pursuit of awareness, wherever that takes us. We come out whole people, not sausages."

"And what, as whole people, do you intend to do with your lives?" Portia said testily.

"Live them," said a boy on another couch. "Live them well, tread lightly on the earth. Leave the planet better than we found it."

"That sounds very laudable. How will you leave the planet better? Will you eradicate disease? You'll need a medical degree. If you want to create new drug therapies, you're going to have to be a research scientist. That's a PhD. Want to defend the innocent and secure justice for all? I regret to inform you that you'll have to go to law school. Maybe you want to lift the indigent out of poverty. I know it's not what you want to hear, but a career in business might be the best way to make that happen. There are plenty of college graduates out there living good lives, treading lightly on the planet, and ardently hoping to leave the world better than they found it. We're looking for those people. There's nothing wrong with sitting in a room for the rest of your life, reading books for your own self-improvement, but if your goal is really to increase your understanding of the world and make it a better place to live, then I think you'd better continue your education after high school."

"Rosa Parks increased our understanding of the world and made it a better place to live," said one of the girls from the corner. She had a dusky gray complexion and beaded cornrows.

"She did indeed," Portia said, sighing. "I'm not implying that education is the only path to making a contribution. But if contribution is your goal, why would you choose to impede yourself, or limit your ability to make an impact? And consider this, please. A college class can give us a clearer picture than the one we might get sitting alone in that room with our books. For example — and I'm going to hijack your own example, if you don't mind — Rosa Parks, remarkable as she was, was not the first black American to refuse to give up her seat on public transportation and find herself in a jail cell. And her act was not the basis of the lawsuit that ended segregation on buses. Seven months before Rosa Parks, there was another black woman who was taken to prison for not moving when a white person wanted her seat. Her name was Aurelia Browder, and she filed suit against the city of Montgomery, Alabama. And that's the lawsuit that struck down segregation, not Parks's lawsuit. Now," she said, surveying their subdued, even stricken faces, "have you wandered into the wrong meeting? Am I really here to talk about the civil rights movement and only pretending to try to sell you on the idea of applying to Princeton University? No. The only point I'm making by telling you about Aurelia Browder is that I wouldn't have known about her myself if I hadn't taken an African-American history course when I went to college. College is where you go beyond the official version. College is where you read the sources and look past the canon. Now, Rosa Parks was a heroine, no question about it, but who thinks we ought to be just as impressed by Aurelia Browder?"

There were stray nods. A couple of them raised a hand.

"Could you have learned about her on your own? Sure. But you didn't, did you? In my college class, we read the trial transcripts. We read the contemporary newspaper accounts. Our professor had written a book about Bob Moses. Who was Bob Moses?"

Blank looks.

"Okay. I rest my case. Now, if I've convinced you to devote the next four years of your life to higher education, I'd like to please move on to one particular institute of higher education. So if there are no further questions — "

"Actually," said her antagonist from the couch, "I still don't understand why you're here. I mean, isn't Princeton already competitive? Why do you need more applicants? Or do you want even more people to apply so you can let in an even smaller percentage? I mean, isn't that the measure of status for elite colleges? That it's harder to get into your place than Harvard or whatever? Why is it necessary for even more of us to participate in this national hysteria about college admissions?"

It was actually quite an impressive speech, and—as it happened— uncomfortably close to the bone. Portia regarded the girl, saying nothing for a moment. She was thinking: I must get her name. This kid was smart, opinionated, stubborn, and thoroughly relentless. Portia could just imagine her in Congress, not that such an acerbic character could get elected to anything. But a mover and a shaker, definitely: Today Princeton, tomorrow the world.

"I came here," said Portia, "to let you know about us, so that if you're considering higher education, you could consider us. Just as we would like to have the opportunity to consider you."

"Oh, right. You mean you'd like to have the opportunity of considering our applications so you can reject them. What are the chances of getting into Princeton these days?"

"We're running about one in ten admits," Portia said tersely. "We have an enormously talented applicant pool, and a very difficult job assembling a class."

"You mean unless the applicant happens to be really rich and just gave a soccer stadium to the school. Then maybe it's not so difficult."

"That's not accurate," Portia said, getting seriously annoyed.

"Wouldn't you agree that the ideal university ought to be a purely need-blind, influence-blind, affluence-blind meritocracy?"

"Ah," she said dryly. "But aren't there many ways to define merit? Unless you'd like to make it a strict question of numbers. But should we really be relying on standardized testing? And is it, in fact, standardized when some students can afford expensive courses to raise their scores and others can't? But let's suppose you did have a single, reliable testing system, that isn't going to solve the problem of who's going to throw the shot put on the track team, and who's going to play tuba in the marching band, and who'll be writing the songs for the *Triangle Show*. Princeton is a community of many parts. We don't just need molecular biology majors and tennis players. We need Gregorian chanters and break dancers. We need people for the math club and the mime troop and the Nepalese student association. We need somebody to chair the gay Republicans group and somebody to lead the Democrats for Fiscal Responsibility. Now listen," she told them. "I could go on talking about Princeton till the cows come home. Literally." She laughed and was relieved to note a few actual smiles. "But before we go any further, I want you to look at this short film. Afterwards, you may know that Princeton isn't for you, in which case I'm sure there are chores that need to be done around here. Am I right?" She turned to John.

"Always chores," he said, looking amused.

"But if you have questions, and some of you might, then we can talk more. Okay?"

She had survived her hazing, she saw. The consensus was: They would now watch the film.

She tried to angle the laptop so that the sun, visibly sinking now at the far end of the field, did not glare across the screen, but even in the six-teen minutes it lasted, the group on the floor first leaned and then shifted, inches, feet, chasing the shadow. She watched them as they watched the students on the small computer screen rhapsodize and crow. She inspected the students of the Quest School, looked at their faces, then at their bod-ies (alert or drooping, leaning against one another), then at their clothing, which on this closer inspection was impressively varied. There was quite a bit of tie-dye, of course, and T-shirts with band logos, and the inevitable jeans, but there was also an Asian girl in a frilly dress and Mary Janes, a wide-eyed boy with a chestnut-colored forelock wearing a smart jacket and khakis (he would not have appeared out of place at a Deerfield master's tea). There was a girl in blond pigtails who wore a loose, zip-up jumpsuit with a gas station's name imprinted on the breast and a name in embroi-dered cursive: "Frank." Another girl, plump and pale with a cap of thin red hair, wore a sweater set that might have come from the Talbot's on Nassau Street, a stone's throw from Portia's office.

That these kids, individually and collectively, had refused to meet her expectations was, after all, not their fault, but she actually felt a little annoyed with them for confounding her. She had weathered nearly sixteen years of teenagers, always at just this moment in their lives, always com-ing up to the same fork in the road. They variously charged ahead or hung behind or else stumbled along because they couldn't care less what hap-pened to them, but in essence they had never changed. Not in hundreds of school visits, and hundreds of thousands of applications, and an untold number of unscripted, unscheduled encounters, when people found out what her job was and dragged over their astonishing niece or godchild or prodigy offspring to talk to her. She knew how to recognize the good girls and the diligent boys, the rebels and fuck-ups, the artsy kids who knew nothing about art and the ones who had art burning inside them. She could spot the blinkered athletes and the pillars of some future community, the strivers of every stripe and shade, the despairing and despaired of. Almost every single one of them occupied a place that had been previously occupied by someone else, and someone else before that—someone elses who looked like them and sounded like them and thought like them. Sixteen years of drummers and different drummers, poets and players. But these students...they were not taking their seats. She was having trouble putting them in their places.

When the film ended, most of them—apparently taking Portia at her word—got up and left, but a few walked straight over to her and began talking. There seemed to be no medium, happy or otherwise, between "I care" and "I don't care." The ones who approached her wanted to know how to apply to Princeton. They wanted to know the essence of what the admissions committee looked for in an applicant and what made them admit the one out of ten and reject the other nine. (She had to repress her natural response; it was so artlessly asked.) They asked what was meant by the idea of diversity and what the political mood of the campus was. The Asian girl asked if she could study fashion at Princeton. ("No," Portia told her. "But you can study art and culture, which are necessary to understanding fashion. And you can create a senior thesis that incorporates fashion design.") The girl in the gas station jumpsuit was writing a novel and wanted to know if she could submit that instead of a traditional application. "You can submit it as part of your application," Portia said. Would it matter, someone asked her in a quiet, urgent voice, if both parents worked in a supermarket?

It was the reader. He stood with his finger wedged into his book, its bright yellow-and-blue dust jacket frayed at the edges.

"I'm not sure I understand what you mean."

"My parents aren't educated. They both work in a supermarket in Keene."

He looked at her with a disarming directness. He was an inch or so taller than her but still somehow gave the impression of looking up. He had very dark eyes, with very dark circles beneath them. His black hair was so imprecisely cut it looked as if he had hacked it himself, perhaps when it had fallen in his eyes one too many times. He wore jeans an unfashion-ably pristine shade of blue and a red sweatshirt with the single word *QUEST* printed in white letters. Noun or verb? she found herself thinking. He con-tinued to stare at her, motionless but not exactly tense. He was merely waiting. There were no social niceties, no verbal lubrications: *Thank you for speaking to us. I'm really interested. I think it would be an amazing oppor-tunity.* It was as if, having finally broken off from his book, he had now found something equally interesting to focus on.

"Oh no, of course not," Portia said, stumbling. "It doesn't matter what your parents do for a living. It's your application."

"Don't you care, though?" he asked, again with that unthinking directness.

"No. We don't care. There are kids from very intellectual, academic backgrounds at Princeton, but there are also plenty of kids who are the first in their families to graduate high school."

"I'm going to apply," the boy said bluntly. "I need to get out of here."

She looked at him curiously. "This seems like a good place to be a stu-dent," she said carefully.

"It's good. I don't mean the school. They just let me read. I know it doesn't sound that great, but it's so much better than my old high school in Keene."

"Why?" she couldn't help asking. "What was that like?"

He shrugged and pushed a black curl out of his eyes. It immediately escaped confinement behind his ear and flopped back.

"I just couldn't get with the program, you know? I just wanted to kind of go off on my own, 'cause my brain sort of . . . it goes a little walkabout, you know?"

Portia, who didn't, nodded anyway, just to keep him talking.

"I mean, I was all for learning, I just did it differently."

She took a moment to absorb this, then converted it to the most likely euphemism and asked, "Oh, I see. You're dyslexic? Or . . . ADHD?"

"What?" he said. "You mean . . . reading? Can I read?"

"Of course you can read," she said, thoroughly embarrassed, as if she were the one to be telling him this.

"Yeah. No, there's nothing wrong with my reading. Except they couldn't stop me doing it. If I was in the middle of something good, I didn't want to go to class. Or if I was in class, I wanted to talk about whatever I was thinking about then, not what the test was going to be about. And sometimes I tanked on the tests and sometimes I pulled it out, but on the whole they couldn't figure out what to do with me. You know, do they skip me ahead a couple of years or make me repeat all the classes I failed?"

Portia nodded. "That's a very unusual problem."

"It's much better here," he said affably. "John and the others, they've been talking to me about going to college." He stuck the same lock of hair behind the same ear, where it remained only a fraction of a moment longer. "Princeton sounds like a cool place."

"It's very cool," she agreed.

"They teach philosophy there? I like philosophy. What about art?"

"Great Philosophy Department. Great Art Department." She nodded to his book, still held open where he had left off, as if he had no wish to waste time finding his place again. "Tell me about Edie," she said.

He lit up. "You know this book? It's amazing, isn't it? It's the first biography I've ever read where the narrative form reflects the content."

She frowned. "I don't know what that means."

"I mean that in this depiction of the sixties, the fragmentation of the experience is mirrored in the use of oral history. You feel as if you're there, because so many impressions are competing for your attention. No single witness can claim to understand the subject of the biography, but cumulatively you do come to see who she was. I'm fascinated by the entire Factory thing, actually. Warhol—I can't quite decide if he was utterly talentless or utterly talented. And his passivity. You know, how does someone so resoundingly passive wind up with all of these forceful personalities deferring to him? Can anyone do that? I mean, can people be trained to be a Rasputin or a Warhol or a Charles Manson? Or is it a sort of chemical thing? Or do certain cultural factors have to be lined up just right?"

"I don't know." She laughed uneasily. "I'm afraid you lost me back at the Factory."

"I know who Bob Moses was," said the boy.

This was a moment of cognitive whiplash. It took her a moment herself to remember who Bob Moses was. "Oh?"

"He lives in Cambridge now. He's trying to teach math in a new way. About a year ago, I had this phase where I was reading books about mathematicians. He was in one of the books I read."

Portia could only nod.

"You know what's strange, though? Really good mathematicians talk like poets. They run out of language, so they twist words together to explain their ideas. Like poets do. But anyway, the book about Moses made some reference to his civil rights work. So then I read something else about what he did in Mississippi."

"What's your name?" she asked him.

"Portia," said John, materializing beside her, "thank you for doing that. And I apologize—you must have thought the initial reaction very odd. I ought to have prepared you—we tend to encourage that kind of participation. Spirited participation."

Rude participation, she thought. "I sort of got that. The culture of the school, yes?"

"Yes. And that particular student is Deborah's daughter."

"The elusive Deborah Rosengarten?"

"Yes. Simone's her only child. She's been raised to make her opinions known."

Portia smiled. Simone Rosengarten. As in de Beauvoir, no doubt. She would write it down tonight.

"Not your typical information session, I suppose," he said, watching her.

"No." She smiled. "I do feel as if I earned my salary today."

"I would have stepped in if I were ever in doubt. You were really remarkable."

"Oh, I enjoyed it," she said, not entirely truthfully. And—" She turned to the boy, the Warhol boy, but he was already halfway to the door. "Hey," she said after him. "Wait a minute."

John turned to look after him. "Hey, Jeremiah?"

The kid stopped, but halfheartedly. "Yes?"

"I—" But she wasn't entirely sure. Wanted to ask him something, but what? His last name? Or whether he would really apply? Or maybe what it was that kept her here a long moment past the point where it made sense to be looking after him.

"Jeremiah," said John, "are you thinking of applying to Princeton?"

"Yeah, maybe." He looked utterly nonplussed.

"Well, I hope you do," Portia told him. "And if you do, please let me know. Here's my card," she said, taking one from her wallet. "Let me know if you have any questions. If you want to come visit the campus, we can match you up with an undergraduate and you can stay with him in his room."

"Okay," he said, looking at the card. "Portia," he read as if she weren't there. "Like *The Merchant of Venice*."

"Yes. My mother had the idea that if she named me that, I would grow up to be very wise. I'm lucky she didn't name me Athena."

"Or Minerva," Jeremiah said. "Or Sophie. But a lot of people are named Sophie. They probably have no idea that's what their name means."

Portia frowned.

"Or Metis. That would be really strange. Or Saraswati. Yeah, I think you probably got lucky. If you've got to be called something that stands for wisdom, you probably couldn't have done any better."

She just looked at him. He stood by the door, his book resting against his thigh. He had delivered this disjointed speech in profile, his rather aquiline nose directed at the great picture windows at the end of the room. Now he lingered for a final minute, utterly without self-consciousness, and finally turned and left.

"Interesting kid," Portia said, removing the DVD from her laptop and placing both into her brown leather satchel.

"I guess. We're so used to him. We let him alone, mainly, but we do make him produce scholarship, otherwise he'd keep going the way he was before. He told you about his old school?"

She nodded. "So...he doesn't take classes here?"

"Oh sure. Well, he attends, but his mind is usually otherwise engaged. We decided not to fight it. That's what they did at Keene Central, to ill effect."

"They threw him out?" she asked, shouldering her bag.

"Well, they were headed in that direction. I met him at a yard sale last spring. He was sitting on the ground reading a 1952 *Encyclopedia Britannica*. Letter S." John grinned. "He said he was looking into the source material for *King Lear*. He told me he was on academic probation. We started getting together at Brewbakers on Sunday afternoons."

"Brewbakers?"

"Only cappuccino in town." He shrugged. "Anyway, he started here this fall, and it's working, as far as I can tell. He's preparing a lecture for the entire school about pop art right now." He shook his head. "On the day we assigned it, it happened to be pop art. If we had assigned the lecture a few days earlier, it might have been the Beats. A few days later, it could have been the Armenian genocide. He's like that game show where they let you loose in the supermarket for five minutes and you have to grab everything you can, except we can't seem to convince him he has more than five minutes. He can take his time."

"He mentioned that his parents hadn't gone to college."

"No. They seem like nice people, but they don't connect with him very well. You know, he was supposed to be playing football at Keene Central by now and racing motocross on the weekends. Jeremiah was never going to be like that."

She nodded. There had often been Jeremiahs in the applicant pool. They were attractive to the faculty, who some years earlier had flatly asked for more of them: fewer golden kids who did everything well, please, and more awkward kids who were brilliant but couldn't tie their shoes. The faculty themselves, she suspected, had once been awkward, brilliant kids who couldn't tie their shoes.

"Are you going back now?"

"Oh no. I'm staying over in Keene tonight. I'm going to Northfield Mount Hermon in the morning, then I'll fly back from Hartford."

"Northfield's a great school."

"Yes. We've had wonderful applicants from Northfield."

She stopped. She was aware, for the first time, of something awkward between them, something she had to call upon herself to ignore, or resist. She didn't particularly want to look at it directly.

"Let me walk you out," said John.

Outside the sunlight was in its last, brilliant blare of the day. The hay in the fields was richly yellow and came glowing, vibrating, out of the dirt in unkempt piles of bales. She could see kids in the cow pasture, walking the herd back after milking, with three or four dogs running around them. Closer, where the volleyball game had been played, the stout woman she had seen in the commons seemed to be setting up for some kind of game, with goals and boundaries. This enterprise, it seemed to her, was not entirely logical, but it was, in some baffling way, cohesive. Even beautiful. This was, Portia felt suddenly, a beautiful place—an astoundingly beautiful place to spend a life, or a work life, at any rate. Whatever their oddities, the project here seemed tangible. Take kids, make them participate in the community, and make them think. It was Princeton's own mission, more or less. Minus the ivy. And the money.

She opened the passenger door, and the car emitted hot air. She closed her eyes, momentarily dizzy. John stood behind her, and there was again that awkwardness between them. She was wondering how to leave, precisely, but in the next moment a boy of about fourteen came rushing up to them and stopped abruptly at John's elbow.

"Dad," he said.

The boy was young but tall—gangly, teetering on long legs. He was a handsome boy with coiling black hair and deeply black skin and a long, sinewy neck too elongated for his wheat-colored turtleneck sweater, which hit rather lower than it was meant to. He glanced at Portia without expression, then focused again on John.

"Portia," he said, "this is my son. Nelson, can you say hello to Portia?"

Obediently, he turned and held out his hand. It was warm and dry and rough, and she shook it.

"Dad," the boy said, his task dispatched, "okay if I go home with Karl? We want to do math."

"Math?" John said wryly. "Or computer games?"

"First math. Then, and only if there's time, *educational* computer games."

"All right," he said. "Be responsible. I'll come and get you on the way home."

"Thanks," said Nelson. "Bye," he said to Portia, and took off.

John looked after him. "Of course he makes friends with the only kid at our school who has a full library of computer games. I'm only hoping they're not of the blood-spattered genre, but the truth is, I'm afraid to ask."

"Denial is a parent's best friend." Portia smiled.

"Yes. Do you have kids?"

She shook her head quickly. "No. No kids."

"Well, it's an adventure."

She nodded, watching his long boy climb into the backseat of a battered Volvo. "He seems like a great kid."

"Oh, he is. He's happy and smart. A little lazy, but why not be lazy when you're young? When else are you going to do it?"

"Good point. Well, listen, thanks for having me. It was very interesting.

You've got some very strong personalities here. I hope we'll get some of them to apply."

"I think you might." He smiled. "I'll work on Jeremiah. And I wouldn't be surprised if you got Simone, eventually. I think she'd do fantastically well at a place like Princeton. Despite her bluster."

"Maybe because of her bluster," Portia said. "Look, if you have questions about the process, please call me. College guidance is such a well-oiled machine at most private schools. I don't want your kids to miss out because this is the first year for you."

"That's really kind of you," he said. He looked as if he meant it. "We should have had you sooner," he said. "And I'm so sorry about Deborah. I will scold her when I see her."

"Oh, not on my account," Portia said, thinking that a scolding was certainly in order. "Hey, can you tell me how to get to the lovely Keene Best Western?"

He could, and did. She wrote down what he said and tossed the piece of paper onto her passenger seat. Then she closed the car door. "Well, goodbye," she told him, forcibly ignoring, once again, that clear discomfort.

"Portia," said John, who wasn't taking her outstretched hand, "before, when I said I remembered you, I didn't mean that I remembered the appointment. I meant that I remembered you. I remember you," he said. "I went to college with you."

Still, ridiculously, she held out her hand. Only the ground wasn't quite there anymore, just a slightly tilted thing underfoot. She frowned at him. "You were at Dartmouth?"

"Yes. We didn't know each other. But I knew you. I knew who you were."

Who she was? It was nearly unbearable to think about who she was.

"Yes?" Portia managed.

"I knew Tom. I was in his fraternity."

She nodded glumly. She looked at him again, trying to imagine him younger, but he already looked young, and with more hair, but that brought nothing back. It had been one of the bigger fraternities, with, thanks to Dartmouth's quarterly sessions, an eternally shifting population in the house, not that she'd ever noticed anything when she was around Tom, on her way to Tom, in retreat from Tom. She hadn't thought about Tom in a long time.

"I'm sorry, I took you off guard."

"No, it's okay. I don't remember you."

"Oh, I was a year behind you. And everybody was always coming and going, right? That crazy Dartmouth Plan. I went to France for almost a year. And you left for a while, too, I think."

"Yes..." Her mind raced. "I was in Europe."

"Ah. When I came back from France, your class had graduated, but then I started seeing you around campus again."

She nodded dully. "I was working for the admissions office."

"You know," he said, "this is sounding a little stalkerish. I apologize. It wasn't like that. But I always thought you were..."

She looked at him sharply, and he seemed to take control of himself.

"Anyway, it's nice to see you again."

"Nice to see you," she said heartily. "Nice to meet you."

"Yes."

They stood for too long a moment. Portia was nursing a sick feeling that began to rattle through her abdomen, dissipating as it radiated. She was forgetting where she was, not physically so much, but in the span of her life, as the curtain she had strung across her wake began to flicker and then ripple, showing little views of herself as she'd been in that fragile, dangerous time. She was no longer in contact with anyone who'd known her then, and for good reason. Now, ambushed, she was surprised by her anger.

"Maybe I should have mentioned it sooner," he said quietly.

"Yes, maybe you should have."

She reached for his hand and gave it a brisk, cold shake. Then she turned her back on him and went to the driver's-side door and got in. She made a point of not looking back, but she couldn't get out of there fast enough. Once she was clear of the driveway, with the crude, homemade sign in her rearview mirror, she drove without direction through the woods, turning and turning as the roads forked and met. She was greedy for the darkness, which grew as she drove, and the cold, which she would not alleviate. It took nearly fifteen minutes to feel safe, but when she did, she pulled off into a stand of white pines, and stopped the car, and covered her face with her hands.

*In the middle of my sophomore year, my father was hospitalized with
depression. This event affected every aspect of my family. For one thing,
I found that I was required to be in charge of my younger siblings after
school, which meant that it was impossible for me to continue to play
on the softball team. I also had to give up my volunteer services at the
hospital, a great disappointment to me. My father is back at work now,
and I have tried to make up for the time I missed in my extracurricular
activities. I wanted to explain this lapse in my participation, in light of
the situation in my family.*

CHAPTER THREE

THE WORST KIND OF FAILURE

When the call came, she was sitting at the round table in the corner of her room, with the heavy floral curtain mostly drawn. There was a grievously overpackaged application unfurled before her on the table and some tasteless tea from the in-room carafe, cooling rapidly in its plastic cup.

That would be him, she knew right away. Anyone else would have called her cell. Anything else could have waited.

The ring was shrill, almost metallic in this anonymous room. She sat up in her chair and placed her palm flat on the cool plastic of the laminate tabletop, her fingers splayed beside the plastic cup, listening to its irritating chirp. Oddly, she was thinking mostly of the applicant, this rigorously organized, prepped, and groomed seventeen-year-old. There was a rule, instilled in her early on—back at Dartmouth, actually—that you didn't start a folder if you couldn't finish it. *Applicatus interruptus,* one of her old colleagues had called it, and he'd been right, because it always happened when you came back to the essay or the recommendation, after the call or the trip to the bathroom or the Girl Scout at the door, that the person you'd been conjuring out of the words and numbers seemed to have slipped away, leaving behind a muddle of the previous application, and the kid from earlier that day with the sort of similar name, or the one who also had a mom who worked as an electrical engineer but who wanted to be a journalist—not, like this one, a pediatrician.

The phone continued to ring. She looked across to the table between her two queen-size beds where it was shrilling, bleating, and blinking, then down at the essay before her, instinctively finding the sentence she had just read: "... I realized that pediatric surgery would best combine my love of children and science, and my profound need to give back to my community." She could ignore the call, and who was making it, and what that meant.

She felt for her sad plastic cup of tea, only to find she didn't want any. Already, she was fighting the urge to know if she had remembered his voice right—not deep, not steady, and with a vein of uncertain intimacy. And besides, she had already forgotten whether the girl from Sudbury, Mass., wanted to be a pediatrician or a surgeon or a journalist, and whether she was a girl at all. So what would it matter, now? Then it occurred to her that he had to know she was here. Who would let the phone ring so long in an empty hotel room? This changed everything. She charged up, knocking the table as she crossed the room.

"Hello," she said.

"Portia?" Whether from the recent or—less likely, but, she supposed, possible—deeper past, she confirmed the familiarity of his voice.

"Yes?" she pretended.

"This is John Halsey. I'm not sure I told you my surname."

"Halsey," she said aloud, stalling. In fact, it wasn't a familiar name. But then, it hadn't been a familiar face.

"From the Quest School. From earlier."

Portia nodded, as if he could see that. "Yes," she said.

"Look, I just feel badly. I'm not sure exactly what happened, but I know I upset you, and I'm very sorry. I probably shouldn't be doing this." He gave a forced laugh. "I mean, I'm probably breaking some sort of college admissions protocol."

That's very possible, she thought. "It's fine," she said neutrally.

"I remembered where you said you were staying. I thought...well, I hoped I could..."

He seemed to hit a wall and stopped, waiting for her to rescue him. She waited, too, but she didn't help. "Have you had dinner?" he finally said.

It was past seven. She had not had dinner. She hadn't wanted it. She didn't particularly want it now.

"No," she said.

"Well, can I take you somewhere? We don't have much here, but there are one or two places you might not find on your own."

Entirely unannounced, the tiniest lick of hunger popped to life inside her. She ignored it.

"Or for a drink, if you'd prefer that." He was sounding frankly uneasy now. "Or Brewbakers, if you'd like some coffee."

"Only cappuccino in town," she heard herself say, instantly regretting even this concession.

"That's right!" He sounded so eager, so grateful to her for remembering.

Then more hunger. Two little matches, alight, joining forces.

She didn't want coffee. She wanted to ask him what he remembered about her. She wanted him to go away, but first to put his hands on her, if he could do that very carefully, without pissing her off. "Where are you?" she asked him.

"Downstairs."

She listened for a long moment. There is a sound to waiting. It sounds like held breath pounding its fists against the walls of the lung, damp and muffled beats. Or was that her own breath? she wondered.

"I don't want coffee," Portia told him. "Give me a few minutes."

She hung up the phone. She was wearing what she'd worn earlier, but only the top half of it, only the cashmere sweater, and underwear. Her tweed skirt was flung across the foot of one of the beds, the crumpled stockings beside them, the brown boots kicked off on the floor. She had only a change of clothes for tomorrow, a pair of green khakis, formal enough to represent Princeton but laid-back enough to connect with Northfield students. She didn't want to put the skirt back on again.

It was hard to resist the urge to rush. She was not late, she was not keeping him waiting, he was not a date. She refused to look at herself in the mirror, to fix anything about herself. She pulled on her boots again, closed the application (*journalist, Sudbury, girl*), and placed it on top of the unread pile, resigned to starting it again when she came back. Then she looked at the folders.

They were not to be seen. They were secret, private. To leave them out like this, when there was the smallest chance of someone seeing them — someone *not disinterested* seeing them — would be negligent. But to put them away was to concede the possibility of another person here, in her hotel room, which was worse than negligent. Which was calculated. She stood, looking at this sad tableau: roughed-up plastic table, orange files, some thick, some thin, in two stacks, abandoned cup, crumpled bit of hygienic cellophane. *You are not to do this,* she heard herself think.

Then she opened her suitcase and zipped the files inside. And left.

He — John Halsey — was in the lobby, perched on the arm of a chair covered in murky green fabric. He had his hands, his fists, actually (she could see them clenching and unclenching, even across the room), in the pockets of his brown corduroy jacket. He stood up as she reached him and extended one of those unfolding hands. "I'm sorry to surprise you like that."

I wasn't surprised, she almost said.

"No, it's all right," Portia told him. She was looking at him, gathering information, testing her earlier impressions: earnest young schoolmaster adrift among New Age flocks. No, that wasn't right, she could see that now. He had a kind of calm beneath the current fluster. And a beautiful throat, indifferently shaved. He dressed to please himself, because no one else cared in the slightest, and what pleased him were these still very crisp chinos and this still very white button-down shirt. He hadn't changed his clothes, a fact that reassured her, though she wasn't sure why. On the other hand, she couldn't understand how he could manage to look so clean at the end of a day. A day that had, at the very least, included an outdoor class on a working farm. "It's very friendly of you to call."

"I'm sure I'm breaking some kind of rule. Taking the admissions officer out to dinner, I mean. I suppose people try to butter you up."

She burst out laughing. This was, of course, such a vast understatement that it could only register as ridiculous. She had been buttered up by any number of acquaintances, alumni, college advisers, endless parents, of course, often with attendant flattery, invitations, offers, not to mention those desperadoes, the applicants themselves. Buttering up, as John had called it, was thoroughly understandable, but it was never a good idea and somewhat akin to slipping the cop a fifty: dubious upside, cataclysmic downside. But then, he had said it so cluelessly, it was strangely beguiling. "Well, that does happen, yes."

He suggested the restaurant in the lobby. It was awful, he admitted, but probably no less awful than anywhere else nearby.

"Well," she said, laughing, "with a recommendation like that...I do have work. I can't take very much time away." This was patently untrue. Of course she had work. There was always work, but that wasn't the point. Even if, like those literate adulterers Paolo and Francesca, she read no more today, there would be no difficulty in finishing the folders she'd brought with her. She was alone here. No one cared what time she went to bed. And in any case, she felt, with every passing instant of this odd, strained conversation, that a sober, solitary, and above all *early* night was the last thing in the world she wanted.

The restaurant, off to the side of the lobby, was called The Grille. She might have recited the menu from the generic plants growing atop the booth dividers, the high-quality silk flowers on the tables. To her own surprise, she felt real hunger when she took her laminated menu from the waitress: prime rib, breast of chicken, Caesar salad.

"Do you eat meat?" she asked him.

He looked up at her and frowned. "I do. But I'm a little hush-hush about it at work. Technically, we don't have a policy about it one way or the other, but the students — or I guess the parents — skew heavily in favor of tofu and seitan."

"I hate that stuff," she said, reading and rereading the description of the New York strip, which used both the adjectives *succulent* and *luscious* and boasted a misplaced apostrophe ("seared with herb's"). "I mean, seitan. I don't mind tofu. But whoever dreamed up seitan should be force-fed bulgur for the rest of his life."

John laughed. "I'm not a bulgur fan myself. I remember they gave it to us on Outward Bound when I was a teenager. We'd just come off these three-day solos, where they'd left us each on our own little island in Penobscot Bay. When it was over, they picked us up and brought us back to base camp, and they cooked us up a big feast of bulgur. Twenty-five starving kids. I mean, *so* hungry. We hadn't eaten in days, most of us. Well, a few of the more ingenious ones managed to remember which plants they'd taught us were all right. But I don't think any of us could get that bulgur down."

She smiled. "Well, I hope you don't mind if I order a steak. Who can resist a dish described not only as luscious, but succulent, too?"

"Don't you love those redundancies? Like 'anonymous stranger.' And 'diametrically opposed.'"

"Don't forget 'proactive.' And 'exact replica.'"

"'Frozen tundra,'" he said. "Well, we might have to take that one off the list soon. Would you like some wine?"

"Oh...no, thank you. Go ahead, if you like."

He didn't like, or said he didn't.

"Should I have suggested beer?" he asked when the waitress was gone. "After all, you're a graduate of Dartmouth College, beer consumption capital of New England."

"You must mean that sticky stuff on the basement floors of all the fraternities."

"Yes." He laughed. "I shouldn't act superior. I told you, I was in a fraternity. For a while, anyway. I lost interest and stopped going to the parties, let alone the meetings. I think they even quit coming after me for dues."

"Why did you join?" she asked.

He shrugged. "The usual reasons. Group of friends. A place to go. I was on the rugby team, and everyone was in the same house. But I stopped playing rugby, too, after my sophomore year. I had this conversion to my academic work, amazingly enough. I'd never thought of myself as a student, though of course I'd been in school my whole life. Suddenly, everything sort of snapped into focus, you know?"

Portia nodded tentatively.

"I was an education major. It wasn't a big major. There weren't very many of us, but we talked about teaching incessantly. We talked theories of education, theories of childhood learning. Waldorf versus Montessori. There were real fights." He shook his head. "But the fact was, when they sent us down to intern in the public schools in West Lebanon, most of us couldn't even control our classes. It was very deflating. After that, a few of the education majors sneaked off and took the LSATs."

"But not you," Portia said.

"No, I still carried the torch. I went off to Groton after I graduated. I was all set to start the Dead Poets Society and teach them to seize the day and all that. But after two years I just had to claw my way out."

"Why?" Portia asked. "Did you hate it?"

"No, no. I loved it. I'd gone to a boarding school, so I knew the culture. But from the other side of the divide, I could see how great the kids were. I loved how they were all excited about going to college and becoming fine, upstanding citizens. But it was such an easy life, with my little apartment in the fourth-form boys' dorm, and three meals a day at the cafeteria, and smart students who went out of their way to appreciate me, if only because they wanted me to write them recommendations. It was like the poppy field in *The Wizard of Oz*. I just could feel myself getting sleepier and sleepier. I thought, I'm going to drop off any minute and wake up in forty years with a Groton writing award named after me and some sort of framed declaration on my wall. It's going to float by me in a beautiful haze of crew shells and foliage and long shadows on the quad. I have to leave immediately."

She couldn't help smiling. The waitress brought them two pallid salads: orange tomato wedges on limp iceberg. She ignored hers.

"So, what, you went to the opposite end of the spectrum, right? South Central? South Bronx?"

"Even farther. Uganda. I enrolled in the Peace Corps. I was there for two years."

"Wow," Portia said, watching him spear his sorry tomato. "Good for you."

"Oh, don't say that." He looked up at her. "I didn't do it to be good. I just couldn't stand feeling like a heel. It wasn't why I'd become a teacher, Dead Poets Society or not. Of course it's valid to educate the wealthy. I mean, what's the alternative? It would be pretty irresponsible of us not to teach those students. They're probably going to end up running the show, right? Better they should be engaged with the past, and the history of ideas. Just because there's an inequity of education in this country, that doesn't mean we should shortchange the privileged. The goal should be to get everyone else up to that level. I mean, I really believe that. But after Groton I felt as if I had to do two years of penance. And I knew, when I left there, they'd just replace me with someone exactly like me, who was just as capable of teaching those kids. I wasn't at all special, you know? It's just I felt like I'd been borrowing from the bank for years, and I had to pay it back."

She listened to him, sipping her water. There was a physical component to all of this passion, she noted: a flush, not to the face, which seemed nearly impassive, belying the clear emotional investment in what he was saying, but to the neck, the throat. She watched it appear and spread, around the neck, up to the ears, down into the visible chest through his unbuttoned collar. She knew this was voyeuristic, improper, but it actually felt clinical, as if she were merely observing some experiment she'd had a part in setting up and hence maintained an interest in. But what was the nature of her interest?

When her steak was set down, Portia felt a jolt of hunger. She made herself wait until he'd been served.

"You know," he said a moment later, "you look exactly the same."

She swallowed uncomfortably, her eyes on her plate. She wanted, suddenly, to be left alone. She needed the protein more than the company, more than the deep, alluring tension at this table and that thin possibility of something good that it conjured. "I doubt that," she said, pointedly cutting another triangle of meat.

"No, you do. I recognized you right away. Your hair is shorter. You dress better. But don't we all? I mean, we're not still going around in down vests, thank God."

"Thank God," she echoed, smiling despite herself.

"And you have that...I always noticed it about you, how much there seemed to be going on with you. There was always more. Under the surface, I mean."

He seemed to have given the matter a certain amount of thought. That in itself was disturbing, but she didn't feel threatened. The only threat, she reflected, seemed to come from herself. Because she had already made up her mind about this. She had already made out her wish list for this one night in Keene, New Hampshire, for this unknown man from her past, with his long fingers and thinning hair and beautiful throat. It did not necessarily involve conversation, though she had nothing against conversation, as long as it revealed nothing about her. Or nothing important.

"I have to tell you," she said, "I don't remember you at all."

"That's okay," John said self-effacingly.

"I mean, it's a little strange. You're sure you were there," she said with forced humor.

"Oh, absolutely. I could probably dredge up the Winter Carnival themes, or some outrage by the *Dartmouth Review*, just to prove myself. Look, it's not complicated. I sort of had a crush on you. I saw you around the campus. I *noticed* you, I mean. But you were taken, and there are rules about that, especially when you know the guy. So I just went along my way and had lots of meaningless love affairs. You know how it is."

"Oh sure." She laughed. It was, it occurred to her, almost immaterial that she liked him. It didn't matter whether she liked him or not. But she did, actually, like him.

"And then, you weren't with him. I don't know the details. We weren't close. He didn't discuss his personal life with me. But I don't think you were that blonde who was always tiptoeing down the stairs at two a.m."

"I was not that blonde," she confirmed, though with some sarcasm. She hoped it sounded like sarcasm.

"I had this idea you'd just, I don't know, left. Or transferred, or something."

"I traveled a bit," she said. "Junior year. I actually graduated a year later than the rest of my class."

He nodded. "I had a girlfriend when you came back. Otherwise..."

She looked flatly at him. She wondered if he knew how offputting it was, this image he was conjuring of their unrealized affair. But then, to her own irritation, she understood that she wasn't feeling nearly as put off as she ought to be.

"How's your steak?"

She looked down at her steak. She gave it a fresh appraisal, trying not to hold against it everything she already knew about it. It didn't look very appealing. It was nondescript in its steaklike qualities and looking less appetizing by the second. "I guess I wasn't as hungry as I thought I was."

"Or it's bad," he suggested.

"No. I mean, it's sort of par for the course at a chain hotel somewhere in America. I feel like I've eaten this same steak a hundred times already. I used to oversee applications from the Pacific region. Mainly California, but also Hawaii and Alaska, so I would travel out there all the time. This is my first year covering New England. Princeton seems to really like Best Western. They always book us here. I don't know," she said with a sigh, "maybe Mr. Best Western is an alum. Maybe there's a special Tiger rate."

"Ooh." John smiled. "It's all so...corrupt. Just what we've always suspected about Ivy League admissions."

The mood between them shifted on a dime. "But I didn't mean that," she said tightly. "The process isn't at all corrupt. It may be complex, but not corrupt."

"I wasn't being serious."

"No, really. I know people think there are all these secret codes, or handshake deals in the back room, or we keep a well-thumbed copy of the *Social Register* in the office, but that isn't what we're about. You have no idea how absurd the situation is. Eighteen thousand applications last year! And the vast majority of them are great—well-prepared academically, interesting kids with plans for the future and talents they could bring to the community. It's just an incredibly difficult job."

"Portia," he said, a palpable edge of dismay in his voice, "I didn't mean to suggest anything."

"But everyone thinks we're just throwing the names up in the air and admitting the ones who land inside the circle, or we're sadists who love to stick it to kids all over the world. I've been doing this for sixteen years, and I have to tell you, I've never worked with a single person who enjoyed rejecting applicants. If you ask any admissions officer what they like about their job, they talk about saying yes, not saying no."

"Well," he said, still trying to break the mood, "they'd hardly admit to enjoying saying no."

"If that were true, it's something I'd see," she said crossly. "Believe me, at the tenth hour of the fifth day of the third week of committee meetings, when people are desperate to get to that last application and make that last decision, there's still no joy in saying no. We're in it because we want to say yes to these kids. They astound us. They have amazing minds and amazing dreams. The rest of it, the saying no, that's just what we have to do so we can get to say yes. It's the worst part of our job. It's the *job* part of our job."

"Okay!" He put up his hands.

"I'm just sick of all the attitude. Nobody wants to talk to *you*. Whoever you are. They couldn't care less where you come from and what matters to you. All they see is the job title, and all they care about is what you can do for them. Like my first boss at Dartmouth told me when I was hired, he said, 'When people find out you're an admissions officer, they'll suddenly become very, very interested in what you do. But they won't give a shit about you.'"

"That must be hard," John said carefully. He had sat forward on his chair and was resting his chin in his hands. He, too, seemed to have abandoned his meal.

"There are only two ways people talk to you. Mostly it's this awful pleading, you know, 'I know the most fantastic kid . . .' or, 'I *have* the most fantastic kid. . . .' You're constantly being bombarded, and all you can do is grin and nod and say you hope this wonderful kid will apply, which you *do* hope. I mean, what do they expect you'll say? 'He sounds fantastic! He's in!'"

"Portia," John said, "we should change the subject."

"But the other reaction," she went on, bulldozing past him, "is much, much worse. Because if, sometime in the recent or misty past, Princeton University has actually rejected some wondrous young person near and dear to them, then you are no friend, and basic good manners are not called for. Because if this brilliant child, so gifted, so sweet, so in love with learning for its own sake, has been deemed, by you, *unworthy* to attend Princeton, then that can only mean that you and your equally corrupt peers have allowed some lesser brat to buy his or her way into our elitist institution, and we're all such greedy shits that we're willing to serve up the very principles of higher education, not to mention the American dream, just so some blue-blooded prep school boy can be the tenth generation of Princeton men in his family."

John sat back in his seat, hands folded. He was waiting for her to finish.

"Or let's say the rejected applicant is, God forbid, the first poor soul in ten generations of Princeton men to be denied admission. Obviously that proves the university is enslaved by affirmative action, and we feel free to discriminate against applicants who happen to be white, which is a disgrace for which I am personally responsible, because after all, I only do this job because I like putting people down, and everyone knows that people who get their kicks out of rejecting other people are the worst kind of failures themselves."

She ran out of breath. Literally. And reached for her water glass, wishing fleetingly that she'd asked for that wine. She was thoroughly ashamed of herself, not because she'd revealed any secret thing about her work—she hadn't, she told herself quickly, or nothing important—but because, with that final thought, she'd revealed some potent thing about herself. Which she now profoundly regretted.

"Well, that's quite a speech," John said mildly.

"I'm sorry!" She was feeling the heat in her cheeks. Intense, tear-threatening heat. "I'm sorry. I don't think you deserved that. It just kind of builds up, you know?"

"Well, I know now."

"Look," she heard herself say, "it was nice of you to call. I'm really sorry, but I think I'd better go upstairs."

"Portia," he said. He looked at her. He wasn't angry. Or even baffled, she saw. Something else, though not quite clear. Or quite clear, she realized suddenly. Only silent.

"No, I...You know, I have a ton of work upstairs, and I have to be at Northfield at ten, so I probably shouldn't even have come down." She was speaking so quickly, she nearly missed the clipped tones of her own mortification. There was only this race with herself, to the elevator and then her room. "But it was really nice to see you again."

"Please don't do that. Let's order some coffee. Let's talk more."

But I don't want to talk, she nearly said. "I can't. I'm sorry. I need to leave."

"Wait," he said. It was a caution, calm and low, but utterly serious. He got deliberately to his feet. He reached slowly, pointedly, into an inside pocket of his corduroy jacket and took out a wallet, never looking away. He removed two twenties and put them on the table. Portia's eye lingered on the bills. There was something vaguely sordid about them, as if the money were for something else, though that was not logical. But the two of them, they looked as if they were in a rush, didn't they? Even though they weren't going anywhere. They weren't. So much for her stupid wish list. So much for this pointless, pathetic distraction. She looked back in the direction of the kitchen. The waitress, at least, was nowhere to be seen.

"Let me walk you to the elevator," John said.

She let him, and she made herself walk. She was aware of her own footfalls on the smooth, hard floor of the lobby. The woman at the desk, not the woman who had checked her in, another woman, looked up at them. She wouldn't know, Portia thought, that John wasn't with her. She wouldn't stop them. No one, she realized suddenly, was going to stop them.

It was night now, and the place seemed oddly inert. Even the Muzak was barely there. She strained to hear it, was suddenly, disproportionately, afraid of what it meant that she couldn't hear it, but she could pick up only its faintest imprint, as if she had suddenly, rapidly, ascended a steep mountain, and her ears were thick, but not so thick that she couldn't hear John, who was trying to speak to her.

"Portia," he said as she stabbed the elevator button.

"It was fun catching up with you," Portia said, turning back to him but declining to meet his gaze. "It was nice of you to call."

"I want to say something to you," he said quietly.

"I wish I could stay up later, but I have—"

"A lot of work. Yes, I know," he said quickly, and she was surprised at how angry he didn't sound. He just seemed to want to get on, to something else.

Behind her, the elevator door opened with a sound of grinding metal. Portia looked into the beige interior. "So...thanks," she managed. "Let me know if there's anything you need. Your students need," she added quickly. She stepped into the elevator and turned around. She made a show of selecting her floor and pressing the button.

"I want you to know something," he said. She had to listen very closely. "I loved seeing you." He seemed to be taking part in an entirely different conversation. She looked at him in mute amazement. "When you forget everything else, I mean, all of this...discomfort. I want you to remember that. I loved seeing you. I was happy to see you. Portia."

What happened then happened quickly. She could not have said, later, what order things took, and who bore which responsibilities, and what might be the reasonable effects of her own step back, or his step forward, the outstretched hand (whose? and to what purpose — handshake or life-line?), all to the rhythm of a creaking, labored noise from the sliding elevator door, though by the time she knew what sound that was he was already inside, and the door had closed, and the two of them were on their way.

*I can remember clearly the day my father threw us out. My mother
pulled me into the car and locked the door. I was crying because my
father was so angry. He threw something at the car window, and it
cracked. My mother was crying very hard. She didn't drive very well,
because my father had always done the driving in our family, but she
managed to drive us away. We went to visit her sister in New York
State, and stayed there for several months. Later, we returned to Maine,
but settled in a different part of the state, where I was able to attend
the Yarmouth School on a scholarship. I am extremely grateful to the
school, for allowing me access to this excellent high school environment,
which my mother could never have afforded on her salary. Now, as I
look ahead to college, I am thrilled by the intellectual vistas opening
to me. Though I may well emerge, five years from now, as the medical
student I imagine myself becoming, I am also open to other possibilities.
The only thing I do know is that I want to use my gifts to give back to
my community.*

CHAPTER FOUR

WHAT WE LET OUT

In the room, it was more than dark. The garish light from the hallway,
light flung geometrically through the opened door—the flung-open
door—disappeared as the door slapped shut behind them. Then darkness
again, with every other sense screaming to fill the void.

Portia felt for the bed. It wasn't difficult to find. The room was all bed,
first behind her and then beneath her. Its cover felt slippery and tightly
stretched. She wanted to be pressed into it. She wanted to feel the heaviness of her own body against it and the heaviness of his body against her.
She wanted a lot of things.

The darkness, that was her doing, too. There had been a moment earlier, as she'd held open the door to leave, to go downstairs, when her hand

had touched the switch and stopped—a long moment in which she had infused this normally mindless gesture with grave implications. Not a matter of saving the hotel chain some expense or the environment a pinch of its failing resources. Like those orange applications folders, safely zipped into her suitcase, the switched-off light meant simply that she had intended not to return alone. Or at least admitted that possibility. And then if—when—if—it did come to happen, this allowed, likely, intended eventuality, her own preference for darkness would preempt without any awkward discussion:

Can I turn on a light?

No.

I want to see you.

No.

It wasn't her own body she didn't want revealed. She was not self-conscious. It was him she didn't want to see, or not yet. She just wanted to be able to concentrate on this: the sound of their clothing in contact, the salted taste on her own tongue, the feel of a mouth at her neck and the hand at the small of her back, pulling her against him in the dark.

Neither of them had said a thing since the lobby, not a thing, not even in the elevator (when he had held her so tightly, her back pressed so hard against the faux wooded plastic of the wall, that she had wondered if they might actually derail), and not in the hall (where he had stood next to her, tense like a runner in the blocks, waiting for her to drop the plastic key card into its slot, then wrenching the door handle himself). There was...not precisely *romance* in the silence, only a plain synchronicity of intent. *What I want is what you want.* But the reasons behind all that wanting—Portia had no idea what they were, neither his nor even her own.

There was hair on his body, long like the hair on his head. She could feel it, slipping between her fingers as she ran her hands over him. He was thin but soft. She liked that. She liked what she didn't feel: ridges and ripples and densities of muscle. She liked the give of him, the concavity of his abdomen, the hollow below his hip bone when he turned on his side, even the long, inelegant scar that seemed to point to his groin. Of course, she didn't think any of these things as they happened, only later, leisurely, somewhat amazed at herself. For now, the impressions tore by like a vivid shifting landscape seen through a train window, and she knew enough to reach for the joy of them. Her breath came quickly, as if the two of them were competing for oxygen. Her hand slipped easily beneath the edge of the pants he wore. His hand made a deliberate journey up her back, as if he were reassuring himself that each vertebra was where it needed to be. When he reached the strap of her bra, he went discreetly past.

"Can I turn on a light?" he asked suddenly.

"No," said Portia.

"I want to see you."

She shook her head and pushed the shirt up over his head. Then, realizing that he couldn't see that she had shaken her head, she said, "I don't want to."

"What?" He stopped everything. His hands on her back, his mouth at her throat. "Do you want me to stop?"

"No." She smiled. "Don't stop. Just . . . I don't want to turn the light on."

"But you're beautiful," he said, not understanding.

That's beside the point, she nearly said. Instead, she kissed him. Already, she loved kissing him. She loved the roughness of his lips and then the dark softness inside his mouth. She loved the way his tongue knew how, precisely how, to glide against her own tongue. She loved the language, first faltering, then fluent, their mouths had devised and how they were congratulating each other for their cleverness. She tried to remember if she had ever been so deeply kissed. She couldn't, suddenly, remember if she had ever been kissed all.

"Let me," he said, somewhat indistinctly, as if she were preventing him. She nearly tore off her own sweater, she was so impatient. Every part of her seemed to be caterwauling, selfish, whining. She felt crude and pushy. She wanted to make him do what she wanted, and he knew exactly what that was, only he wasn't doing it fast enough, and that was maddening. She found his head at her abdomen: not high enough, not low enough. His cheek turned against her skin as if the universe attended his wishes. She moved against him, thinking, *Come on.*

From outside, the night-splitting noise of a motorcycle, out of nowhere, heading off to somewhere. It was a rude noise, like something guttural and enraged. It stopped them both. "Born to be wild," said John. She understood that he was smiling.

She tugged at his shirt.

"We don't have to rush," said John.

But we do, she thought, actually disliking him for that instant.

The bed seemed to tip in the darkness. It felt contrived, controlled, as on a fun-house ride. She nearly rolled away from him and had to pull herself back, hauling her own weight along his length. Why was he so contained? Wasn't he the one with the long-ago crush? Wasn't lust cumulative? She had the briefest instinct to slap him, but then she felt his hands between her legs and forgot what she was so angry about.

There was, when they were finally naked, a sort of exhalation between them, a kind of mutual calming or resetting of the metronome. She found herself slowing down, touching with new care: his chest, his nape, which was oddly sharp, the twin depressions at the base of his spine. Their limbs tangled together; she lost track. Rib cage jutted rib cage. His mouth was no longer too high, no longer too low. How insightful he was, she thought, after all, how sly to pretend all that ignorance when he was this clever, this passionate, all along. She wondered who else must be in the room making all that noise. Only an unfurled pant leg still caught her by the ankle, like a Peter Pan shadow, but Portia didn't kick it away. She liked the feeling of being tethered, of this one filament tying her to whatever propriety she'd jettisoned, a chance of finding her way back. She would need to find her way back when this was over, when John Halsey was no longer making love to her in a nondescript hotel room in Keene, New Hampshire, an act that somehow banished all banality from the setting. She could, and did, forget herself, and where she was, and who she was, and the myriad reasons she ought to have resisted. But for the time she held him—and she did hold him, both as he moved inside her and after, still and damp and curled against her—the points of contact they made seemed more compelling than anything else she could summon to mind. At rest, he breathed heavily into her hair. He said her name, once, then seemed to think better of it and settled for touch. One hand came to rest on her hip; the other reached deep into the hair behind her ear. Both were so inexpressibly tender that Portia felt suddenly, alarmingly, in danger of tears.

"Tell me about Nelson," she said, to save herself.

"Nelson?"

Now that it was fully night, the white lights of the parking lot found the edges of the curtains, making them both bluish at the edges, just visible.

"He's not . . . I'm assuming he's not your biological son," she faltered.

"No, you assume correctly. I adopted him at six weeks."

"In Africa?" she guessed. "While you were in the Peace Corps?"

"Well, yes and no." He sighed. "I was there for two years, mainly in Kampala. The school I taught in was part of a Catholic compound in the city, run by a priest named Father Josiah. Fantastic man. He'd gone to university in Italy, and he'd lived in Europe and the States before going home to Uganda. He was insane about backgammon. We must have played a thousand games of backgammon. He didn't have the slightest interest in converting me, but he was extremely interested in beating me at backgammon." John laughed.

"Did you play for stakes?" she asked.

"No. Nothing like that. But we had wonderful conversations. I got more of an education from him than I got anywhere else. Very brilliant, decent guy. Very stoic. You know, the communities we worked with, everyone had HIV. The kids in the school had it. The parents were just withering and dying. First the men would die, and they'd infected their wives, so then the wives would die, and that left all the kids to be raised by their grandmothers. And the kids, of course, were infected in utero. You'd just watch them get listless and skinny."

"It must have been very hard," she said, feeling the inadequacy of that.

"It's more like a learned skill. You talk to Peace Corps folks, only the details change. Otherwise, there's this complete uniformity of experience. It's like emotional hazing. You trot on over, thinking you're going to fix everything. Or, even if you won't admit to thinking that, you at least want to fix *something*. Then, when you get there, you find yourself under this hammer that just tap, tap, taps you into the ground. The problems are so relentless, not only can you not fix them, you can't really fix any part of them. And people just lose it. They sign on for the Peace Corps because they think of themselves as problem solvers, and here they've come to the ends of the earth and they can't do anything—I mean, not anything substantial—about what they're seeing. And this is on top of all the other stuff, like the deprivations and the isolation, not to mention the microbes. So you quickly get to a crisis point, where you either go back to wherever you came from or you undergo a third world readjustment. Actually, *correction* might be a better word. It's sort of bizarrely freeing. You get to this point where it's okay that you can't fix it. You just don't want to make it any worse than it was before. Making it a tiny bit better is now your most ambitious desire."

"And you got to that place, I take it." She rolled onto her side and found that she could see him, more or less. He had his arms up over his head and was lying flat. The hollow below his rib cage rose and fell. She found that long, ragged scar on his abdomen and traced its curious length with a fingertip.

"Yeah. It wasn't that hard for me, actually. Probably because of this priest. He basically told me there was no point in falling apart. I'd just be wasting time. His time." John laughed. "And he was a busy man. He had a clinic to run, and the school, and an orphanage, and a food program. He ran a literacy program and a sponsorship program. And of course, there was all that backgammon he needed me to play." He shook his head.

Portia smiled. "So that's where you adopted Nelson? You brought him home with you?"

"Not exactly. I finished up my two years in Africa and then I went traveling. Mostly in Europe. And then I came back to the States. I'd left Uganda, let's see... about eight months earlier. Father Josiah wrote to me at my parents' address. He was very cunning about it. He didn't say anything about coming back. He just wanted to let me know that my son had been born. The baby was in the orphanage and he was very healthy. You'd think I would have been angry. Or baffled, anyway. You know, had I forgotten I'd had sex with some woman before I left? But that wasn't what he meant. He meant that I was supposed to take care of this particular child. This was my child. And I remember, the whole thing was so calm. You know, there I was in the living room of my parents' house outside of Philadelphia. They'd kept the letter for me — I was away, visiting some friends in the Midwest, and now I was back and I was supposed to be looking for a teaching job. So it was already a month old. I remember sitting there on my mother's very proper chintz-covered sofa, looking out the French doors at the backyard. And my mom was out there, weeding the peonies. And there was not a moment of uncertainty, that's what was so bizarre. No *Should I? Shouldn't I?* Of course I was going back to get this baby. He was my son. I mean, already. And he was born, and he was healthy. You know, he was *waiting* for me. Actually, the only thing I was stressing out about was how to tell my parents their first grandson wasn't going to have the family chin."

Portia laughed, a bit uneasily.

"It sort of makes you wonder what this biological thing *is,* you know? People make such a fuss about having their own genetic children. I'd never really thought about it before Nelson. I guess I just assumed I'd have biological children. But even sitting there, half the world away, without even laying eyes on him, he was already mine. Just because someone had told me so. Just like that. I didn't even have a snapshot."

"And you felt the same way when you got back to Uganda and met him?"

"Yes. Absolutely. I picked him up out of the basket, and I didn't put him down for the next three years, basically."

They lay without talking for a few minutes. Cars *whoosh*ed and groaned up the road outside the hotel. Once, a flap-flap of footsteps sounded down the hall outside.

"Does he ever ask about his biological parents?" Portia said.

"Actually, no. I've always wondered about that. I've always wondered why he wasn't more curious. He's never asked me to take him back, to find a cousin or an aunt or a sibling. Somebody. He never seemed interested. And I never suggested it. Maybe I'm afraid of it, I don't know."

"You shouldn't be. I'm sure you're a wonderful father."

"Thank you," he said. He sounded actually moved. "We all make it up as we go along. I'm sure the biological dads are just as clueless."

"I guess." She smiled. "Though my mom always acted as if she knew what she was doing."

"Well, that's what matters. It's what experienced teachers always tell new teachers: 'Act like you know what you're talking about.' We all do it. Then, one day, we magically realize that we do, actually, know what we're talking about."

In the darkness, she nodded, not for him but for herself. Maybe everything was like that, she thought. She remembered the first years along her own odd career trajectory, fudging statistics when asked, trying to act as if she understood the strange and unwieldy behemoth that was college admissions, reading its runes to glean some semblance of logic when there was little logic. Whim and art, she would tell herself, as if that made up for not knowing what she was doing. And then one day she realized that she did, in fact, know what she was doing. She just didn't really know why.

John was quiet for another moment, then he got up to use the bathroom, and when he turned on the light, Portia saw him for an instant in the open doorway. He was beautiful. She hadn't really understood until that moment how fluidly the parts she had felt with her hands and mouth were joined, how unified and lovely. He was muscular but not padded and, even in the garish bathroom light, a kind of lemony pale, a shade both false and appealing. She felt a quick pulse of longing—informed longing, she told herself, because she knew now what he looked like and what he felt like and what he could do to her. She waited for him to finish.

When he came back, he sat at the foot of the bed and looked at her. He had left the door to the bathroom open a bit, and the light cut into the room in a thin wedge. "You know," he said, "I feel as if there's some basic information we haven't covered here."

"I'm of age, thanks," she said, smiling.

"Yes. I mean, no, I wasn't thinking that."

"Of sound mind. Of sound body."

"Very sound. Clearly. I was thinking...you know, I wanted to tell you that I don't do this. I wouldn't say never. But what I did tonight, coming to the hotel like this. I've never done it before."

"I thought you were just coming to take me to dinner," she said coyly.

"I was! I really was."

"But hoping for something else."

"I don't know...." He gave up on this thought and regrouped. "I don't know anything about your situation. I don't know...for example, I don't know if you're involved with anyone."

"Are you involved?" she asked.

"No. I was for a long time, but we've separated. It's complicated, because we work together, and we're close friends. And we've helped to raise each other's children. But no, not involved any longer."

"The famous Deborah Rosengarten?" she asked.

He looked surprised. "How did you know that?"

"Educated guess."

"We really are friends," he offered. "I know it sounds lame."

"Not at all. It's great that you're still on good terms. I'm not on good terms with anyone like that."

Tom, she thought, and she could see he was thinking it, too. But he had learned, evidently, from the last time and didn't say it out loud.

"Are you involved now?" he said instead.

She considered this. The truth, whatever it was, was not her only consideration. There were other, complicating factors, like the past and the future. It was a question she had not given nearly enough thought to for far too long a time, and now, instead of having a settled, concrete sense of what the answer was, where her life was, whom — if anyone — she was tied to, she found she had nothing at all.

"Are you not sure?" he said with false levity.

"I'm involved," she said quickly. "I'm sorry."

"No, no. Don't be sorry. I had no . . . I don't have an *agenda*. And it's none of my business."

"I wish . . . ," she said before she could stop herself. She'd meant, it was obvious, that she wished it were. His business. But she didn't, she couldn't. It was all complicated enough without that. And she couldn't really want him badly enough. Not out of the blue like this, with a chance meeting, a jolt from the past, that part of her past she had worked mightily to excise from her sense of self, and a single night in a thoroughly anonymous hotel room. Lives didn't change so suddenly. Her life couldn't change.

"You wish . . . ?" he prompted after a moment.

"No, it's nothing. I get very tangled up sometimes. I feel as if I don't know anything, you know, even after all this time. Sometimes I think I knew more half my lifetime ago. Which begs the question, What have I been doing with the second half? I have these vivid memories of the books I read in high school, and the things I did and thought about. Now I can hardly remember the novels I read for my book club last year or the last real insight I had."

"It is strange," John said, but tentatively. He wasn't necessarily agreeing with her, she understood. He might be having a different sort of life, a better sort of life, she thought, and pitying her.

"I mean, do you remember getting your acceptance letter from Dartmouth? I remember it, in Technicolor. It was just after I turned eighteen, and I actually remember what I was wearing and what my mother and I cooked for dinner that night. Now I'm the one putting the letter in the mail, and I know less than that eighteen-year-old girl. That's not the way it's supposed to work, is it?"

"No," he agreed. "But somehow that's how it always does work. You shouldn't feel embarrassed," he told her, embarrassing her more by knowing she was embarrassed in the first place. "You'd be amazed how often I seem to have this conversation, or some version of it. We're in Dante's forest, you know. Wasn't he thirty-five in *The Inferno*? We're all like this, wondering if we did the right things, how it would all have been different if we'd turned left instead of right. Besides, we can't expect to understand what the hell we're doing," he said, moving up the bed. He lay by her side and propped himself up on an elbow. "You know what Kierkegaard said about living life forwards but understanding it backwards."

"Backwards?" she said, feeling even duller.

"'Life can only be understood backwards, but it must be lived forwards.'"

"Now that's impressive." She laughed. "Dante and Kierkegaard in one shot. Let's hear it for a liberal arts education."

"Rah," he said, kissing her almost chastely on the cheek. "This is what I tell my students. My male students, anyway. Go to college. It will help you impress women in bed."

"What do you tell your female students?" she said archly.

"I tell them not to give up on the boys. Just let them have a few years to catch up. Some of them will turn out not to be complete idiots."

Portia smiled. "And they believe you?"

"Of course not. They think I'm the worst kind of gender apologist. They know perfectly well the only rational response to a teenage boy is total disgust. These girls recognize a weaker vessel when they see it."

"Except for your Jeremiah, I take it."

"Well, Jeremiah." He shrugged. "Jeremiah is off the charts. In a number of ways. He's not what you might call a socially successful kid. But I doubt Bill Gates had girls lining up for him in high school either. The other students, they certainly keep their distance, but they do respect him. I can see that. It's sort of heartening, actually. Compared to what he went through at his old school, benign neglect from the student body is a fantastic state of affairs. But now," he said sternly, "this really is beyond the pale. Here we are, stark naked in bed together, schoolmaster and college admissions officer, discussing an applicant. That's surely not kosher."

"He's not an applicant yet," she pointed out, knowing he was perfectly right.

"No, but he will be if I have anything to do with it. Princeton would be a paradise for him. Not that you heard me say that," he said, shaking a finger.

"I didn't hear a thing," Portia said.

He leaned over her and kissed her again, this time less chastely and not on her cheek. "You know," he said, "I'm surprised to hear you say your work isn't meaningful."

"I didn't say that," she objected.

"Well, implied it. Or that you felt less qualified to send the acceptance than you did to receive it."

She heard this, somewhat dumbstruck at its accuracy. "It isn't true," she managed to say, though she felt, more than ever, and hearing it put so succinctly, that it was. And also she was getting distracted.

"Good. Because I think your work must be incredibly fulfilling. You can change lives, can't you? I mean, it must be wonderful to take some kid who's fully capable of getting his teeth into a first-class education and then giving that to him. You must love doing that."

She nodded. It sounded good.

"All that saying *yes* you talked about. Downstairs."

"Yes," Portia said, but she wasn't sure what exactly she was saying yes to. John's hand was in the hollow of her belly, and nothing was holding still.

"Besides," she heard him say, "it's not like it's a simple thing. Admissions. *Admission.* Aren't there two sides to the word? And two opposing sides."

"What?" she asked him indistinctly. She was feeling something, definitely. It was harder to focus.

"Admission. It's what we let in, but it's also what we let out."

"Let out?" said Portia, trying to catch her breath.

"Our secrets," he whispered, enjoying himself. He had kissed her legs apart and was moving between them. "Of course. We admit a stranger to our homes. We admit a lover to our bodies, yes?"

Well, yes, she thought, losing, for the next moment, the train of their conversation.

"But when we admit something, we might also let it out," he said. He seemed, rather maddeningly, not to have stopped thinking. "That's true, isn't it? That we admit our secrets?"

Secrets, Portia thought. She was not inclined to speak. She had no breath to speak.

"I have them. You have them. Well, I think you have them."

She closed her eyes. She had them.

"Can I stay a little longer?" he asked. "I'd like to stay."

He was very close to her, close from chest to calf. It had come back, fast, the specific feel of his skin against her skin.

"Where is your son?" she managed to ask.

"He's playing illicit video games at his friend's house. He's going to spend the night."

She nodded, but it wasn't a nod, really. "Yes, you can stay," she told him. They could both stay, a little longer, at least.

I have always felt that it was my destiny to attend a first rate college or university like your institution, and with the help of your institution I can achieve all of my potential. I know that I will bring to your institution all of my intellectual and extracurricular gifts, and I will add to the life of the campus in a myriad of ways. My aim in life is to use my abilities to make the world a better place, and I am sure that your institution can help me accomplish that.

CHAPTER FIVE

CHICKEN MARBELLA

Princeton's Office of Admission had both a public and a private face. For the scores of visitors to the university, tremulous high school students with their families (sometimes in tow, sometimes firmly in the lead), there was the impressive Clio Hall, a white marble mausoleum complete with classical pillars and Groves of Academe steps, located directly behind Nassau Hall in the heart of the campus. Inside Clio, these visitors registered for their information sessions, picked up their Orange Key tours, helped themselves to gratis coffee, and nervously eyed the competition. Portia and her colleagues took turns manning the sessions, but this was an element of her job she had liked less and less as the years went by and the atmosphere grew ever more toxic. A decade earlier, when she'd first arrived at Princeton, she had enjoyed the challenge of responding to whatever might come up: a father's question about the Ultimate Frisbee team, a kid from Mexico City wanting to know if he'd be able to study in China, tongue-in-cheek questions about *This Side of Paradise,* thoughtful queries about social issues on campus, including the eternal curiosity about the eating clubs and their influence. She had prided herself on not getting stumped, even during those first years when she was learning the material herself, and later, as her affection and respect for the university became genuine, it pleased her to communicate how extraordinary she thought it.

Eventually, though, the sessions became stressful, then oppressive. There was something about how the mothers sat, knees tightly together, mouths painfully tense. The anxiety in the room was free-flowing. And the hostility. The visitors had a way of checking out their designated tour guides, as if trying to guess the pertinent statistics, the hooks or — worse — tricks that had brought him or her to Princeton, as if this unsuspecting student had directly usurped their own son's or daughter's future spot.

Still, no matter how severely the applicants and their families inspected the student guides, it was nothing to the way they sometimes looked at Portia. *Who was she,* their sharp eyes seemed to ask, *to sit in judgment on them or their brilliant children?* And when they asked, as they often did, whether she herself had graduated from Princeton, and when they learned that she had not, there was palpable disdain. *She couldn't even get in herself!* (This sentiment had reached its apotheosis the previous year, when the director of admissions for MIT had been exposed as lacking any college degree at all.) For Portia, the last straw had been a visiting boy from the South with a lock of nutmeg-colored hair dipping over one eye, who had asked with great false solemnity what advantage he might expect from the fact that both parents and both grandfathers had attended Princeton. There was a shudder of distress throughout the crowd. Portia, repelled, made sure that she took down his name, though not for the purpose the student so clearly hoped. After that, she had asked Clarence to give her a little hiatus from the information sessions, and he'd agreed, but only for a while and only because he had two new hires, both newly minted Princeton grads who were still, in some small way, celebrating their own letters of acceptance and too brimming in goodwill to take anything personally.

Catty-corner from Clio stood West College, the more modest but far more crucial private face of the university's admissions apparatus, where the heavy lifting was actually done. In the fall and winter, hundreds of thousands of pieces of mail arrived here in trucks from the post office, FedEx, and UPS and were hauled into the building, crate by crate. They went first to the sorting stations in the back of the ground floor, where they joined the paper output of a dozen purring fax machines and as many printers, churning out hard copies of e-mail correspondence and the ubiquitous common application. Everything was sifted, inspected, shifted, and dealt, sorted and sorted again by the permanent staff and student employees until they landed — ideally, at least — in appropriate individual folders and there merged to form a cohesive whole in theory greater than the sum of its parts: *The Ballad of Johnny Schwartz from Shaker Heights; The Saga of Robert "Bo" Wilson-Santiago from L.A.; The Tale of Betsy Curtis, Manhattan via Exeter; The Broken Narrative of Xiao-Gang "Kyle" Woo, Shanghai by Way of San Diego.* And on.

There was concentrated, detail-obsessed attention in this office. When Portia came down, as she often did, to pick up files or avail herself of the confectionery smorgasbord (by tradition, baked goods and other delicacies submitted in misguided support of applications were promptly parted from their senders' identification and set out on a table in the corner, beside the coffee machine), she was quite often reminded of a fairy tale that had fascinated her as a child, in which scores of devoted ants worked without respite on an intermixed mountain of black and white sands, separating them into perfect, segregated hills. There were, of course, occasional errors—Cindy Lin's effusive teacher recommendation landing in Cynthia Liu's application folder, that sort of thing—but nothing irreparable. With so many filaments of information flying around and so many hands stirring the soup, it was surprising how few applications turned up incomplete. (When they did, when a folder lacked its letter of recommendation or a transcript, the student was given an opportunity to resend whatever was missing. In general, applicants to Princeton tended to be as highly detail oriented as the officers evaluating them; if their folders lacked some critical element, they wanted to know about it. They wanted, most fervently, to redress the flaw.)

When Portia returned to Princeton late that Friday afternoon, she drove directly to the middle of town, lucked into a space on Witherspoon, and hauled her laden bag to this warren of activity in West College. She greeted the women in their cubicles, but the truth was that she didn't know half of them by name. There seemed to be a fairly high outflow from this office to administrative posts in every corner of university, the theory being, she supposed, that if one could handle being on the receiving end of an entire country's application panic, one might easily parry a few philosophers or chemists. And after a year or two down here, people were usually quite content to move on to more sedate work environments.

Only Martha Prestcott was eternal. A woman whose figure seemed to spring from a Helen E. Hokinson cartoon—all thrusting bust and linebacker shoulders—she ran this nerve center as a benevolent dictatorship. "Hey there," she hailed Portia. "How's my gorgeous niece?"

"She's terrific," Portia said. Martha's niece, Princeton graduate and math teacher at Northfield, had attended her session that morning. "She said to give you a big hug and remind you that you promised her Pillsbury crescents on Thanksgiving. I assume this is some kind of secret code, because I know you wouldn't be caught dead serving Pillsbury crescents."

"Oh dear. I forgot about that. I promised her," Martha said with evident regret.

"Are you expecting a big crowd?"

"Well, I'm up to fourteen and it's still three weeks off, so I'm thinking twenty. George usually brings home a few strays."

George Prestcott taught in the Engineering School, where a concentration of international students tended to linger over holidays.

"That's nice."

"Well, it makes a challenge. This one won't eat meat. This one won't eat pork. They've never seen yams and cranberries before."

"Or Pillsbury crescents."

"Oh, they've probably seen those." She laughed. "We know the college diet is largely composed of refined sugars and bread from a cardboard tube."

Portia smiled. She went to the corner and surveyed the offerings. Brownies with orange icing, two tins of cookies, some squares of indeterminate nature. She helped herself to a cleverly decorated cookie in the shape of a *P*.

"I wouldn't," said Martha. Martha's tenure in Princeton admissions was easily double Portia's own. She had seen — and, given her girth, more than likely tasted — everything. "Hard as diamonds."

"Oh. They look so pretty. And I'm so hungry."

"Try those." Martha pointed. "They came with a note about a vegan cookbook."

"Vegan?" Portia frowned. She looked into the box on the table. It was a shoebox lined with waxed paper. The squares inside looked dark, moist, and dense.

"Her own recipe. For her vegan cookbook in progress. They're called 'Health Bars.' Don't worry," she told Portia, "they arrived this morning. By overnight express."

"I thought you threw the written stuff out," Portia said, lifting a health bar from the box. Fulfilling her expectations, it was weightier than it looked.

"Oh, we do, but I always read them first. There might be some information to transfer to the file. Besides, I feel bad for them. I mean, these kids have gone to the trouble. Somebody should read what they have to say. You know," she said, eyeing Portia, "they're actually better than they look."

Portia inspected the square, supporting it with two hands. She took a cautious bite, filling her mouth with molasses, honey, and packed dried fruit. She folded the rest into a paper towel. For later, she explained. "Corinne been in today?"

"Sure." Martha nodded. "She was here. Loading up for her trip. What do you need?"

"Oh...whatever you have ready."

Martha nodded. She got up and went to the files, where she pulled about fifty orange dockets identical to the ones Portia was turning in.

"Where's Corinne again?"

Martha considered. "Castilleja, I think. Is that just girls?"

"Uh-huh. Silicon Valley."

"That's the one, then. And a couple of schools in the East Bay. It was rescheduled from that time in May she hurt her back."

"Right." Portia nodded. It gave her some not very laudable satisfaction to think of Corinne Schreiber on a westbound flight on this clear blue autumn Friday. Corinne, who had taken over the Pacific region with a certain poorly suppressed antipathy toward her new assignment—indeed, the entire office had been treated to her ongoing and all too vocal resentment—had coasted for years on the excuse of her young children at home, clinging zealously to her prior geographic area, the Mid-Atlantic. She'd come to Princeton, her alma mater, from a college-counseling job at a private school in D.C., preceded by a decade in the English Department at the same school. The Mid-Atlantic, she'd argued, allowed her to travel to schools and still be home for her kids, a need few of her colleagues (recent college grads, the unmarried, and, like Portia, the childless) could claim. Portia, naturally, had declined to be persuaded by this rationalization after the first couple of years. She felt penalized for her childlessness, for her asserted independence, while she was every bit as old as Corinne and every bit—she was certain—as tired. When Clarence had given her New England, she'd made free to suggest Corinne as her successor.

"Corinne doesn't like to travel," Clarence had remarked. "Because of her kids."

Portia had frowned. But...weren't Corinne's kids both at Andover now? Her oldest was in his third year. Her youngest was starting in September. Or perhaps she was mistaken.

She was not mistaken. The following week, after a high-decibel exchange in Clarence's office, Corinne had become the admissions officer in charge of the Pacific: California, Alaska, Hawaii, Washington, Oregon. There would be many long flights in her future and many school visits, from sunny San Diego to snowy Nome and all points in between. Portia had offered to share her list of great San Francisco restaurants. The offer was declined.

The Office of Admission, two flights up, was a corridor of small offices with pretty, leafy views. A few of Portia's co-workers preferred to take files home during the most intense reading periods, but most spent their autumn and winter months in these rooms, crawling through their allotted folders and fielding calls from contacts in their regions. At the end of the corridor was Clarence's office, notably a far grander establishment than the smaller rooms Portia and her fellow officers occupied. It had, for example, windows on three sides, a couch, and a small round table, and it came with a nonfunctioning but very dignified fireplace. It also came with an assistant called Abby, who sat in an alcove just outside Clarence's door, in a cubicle plastered with photos of her Russian grandson. Abby, who had also worked for Martin Quilty, possessed an easygoing nature in combination with organizational skills of military caliber. She had—and this was equally important—a range of phone voices extending from sweet simulated ignorance to cunning brick wall and an uncanny knack of choosing the correct one for whoever was on the line.

Portia carried Martha's fifty files into her office and set them down on top of another stack, this one bound in a rubber band and bearing a note from Corinne. Each application was reviewed by two officers before going to Clarence, committee, or both, and Clarence had requested she serve as second reader on Corinne's folders for this, her first year in the Pacific schools. With the admissions season only just under way, Portia was already irritated by her colleague's idiosyncratic spelling and elusive script, not to mention her evident paranoia about coached applications.

Of course, Corinne was not alone in her antipathy toward paid college consultants and their influence. They all knew perfectly well what was out there, primarily in the cities and wealthier suburbs, but now also, democratically, on the Internet, where consultants of every stripe had hung out their virtual shingles, offering some artificial Rosetta stone for top-tier college admissions. All of them shared her opinion of applicants "reverse engineered" by some self-proclaimed expert. How could any admissions officer know — truly know — whether an applicant had honestly fulfilled the declaration he or she had signed on the application itself — the one that read, "I certify that the essays are entirely my own work" — or whether some other person or persons had advised, revised, or even written their essays for them? It was a laudable but doomed crusade. Yes, it went without saying that students capable of paying up to $30,000 for a consultant to "work with them" on their essays and design their applicant profiles had an unfair advantage, but it was also shortsighted to assume that any applicant to Princeton had not had his or her essays at least vetted by *somebody*. The least savvy among them most likely had a parent check the spelling or an English teacher look over the syntax. Even overworked college counselors with hundreds of college-bound seniors might take a moment to skim the essays of an applicant to Princeton, especially if she or he intended to write a recommendation for that student. Trying to detect the sticky fingers of a paid consultant seemed a poor use of time. And time was short enough.

There were mercifully few e-mail messages waiting for her. Some, from applicants in her region, reporting some new honor or panicking about a perceived flaw in their applications, had been forwarded from the central admissions account downstairs. She had e-mail from the college counselors at Boston Latin, Groton, and Putney, wanting to set up phone appointments, and a message from Clarence asking if she'd gotten to the student from Worcester, Mass., the one the ice hockey coach had been on his case about. She hadn't. She couldn't recall any hockey players at all, so far. This was the only e-mail she returned.

It was near dark by the time she left, that slender interlude when there is no more sunlight and the shadows begin to stretch. Princeton, always beautiful, was somehow at its best just now, with the faintest smell of pine reaching her. She walked alongside Cannon Green, so named for the Revolutionary War cannon buried muzzle down at its center — an ironically pacifist statement for a university that had sent its sons to every American war since. She moved among the students, unable to resist her habitual curiosity about them. Always, she wondered if she might recognize this petite girl in the oversize Princeton sweatshirt, or this lanky

African-American boy with the ponderous backpack, or the blond young man with a swimmer's haircut and shoulders who was laughing into a cell phone, merely from the on-paper selves she might have pored over, one or two or three or four years before. It was an oddity of her work that she might know these young men and women so intimately from the records of their accomplishments, their confessed secrets, their worries and ambitions, and yet when the flesh-and-blood applicants arrived on campus a few months later, they were always strangers. Somehow, the folders turned into these bodies: high-spirited, intense, beauteous, or plain, usually clever but sometimes quite dull. They looked like teenagers walking the campuses of Notre Dame or Texas A&M. They sounded like kids at the mall or on the subway. The special, unique eighteen-year-olds, whose applications had so thrilled Portia and her colleagues, or made them argue passionately for admission over wait list, or wait list over rejection, had somehow morphed into these strangely ordinary beings. They chatted and texted away on their cell phones incessantly. They clutched identical Starbucks containers and shouldered identical backpacks. They went to the U-Store and bought their Princeton garb and so completed their transformations into Princeton students, disappearing into orange anonymity. This was not, of course, to take away from their brilliance. They were still brilliant, still gifted, still passionate about everything from Titian to nitrogen fixing in soybeans. They still wanted to give back, make things better, cure disease, and alleviate poverty. They were good kids, ambitious kids. But they were so ordinary, too.

She drove home along Nassau Street, the bag of new files on the seat beside her and the window down. Now only minutes from her house, she let herself feel, entirely feel, the stress and fatigue of the last couple of days—two flights, three school visits, and a night in which surfeit of emotion had met lack of sleep. And sex. And, not least—though she was only, shamefully, getting to this part now—the fact of her own transgression. The weight of it all exhausted her, and there was little she craved more than a hot bath and an early night, to bed with her files, at least, if not early to sleep. She didn't know what was in the house to eat or what Mark's plans were, but she didn't want any distractions from the plan or, needless to say, any discouragement. Turning onto her street, with the towering cherry tree in her front yard already visible at the end of the block, she allowed herself the first hit of relief.

This was their second home in Princeton, the first being a nondescript ranch at the north end of town, not far from the shopping center:
a sterile place, irredeemably ugly. They had moved here five years before,
to this neighborhood known as the Tree Streets for its arboreal street
names—Maple, Pine, Linden—but also as the Gourmet Ghetto because
of its concentration of good places to buy food and dine out. In Princeton,
sadly, this was saying a good deal. On their arrival, the town had been
a culinary wasteland, with a single dull supermarket and only one other
shop of note: an excellent fishmonger. The wonderful Princeton purvey-
ors she had read about in Betty Fussell's gastronomic memoir, *My Kitchen
Wars*—like the butcher who gamely ground pork and veal for clever, frustrated housewives in thrall to Julia Child—seemed to have perished, and
all good restaurants, if any had existed, had evidently fled along with them.
But some small transformation seemed to have taken hold, much of it in
this cluster at the end of her own street: a natural foods market was now
open and a fish restaurant, a good coffee shop, a decent Chinese. These
establishments kept Princeton hours, it was true, but Princeton hours were
themselves an improvement over Hanover, New Hampshire, hours. So she
wasn't unhappy. At least, not about food.

The house was a product of the town's 1920s building boom, and it had
a grace that had grown rarer with each passing decade of Princeton construction. Few twenty-first-century tenants, like few twentieth-century
tenants, had had the wit to leave well enough alone, but this house had
somehow managed to survive with what the magazines so annoyingly
referred to as "good bones." Still, and in spite of the fact that she had post-
poned caring about things like how nice her house looked until she actually
lived in such a house, Portia could not seem to work up much enthusiasm
for it. She ceded the decorations to Mark, choosing only the deep green
couch and the living room rug, which even she now acknowledged clashed
uncomfortably with the walls. Mainly, she kept it clean. Mark couldn't.
He was a tidier, but dirt...dirt was beyond his abilities. He seemed not
to understand the science of removing it. Worse, he seemed not to notice
its existence, which frankly baffled her. Once—following an experiment
in which she had left a pile of swept dust in the center of the living room
floor for six days, ten days, two weeks, watching to see when he would,
first, notice it and then, hopefully, take action to remove it—they had had
a terrible quarrel. It was the night of their party, the party they usually had

in the week between Christmas and New Year's, mainly for his colleagues in the English Department, but also for academics visiting from overseas ("strays and waifs," he called them), and Mark had spent the day dutifully making the house ready, ferrying glasses from the basement, placing the chairs, setting up the bar, all the while stepping carefully around the pile of dust on the floor. He didn't see it. Or he didn't register it. Or he didn't mind it. And as the hours ticked closer to the hour of the party, her nerves frayed. Around five, she lost it and started screaming. By five twenty-five, she was thoroughly depleted and not remotely in the mood for their now imminent party, but she had at least come round to his stated view on the matter: that her resentment was displaced, excessive, not logical. After all, if she was so very troubled by the dirt on the floor, why hadn't she removed it herself? Why did she not remove it now? What was the point in being angry about it? And if it was true, as she claimed, that there were certain things, certain difficulties, he simply failed to note, then weren't there some synapses in her own domestic perceptions? That porch fixture bulb he'd asked her to replace the day he'd left for a semester's sabbatical in Oxford the previous year, only to find it encrusted by cobwebs and every bit as dark on the day of his return? The fact that she had done not one thing to implement her own aspirations for the "garden," as she rather pathetically persisted in thinking of their uncultivated front and backyards, had in fact done nothing for them at all beyond the overpriced mums she dutifully stuck in each fall and the pansies from the supermarket she dutifully stuck in each spring? Her gardening aspirations had outlasted her shelter magazine phase by a few years, but while she had gotten as far as charts and diagrams for the intended plantings, nothing had come of them. She had made nothing come of them. Nothing grew.

It was strange, she thought now, easing into the driveway. The house she had grown up in had been a control center for clubs and causes and campaigns, where the masses were fed and plans hatched. Back then she had indulged in an idea of home, a home with frills and decoration, but even after all this time, their house had a *for now* feeling about it. The furniture, good enough *for now*. The colors, likable enough *for now*. As if it were not worth taking action against the generic ceiling fixture in the hallway, which a previous tenant had left in place of an original (probably gorgeous) item. As if there were some not yet articulated thing that had to happen before the living room got its truly intended blue and the right sleigh bed was even looked for, let alone found. Only every time she got close to wondering what that event might be, she found herself so thoroughly exhausted that she quickly made herself stop and think about something else.

There was a wonderful smell inside when Portia unlocked the front door, a smell that nonetheless carried with it some vague anxiety she wasn't inclined to identify. She heard the loud suck of their refrigerator unsealing and the almost immediate slap as it was shut again. Mark cooking, NPR from Philadelphia, a little on the loud side (he being a little on the deaf side). She put down her bag beside his briefcase. She put down her purse on the hall table. She didn't call out right away. The smell was rich and sweet: like fruit, but heavier. Chicken Marbella, she thought, snapping to attention. Chicken Marbella, the signature dish of an entire decade (namely, the 1980s), the dish you were more likely than not to be served at any dinner party given by any member of the bourgeoisie, or in any academic enclave from sea to shining sea, was nonetheless Mark's dish of choice when company was expected, because it was simple (after the first forty or so preparations), and because one could forgo the recipe and throw everything into the same casserole with abandon, and because most of the work could be done the day before. They never ate chicken Marbella when they were at home, alone. With dread, she stepped gingerly into the living room. All was worryingly tidy. A fire was laid. And beyond, through the open doorway, clean glassware twinkled from the dining table. Five places, but asymmetrical, as if one had been lately inserted and the others not yet adjusted to make this number seem intended, not accidental. This was more troubling than she could say.

Four places at the table . . . that, she realized, would have had a strangely familiar tone to it: two guests for dinner, obviously, on the night of her return, and Mark saying he would take care of everything, though she couldn't, just now, think who those two guests might be, and even if she could, what did it mean that there were five places? A stray-and-waif? A guest of their guests? The unmistakable pop of a cork from the kitchen. Red wine, opened to breathe. Clos Du Val most probably, twin of the bottle poured over the chicken an hour or earlier. Cousin to every bottle Mark had ever bought to serve with every preparation of chicken Marbella he, or she, had ever prepared, for far too many of the dinner parties they had ever given. And she was so tired. She turned and went back to the doorway and picked up her bag. She fought a brief, almost giddy urge to go back out to her car, to a motel on Route 1 with a queen-size bed and a remote control. Beside her purse there was a slip of paper she only now noticed, actually the back of a Wild Oats receipt, white with that pink stripe along the side that means: Replace the roll. It said, in his terse British print: "Your mother rang."

I would appreciate the opportunity to clarify a situation that occurred in the spring of 9th grade, when I was suspended for one week for alcohol offenses. This incident occurred at a time when my family was undergoing a difficult period, and, to put it bluntly, I had made some poor choices in the friends I was spending time with. One of these friends had an alcohol abuse problem, but I take responsibility for participating in his abuse. I have regretted this incident many times since it happened, but it also helped to make me the person I am today. I certainly hope that this single youthful mistake will not adversely affect my application.

CHAPTER SIX

ACADEMIC FOLK

Your mother rang," Mark said. He came out of the kitchen wearing a green Whole Foods apron and holding out his hands, which were wet and stuck with tiny bits of mesclun.

"Hi," said Portia.

"Mwa." He kissed her on the cheek. "Was it dreadful?"

"What? No, not at all. It's the best time to be in New England."

"Oh yes."

His hair smelled of oregano. He was an enthusiastic and untidy cook, who left no utensil unturned in the kitchen. In vain had she once attempted to understand how a zester featured in a meal of shepherd's pie and green salad, but with time she had learned not to argue with the results.

"Chicken Marbella?"

"I know. It's too boring. But there was a meeting all this afternoon. I knew I wouldn't have time for anything else."

"No, it's fine. Everyone loves chicken Marbella." She looked past him at the table. "Who's our fifth?"

It was a calculated end run, this question. The third might reveal the first two, without her having to admit she'd forgotten.

"Rachel rang to ask if she could bring our new hire. It's fortunate, actually. I've been feeling bad about it. We're in November and I haven't lifted a finger. And she's my countrywoman."

"Oh." Portia frowned. "From Oxford, right? Virginia Woolf?"

"Yes." He turned and observed the table. "All of Bloomsbury, actually. Can you fix it up a bit? You're good at that."

"Yes, but..." He looked at her. "Do I have time for a bath? What time are they coming?"

"Seven. You have time. And ring your mother."

He went back to the kitchen, and she watched him: white shirt untucked, shoeless, hands aloft. He had, for all his heft, an almost irritating boyishness, no doubt to do with the soft English skin and overendowment of thick curling hair, once dark brown but now at least graying. She hung up her coat and went to the table. The table was dirty, so she removed the place settings, went to the cleaning closet, and came back with a rag. After she'd finished wiping the dust, she put everything back, straightening the place mats and placing the plates and glasses. One of the glasses was a flat tumbler, not a wineglass. She took it into the kitchen.

"Are we short a wineglass?"

"What?" He had the chicken Marbella on the stovetop and was stirring it with a wooden spoon.

"This is a water." She opened the cupboard and took out another wineglass.

"Right. Oh, I had an e-mail from Cressida. She says she wants to go to university in the States."

"Hey, that's great," Portia said, putting the water glass back on the shelf. "What does her mother say?"

"I doubt she's told her. She won't, if she has any wit, not till she has one foot on the airplane. Can you imagine Marcie letting her come here?"

"She'll have to follow," Portia said.

He laughed. "Yes. Of course."

"And move into the dorm."

"My God."

"It smells good," she told him. "Just give me half an hour."

She went back to the table and replaced the glass, then took her bag upstairs. The fact that she now remembered what was supposed to be happening tonight, and when they had discussed it (only a couple of days earlier, at the beginning of the week), and what they had said about it (about David, Rachel's husband, who—being a philosopher—had idiosyncratic social skills), and how Mark had talked her into a dinner party on the night of her return (he would cook *and* clean up, he promised), was little comfort to her. She ran her bath and placed the new folders she had taken from the office on her bedside table. Had it been an ordinary trip, she might simply have made the transition: traveling saleswoman to hostess, perhaps even via the kitchen. She would have been tired, of course, but not so fundamentally worn out and...yes, actually, bereft. The bereft was new. And the guilt, of course. She was just now taking the measure of that guilt.

Drifting up the stairs, she recognized the theme music for National Public Radio's *Marketplace*. She ran her bath and climbed into the tub, fighting an urge to submerge herself entirely: the ritual purification for unclean women—that is to say, all women. Like most atheist Jews, Portia had never actually visited a *mikvah*, but she had always been curious. It just sounded so clean. Like a spa of soul-scouring proportions. Clean interested her. Did you have to believe for it to work, or did it work the way acupuncture worked, whether or not you accepted that currents of energy ran through your body? And what if it really did function as an absolution, the watery equivalent of assigned penance in the confessional? Then she could wash away the residue of the fingerprints of John Halsey, along with what they had meant and how they had felt, things that were still so vivid there was nothing left to the imagination, and the unmistakable but impermissible and thoroughly troubling wish not to never see him again. Clean slate, she told herself, washing. I'm home. I'm involved. As I said, she thought, somewhat defensively.

In sixteen years, this hadn't happened. For either of them, she was certain, though there had always been another woman in their lives: Cressida, the daughter who was only twenty months old when she and Mark had met. Two other women, if you counted Marcie, Cressida's mother, though Portia had never actually met Marcie. Mark hadn't deserved the punishing stress of an enraged ex-girlfriend and the occasionally litigated afterlife of that long-ago relationship, not to mention the longing he felt for a daughter he never saw enough of. He was a good person. He was too good to deserve what she had done. She washed herself again. She wished she could not remember—so clearly, so pointedly—the heat of John Halsey's skin.

By the time she was ready, *Marketplace* had been supplanted by jazz and a plate of Camembert was in place on the coffee table. Portia put on the porch light when she came downstairs and lit the fire Mark had set. They were practiced hosts. They had spent the first years working out the kinks and now enjoyed a small reputation, very localized, among their friends. Dependable food: comfortable, not flashy. Dependable cast of characters: articulate, opinionated, usually affable, usually university affiliated. No fireworks. It didn't sound particularly exciting, but despite their reputation, she had found, academic folk liked peace and quiet when they went out for dinner. Princeton, like many another university town, had a certain repu-tation for domestic Sturm und Drang. Before moving here, in fact, she and Mark had both consumed Rebecca Goldstein's *The Mind-Body Problem* (which skewered the Philosophy Department) and Eileen Simpson's *Poets in Their Youth* (booze and bad behavior among the Princeton scribes), in addition to the oft-cited *My Kitchen Wars* (bed hopping in the English Department); but things seemed positively sedate by the time they turned up in the mid-1990s. The bad old times, still fondly recalled by long-in-the-tooth professors, had given way to Gymboree and SAT prep, ubiquitous soccer, and benefits for the local hospital. People were too tired to sleep around, it seemed. Or so tanked up on antidepressants that they no longer felt the itch.

"You sit," Mark said, taking a glass from the table, pouring her some wine, and bringing it to her. "I said I'd do everything."

"I know. It's so nice of you. I feel like a guest in my own house."

"I can't get used to these short trips. I keep thinking you're going away for a week or two."

"Yes, I know. But this is so much better. Those West Coast trips just took it out of me. And I used to miss a lot while I was gone. I'd come back and some crisis had happened in the office. And I'd be going, 'What? What?'"

"Sounds ideal." He laughed shortly. "I wouldn't mind missing some of the crises."

Mark had taken over as interim chair the previous spring, when the august, longtime head of the English Department had been diagnosed with terminal cancer and abruptly retired. His tenure was supposed to be temporary, but there was a definite move afoot to draft him for something at least semipermanent. He was good at the sort of benevolent dictatorship required, it turned out, his light touch with the considerable egos involved matched by the sort of firm control the celebrated former chair had abdicated. The only undertow had to do with Mark's own scholarship, including a second book that was supposed to have been finished last year and now seemed even further from that goal than before the upheaval. He hadn't talked much about it in some time, since coming back from his Oxford sabbatical, actually, and Portia sometimes wondered if he had taken to this administrative work so eagerly because it buffered him from his colleagues' expectations or from—and this was, of course, far worse—their lowering expectations. Hired on the promise of his first book on Shelley, he'd been working on a long study of American and English Romanticism ever since. These days, consumed by the running of the department and the management of certain high-strung academics and scores of high-strung Princeton students, he didn't talk much about it.

"Here they are," Mark said. He moved past her and met them at the door. "Rachel, hello!"

"Hello," Portia heard. "David's just parking. I've brought Helen."

"Yes," he said. "I'm so glad. Please come in."

Portia stood and turned, feeling—awkwardly—less like the hostess than like the first guest to arrive. She kissed Rachel and shook hands with Helen, who was small, with blond hair piled artfully on the back of her head (Like Virginia Woolf? she couldn't help thinking), and was wearing a silk scarf knotted around her throat in the way only European women seemed to master. "I'm so glad you could come," she said brightly. "We've been meaning to have you over for ages, but the term just got away from us."

"Not at all," said Helen. "I know how busy Mark is."

This was an off-script remark, Portia thought. Wasn't Helen supposed to say something about how overextended they both must be, host and hostess alike? Or all three of them—collectively busy! Or even just she herself overwhelmed, with her move to a new country, university, apartment. Portia was immediately irritated, which was unfortunate, as the evening had only begun and the woman in question, after all, already had tenure. But she felt dismissed, which was . . . well, an overreaction, of course. Certainly not enough to *dislike* Helen, Portia scolded herself. Obviously, Helen saw

Mark in situ at the department. Obviously, she saw him doing fourteen things at once. And he had hired her. And plainly, she didn't know the first thing about Portia. Why should she?

"Can I get you something?" she asked. "Would you like some wine?"

"Do you have sparkling water?"

"We have Perrier," she said, hoping they did.

"Yes. What an enormous couch."

Not "pretty," Portia noted. Not "comfortable." Now she was offended on behalf of their couch, a deep, boatlike item covered in a green velvetlike fabric. It was her favorite place to read application folders when the bunker mentality of reading season set in. Admittedly, it was not very well suited to guests. At least not to very formal guests. Helen seemed to be a formal person. She perched on the edge of the couch and crossed her legs. Her dangling foot, clad in an expensive-looking T-strap leather shoe, pointed straight down. She looked up into Portia's eyes. She was waiting for her Perrier.

Portia went to get it. In the kitchen, the rice maker was percolating on the countertop, giving off a yeasty smell. A crisp salad was waiting to be dressed, and a cake box from Bon Appetit, Princeton's uppity gourmet emporium, seemed to indicate Mark's plans for dessert. She took from the cupboard the same water glass she had lately put there and poured Perrier into it. She heard Rachel laugh.

When she got back to the others, David had arrived. He sat beside Helen on the deep couch, his knees apart, mauling the Camembert with a cheese knife. David was a philosopher, a term it had taken Portia some time to embrace. Not: "Taught philosophy." Not: "Was in the Philosophy Department." He philosophized; this was the term given to his work. It said something, she supposed, that she now lived among people who actually were the things they taught: poets, rocket scientists, diplomats, philosophers. And David was actually known for the work he did. There were people out there, she had learned, who avidly paid attention to what emerged from his utterly convoluted mind. She had been asked about him on recruiting trips by similarly brilliant, similarly antisocial high school students. She had even read admissions essays about his apparently world-famous abstract, "Metaphysical Reduction and the Reality of Numbers." David was a loyal and good-hearted person, though she had never once felt she had gotten past the most superficial of his layers. Maybe there wasn't anything under there, or at least anything available to her, most of him having been shunted to the work, and of course the children—he and Rachel had two, in grade school. But it had amused her to learn years earlier from Rachel that David was what passed for socially gifted in the world of philosophers, a world populated by seriously obstructed individuals. It was a world full of men (philosophers, it turned out, were mostly men) who looked at Rachel's breasts, rather than her face, on being introduced. Rachel had laughed when she'd described this, but Portia had a feeling her levity on the subject was hard won. Rachel herself came from English (Bryn Mawr and Yale, before Princeton), where the men apparently looked you in the eye, at least at the cocktail parties, and when she began to meet her boyfriend's, then fiancé's, and then husband's colleagues, she had found herself alternately appalled, repelled, amused, and finally...philosophical. To motivate herself to attend David's professional events, she once told Portia, she had instituted an add-a-pearl reward system, requiring that David purchase a pearl for this theoretical necklace every time one of his colleagues cast an untoward eye (never hand) south of her collarbone, or if he ignored her completely for a long evening as he and another philosopher lobbed theorems and formulae across her place at the table. (The formulae themselves had also taken some getting used to, Rachel explained. On sitting down together, apparently, philosophers immediately produced bits of paper and leaky pens from their jacket pockets. Then, very soon, they would begin illustrating their conversation with formulae scribbled on the bits of paper. They could not seem to talk without these bits of paper, Rachel laughed, as Portia, who in her ignorance had not even known that there was some kind of overlap between the worlds of philosophy and math, frowned in confusion.)

Rachel had attained her pearl necklace by the time she and David married. In fact, she had worn it at the wedding.

"David," Portia said. She leaned over him and kissed his cheek. "Don't get up."

He hadn't, actually, made a move to get up.

She handed the Perrier to Helen, who took it without even looking at Portia.

"Yes, it's been a bit of a problem," Mark was saying. "And there are a few in the department who just want to let it go, so that's become a difficulty in itself."

"Not me," Rachel said to Helen. "Of course, we're limited in what we can actually do. The student graduated three years ago. We can rescind the prize, of course. We can even request the monetary award, not that we could compel him to repay, but does that have any practical meaning at this point? And we don't have the other essays anymore, so even if we wanted to, we couldn't pick another winner. Not to speak of the legal issue of going into the endowment for a second awarding of the prize."

"What about criminal charges?" Helen said. "What about rescinding his degree?"

"Well, we'll be considering all of that when we meet next week," said Rachel. "But I can make all of the arguments against doing either of those things, much as I personally would like to see them done."

"What is it?" Portia said, taking one of the chairs and picking up her wine. "What's happened?"

"Absolutely, his degree should be rescinded!" Helen said sharply. "Why is it even up for discussion?"

"The student who won the Fritz Prize three years ago," Rachel explained. "It's for an original work of literary criticism. Not something done for a class, you know. The student who won wrote about John Berryman."

"That should have been a clue!" Mark said genially.

"He cheated?" Portia asked. The conversation seemed to allow no other possibility.

"We would never have known," said Rachel. "And that, I think, is a big part of why we seem to be taking it so personally. You know, it's gone beyond our being furious at the student. Now we're humiliated, not just for not picking it up at the time, but for having to be told by another undergraduate."

"Who was the undergraduate?" asked David, still in his sprawled posture at the back of the couch.

"A senior. She came in a couple of weeks ago to look at past winners of the prize, before she started her own paper. But of course, being the very thorough Princeton student she is, she also went online and started looking at the prizewinning essays at Yale. Yale has an identical award, endowed by the same family. And there it was, the winner of the Yale prize in 1983. Different title, but the same subject, 'Jazz in the Dream Songs.' He hadn't changed a comma. The student brought it to us last week, and we've been barely keeping the lid on until we can hold an internal meeting."

"Has the student been informed?" David wanted to know.

"That he's a cheat? I'd imagine he doesn't need to be told." Helen shook her head. The great loose bun, Portia noted, moved dangerously.

"That we know about it? No," said Rachel. "Not yet."

"I don't want to go to the dean without a departmental recommendation," Mark explained. "It's a far less straightforward thing to get than I imagined it would be. There's a certain little-to-be-gained, much-to-be-lost school of thought, you see."

"I do not see," Helen said. "You'll have to forgive me. I am a newcomer, and it all looks blindingly clear to me."

"If it gets out—" Rachel began.

"*When*," Mark corrected. "When it gets out."

Rachel sighed. "It becomes an irritating little item that won't go away, or at least anytime soon. A student cheats, but the high-and-mighty Princeton English Department doesn't even notice." She held up her glass to Mark, and he refilled it. "Granted, it's not an all-out disaster, like plagiarism from the faculty, but those two ideas, *cheating* and *Princeton*, would still be sitting right up next to each other. And that affects all of us, not just the department."

"Well, it's not good, of course. But why is the university afraid of showing a flaw if it's in aid of a greater principle?"

Any of the three of them could have answered, Portia thought. But no one spoke, and in the ensuing moment, which was not a comfortable moment, not a *pleasant social* moment, she understood that it fell to her. As the nonacademic, she supposed. The one most enmeshed in Princeton-as-financial-construct, that unfortunate nod to commerce, which too many faculty members, she knew perfectly well, did not deign to acknowledge unless they absolutely had to. She was not an artist or a scholar. She wouldn't cure cancer or even illuminate the humblest property of the humblest life form or generate a single new idea to be added to the evolving total of new ideas. There would never be a book title beside her name, unlike the rest of them. She merely helped turn the wheel that kept them all sheltered and fed, not to mention free to do whatever it was they did to make their mark. Well, she wasn't going to apologize for that.

"Among the top American colleges, there's a constant shuffle for position," Portia said, addressing Helen. "Harvard and Yale and MIT and Stanford, all of us compete for the best students and the best faculty, not to mention funding from both private and public sources. Where we stand, in comparison with other great universities, is important to us, because that position impacts us in a lot of ways, some more obvious than others. It's kind of a contentious issue right now, actually, the whole ranking thing."

Helen seemed to perk up at the idea of a contentious issue. "Oh yes?"

"*U.S. News and World Report* has been ranking American colleges and universities for about twenty-five years. The rankings are very closely followed, though there's a great deal of disagreement about whether they're a good thing overall. In fact, there's a movement now to withhold data from the magazine. Not to participate, in other words."

"Yeah?" David said. "Since when?"

"A couple of years." Portia shrugged.

"And how do they arrive at the rankings?" Helen wanted to know. "Is it by academic results?"

Portia shook her head. In Helen's Oxbridge universe, the reputation of individual colleges rose and fell by the annual examination rankings. She couldn't even conceive of a comparable system here.

"That's part of the problem. There are a number of factors, like faculty-student ratio and selectivity, and what percentage of the admitted students were in the top tenth of their high school classes. But then there are also things like the rate at which alumni give money to the school."

"You're joking," Helen said, appalled.

"And on the other hand, it doesn't measure things like public service or how many students go on to do graduate work. I mean, you would come up with entirely different rankings if you changed the formula, but *U.S. News* seems to have dominated the market with one set of factors, and it really does affect the numbers who apply. Students want to get into the school with the number one next to its name just a little bit more than they want to get into the number two school."

"And Princeton is...?" Helen asked archly. She plainly expected its ranking to be neither of these.

"Number one. This year. But that's not the point."

Helen looked satisfyingly surprised.

"A situation like this, in the English Department, is not going to affect the *U.S. News* rankings. And rationally, we could look at it and think, Well, it's not an institutional problem. It has nothing to do with 'Princeton,' you know? It's a small, localized situation. Just...one bad apple. But unfortunately, people love a story about a great university with mud on its face. So then...well, let's say someone is trying to decide between two universities he's been admitted to. Those tiny little things can become tipping points for the applicant. Or his parents."

"Applicant?" Helen said, actually turning to face her for the first time. *"Parents?"* She gave Portia a frankly curious look.

"The fact is," Portia went on, "we encourage a large applicant pool so that we can select the students we want. And then, once we've selected those students, we often have to work to get them. The same Intel winner or National Spelling Bee champion or...I don't know, Academy Award–winning actress who applies to Princeton has almost certainly applied to other Ivy League colleges, or Stanford, or MIT and Caltech. Those colleges will make an offer of admission as well, or some of them will. So now, suddenly, instead of students competing to get into Princeton, Princeton is competing to get the student. And that's when our tipping point comes into play."

"Oh, I think this is a little paranoid," Helen said.

If only it were, thought Portia. This scramble at the tail end of the admissions calendar seldom got much scrutiny from the public, but it was critically important to the universities involved. The fact was that once an offer of admission had been made, the entire game changed and the roles reversed: now the school was the one on bended knee. Having gone to the trouble of winnowing the stupendously remarkable from a vast field of the only normally remarkable, Princeton did not want to lose that stupendously remarkable student to Stanford. Or Harvard. Or—gnashing of teeth—Yale. There had been more than a few of these students over the years. She had agonized over their applications and been moved by their stories, impressed by their essays and achievements. She had stood up for them in committee and felt immense satisfaction as she persuaded her colleagues to admit them. Then she had watched them blithely go elsewhere, and while the choices were often understandable (some students were always going to choose Harvard, weren't they?), sometimes they were baffling. She remembered in particular one boy from Arkansas who had won Princeton's international poetry competition for high school students—a very useful thing to have done if you cared to be admitted to Princeton. This kid had grown up in extreme poverty and was a loner in school, but also a student his teachers were enraptured by, and his essays were beautifully realized evocations of the life he had lived and the one he hoped to live. (He was, Martin Quilty had noted at the time, one of those kids who had somehow picked up Princeton on their radar—you were never sure how. A poster outside his English teacher's office? F. Scott Fitzgerald? Brooke Shields?) In committee, there had been so much enthusiasm for his application, Portia remembered. The admit vote had been accompanied by actual applause. But the applicant had chosen to go to a state college down south. Years later, Portia still thought of him, baffled and disappointed at his escape, or failure of nerve, or their own failure to bring him in.

She was not going to share this story with the acerbic and brittle Helen of Oxford.

"Well, think of it this way," she said instead. "Let's say a girl in Iowa is accepted at Princeton and at Stanford. Let's say this student wants to be a literary critic or a novelist. Maybe the fact that our English Department has a cheating scandal and Stanford's doesn't will be the one small thing that makes us lose her to Stanford."

"Which affects the . . . what's it called?" said Mark.

"Yield!" Rachel laughed. "Jesus, Mark. How long have you been living with this woman?"

"Right, the yield."

"Which affects our ranking, however we feel about ranking. Which affects our alumni, who like it that we're ranked first. And that matters to us, because our alumni matter to us. And it affects our applicant pool, which may well be smaller for the school ranked number two than it is for the one ranked number one. Which gives us fewer applicants to choose from the following year. Which gives us a very slightly less strong incoming freshman class for the year after that. Do you see?"

Helen did not appear to see. She frowned first at her knees and then at Mark, before turning at last to Portia.

"What did you say you teach, again?" said Helen.

"I don't teach. I'm an admissions officer."

Oddly, Helen turned back to Mark, as if for clarification.

"You know," he said. He seemed to be forcing some kind of levity. "Portia guards the gate. Picks the best of the lot for the incoming class."

"Sits in judgment!" David said brightly. He was, in his odd way, trying to be helpful.

"David," Portia said wearily.

"David!" said Rachel. "You know there's a lot more to it than that."

Mark got to his feet. "Let's go and sit down. Dinner's ready. Portia? You'll tell people where to sit?"

She got up. "Yes, please come in. I'm so hungry, actually. I just got back from a trip an hour ago. Mark has done all the cooking."

"It smells wonderful." Rachel walked to the table and set down her wineglass.

"Helen?" Portia touched the chair beside her. Mark came in with the platter. Green olives and chunks of chicken glistened in dark sauce.

"Oh, that looks divine," Rachel said, sitting. "Mark, you cooked this?"

"It's a simple dish," he answered modestly. He set down a bowl of steaming rice.

"It must all seem very strange to you," Portia said to Helen. She was trying to extend herself. "I'm assuming you came through the U.K. system yourself?"

Helen merely regarded her.

"When you applied to university, you took A levels? Perhaps you interviewed with a tutor at the college you wanted to attend."

"Of course," she said shortly.

"Was there any kind of essay in your application?"

"Naturally. I wrote about Mary Wollstonecraft and the Gothic."

"But not a personal essay. Nothing about your extracurricular activities or a person who had influenced you."

Once again, she gave Portia a blank look.

"Well, it's very different here. Intellectual potential is extremely important to us, of course, but it isn't the only factor. We want to create a community that can produce all kinds of things, not only academic work. We want athletic teams and arts events and political activity. So we ask them to tell us about those aspects of their lives as well."

"But that's ridiculous," said Helen. "English universities manage to produce athletic teams and the arts. If they want to come in and row for the college or join the union or do theater, that's fine, so long as they can do their work. We've managed to produce athletes and actors and, God knows, centuries of politicians, without asking them what club they want to join."

"So, when you interview applicants at Oxford, you wouldn't consider their other interests?" Rachel asked, ladling chicken Marbella onto her plate.

"What do you mean?"

"I mean... well, if they play an instrument. Or if they've done some kind of volunteer work."

"Volunteer work?" Helen looked baffled.

"We've had applicants who went to work in refugee camps or battered women's shelters," Portia said.

"I have a girl who spent six months in Thailand after the tsunami, working with refugees. She's in my Frost seminar right now," Rachel said.

"I have the national table tennis champion in my introductory logic seminar," David added with notable pleasure.

Helen looked at them as if they might be mad. "No. Nothing like that. If they've done those things, they don't tell us, because they know it's not pertinent to the application. Well, sometimes the school report will mention they row or they play rugby, but we're not hurting for athletes. God knows we always manage to fill up the boats and field a rugby team."

"But what if their extracurricular interest is academic? Somehow related to what they want to study?" Portia asked.

"I don't understand," Helen said. She had covered her plate with salad and a couple of pieces of chicken, seemingly liberated from any sauce.

"Well," said Mark, "what if you were considering a student who wanted to read English, and they had won a prize for their poetry?"

"Oh, they all write poetry," Helen said dismissively.

"Okay," Mark went on. "But what if one of them had already published a poem. Say, somewhere important. The *TLS*, or *Poetry Review*. Would that affect the application?"

"That did happen," she considered. "Well, just about. We had a boy who had published a novel. Or, not published yet, but a publisher had bought it. Some teenage angsty thing. But he was quite arrogant. He let me know at the interview that he would need to be let off essays now and then, if he was writing."

"Did you take him?" Portia asked.

"Not at all. Not because of the novel. Or even because he was a prat. He just wasn't terribly good. We had some quite strong applicants that year. Somewhere else took him. Oriel, I think."

Mark reached across the table to pour more wine for David. "What happened with the novel?" he said.

"Oh, it was published. And it got some attention, I seem to recall. He was interviewed in the *Times*. But he didn't do at all well on his exams. He got a lower second, in fact, so it was just as well we hadn't taken him." She speared a piece of chicken with her fork, examined it briefly, and took a cautious bite of it.

"Well…" Portia sighed after a moment. "As I said, it's very different here. An entirely different system, the major difference being that the faculty aren't directly involved."

"Ah." Helen nodded into her salad. "But ultimately, it's a question of which system produces the finer student, isn't it? And that remains to be seen."

By you? Portia thought, giving in, finally—and after, she thought, abundant provocation—to her serious dislike of this woman.

"The system we have now, at Princeton and other selective colleges, has evolved continually since its inception," Portia explained, but with resignation, since she doubted Helen would care. "For the last hundred years, it's been a constant ricochet among academic standards, diversity, and tradition. In the nineteenth century, all you had to do to get into Princeton was be a white male from one of a handful of prep schools. But when faculty began calling for higher academic standards, those conventional Princeton students started getting squeezed out, and they didn't like it. So there was a swing back. Which pleased the traditional applicant pool but made the faculty angry. And so on through the twentieth century. Which is not even to speak of ethnic minorities and women."

"Still, the faculty are right," Helen said with annoyance. "A university is first and foremost a place of learning. Not table tennis or refugee work, however noble that may be. Princeton should be an academic meritocracy, like Oxford. That is the only criterion that matters."

"But isn't academic meritocracy a relatively new admissions philosophy at Oxford?" Portia asked. "Think about it: In an eight-hundred-year history, how recently did the colleges care more for academic promise than for social standing and wealth? You may not be factoring other elements into your application process now, but until a very short time ago, men were just set down for Oxford at birth. It didn't matter how brilliant they were. Class was the only thing that mattered."

"Witness poor Jude the Obscure!" Rachel laughed.

"Have you been disappointed by your students at Princeton?" Portia asked Helen, noting and ignoring the strong beam of warning emanating from Mark.

"They're absolutely charming. They're bright. Of course, they don't know anything about English literature. You can set them down with a poem and ask them to write for half an hour. Most of them won't recognize the poem, but even if they do, they're completely incapable of doing any practical criticism at all. They don't have context, so they can't bring in other work. They don't know history, so they can't comment on what the author may have been trying to do. They've never seen theory, so they can't make any kind of argument about the text itself. All they can do is comment on how the poem makes one particular reader—*them,* in other words—*feel.* Which"—she looked at Mark—"I think you will agree, is of limited value. They simply don't understand that I couldn't care less how they feel about the poem. I'm interested in what they have to say about the poet's ideas. And the notion of that is utterly foreign. That's the problem."

"Of course, it's a function of how they've been taught," Rachel said carefully. "It's very different here. We've learned to be grateful if they come through secondary education with any feel for poetry at all."

"Yes…" Helen waved one bony hand in Rachel's direction. "Of course, I'm fully aware the students are among the best this system can produce. So I was prepared for it. And," she added as if to placate, "as I said, they are charming."

"Well, isn't it nice not to have to devote all that time to admissions yourself? More time for your own work," Mark said. "I imagine."

"Yes, that is a good thing," she agreed. She was cutting her chicken into very small pieces on her plate. "But on the other hand, I'm now being assaulted by students who want me to write references for them. Rhodes scholarships. Marshall scholarships. Rotary scholarships. They're all relentlessly ambitious. Whatever they've accomplished, they have their eye on the next step. They want their options open. And they all seem to want to go to Oxford. So I'm still putting in my time for Oxford admissions."

Rachel smiled.

"Just when I thought I was out, they pull me back in!" said David.

Mark and Helen looked at him, alarmed.

"It's from *The Godfather*," Rachel explained.

"Is there more chicken?" said David.

"Where was your trip, Portia?" Rachel asked. She was a capable hostess herself, and practiced at diverting the conversation when necessary.

Portia told them about Deerfield and the boy who had been wrapped in an orange blanket at birth. She told them about Northfield, where a girl had asked about Princeton's portfolio because she had made a decision to apply only to institutions of higher education that invested along sustainability and humanitarian principles. (Good luck with that, Portia had thought at the time.) She chose carefully what she told them about Quest. She was not willing to have them laugh at its idealism, even at the extremes of its idealism. She did not tell them anything important. She told them the students had challenged her about higher education itself, which was unusual and, she had to admit, sort of refreshing. She told them about the boy she had met, the odd boy reading the biography of Edie Sedgwick, who had casually tossed half a dozen goddesses of wisdom in her direction and whom the school had more or less left to his own devices.

"He sounds like a future philosopher," Rachel said wryly.

"What do you mean?" Helen asked, accepting—though it seemed rather reluctantly—a tiny additional portion of chicken from Mark.

"That's what David's crowd were all like when they were teenagers. They hated having to take classes in stuff they couldn't care less about. They just wanted to be left alone so they could learn. They sat there in their fetid little rooms reading book after book and refusing to bathe."

"That's completely untrue," David informed the table. "I had excellent personal hygiene. I still have excellent personal hygiene."

"No comment!" Rachel laughed. "So"—she turned back to Portia—"you liked this kid."

"Well, he was very memorable. But we'll have to wait for the application. He didn't strike me as someone who'd given much thought to attending college, let alone applying to college. To say that's extremely unusual in our applicant pool is a vast understatement. If he can pull it together, and of course if the test scores support what his teacher told me, then yes, I would try to get him admitted. I don't suppose we'll get much from a tran-script. It sounds as if the public school he attended was about to fail him."

"I failed French in tenth grade," David announced proudly. "Actually, I failed it in eleventh grade, too. And band. I failed band."

"It hasn't held you back," Mark observed.

"Actually," Rachel reported proudly, "his high school wanted to suspend him."

"They did suspend me," David corrected her. "In my junior year. I kept cutting classes so I could take the train into the city and sneak into phi-losophy lectures at Columbia. No one ever stopped me."

"Why would they?" his wife said dryly. "He looked exactly like the other philosophers. He even sat the exams. Even though he wasn't enrolled!"

"One exam." David grinned. "Advanced epistemology. This guy was so amazing, who taught it. I never spoke to him, of course. I mean, I wasn't supposed to be there."

"But you audited the class and actually took the exam?" Mark asked. "Did you take it anonymously? What did you write on the exam booklet?"

He had written his name and address, David explained, because he lacked a student ID and campus mailbox, the requested information. He hadn't really thought about it. A week later, his blue booklet had turned up in the mail at home, with a red A and an indelicate query scrawled beneath it: "Who the fuck are you?"

"So naturally he decided to go to Columbia," his wife concluded.

"Do you think those F's would have kept me out of Princeton?" David asked Portia.

"Back in the eighties? They might have. Hey, you failed band! But that was the bad old days. Isn't it lucky the university's in the hands of such qualified admissions officers today?"

Mark got up to make coffee. Portia reached for the wine. She was nearly enjoying herself now, though the advent of coffee, which meant the begin-ning of the end of the dinner party, certainly cheered her, too.

"What makes you qualified?" Helen said abruptly. When Portia turned to look at her, she said, "I'm just curious. Again, I'm a stranger in a strange land. I really haven't the foggiest."

"I beg your pardon?" Portia said.

"You said 'qualified.' I wondered. What does that mean? How does one train to become an admissions officer? Is it a degree course?"

From the kitchen, there was a brief sputter of grinding. Then the tap, tap of coffee grounds emptying into the coffeemaker.

"No. There isn't any set degree. In fact, admissions officers come from a variety of backgrounds."

"Such as?" Helen asked.

"Many come from college advising. In other words, they've counseled high school students on applying to college. Some are teachers. Some people just begin working in an admissions office — for example, in some clerical capacity. Then they move into the actual admissions work."

"So you're not qualified, exactly. It's more of a seniority track."

There was now official discomfort at the table. Rachel seemed to be looking past Portia entirely, her gaze vaguely on the wall of bookshelves at the far end of the room. Even David, not the most sensitive follower of human interchange, was looking at Helen in an openly perplexed way. When Mark came to the table, he sat down quickly and looked worried.

"I suppose." Portia nodded carefully. "We don't have formal preparation. Admissions work is something people just find they're good at. Or they don't. Or they may be good at it, but they discover it's very difficult for them emotionally. It does affect you. You're very aware of what's out there, and the stress these kids are under. And they're very deserving. You want to say yes to them all, but you can't. People either make their peace with that or they need to do something else."

"And you've made your peace with it, then." It wasn't a question. It was a judgment. Helen sat back in her chair, looking diverted. Portia let the wisp of earlier distaste come flooding through her. This, after diligent good manners, was actually a relief. She said nothing but allowed herself to feel the pleasure of pure, almost gleeful loathing. It had been a long time since she had hated anyone so fully and with such little cost to herself. She was even able to laugh as she answered the question that was not a question.

"It's a process." She forced a smile and wrenched the subject away. "Mark," she said, "that looks so good."

He served the rather ordinary fruit tart, and the evening limped along to its end. She heard about Helen's first American Halloween, at the Friedmans' on Wilton Street, and her perambulation through the neighborhood with ten-year-old Julia Friedman, who was dressed as a white-faced ghoul in a mask that somehow pumped fake blood over its own cheeks. The parents they met in the darkened streets had been horrified, Helen reported, and covered their young children's eyes. One had even scolded Helen, mistaking her, Portia supposed, for Julia's mother, complaining that the dreadful bloody mask was too frightening for the children.

"Which is absurd," Helen announced. "Of course, we invented Halloween. In England, it's meant to be bloody. The fear is the point. This costume parade of cartoon characters and superheroes, I can't fathom it."

Portia practiced her weary smile and feigned interest. She suppressed her dismay when Mark offered, and then made, a second pot of coffee. She was close to Rachel. Sometimes they went for walks along the canal, accompanied by the Friedmans' portly chocolate Lab, or met at Small World Coffee on Witherspoon Street. She found David adorable in a profoundly glad-I'm-not-married-to-him way. But tonight, after two such wearying, emotionally exhausting days, she could bear little more of them. She wanted them—*please, please*—to exhale, push back from the table, arise, withdraw, depart. And this woman. Who was this terrible woman?

"Who was that terrible woman?" she asked Mark, following him into the kitchen with the glasses in her hands. David and Rachel had finally gone, taking Helen away with them. "Apart from a colossal bitch, I mean."

"That terrible woman," Mark said testily, "is one of the most eminent Virginia Woolf scholars in the world."

"Don't you mean Bloomsbury as a whole?" said Portia, setting down the glasses beside the sink.

"I mean," said Mark, "that we're lucky to have her. She brings a good deal of prestige to the department. And the university."

"Well, she brought a good deal of bad temper to our house tonight. I didn't hear her say one pleasant thing all evening. She didn't even compliment you on your dinner. Which was excellent, by the way."

Mark ignored this. He had his back to her. He stood at the sink, running plates under the tap and setting them down into the dishwasher.

"Mark?"

His shoulder flinched. This actually made her furious.

"Mark. Is she . . . was tonight typical for her, or do I need to give her the benefit of the doubt?"

He whirled around, his hands almost comically flicking soap onto the

floor, but there was nothing comical in his face. It made her want to step
back.

"I thought that was inexcusable, if you want my honest opinion. Going
on like that about the university. Like a saleswoman."

"I don't—"

"You don't need to peddle to us, Portia. We live here, too. Our paychecks
say Princeton, too."

"It's a very nice paycheck," she reminded him, wondering that she had
to remind him.

"I know it's a nice paycheck!" he said.

His voice was quiet, but suffused with anger. She stared numbly at him.
She had heard this voice before, but only when he spoke to Marcie, or
about Marcie, or to the lawyer on the subject of Marcie. Never to her.
She remembered the day they had driven to Newark Airport to pick up
Cressida, only to find that she was not on the plane, was not even booked
on the plane. He had gone to a corner and called Marcie, swaying in rage
like a davening Hasid. And the time, just this past July, when he had gone
to London for his visit, only to find that Marcie had decamped to a friend's
house and refused to release Cressida until Mark signed some document
promising he would drive only on secondary roads, because she had reason
to distrust his ability behind the wheel. For years, forever, Portia had taken
the attendance of Mark's rage. She knew it was there, but what had it to
do with her? She had always been the one standing slightly off to one side,
watching the white beam of that anger find its target—like the supportive
teammate or faithfully recording secretary. This wasn't right. She stared at
him: green eyes, graying hair, poorly shaved jaw. And then the idea came
surging up into the space between them, erupting from the blue-painted
floorboards, exploding through their kitchen and their house and their
conjoined lives: *He knew.* Somehow, she had no idea how. He'd known
all evening. He'd known since before she arrived home. He'd known the
instant John Halsey had left her body.

"Mark?"

"I bring home a new colleague. A valued colleague. And incidentally,
someone I've known for a long time. And you treat her like she's applying to
Princeton but hasn't bothered to read the catalog."

Despite herself, Portia nearly laughed. This was, in fact, a fairly suc-
cinct description of Helen.

"I do wonder why she came here, if she's so down on the place. I mean, if Oxford is so perfect and the students so superior, why on earth did she leave?"

"Why, I don't know," Mark said caustically. "Maybe it has something to do with a higher paycheck and a lighter teaching load. She's a scholar, Portia. She has work to do."

Portia noted the dig—her own work being more toil than vocation, in other words—but chose not to react.

"Yes, but Mark, she just came in here and started criticizing everything. You have to admit she was far from gracious tonight. And she was thoroughly unpleasant to me."

"*You* were thoroughly unpleasant to *her*," he corrected. "I was ashamed of you."

Portia looked at him in disbelief. For a long moment, neither of them spoke. Then, seemingly with great effort, Mark broke away and turned back to the sink. Painfully, he took up a plate and painfully, deliberately, ran it beneath the water.

"Mark," Portia said quietly. "What is this?"

His shoulders tensed. He gripped the edge of the sink with one hand and leaned slightly forward. The water ran on, bouncing up off the surface of the plate.

"I think," he said finally, "I need to go back to the office for a bit."

Automatically, she looked up at the kitchen clock. It was half-past ten.

"Now?" she asked.

"I just need some time. Everything's all right."

Strangely, she did not feel at all reassured.

"Could you bear to clean up? I know I said I'd do it."

He wasn't looking at her, though he had turned off the water and stepped back from the sink.

"All right," she told him. "I don't mind. But we'll have to come back to this at some point."

"Yes." He nodded. He looked horrendously depleted. "I know. But tonight, I can't. I'll just be a couple of hours."

"Okay," she said.

He walked past her, moving the air. He went straight to the hallway, picked up his keys from the table, and left. The door behind him failed to click shut. Portia looked after him. She stood for some time, rooted and amazed. There was a subject between them now, as yet unidentified but quite real, and likely not evadable, or at least not without cost. She had grown comfortable here, with Mark, or if not comfortable, then stable, safe from the barbed thing she had done a very long time ago. Now, suddenly, that thing was utterly present, sharp, and terribly sad, demanding attention and redress, and she was as ill prepared now to face it as she had been then, in spite of being so much older and theoretically more capable. Theoretically, Portia thought, astonished. Alone in the house, alone in her life, alone with the aftermath of a bad dinner party and an old, old transgression. What was there to do but follow him to the front door and shut it the rest of the way?

*I have experienced a myriad of challenges in my young life, but I am
not sorry for myself, because they have had an important affect on me.
I know that I am a better person because of the things I have faced.
I try to remember that everyday.*

CHAPTER SEVEN

TEAMMATES

At the age of sixty-eight, Susannah Nathan was still, somehow, a fire-brand in the making. Despite committed attachment to a long series of social, political, and creative endeavors, Portia's mother had never found the vector capable of transforming her into a Gloria Steinem, Alice Waters, Wilma Mankiller, or Twyla Tharp. She could last only a brief time in any setting before becoming convinced that she was needed elsewhere. She had campaigned for women and immigrants, early sex education, and subsidized housing, sanctuary for victims of male violence and of mandatory drug sentencing. She had toiled against consuming the flesh of animals and the slaughter of virgin forests. She had marched and rallied and fundraised and lent her considerable energies to any number of efforts both local and global, but always as a foot soldier, never a general—forever the woman holding the sign in the background, as some astonishing beacon of energy and inspiration stepped up to the microphone. Outwardly, over the years, very few things had remained constant in Susannah's life. In fact, there was only one thing that had traveled with her wherever she went. That thing was money, and lots of it.

Regrettably, for an aspiring revolutionary, she had been born into a family of materialism and privilege, and unlike some of the others, she had never quite had the wherewithal to let it go. Initially, she had stuck to the proven path, commuting to Barnard from her parents' home in Great Neck and making a real effort to do the great work expected of her, which was to secure a Columbia-educated future physician or attorney and marry him. Even as graduation neared without her having accomplished this basic goal, no one in her family admitted to any apprehension about her. Susie was an excellent student, and her parents were modern people: Didn't Judaism celebrate the intelligence of women? Why shouldn't she get another degree? A master's, or a...teaching thing? (It was good to work with children before you had your own. It showed you what to expect.) The alarm bells failed to ring as Susannah made her application to a university far, far away in California, an about-to-be-roiling university, a university already uncomfortably odd. Ostensibly, she had gone west to study psychology, but her interest, already tenuous, did not survive the realization that graduate work in the field focused less on feelings than on dry assertions tested with live mice. Also, she was not personally courageous. During her first year on that soon-to-be-tumultuous campus, she joined a sorority, the only graduate student in the university to do so. At best, she was fixed in place. At worst, moving backward.

Then, finally, she got the jolt she was waiting for. That spring, only months before Mario Savio would seize a microphone on Sproul Plaza and declare Berkeley, California, the center of the new universe, Susannah, who was manning a fund-raising stand on Shattuck with some sorority sisters, was noticed by an artist (also dope dealer) from St. Louis, whose street sculptures were arrayed for sale on the pavement. The artist (and dope dealer) had cast aside his own familial trappings and invested his tuition money (originally intended—O irony—for Princeton) in a particularly fecund patch of Northern California, where a hale and potent strain of cannabis grew as cheerfully as the kudzu back home. He beckoned Susannah to his makeshift stall on the pavement. So much for that elusive Jewish physician. So much for psychology.

He, at least, was entrepreneurial. Many years (and two prison terms) later, he would still be living on the proceeds of that thwarted Princeton tuition and that very prosperous hectare of soil. With him, the following year, Susannah would leave Berkeley and move north to live at peace with nature. With him, a couple of years after that, she would try urban homesteading in Harlem. Without him, when that went south, she herself would head south to attempt life as an emancipated human in a womyn's collective, in Baltimore. Then north again, first to tidy up odds and ends (and collect the lion's share of her fortune) in the house her parents had left her in Great Neck, and so to Northampton. Ah, Northampton. Home of the listing Victorian painted some unusual color. Home of the rigorously divided household responsibilities and rotating cooking duties. Home of the Bluestocking, the deconstructing genius scholarship girl, the earth mother therapist who moonlighted with her guitar at the Iron Horse Music Hall, singing, "There's something about the women in my life . . ." In Northampton, Susannah picked up a legal mate and produced a daughter, not that those two acts were at all connected, and continued to pass from stand to stand, from purpose to purpose, from partner to decreasingly viable partner, before, at last, migrating north to the eventual destination of not a few of her friends: Vermont. But through every outward change, she held on to her money. And despite the chorus of disapproval, the dressings-down at consciousness raising, the patient counseling of gurus and sisters, not to mention the pointed and powerfully articulated views of the men she sometimes cohabited with, Susannah declined to consider that a problem.

The money, which had been tied up in trust until Susannah was twenty-five and was hers outright thereafter, came from two sources: first, a maternal grandparent who had been consumed by anxiety all through the summer of 1929 and finally given way to it in early October of that year, fleeing the stock market to the derision of his friends; second, her own father, who had a (not quite aboveboard) knack for knowing where most of the postwar Levittowns on Long Island were going to get built. The fortune these visionary men would leave to Portia's mother was not of immense proportions, but it was unignorable money. Safety-net money. Property-in-the-community-of-one's-choice money. It was don't-have-to-work money, fuck-you-I'm-out-of-here money, and at-least-I-know-my-kid-can-go-to-college money, just the thing for a responsible citizen who needed to make art or wanted to give everything to the poor. But Susannah was not an artist, and though she dutifully raised funds for the poor in their many guises, she never gave away any of her own money. Instead, she put it into quite a sophisticated portfolio, had it managed by a series of extremely smart young men at a white-shoe firm on Water Street, and directed a laudably modest percentage of the interest to be deposited regularly into her checking account, where it mimicked a subsistence wage or welfare stipend.

She refrained from telling any of this to her daughter, who was accordingly stunned, years later, to happen upon a $20,000 check for her college tuition, printed in an old-world typeface on a pale beige check and from an extremely WASPy-sounding bank in New York Portia had never heard of. It would shame her, later, that she had just assumed she was on financial aid at Dartmouth, like everyone else up there who didn't come from obvious wealth. When she confronted her mother it all came out, and without shame. So she had some money saved. So what? Was Portia implying that she had led a life of deprivation? Was there some terribly important thing she had been denied? Some crucial possession she had been forced to forgo? Had she suffered terribly?

Of course, she had not. In fact, Portia had some difficulty articulating the sense of dismay, of...well, almost *betrayal,* she was feeling. It went without saying that their life, the life of her childhood, had not been one of suffering and deprivation. It hadn't been luxurious, of course. Their bookshelves were salvaged boards and cinder blocks, like the bookshelves of everyone else they knew (and, for that matter, laden with most of the same books). They ate their own tomatoes, and Susannah bartered babysitting for the services of a handyman when the ceiling started to bow. Her mother hit the yard sales and rummage sales for every thread Portia wore, every toy she played with and book she read. Food came in bulk from the Co-Op. Gifts were handwritten cookbooks containing Susannah's recipe for wheaten bread, her brown rice stir-fry. She also knitted a lot. But while there were utilitarian things around them, things they needed, things to make life simpler or better organized, Susannah seemed thoroughly averse to the idea of acquisition for its own sake and terribly proud of her abstemious character. (Portia had sometimes heard her mother proclaim, with glee, that an entire society of consumers like herself would bring the economy crashing down within days.) She and her mother did not take the kinds of vacations her future classmates at Dartmouth were taking, to winter sport meccas, capitals of culture, white beaches. On holidays, mother and daughter visited friends and Susannah's former lovers in their mindful communities or off-the-grid last stands. It helped that Portia was not covetous herself. But the oddity of it, the irony of it, was something she had never been able to stop chewing over. After all, it was one thing to *have* money and something else *not* to have it. But to have it and, as far as she could tell, ignore it? For all that time? This paradox would preoccupy her for years. If you had money and didn't want to spend it, why not give some of it away? On the other hand, if you had it and didn't want to give it away, why not, you know, buy yourself something nice every now and then?

The year after her daughter started college, Susannah sold the Northampton house—at a loss, of course. (That plumber? Whose services she had bartered for babysitting? He was neither gifted nor licensed, let alone bonded. The resulting mess would require a massive reduction in the sale price.) Then she resigned her chairmanship of the Pioneer Valley Food Co-Op and her membership in the Northampton Fellowship of Reconciliation, found a successor to lead the Pioneer Valley chapters of NARAL and Amnesty, and moved north.

Vermont, it seemed clear to Portia, was destined to become one great retirement complex for lefty seniors, not to mention an outstanding investment opportunity for the right kind of entrepreneur. (Organic all-you-can-eat buffets? Collectively run and Hemlock Society–endorsed continuing care facilities? Health clubs pulsating to a Jefferson Airplane sound track?) Specifically, Susannah was bound for Hartland, where two of her friends had decamped some years before, pooling their funds to buy, renovate, and generally civilize a hundred-year-old farmhouse on twenty hilltop acres. The friends, both women, were cohabitants but not lovers. One was a weaver, one a schoolteacher-turned-folksinger, both committed vegans and technophobes. Their domestic arrangement, in its eighth year at the time of Susannah's arrival, had lasted longer than both women's marriages and was, by any account, a success. Then Susannah moved in.

"Call your mother," Portia thought, jolting awake the morning after the dinner party, the cold air hitting her exposed shoulder as it came uncovered. She was alone in the bed but hadn't been for long. At three she'd been wakened by the suck, slap, of the refrigerator downstairs and noted then that Mark had only just gotten up. Which meant that he had previously come home, undressed, and entered the bed—all without waking her. Now he might be anywhere: in the bathroom, the kitchen, his office. He might be at Small World, drinking his habitual wake-up espresso and plowing through the *Times*. He might be at his desk in McCosh Hall. How much time would pass before they came back to it? And would they come back to it at all? This sort of thing had happened before, she freely admitted: little jolts of the needle, measuring the years they had lived together, little dots that had never connected to form any sort of linked narrative but remained in situational isolation, though Portia could remember each and every one of them, pain-filled nights of no sleep, bleary, acrid mornings. Somehow they had always passed. And this one, she supposed, would as well.

After all, it came to her, making her way downstairs and pouring herself what remained of the coffee Mark had made earlier that morning, they had both been tired. Mark had cooked single-handedly to give dinner to his friends and colleagues, and the evening had mired in...well, not strife. Not acrimony. But there was perhaps an absence of good feeling. It hadn't been a disaster, just not a success. Not the warm welcome he must have wanted to extend to his new colleague from the old country. She ought to have tried harder, Portia thought. Stuck to local real estate (that staple of Princeton conversation) and supermarkets, the new plan for downtown, the ongoing restaurant black hole in which they dwelt. She ought to have sold the town the way she sold the university, and she had not done that, and for the worst of reasons: because she was tired and cranky and racked with...well, *something*, about the fact that she had gone to bed with a man who wasn't Mark, and she had forgotten about the dinner and was predisposed to dislike *anyone* who walked in her door and required more than the most modest of effort on her part. She would apologize to him. Then she would call Helen and offer to take her to lunch, or out to the flea market in Lambertville, or something she might enjoy, and through this penance she would restore herself and her home.

Reaching into the refrigerator, she looked past the plastic wrap–covered bowl of goopy leftover chicken Marbella, not because it seemed unappetizing (the dish was, annoyingly, often better the next day), but because it now felt entwined with what had happened last night and bore a kind of taint. She put milk in her cup and placed the carton back on the shelf.

Portia resisted the unfurled *New York Times* on the kitchen table and took her coffee back upstairs, intent on working through four or five of the weekend folders before she got up properly. The Wild Oats receipt and its note were on her nightstand, left atop the unfurled paperback novel she had given up on the previous month. Portia's heart sank anew. Her mother's tone of command had an uncanny way of working itself through all media, no matter the filter or the remove. Even here, on this pink-striped slip of paper, there was a sense of imperative and imminent offense. How much time had passed since her call? The clock was ticking.

Mother and daughter had once been teammates, but never quite friends. Teammates, as Portia would discover in high school when she had actual teammates, were fine things. Piling onto the bus before the game, edgy with shared nerves, egging one another on with the genial, meaningless phrase *C'mon, you guys!,* collapsing back into the same seats for the ride home—that sense of striving in accord had been a sweet part of high school. Possibly the sweetest. But the camaraderie had not survived graduation, or even the off-seasons. Her teammates, passing in the school corridors in winter or spring, were downshifted to nodding acquaintances who had once been close, that past connection floating off like cotton candy on the tongue. They were not friends like the friends her mother instructed her to find, the kind her mother had in, it seemed to Portia, embarrassing excess.

Women friends, to be specific. Susannah was passionately clear about the necessity of women in a woman's life. And not too many of them, but only the right ones. "You don't need fifty best friends," Susannah had told her after one especially gruesome day in seventh grade, when Portia had been roundly shunned by the rigidly patrolled popular crowd at Northampton Middle School. These girls, uniformly lithe and light of hair, held unchallenged sway over the choicest lunchroom tables (best visibility, best vantage, just . . . best). When Portia, employing a very deliberate air of cluelessness about the hierarchy of seating, had attempted to sit at the most rarefied table of all (she had rushed to the cafeteria to be first in line, for this very purpose), two extremely strident and highly amused blond girls had sent her very publicly packing.

"Why are you running after a crowd?" Susannah had said that night, over vegetarian chili and green salad from Bread & Circus. Her lack of sympathy, though hardly unexpected, was salt in her daughter's wound. "Even if you succeed, what have you got? You're just another face in the crowd. And *that* crowd," said disapprovingly.

"But they're *nice,*" Portia had said in pointless disregard of recent history.

"That I doubt. And even if it were true, *nice* is very much overrated. I'd like to see you go for more than *nice.*"

In any case, Susannah had gone on to explain, women do not bond in packs, or if they do, they do falsely, in the manner of clubs or sororities, with their artificial enclosures of dues-paying "sisterhood." Portia should have real friends, soul friends, not birds-flocking-together-in-their-common-plumage friends. Not, Susannah would undoubtedly have said, *teammates.* Portia was going to require companionship through life. Confidantes. Counselors. Comedians with perfect timing. *There's something about the women in my life.* Like the women who loved and valued Susannah herself.

Right, Portia had thought, despondent and irritated. The irritation was for her mother, for making such a thoroughly unrealistic injunction. (In seventh grade, who has friends like that?) The despondency was for herself, because she suspected even then that she would never have friends like that.

And in fact, she had never had friends like that.

A quarter century after her exile from the coolest of tables in the middle school lunchroom, Portia had found neither those intimate traveling companions her mother had prescribed nor even the superficial reassurance of a group of women friends. She enjoyed her colleagues — or some of them — here at home and generally looked forward to the annual NACAC meetings, where she often joined a group of long-acquainted comrades to indulge in soul-cleansing portions of alcohol. Were these the friends her mother had alluded to? They were not. She never spoke to any of them between conferences, unless some professional necessity arose. Their interactions were limited to e-mail health alerts and holiday cards containing snapshots of their families. But she was not isolated. Who could feel isolated when bombarded daily by hundreds of teenagers? And she lived with Mark, after all! She went for walks on the canal with Rachel and Rachel's dog. She was in a book group, though she tended to duck out at the height of the admissions season. (And whenever she didn't like the book. Which actually happened quite a lot.) But it wasn't the same.

It wasn't what her mother had, had always had. In the Northampton kitchen the phone rang incessantly, not only with organizational updates for the myriad collectives, task forces, and Amnesty groups, but with glad women, distraught women, women in need of Susannah's counsel and support. When Portia came home from school, they would be there before her, as often as not, cups of rapidly chilling herbal tea on the kitchen table and little soggy teabags oozing into the tabletop. The women would look up when she came in, their faces full of residual pain. (Her mother excelled at residual pain, Portia sometimes thought. She had a calling for it.) They seldom broke away from Susannah, and if for some reason they had to leave Northampton, they became the very women Portia and her mother would visit during school breaks: days of local culture and activity punctuated by more of those long, long evenings over the kitchen table (nicer kitchen tables, generally, in much nicer kitchens). Her life with her mother had been a travelogue of these dearest friends, like the one who committed to her lover and followed her to Tennessee, and the one who left her husband and was suddenly a Harvard Law student. (She must have been planning *that* for a while, Portia would later understand.) Embarrasingly, even at the height of her high school career, the ringing phone was always for her mother. Even more oddly, this would not strike Portia as odd until years later.

Still, as the only fruit of Susannah's loins, Portia had not exactly faded into the crowd of her mother's women. She was special. She was perennially important, like the permanent number one slot on the to-do list. She was, she saw very early on, Susannah's purpose and justification: her life project. And it would be wrong to suggest that this had not been heady stuff for a very long while. Portia had been introduced to her mother's circle as a heroine taking shape before their eyes, Susannah's own *little light of mine*. She had been the future something amazing, the proof in the pudding of what could happen when women did not allow themselves to be thwarted, limited, disrespected. She turned cartwheels at the potluck in somebody's Northampton backyard, the joyful girl at whom everyone else smiled and nodded, the powerful example of what a free and strong female was supposed to look like.

Sadly, by adolescence, Portia was finding it harder and harder to keep that up.

Shining examples were not supposed to get sent packing from the cool tables, were they? Joyful girls were supposed to have friends, or at least scads of people who wanted to be friends. And free and strong women? Surely they never felt about themselves the way Portia felt about herself: addled by insecurities, endlessly halted by doubt. And also sure — quite sure — that she was losing, filament by filament, the respect of Susannah, her creator, who was going to be very disappointed when she discovered that her daughter, in whom she had invested so much effort, was turning out to be deflatingly normal, a garden-variety self-sabotaging female after all. This normal Portia would turn out to be a woman of unobjectionable looks (trim enough, tall enough, with brown hair like her mother's and brown eyes like her mother's and pale, freckled skin. Like her mother's). Normal Portia would be obviously intelligent, but not what you'd call scary smart. Normal Portia was one of those people you could count on to listen to what you were saying and say, more or less, the right thing in return, but she wasn't exactly a font of wisdom or comfort. Like Susannah. In her serene and knowing way. To her many dearly loved and loving friends.

Later, she would try to convince herself that the renegotiation of power in a mother-daughter relationship was an essential part of growing up, and perhaps that was a little bit true. She would also tell herself that she and her mother had grown apart at the normal time, when she was in high school, when daughters were simply supposed to leave their mothers in the dust. But that wasn't quite true. She would try hardest of all to believe that there had been no incident, no great traumatic event parting daughter from mother, severing the unspoken bond, et cetera, et cetera, but that the coming apart had happened in increments so slight, she had not even noticed: glacial disentanglement, continental drift. And that, Portia knew perfectly well, was an outright untruth.

An incident. An accident. A rift.

All of the above, she thought grimly, which made her mother's increasingly desperate, then increasingly hopeless, overtures ever more poignant. They went on for a long time: the last year of college, the first years of Portia's new career (which baffled her mother), and all through the past decade at Princeton, when Susannah seemed at last to have begun to give up. Now their phone calls and visits were acrid, hollow ordeals of proximity and pretending, painful to all concerned but hardening, at least, into routine. They did not begin without anxiety on both sides, Portia knew, and they did not end without relief, also on both sides. And it might all have been avoided. And it might still be somehow salved, if Portia one day decided to take her mother back into their long-ago confidence. But that would never happen.

She took the first four folders from the pile and set them down on the bed, then climbed in with her coffee. The bed was simply made but warm, Mark having introduced her to certain European necessities like the divine duvet. She plumped the pillows behind her back, sipped her coffee, took up her pen, and read.

Stressed-out girl from Belmont, math team, tennis team, violinist in the local youth orchestra, fund-raiser for the women's shelter. Mom an engineer. Dad an engineer. Older brother at Yale. She wrote about her grandmother, who'd left Ireland in the 1950s because no one seemed willing to educate her and came to Boston, where she remained uneducated. "Going to college has been my goal since childhood," the girl concluded her essay rather portentously. "I've seen what happens to people who are not granted this opportunity."

Maybe Yale would take her, Portia thought, marking the reader's card with comments from the two enclosed references ("One of those faces I look forward to seeing in my classroom." "Hardworking and sensitive student." Sensitive? Portia thought). Colleges, Princeton included, did try not to create dire family stress by admitting one sibling and rejecting another, unless there were overwhelming differences in the quality of the applications. No undeserving applicant ever rode in on the coattails of a brilliant older sibling, of course, but no admissions officer relished being the cause of some drunken outburst at Thanksgiving twenty years hence, along the lines of: "You know you're not as smart as Johnny. *You* couldn't get into Princeton." *Good luck at Yale,* she silently told the girl, shutting the folder and putting it aside.

The next folder belonged to a classic campaigner. In addition to the common application with its Princeton supplement material, transcript, test scores, and recs, he had accumulated a two-page CV that memorialized every move he had made since entering the ninth grade, an eight-by-ten glossy photo in full baseball regalia, and a page of game-related statistics. There was a packet of newspaper clippings, and three unrequested testimonials illuminated the applicant's team spirit, competitive rigor, and moral caliber. Portia, alerted to the presence of this extra stuff by the thickness of the folder, rigidly avoided looking at it until she had made her way through the application proper, in the same order and at the same pace she read every other. That way, when she finally arrived at this figurative and literal padding, she was reassured by the fact that her impressions had already been formed not by the egoism of the publicity blitz, but by the lack of academic intensity already inherent in the transcript, the serviceable writing of the essays, the hearty but nonspecific recs. Then, having ascertained the gist of the unsolicited material, she put aside these later impressions and tried earnestly to forget them, forcing herself to think her way through the application one more time, making sure that her resistance to his personality had not overly directed the box she checked.

Go for It! was his mantra, she supposed. Or, *Sell Yourself! The Squeaky Wheel Gets the Grease! Don't Hide Your Light Under a Bushel! Ask for What You Want! Never Ventured, Never Gained!* The impulse to hawk one's virtues, to demand affirmation, to politely but firmly request the prize, was so American, she thought, sighing. Being unmoved by it seemed unfair, like an unannounced reversal of the rules. In this dossier, after all, was the spirit that had crossed the prairies, the go-getting attitude that had built empires of business and culture. The fact that it so turned her off was downright unpatriotic, she thought regretfully, setting aside the folder and taking a long drink of her now tepid coffee. Two down. Two more and she would get dressed and go into the office: a decent overture to a decent day's work.

She hadn't made it past the data pages when the phone rang. Portia looked at it, considering. The bedside phone had no caller ID, but far away downstairs a stilted, computerized female voice made an accompanying declaration to the empty kitchen:

"Call from...a...nony...mus....Call from...a...nony...mus."

This little feature was supposed to make life easier. It was supposed to give you a heads-up that a pollster or telemarketer or simply the person you least wanted to talk to was on the line, but in practice there were far too many calls that seemed to carry the designation "a...nony...mus." The antiquated phone in her mother's house, and the undoubtedly antiquated Vermont network it was attached to, quite often announced itself as "a...nony...mus" but sometimes, maddeningly, as "Out of...area" or even "Hart...land...Ver...mont."

Sighing, she closed the folder.

"Portia?"

She still had her finger in the file, as if she had the option of declining contact. "Hey, Mom."

"Mark tell you I called?"

"I got in late, I'm sorry. I didn't have a chance. You know, you can always try my cell if it's important."

Instantly, she regretted this. What was she saying? That her mother shouldn't call unless it was important? That there had to be an "it," and it had to be "important"?

"So did he tell you?" her mother asked. Even from this distance, she sounded on the edge of some hysteria. Was it a disease? Was that it? And Mark had known and somehow forgotten to mention this? Because he was angry at her? Because she had supposedly been rude to a woman who was rude to her first? And in her own home!

"He didn't tell me!" she said, sounding a little hysterical herself. She was bracing herself for words with Greek roots: *metastasis, diagnosis*. Things ending in *oma*. Technical terms that everyone understood. *Stage three. Stage four. Palliative. Hospice.* But her mother was talking instead about a girl who had a baby. Or wanted a baby. Or—no, this was it—had a baby she didn't want. What did it have to do with anything? And she was laughing about this now:

"It's been years since I changed a diaper! But I'm telling you, I can't wait."

Portia, who knew only that none of the words she had been expecting were part of this, found herself tuning out the manic buzz from the other end of the line. She looked at the file in her lap. "Terry Wang," it said. She had no memory at all of Terry Wang, despite the fact that she had nearly reached the essays when the phone rang. In theory, many numbers and letters and words of great importance to Terry Wang had already wafted from these pages, coiling up into the great cauldron of her own presumably adequate intellect and capacity for judgment. Something about a mother? She had a deceased mother. Mandarin spoken in the home. She was in a choir, yes? Or a...chorale of some kind. Likely major: molecular biology. Or...Latin? Was she, in fact, a she at all? Portia had many times been pulled up short by a pronoun at the very end of an application. Sometimes with a name like Chris or Terry. More often with names foreign to her, Debdan or Meihui. She would nearly have a fixed idea of this girl who played speed chess to relax, or this boy who had broken every freestyle record his high school could throw at him, only to have some teacher remark, "He is such a pleasure to teach." Or, "She is the only girl presently in my advanced calculus seminar, and refuses to be intimidated."

"Portia," her mother said shortly. "Can you believe this?" Clearly, she was relishing some kind of moment.

"He didn't say anything," Portia said apologetically. "Are you okay about all this?"

Her mother laughed. She laughed, Portia thought, without context, for the sheer, inappropriate pleasure of it. Portia sat on her bed, her finger inserted between the pages of Terry Wang's short, focused life, listening to her mother laugh, far away up north. She saw Susannah in her warm, messy kitchen, an ancient cat under the table, four days' worth of *Boston Globe*s on the counter, dangerously near the stove. Where was Frieda? Portia wondered. Frieda was her mother's remaining housemate. Why didn't Frieda stop her laughing?

"Tell me," said Portia, reaching for the safest thing, "how did this happen?"

"You remember Barbara? Teaches anthropology at Cornell? We stayed with them when you were looking at the school."

"Sure I remember," Portia said, though it had been two decades ago. "Them" had been a houseful of women, very messy women, some affiliated with the university, in the College Town section of Ithaca. She and her mother had slept on a miserable twin mattress on the floor, in a room off the kitchen. No wonder she hadn't wanted to go to Cornell.

"Barb's been working in Wyoming," said Susannah, as if this were some sort of explanation.

"Mom?"

"She's doing a book about feedlot culture."

"For cows?" Portia asked, baffled.

"No, Portia. For people. It's a new economic model. No one's looked at the social impact yet."

"But..." Her head was meandering. She was actually fighting an urge to reopen Terry Wang's file, to solve the now thorny issues of major and gender. "Mom, Barb from Cornell is writing a book about feedlots in Wyoming. What does that have to do with...did you say you were getting a baby?"

"So she's been mentoring at Planned Parenthood, like she used to do in Ithaca. One abortion provider for a thousand miles, and surrounded by the crazies, you know? And this girl came in a few weeks ago, but she seemed ambivalent about terminating. This girl wanted to finish school and go to college, but she couldn't continue the pregnancy at home."

"Why not?" Portia asked.

"Various disapproving family members, I assume," Susannah said shortly. "Anyway, Barb called me. This is two weeks ago. And I said send her here. So Barb put her on a plane."

"Wait..." Portia was shaking her head in disbelief. "When you say 'girl,' how *girl* do you mean? You didn't kidnap a middle schooler, did you?"

"No, no. Caitlin's seventeen. She wants to go to college next fall. Her parents think she's on a high school exchange program. Which she is, more or less. I enrolled her at Hartland Regional. It's like Harvard compared to the lousy school she went to in Wyoming, you know?"

Portia was briefly distracted by her own internal review of Hartland Regional, which was unlike Harvard in every way she could think of. "Well...," she faltered. "Good for you. You took in an unwed mother. That's great. And what happens when the baby's born?"

"Oh," said her mother with maddening nonchalance. "She thinks I'm adopting it. But it won't come to that. Not that I'm opposed to taking care of the baby. I'd love having a baby around again. Frieda's giving me a hard time about it, but she'll come around."

Now Portia was reeling. Somewhere between "she thinks I'm adopting" and "won't come to that" and Frieda needing to "come around," there was a crisis afoot. But what specific breed of crisis?

"Mom," she managed, "you're"—she frantically did the math—"sixty-eight."

"I know how old I am," her mother said tersely. "And very healthy, I'm sure you'll be happy to hear."

"Of course I'm happy to hear it," Portia said, in shock. "Why would you want to do this, at this time of your life?"

"Because I can, right? And I happen to think it's important. And it needs doing. There you go, three excellent reasons. And you only asked for one."

"But you can't adopt a baby!" she said, baffled that she had to be saying this at all.

"I'm not adopting. Didn't you listen to what I said? Caitlin isn't going to let that baby go. She doesn't know it yet, but when the baby is born, she'll see. And I'm happy for her to live here. She can finish high school here. She can even start college in Vermont if she likes. She has no idea how she's going to feel once the baby is actually here and she can see it and hold it. And even if she doesn't feel that right away, she'll come home and stay with us, and she'll bond with the baby."

Portia felt ill—physically ill. She was now sitting bent forward, hands wrapped tight around her knees, as if bracing for an unsurvivable plane crash. She wanted to slap her mother, or scream at her, at least, but what would she say? How dared Susannah assume to know how a seventeen-year-old would feel about a baby she wanted to give up? How dared she lie to a pregnant girl about something as critically important as this? Once, she might have been able to say these things to her mother. Now just the idea of them filled her with horror.

"Mom, don't." This was all she could manage.

"Don't? Don't what?" Susannah said tersely. "Don't open my home to a young woman who needs help? Don't give her the opportunity to change her mind about something this profound? You know, Portia, you may have decided not to have children, but that does not diminish the mother and child bond for the rest of us. I happen to feel it's quite powerful."

Portia was shaking. Bent over, the phone mashed to her ear with a clammy hand.

"She thinks she can just give birth to a baby and get on a plane and leave it behind. Back to her life and her family, whatever. And that's understandable. She's a baby herself. She has no idea how it's going to feel, but I do. And any mother does. I know, when she sees her child, it's going to change. And when it does, the door will be open for her, to take back her child. All I'm doing is making it possible for Caitlin to change her mind."

"And what if she doesn't?" Portia heard herself say. "What if she has her baby and gets on that plane and doesn't change her mind? What if you're left with a baby to raise?" *At your age!* she almost added, but fortunately caught hold of herself.

"You must think of me as very frail," Susannah said icily. "I had no idea."

"No, no," she objected, but feebly. Susannah had never been frail. Susannah was the opposite of frail. "Obviously, you can do this."

"Well, thanks for that," her mother said with abundant sarcasm. "Look, there's no point going on about it now. I get that I'm catching you off guard, and you're finding it difficult to pretend you're happy about this."

She was certainly right about that, Portia thought.

"Why don't you just call me back when you're ready to have a real conversation. In the meantime, we're not going to do Thanksgiving, in case you were thinking of coming up. We're just getting Caitlin settled in. I don't want to overwhelm her. I'd rather you and Mark waited till next month. Then you'll get a chance to meet her. She's very intelligent, by the way. I mean, maybe not *Princeton* material, but still intelligent." This last was said with a definite sneer—identifiable even across the miles and the less than state-of-the-art telephone connection.

"That's not fair."

"Well, life isn't fair," her mother said, and hung up smartly.

*As an ninth grader, I was fortunate to win a scholarship to Andover
through a program that prepares minority students for college. The first
year here was very difficult for me. I felt alone. I was one of very few
Latina students on campus. The other students tended to be from very
privileged backgrounds, and though they weren't unkind to us, it was
clear to me that they didn't really have an ability to communicate with
us in any meaningful way. In my sophomore year, however, I joined the
crew team, and gradually crew became a common language. Some of
my crew teammates became my friends, and while none of them have
ever come to visit me in my hometown of Holyoke, Massachusetts, I
have spent a lot of time in their homes. The father of one of my teammates is a Princeton alum, and he first talked to me about the school.
I want you to know that I am aware my SAT scores are significantly
lower than what is typical for a Princeton student, but I am used to
working very hard, and I am determined to thrive in college.*

CHAPTER EIGHT

FICTIONS OF LIVES

Mark seemed to take the news of their Thanksgiving banishment with
equanimity, if the shrug he offered in response might be termed
equanimity. In fact, there was a certain reserve of emotion in the days
that followed the dinner party, days in which they woke and spoke and
made plans and shifted them without ever having what might be termed
an important conversation. Certainly they never returned to the crucial
moment, the moment she would later know to be a definitive kind of rift,
but only seemed instead to lay a walkway over it and get on with things.
Portia considered this, if not precisely satisfying, then oddly mature, as
if they had somehow arrived at a place in their life together where not
every moment of conflict required a deconstruction and then a reconstruc-
tion of souls, individual or entwined. Like silence in a long conversation,
what had happened felt, in its immediate aftermath, like a sigh, a shake of

the head, or perhaps even the shrug Mark himself had offered when she'd told him—not, perhaps, in these particular words—that Susannah did not want them after all, that they were off the hook. Surely he was glad not to face that grueling drive, eight hours at the mercy of their fellow travelers on the wintry roads, the odd American ritual at this even odder American table in this oddest of all American households. It meant even less to him than it did to her, surely. Why he had even tolerated it all these years... well, it testified to his general forbearance, she supposed.

But then again, he didn't seem relieved. He carried this dismissal like a very small but accrued burden, part of an ongoing increase in small burdens. He made no suggestion for an alternative plan for the holiday, nor did he ask whether she cared to make a plan. She had just begun to feel real concern for the situation when, three days before the holiday itself, Mark came home in a state of some agitation and reported an unfolding crisis within his department, one that had been consuming him—as it turned out—for the better part of a week, and which, reassuringly, had nothing whatsoever to do with him, with her, or—most important of all—with them.

Gordon Sternberg, for decades the most celebrated member of the English Department (as likely to turn up on Charlie Rose as he was to grace Princeton's Web page with the news of some new book or honor), was undergoing a breakdown of spectacular proportions, encompassing—so Mark explained to Portia—every aspect of his life. Sternberg, the author of classic works of scholarship on a staggering array of literary subjects (he was a nineteenth-century man on the whole, but so brilliant that a brief, aberrant fascination with Spenser had resulted in an instantly classic work of criticism on *The Faerie Queene*), was a former chair of the department and current power behind the throne—Mark's throne—simply too important not to consult on matters minuscule or major. He lived a few minutes' walk from campus, at the end of a long street of stately homes, with his wife and whichever of his six children might be drifting through, writing up their PhD theses or taking time off between stints of fieldwork. Famously raucous faculty parties took place in the classically proportioned rooms, with legendary bad behavior and marriages rent asunder. (Portia had herself attended many of these parties, often finding herself in the kitchen with Julianne Sternberg, who—hailing from the Betty Fussell years of competitive Princeton entertaining—refused to hire a caterer or even allow the university to assemble the buffet.)

Now, with a clamorous jolt, it was all over—the marriage, the family, the career.

Sternberg, always a drinker, had imploded in a series of crises, domestic disturbances, a weaving car down Prospect Avenue, an outburst from his seat at a visiting scholar's lecture on Tennyson. Campus security had found him under his own office desk at four in the morning. One of his children had gone to the dean of faculty, pleading for help. Julianne Sternberg was not talking to that child, who was not talking to two of her siblings. The house, it turned out, was quite literally falling down, with the ceiling of the large living room—scene of so many famous bacchanals—actually scattered over the carpeting and the walls puckering from damp and carpenter ants.

The first midnight call came the week before the Thanksgiving holiday, and when Mark returned home just before dawn, it was to deliver the news of Gordon Sternberg's hospitalization at Princeton House, the addiction treatment facility of the local medical center. "I knew this was coming," he said wearily, pulling off his shoes again and lying on top of the covers. "Gordon has been in terrible shape for a couple of years. I'm glad he's had the crisis, in a way. Now he'll get the attention he needs, and they can help him."

But three nights later another call came, this time from the police. Gordon had made some sort of escape from the facility and next appeared at his family home, armed with a long piece of wood he had evidently lifted from a neighbor's garbage pile. His turncoat daughter had called for help as her mother sobbed upstairs. Now there were criminal charges to contend with. This time, Mark didn't come home till nearly ten the next morning.

Meanwhile, there was Sternberg's advanced seminar on the Romantics, which had to be reassigned (Rachel, taking one for the team, volunteered to step in), and the weighty matter of the great man's junior paper students, and the half-dozen thesis advisees, not to mention the graduate students and Rhodes and Marshall applicants to whom he'd promised life-altering recommendations. There was Julianne Sternberg, who was herself becoming unhinged by the rapid implosion of her entire life, the sudden, brutal divisions among her children, the financial body blow of what promised to be intensive and chronic care for her husband, coupled with his abrupt lack of employment in circumstances that didn't at all guarantee the seamless continuation of his salary, not to mention the growing laundry list of legal expenses. And there was the small difficulty of one Ezme Johanna Castillo, the unwitting catalyst for all this heartbreak. Castillo was a doctoral candidate from NYU who had been invited by Sternberg to co-teach an advanced seminar on demonic preoccupations in nineteenth-century American poetry and to whom Sternberg had apparently been declaring extreme devotion since the beginning of the fall term (to, she was insisting, her intense chagrin). The English, comparative literature, and even, in a couple of cases, creative writing faculty had leapt into this sordid human mess and begun thrashing about, milling gossip and schadenfreude out of the muck, calling Mark to register long buried grievances against Sternberg, or little warning signs they'd noted, or confidences he'd entrusted to them, which they—being loyal, honorable people—had kept silent about, despite their better judgments (which—seeing the clear price of their silence—they certainly regretted now!). Everyone, naturally, wanted to talk about Ezme Johanna Castillo. Was she? Were they? Was it a case of an unwitting pawn, lodged in the tractor beam of the great man's stature and brilliance? Sorting out the complicity or innocence of this person, which was technically not even relevant to the nuts and bolts of the Sternberg situation, and figuring out what to do with her from the university's official standpoint, began to consume more and more of Mark's energy, as far as Portia was concerned. As if, she thought, all would hinge on whether it was an actual affair, and if so, a consensual affair or a coercive affair, or instead something confined to the now unbounded imagination of the rapidly deteriorating Gordon Sternberg. So Mark interviewed her, and because he couldn't in good conscience ask anyone else for an opinion on Sternberg's and Castillo's private lives, he interviewed her again. And again. Then, apparently distraught, she disappeared, with nothing settled. And who could blame her?

Sternberg himself at this point was ensconced at a treatment facility outside of Philadelphia and in some legal limbo. Officially he was on medical leave, and the university was maintaining an attitude of prim silence on the whole business, but the entire Modern Language Association seemed nonetheless to be on intimate terms with what was happening. At Thanksgiving dinner, which Portia and Mark ultimately attended at Rachel and David's house, at a table populated by no fewer than four other department-affiliated couples (plus the ever disagreeable Helen of Oxford), no one spoke of anything else, and in the days following the holiday, the scandal only waxed. Mark's phone seemed to ring all the time—at home, too, as if the situation called for a suspension of that civilized separation between time on and

time off. Portia, who was attempting to get through thirty application folders a day in her armchair in the corner of the bedroom, began to anticipate
the interruptions and found herself becoming syncopated, disjointed in her
reading, which forced her to go back and reread, which slowed her down and
confused her. She tried turning off the bedside phone but then only heard
the downstairs phone and the disembodied voice coiling up the stairwell.

By the following week, the wave of alarm among Sternberg's colleagues,
critics, children, nominal friends, acolytes, students past and present,
editors, and now, ominously, creditors seemed to be cresting, so on Tuesday morning Portia relocated her operation to West College, with a box
of Constant Comment teabags and the back pillow from her sadly abandoned armchair, a move that might have signaled—to her colleagues, at
least—an unusual situation at home. There, however, she was scarcely
less distracted.

Corinne stopped by early, to rhapsodize about her children (Bennett,
the elder, had won some wrestling prize, and Diandra had been invited to
join the Andover debate team, even as a freshman!) and, with a martyred
blush, announce that she had *single-handedly* fed twenty-five for Thanksgiving. Clarence, too, stopped by to sympathize, barely concealing his own
interest in the English Department morass.

"Mark must be stuck in the middle of this Sternberg mess," he said
without preamble.

"Right in the middle," she told him. "The phone rings off the hook.
Which is why I came in," she said, answering his implicit question.

"Ah." He nodded. "Sad for the wife."

"Yes. And the kids."

But he was already distracted and moving on. "How's your region
looking?"

"Well, it's early, of course. But the numbers are pretty much in line with
last year."

"Good, good," Clarence said absently. "Do me a favor and look out for a
Milton Academy student named Carter Ralston. Development has already
called twice about him."

Portia wrote down the name on a Post-it note and stuck it on the end of
her lap desk. "You want me to look for it?"

"No, no. It's either here or it's coming. Just make sure we talk about it.
Anyone else?"

"We have a fourteen-year-old from Woonsocket, Rhode Island. Home-schooled. He has eight hundreds just about everywhere, and six AP fives. His mother sent a letter saying she wants to come with him and have him live with her off campus."

Clarence sighed. There were a few of these every year, brilliant kids twiddling their thumbs in high school or even middle school, screaming to be let out. Emotionally, of course, they were unprepared for college life, and in general they were noncontributors to the extracurricular life of the community. But even so, there was sometimes a place for them.

"Leave it on my desk," he said. He turned to leave, then stopped. "How was that school you visited? That new school."

"In New Hampshire?" She frowned. "Quest?"

"Yeah. I had a letter from someone on their board, a Class of '60-something. He said they were doing amazing things."

"Well . . . ," she said skeptically, "*amazing*. I don't know."

"How'd it seem to you?"

"Like a work in progress." She shrugged. "I mean, they've got the students milking the cows, but they've also got Harkness tables. The kids are kind of different. Very secure and opinionated. I had one girl arguing with me about whether college was necessary and whether Princeton was only branded prestige. I don't know if the school is going to wind up looking like Putney or Choate, but I can tell you they're very serious about what they're doing."

He nodded. "We shouldn't see applications for a couple of years, then."

"Actually," she told him, "I'm pretty sure we'll get at least a couple this year. There's one kid I met, I hope he applies."

"Oh?" Clarence said, looking at her.

"Very gifted, and a little bit odd."

He gave a tired sigh. "One for the faculty, then."

"Whatever works." She laughed.

"All right, I'll let you get back to it. Remember to look out for the Milton kid."

"Carter Ralston," she read off the Post-it note. "I will."

He moved off in the direction of his office, trailing cologne.

Portia read on. It was early in the pool, still before the official deadline, but the applicants and the high schools were still adjusting to the post–Early Decision era, and it seemed as if a lot of these kids (and their advisers) were just programmed to get their stuff in early. Maybe they wanted it done so they could get on with the out-of-my-hands portion of their senior year. Maybe they wanted to convey that they were so together, so on top of the task at hand, that the deadline was incidental. She had read a number of notes from applicants assuring her that while Early Decision might be a thing of the past, Princeton was their first choice, and if admitted, they would certainly attend; but she put aside this information—if it was information. Without the binding contract of Early Decision, they might be making the same vow of commitment to every college on their list.

The art of admitting students to selective colleges had never really stood still, but the shifts and reversals seemed to be coming thicker and faster, and the end of Princeton's Early Decision option was only the most recent course correction. The previous century had been a continual shuttle between academic excellence and "our kind of fellow," and no move had been made without a corresponding chorus of disapproval. Placate the faculty by tightening academic standards, and certain objectionable immigrant groups became a bit too well represented on campus. Introduce the notion of "character" into the process to salve the wounded alumni (and keep the Jews out, or at least down), and the faculty let you know how disgusted they were. Let in women: Piss off the traditionalists. Beef up the football team: Watch the academics slide. Show diversity: Insult the traditional applicant pool. Open the door to impoverished students from all over the world: Turn your back on children of the American middle class. A Princeton class of one hundred years ago looked very different from the way it did today, which was of course no bad thing, but Portia sometimes had to remind herself that they would probably always be tinkering with the idea of what a superior applicant looked like. In her brief tenure alone, for example, a new focus on scholarship had seemed to take hold, and a disregard for dabbling in any form was now entrenched. Gone—or going fast—was the reign of the all-around kid, the tennis-playing, camp-counseling, math-tutoring, part-time-job-holding A student who was pretty sure he wanted to be a doctor or an investment banker but was also considering law school. These kids had to know, from the cradle, it seemed, that virology or avant-garde music was their destiny. Portia was sorry to note this change, not because it made her job harder to see the thoroughly specialized, committed, and wildly accomplished applicants she saw now (it didn't, actually), but because she herself had been the epitome of an all-around kid: soccer team member, Amnesty volunteer, stage manager for the musical, book reviewer for the school paper, honor roll perennial. Her own era as a desirable college applicant was now, clearly, past.

Officially, of course, colleges did not comment on such things. There was hardly an Ivy League press office declaring the current fashion to potential applicants with *Vogue* magazine authority, and it took time for the new reality to permeate the culture. These kids were at the mercy of their parents and advisers, too many of whom were still rooted in out-dated thinking about what Princeton was sifting the applicant pool to find, and it pained her to pass on these students who had clearly done, and done well, the precise things they'd been told to do, who had become the very seventeen-year-olds they'd been encouraged to become, a project that sometimes reached back to their infancy, with Music Together and toddler gymnastics. What it did to the kids — she saw that every day. But what it did to the parents! One day a few years earlier, she had been stripping off her sweaty clothing in the locker room of her gym when she overheard two Princeton Day School mothers lamenting the state of their children's seventh-grade science fair projects. One was distressed because a research partner would share the credit for her son's experiment design. The other lamented the fact that her daughter's project did not constitute an original contribution to science. Portia, who was struggling to pull a wet Lycra top over her head at the time, looked intently at the two women to reassure herself that they were joking.

They weren't joking.

More to the point, it was like this everywhere now. Toddlers herded into early enrichment so they could get into the right nursery school, segue into the best elementary school, compete for the most intense high school, and, finally, break the ribbon for one of the right — the so very few right — colleges. She remembered a speaker she had once heard at Rachel's children's private school, a man who had founded a campaign to wrest parental (and child) sanity from the scheduling nightmare that family life in middle-class and affluent communities had become. "Look at us," he had scolded the audience. "We're driving our kids around like maniacs. They're changing into the Girl Scout uniform in the backseat after ballet class. We're feeding them fast-food dinners between the clarinet lesson and the math tutor's house. Why," the man had asked them, "do you think we're behaving this way?"

A woman in front of Portia had raised her hand and stood up. "Everyone knows," she announced, "that Ivy League schools want well-rounded students. We're only trying to do the best for our kids."

It had been a gradual build, the advent of this new parent. Millennial parents, she'd heard them called, and took some comfort in the fact that they now constituted a recognized phenomenon, with a cold, precise, academic-sounding label. Millennial parents were baby boomers, of course, and had always enjoyed the generational perk of being part of a big, big crowd, capable of influencing policy and politics, fashion and music. Now, their offspring had a bubble of their own, and for once, bigger wasn't better. These parents had never been so out of control as they were now, watching their carefully nurtured children discover that they were the camel and Ivy League admissions offices the eye of the corresponding needle. Nothing could be done to make them all fit through, not SAT prep courses and private tutors, CV-enhancing internships, or service trips to Costa Rica. Letters from CEOs could not help them, nor—despite what they desperately sought to believe—could private college counselors, and the helplessness they felt was like a silent but vibrating sound track, just outside the walls of West College.

It was still safe to call Princeton with a question about your child's application, but Portia knew of at least two other Ivies that had begun keeping track of parental contact and adding that information to the applicant's folder. She knew of a small, highly competitive liberal arts college in New England that had begun to employ "parent bouncers" for orientation weekend, in an effort to get them off campus as soon as possible. She had heard from numerous professors about parents calling to discuss their children's grades or negotiating to submit a revised paper. (Revised by whom? A worrying thought.) And she had herself, on occasions too numerous to count, been forced to overhear the student walking beside her across campus whip out his or her phone to call Mom with the results of the Spanish quiz or statistics midterm.

What was behind it? A fear that to let go meant they were no longer parents? Or no longer young? Was it some tragically outsourced pride that began with a MY CHILD IS AN HONORS STUDENT IN KINDERGARTEN bumper sticker, swelled with every SAT percentile or coach's letter, and ended with a Princeton decal in the rear window? What happened to perfectly capable kids who'd been so bombarded with help that they felt helpless to do anything on their own? Or the kids who'd been so driven at home, they'd never had to find their own drive? It couldn't be good, she thought.

Late in the afternoon, one of her youngest colleagues knocked tentatively on her door. This was Dylan Keith, three years out of Princeton himself and newly elevated to associate director. "Portia?" he asked politely, and waited.

She looked up. She was writing her summary on a girl from Maine with a baffling transcript—devoid, it seemed, of any hard science or language but crowded with rhythmic dance, Photoshop, and something called "Creative Expression."

"Sorry, you want to finish that?"

"Yes, if you can wait."

He could wait. She wrote: "Likable girl, and I appreciated her essay on her mother's influence and encouragement to explore her artistic inclinations, but scores are weak and she clearly has not challenged herself academically. Wait for reports from Dance and Art Depts—otherwise unpersuasive." She checked "Low Priority—Unlikely."

"Okay, thanks." She smiled, closing the file. "How's it going?"

"Fine," he said, clearly looking as if it weren't.

"You getting slammed?"

"No. Not yet. I was traveling last week. You have a moment?"

She put her lap desk on the floor. He took the swivel chair and swiveled in her direction.

Dylan was a slight man with a hairline already under assault, sweet and extremely kind. He had come to Princeton from a Houston prep school and had never been north before his college tour, but he had fallen so in love with seasons that Portia doubted he could go home now. Close enough in age to the applicants that he seemed still to bear the marks of his own admissions passage, he was full of empathy with them. That would change, Portia suspected, over time. In a few years, he would grow less patient with them, less able to dismiss self-indulgences and cultural myopia. But not yet. For now, he was their advocate and apologist, a famously soft touch in the department. He had just been assigned to the Southwest.

"Where were you?" Portia asked him.

"New Mexico. And Arizona. I went to the Native American boarding school near Taos."

"Oh. Good," she said, wondering where this was going.

"It's a very inspiring place." She nodded, waiting. "I've been meaning to ask you, you were at Dartmouth, right?"

Portia frowned. "As a student? Or an admissions officer? Well, yes to both."

"Right. I thought so. I just wanted to ask what your experience was there, with recruiting Native American students."

"Well, we had a designated admissions officer for Native American students. It wasn't my area. If you have a specific question, I mean, I did observe while I was there, obviously. But you know, Dartmouth has a historical relationship to Native Americans."

Dylan frowned, demonstrating a forehead creased beyond its years.

"The college was founded to educate them. Well, the point was to *convert* Indians in New England, and then ordain them so they could go out and convert more Indians. *Vox clamantis in deserto* is the college motto. You know, 'voice crying out in the wilderness'? But they were matriculated students at the beginning, alongside the others. All training to be clergy. Like here," she said, alluding to Princeton's own Presbyterian roots. "But then they disappeared from the student demographic for a hundred and fifty years, give or take. We had to get a liberal president in before we got them back on our radar. He came from Princeton, actually."

"I didn't know that," said Dylan.

"Yes. Anyway, in his inaugural speech he rededicated the college to its original purpose, and that meant getting out to the reservations and the Native American schools, and recruiting. So I guess we had a little head start on the other Ivies. Or else we were really late fulfilling our own obligations."

"But," said Dylan, "how did they know which kids were going to make it through?"

"They didn't. And a lot didn't. Of course, there were kids with Native American heritage coming through the general pool, and they did fine. You know, a parent or grandparent had a tribal affiliation, but they were mainstream. The ones we had to go out to find, it was rough for them. On the other hand, the college is very proud of how well some of them have done. And they're committed to continuing. Was there someone in particular you wanted to discuss?"

He nodded, his eyes downcast. The light caught his scalp, already visible. She tried to age progress him a couple of years and found, to her regret, that he would not be an attractive man.

"I met this great kid in New Mexico. At the boarding school. He's a Chippewa from Minnesota. He did horrendously in public school, and they took a big chance on him and let him transfer in last year."

Portia nodded and waited.

"He wants to be a doctor, but if he came here, he wouldn't be as prepared as a typical freshman pre-med. Actually, he's behind across the board: English, languages. He'd need a lot of support with writing...." Dylan trailed off.

"There's a 'but' here," she said helpfully.

"Yeah. But. He's this amazing kid. He's so alive. He's eating everything up there. It's like he's been waiting for some growth hormone, and they've got him on IV. He asked me all these questions about Princeton, and the culture here, and whether they'd let him catch up and keep going. He has a pretty clear grasp of what he needs to do. It's just that I have this awful sense of him getting here and being overwhelmed by the workload, and just falling apart. I don't know if we can support him enough, you know? And I wonder if it's doing him a disservice, in the long run. Maybe if he went somewhere less challenging, he'd be successful, and he'd get there sooner. If he comes here, he might not get there at all."

Portia considered. This was a discussion she had had many times, with many colleagues, and it was an even more frequent internal preoccupation. It wasn't a question of who deserved. They all deserved. But the very delicate balance between ambition and accomplishment, daring and security, made more volatile still by the essential adolescence of the average college applicant, made these decisions of massive—but unknowable—personal impact. When her geographic area included (and was dominated by) California, she'd been able to enjoy a considerable buffer for her anxieties, because the excellent students she rejected for Princeton had an enormous safety net in the form of Berkeley, the jewel in the crown of California's public university system and the likely destination for any high-achieving students who fell short of the Ivy League. The chess master valedictorian from Los Angeles, the brilliant mathematician from San Diego, the meticulous girl from Santa Cruz who had worked so hard, only to be the tenth or fifty-eighth or ninety-first hardworking girl from Santa Cruz to come before the Princeton committee: All of them would be offered admission to Berkeley, and once there, a superb faculty could get them where they needed to go. Now, with Portia's focus on the other end of the country, she felt the lack of such a secure fallback. Not that there weren't state universities for these accomplished applicants, but the University of Maine wasn't Berkeley. Applicants from New England had more to lose, and she—as a result—had even more sleep to lose over them.

As for Dylan's Chippewa student, he could certainly go to Minnesota State. He could take the time he needed to graduate, go on to medical school, and return to his reservation to become the beacon of his community, inspiring generations of other bright kids to see beyond the horizon. On the other hand, he might come to Princeton, or a place like Princeton, and buckle, leaving school altogether and never achieving what he might achieve. On the other hand, a Minnesota State might lack Princeton's abilities to carry him, support him, bear with him. It might lack the scholarship support Princeton could provide, and the mentorship. On the other hand, Princeton's foreignness, its diversity, its raw pressure, might prove unnecessary distractions to someone who would otherwise focus on the matter at hand: to establish a bedrock foundation for the ultimate goal of becoming a doctor. On the other hand, what if this student wasn't really destined for medicine at all, but only awaiting the film studies or religion or art or Chinese mythology class that would set his path in a radically different direction toward an unsuspected vocation? Princeton did that for so many students. And this alive kid, this hungry kid, shouldn't he have the broadest possible range of brilliant outcomes?

Unfortunately, there was no gain in looking to the past for guidance. Over the years, she had taken various deep breaths over various marginal students, some of whom had sailed through and some of whom had faltered and then failed. That girl from Sitka, now at Oxford studying economics on a Rhodes, had been horrendously prepared for Princeton, but once on campus (and with massive support from the writing program), she had found her footing. But there were others who had not been able to stay, and they were like little stigmata to the admissions officers who had fought for them. Portia, like every one of her colleagues, carried her own secret retinue of sorrows: the single mother from Oakland who had fought her way through high school, taking six years to do it, and who had ardently (if inarticulately) pleaded for the chance. She had had to leave after freshman year. The boy from Hawaii who had spent his life in foster care, finding a relatively stable home only in the last two years. It hadn't been enough. Sophomore year, he had bought a history paper off the Internet and been suspended. The fact was, they didn't know. They couldn't know. What would happen if we said yes? What would happen if we said no? Sometimes she thought that every new admissions officer should be issued a Ouija board.

Dylan was waiting patiently, if grimly. "How bad are the scores?" Portia asked.

He seemed to consider this with a weight the question didn't quite indicate. "Bad. Low five hundreds."

"Science aptitude?"

"Unreflected in the transcript, but I do think so, yes."

"Can he write?"

"Passionately. But not very well."

Passion, Portia thought. It was what they were all about. But passion underscored by the attendant numbers and letters. This was not looking good.

"Have you considered asking them to keep him for another year? It sounds like it could make a big difference for him, wherever he ends up."

Dylan sat back in the swivel chair and folded his arms. He looked suddenly calm and pleased. "Yes, actually. I was waiting to see if you had the same thought."

"Do you have a good rapport with the college counselor?"

"Well, it's new. But I liked her. I think the school would support him." He got to his feet. "I'm going to run this by Clarence. Can I say I discussed it with you?"

"Absolutely. And you always can. These are the cases that take it out of you. Well"—she laughed—"most of them take it out of you."

"Right. I was Mr. Universe when I graduated. Look at me now."

She smiled at him. "You're doing fine."

"I'm thinking this isn't for me, long-term."

Portia looked at him. "I'd be surprised if it were," she said, but in fact she was surprised. He'd been a find. Most of the young hires left after a year or two, bound for graduate school or teaching, sometimes college counseling, but she'd had hopes for Dylan. He was an orderly type who went with the gut. Indeed, he possessed that odd (and very rare) combination of opposing characteristics that the best admissions officers had: a capacity for massive detail retention and a converse ability to let go of everything but instinct. Lacking one or the other of these, you could certainly do the work, but it would always be a battle. "We'd be sorry to lose you," she told him.

"Well, it's something I'm thinking about. I miss Latin. I miss Latin geeks."

Portia smiled. Dylan had been his class's Latin orator at commencement. Thoughtfully, he had provided his classmates with a translation, letting them know precisely where in the speech to laugh and where to cheer, which impressed their parents no end.

After he had gone, she sat for a long, illicit time, watching the late afternoon darkness fill her window. She was not in a hurry. There was nothing to go home for; Mark was out, somewhere. Her only tether was to the armchair and the orange folders, traveling slowly from stack to stack across her wooden lap desk, like that T. S. Eliot poem about the life measured out in coffee spoons, except that she was measuring hers with other people's lives, which they had measured into these life-folders. Short lives, slivers of lives, fictions of lives. She opened the next folder.

Sarah Lenaghan, Brookline, Mass. Dad an attorney, went to Cornell. Mom a homemaker. Princeton alum, class of 1991. Portia frowned. Nineteen ninety-one happened to be her own class at Dartmouth, though she hadn't actually graduated until the following year. Sarah's mom must have had a baby right out of college. There were other siblings, younger siblings. Sarah's mother's name was Jane. Portia kept looking at the dates, as if they didn't make sense. Why should they not make sense?

So she was now old enough to have produced a Princeton applicant. So her contemporaries, in the time Portia had been reading thousands and thousands of applications, living in New Hampshire, living in Princeton, living with Mark, had produced one child, two children, four children in the case of Sarah Lenaghan's mother, the homemaker. All those little lives, those clarinet lessons and traveling soccer teams. What had she done?

Sarah was a runner. She had run the Boston Marathon. Her writing was vivid, so vivid that Portia could feel the pain in her own lungs as Sarah hit her wall at mile nineteen. The girl was a wonderful writer. She wrote poetry. She loved Princeton. She had marched in the P-Rade since the age of five, her mother's first reunion. If Portia met the mother, Jane Lenaghan, née Paley, what would they talk about? Their memories of the moon landing? The terrible hairstyles they had worn in middle school? Had they watched the same television shows? Listened to the same awful music? She had a strange, thankfully passing impulse to pick up the phone and call the number on the application to ask her, Jane Paley Lenaghan: "How can you have this child? How is it fair that you have this child?"

"If I still had the opportunity to apply to Princeton Early Decision," wrote Sarah Lenaghan, "I would be doing so. For many years I have hoped to follow in my mother's footsteps and attend this great university. Please know that, should I be fortunate enough to be accepted to Princeton, I will absolutely attend."

She closed the folder, then, gripped by a new idea, an awful idea, she opened it again and scanned the first page, the detail page of names and addresses, e-mails, phone numbers. And dates. Sarah was born in December 1990. Portia's fingertips felt numb. She reached down for the pile of folders she had read through the afternoon and opened the first. Sunil Chatterjee, born September 14, 1990. Beatrice McHugh, born July 24, 1990. Lucy DiMaggio, born September 9, 1990. Anna Cohen-Schwartz, born May 1, 1990. Brian Wong, graduating as a junior, born February 23, 1991.

So it's here, she thought. As if she hadn't been waiting, and for years, for just this moment.

Ten years ago, my mother and father left China to move here. My father had been a research scientist in China, and my mother was a civil servant. Here they run a take out restaurant, where I also work on weekends and during the summer. I must be the translator for my parents, because they still do not speak very good English, and it is difficult for them to fill out government forms and conduct their business. We live over the restaurant, so we are never far from the business. I see every day how hard my parents work, and I am always aware of how much they gave up so that I could come to America and have a chance to go to a great American university.

CHAPTER NINE

AN ACTOR PREPARES

Four days before Christmas, Gordon Sternberg walked out of his treatment facility on the Philadelphia Main Line and disappeared into a Yuletide confection of affluent suburbia. One of Sternberg's daughters filed a missing persons report, another spirited their mother away to her own home on the West Coast. Mark was called in, of course, though there was little he or anyone else could do. Still, on the morning of their departure for Vermont, he went into his office to make some calls, and Portia went for a walk with Rachel and the dog.

It was a cold morning, comfortably seasonal. The dog, a Labrador retriever of uncommon stupidity (even for a Labrador retriever), was in high spirits and pulled relentlessly at the lead, especially when he sighted another dog. They walked along the lake as far as the boathouse and then turned back, making their way up through the campus and along Prospect. As they neared the Sternberg home, down past the depopulated but still magisterial eating clubs, they both slowed. In other years, these parlor windows had showcased a bigger-than-yours Christmas tree, chockablock with gold balls, and the porch pillars had been coiled with pine boughs. Now, silence and darkness in the huge house, and an air of thorough abandonment, seemed to mark the place. Portia was struck by how shabby it seemed on this street of camera-ready holiday cheer, with its drab and spotty stucco and still unraked leaves. It blared discontent and disarray, but for all its disturbances it had been a living place, a place of contact, conflict, life. That, and not the silence, was what had made them stop.

For a long moment, they both stood looking. Neither Portia nor Rachel was sentimental by nature, but both knew they were thinking the same thing: how they had met in this house ten years ago, at a large and loud gathering of English and comp lit faculty. Mark had been newly hired, and the party technically had been to welcome him, but there was no sense of occasion about it and no real order. Gordon Sternberg left Mark to fend for himself, and he seemed not to recognize Portia from the recruiting trip the previous spring, when he had taken them to Lahiere's for dinner. So she simply wandered, looking at the knots of men and women in the hallways and rooms, noting the dusty prints of eighteenth-century London and Paris, the worn sofas and downtrodden rugs. The guests, who were veterans of many Sternberg parties, knew that there would be platters of dolmas in the dining room and spicy nuts in the living room. They knew the bottles of wine and Scotch were on a long table in Sternberg's study, cleared for the occasion of whatever the great man was working on. They simply entered the house, filled up on food and drink, and went to their favorite spots to talk loudly with their favorite fellow partygoers. Everyone looked so comfortably ensconced that she found herself unable to pick out her hostess (Julianne Sternberg had not, naturally, been at the recruiting dinner), and in fact Portia—who couldn't have imagined that Mrs. Sternberg would hardly leave the kitchen that night—would not meet Julianne until some months later. She discovered a pregnant Rachel Friedman in the living room with Sternberg himself, who was by then very drunk. Gordon, apparently the last human being on the planet to understand that alcohol was injurious to a fetus, was exuberantly pressing an enormous gin and tonic on his guest, and Portia, in disbelief, had reached out and taken it from him, distracting Sternberg long enough for Rachel to slip away (this was truly a selfless act, given that it then condemned her to ten long minutes of intense face time with Sternberg himself). When Rachel caught up with her later in the evening, she professed her eternal gratitude, then her astonishment to learn that her savior was the companion of the guest of honor. Then baffled surprise that there was a guest of honor in the first place.

"What will happen to it?" Portia asked, meaning the house.

"Oh, the university will buy it back, of course. Then they'll sell it, I suppose. Probably to another faculty member."

"That's so final," Portia said. "I mean, couldn't he come back?"

"Well, Mark knows better than I, but from what I've heard, I don't think so. Not after teaching drunk. And the baseball bat incident."

"I heard it was a piece of wood."

"Whatever." Rachel shrugged.

"I feel bad for Julianne."

"Julianne should have gotten out years ago," Rachel said with a chilly voice. "I can't fathom that kind of entropy. I mean, my God, what must it have been like to be married to him? What did she get from him?"

"Six kids?" Portia said tentatively.

"Six grown kids. *Please.* I hope she'll have a wonderful new life now. I hope she'll have a wild affair. I hope she'll dye her hair green and go back to graduate school. Wasn't she in graduate school when she married him? Girl interrupted! That's quite an interruption."

"It was a different time," Portia said gently.

"Poppycock," said Rachel.

They walked on, turning at Harrison in the direction of their houses.

"How's Mark holding up?" said Rachel, pulling the dog back from an open garbage can.

"I'm not sure," Portia said truthfully. "He doesn't talk about it. Actually, we're not communicating very well at the moment." She was aware of her hands as she said this, swinging, mittened. Then of Rachel's hand, being pulled forward with the leash. Rachel did not look at her, but she had heard.

"Rough patch?" she said after a moment.

"I suppose. Do you remember that dinner party at our house? With your friend from Oxford? He thought I was rude to her. Do you think I was rude?"

"You? She was a horrible bitch."

Portia burst out laughing. "I thought so."

"I was appalled. I said to David, after we dropped her off, I had no idea she was so awful. She'd been extremely pleasant when we took her out last spring. But he defended her, because she cried."

Portia looked at her. "What do you mean?"

"She was crying. In the car. In the backseat. It was *very* strange."

"You mean . . . wait, you mean she was bawling? Or—"

"No. Quietly. We didn't hear her. But when she got out, we saw that she'd been crying. Honestly, it was really odd. And then the next day she phoned us and apologized. She said she was just hormonal."

"Well, it would have been nice if she'd called me," Portia sniffed. "I mean, I'm the one she was rude to." After a minute, she said, "Hormonal?"

"Pregnant," Rachel said shortly. "You knew that, right?"

Portia shook her head. She suddenly felt very numb. "No." A block later she said, "How pregnant?"

"I don't know," said Rachel, hauling back the dog, who had spotted another dog across the street. "Who knows? A week? Six months? She's so tiny, how could you tell? When I was one month pregnant I was already enormous and covered in acne. Fred!" she said to the dog, who was whining.

Portia walked, her head down. She was thinking of something, or trying to think of something. Just beyond her grasp, her ken, flittering away.

"Anyway, you mentioned that night?"

"What? Oh, we sort of quarreled that night, after you guys left. I mean, it's fine now, I'm sure."

"Which is why you sound so sure when you say that."

"Don't I?" She laughed, but the laugh was not convincing. "I don't know. I guess it's only noteworthy because we've never really been a contentious couple. We've always gotten along so well. We still get along," she insisted.

"And this is what you want," Rachel said, her gaze fixed to the dog's meaty back.

"What?"

"To get along. I'm just pointing out the language, Portia. I have no idea what goes on in anyone else's relationship. I barely understand my own. But I do know that some people — and they may be delusional or histrionic or shallow or any number of things — but some people want more than getting along. Or, let's say, different. They want different. They want a deeper connection."

They had reached Nassau Street. On the corner was the yellow brick house that contained the Michael Graves architectural firm. There were a few people here, waiting for the light.

"We *have* a deep connection," Portia insisted, trying not to sound as irritated as she felt. "Rachel, we've been together for sixteen years. I mean, Jesus, that's a marriage."

"If it were a marriage," Rachel said with in-for-a-penny abandon, "you would be married."

This was stunning. Portia stood, even as the light changed, motionless and aghast. She and Mark, calm in stasis through the years as their peers coupled and came apart, sadly, angrily, viciously, tearing their children and friendships asunder as they disentangled themselves...no one had ever said this to her. No one had questioned the understatement between them, or so directly, at least. And she, if she did question, had never confided a thing, to Rachel, to her mother, naturally not to Mark. It had been such a long time, their two names on the mailbox, on the checking account, on the mortgage. On the invitations Mark liked to display on their mantel, which she never understood until her first trip to England when she saw that everyone did it there. "Mark and Portia," "Portia and Mark," the invitations read. They had outlasted far too many of the marriages they'd witnessed, expensive wedding confections of silk and rose petals and champagne. Why shouldn't she feel smug? Even Rachel had struggled with David's myopia, his habit of getting up and going to the office as if he were a single man without ties, every morning, every Saturday morning, every Sunday morning, every holiday morning, while "Mark and Portia," "Portia and Mark" made coffee, ate bread and Harrods's apricot preserves, and read *The New York Times* at their kitchen table, in silence.

They were made for each other. They were, she had sometimes thought, resisting and resisting the fading impulse to say how much, in their preoccupations, perfectly aligned. They simply did not have that kind of relationship, that sharing intensity, which was never, in any case, what she had wanted. What she had wanted—what she wanted still, she told herself—and what she had, was peaceful companionship in their home, and respect, and affection. She did love him, she sometimes thought, but mostly she appreciated him, and the ways in which he had suffered, and how kind he was. And when she looked around at the relationships of her peers, it was hard not to feel that she had chosen well.

"Portia," said Rachel, "I'm sorry, it didn't come out the way I intended. Yes, I see that you are in a committed relationship. What I don't see is whether you're happy. Are you happy?"

Portia stared at her. The others, who had edged away from them, sensing the conflict with animal precision, now crossed with relief as the light changed. She and Rachel and the seated dog stayed behind.

"I'd like you to be," Rachel said. "I hope you are, but I don't actually know."

"I just don't think like that," Portia finally said. "It doesn't mean I am, or I'm not. I just don't think that way—"

She stopped. Before she could get to the next word, that door in the shape of a word, which opened to a place where she, like Helen of Oxford, might well burst into lamentations, and not, like Helen of Oxford, silent lamentations, and not because she was pregnant. That word was: *anymore*.

"That's fine." Rachel smiled a brittle smile. She seemed more than willing to leave the subject, and the corner. "Because you're my friend. And I care about you."

"Yes, I know," Portia said miserably. "I don't know how we got here."

Puzzled, Rachel looked around.

"No, I mean, one minute we're talking about Gordon Sternberg and the baseball bat and the next minute it's, 'Is Portia happily . . . unmarried?'"

"Right." Rachel shrugged. "Well, I don't give a fuck about Gordon, for the record. We're going to be a lot saner without him around. He was a very brilliant critic, but as a colleague . . ."

"Yes. Though I'm afraid he's going to haunt poor Mark for a very long time. Mark had to go to Pennsylvania yesterday. He spent most of the afternoon with the police, and they said he had to come back in a couple of weeks and meet with someone else about the case. It's a *case*, now. And with the family absconded, Mark has somehow become in loco parentis, or in loco *child*. Or something. Plus, Marcie is making noises about not letting Cressida come over for her visit after Christmas. She says Cressida has to study for her A levels. Which is bullshit. And Mark hasn't seen her since that trip in July, when Marcie was so awful. Not to mention," said Portia, "the fact that we're about to drive for hours on crowded roads to Hartland, Vermont, a place Mark hates, to a house he detests, to visit a woman he can't stand. Seriously, I just don't want to make it worse. I feel bad for the guy."

"Okay," Rachel said. "And now that you have taken a potentially very serious conversation about you and somehow diverted it into a defense of Mark, who I wasn't attacking in the first place, let's just leave it. But you'll remember what I said, please, because I actually do worry about you." She tipped up her face, catching a moment of bright winter sunlight. She had the beginnings of lines, faint filaments at the corners of her eyes, and silvery hair at the temples. She was without vanity, Portia thought. A happy woman who had measured the years of her adult life neither by coffee spoons nor by application folders, but by the children she was raising and the books she was writing, who didn't care that those same years were beginning to show on her face. She didn't even wear makeup, which was not something Portia herself could say. And Portia was younger by four years.

"Rachel," Portia said.

"Here's the thing," said Rachel, turning to her with renewed intent. "You are thirty-eight years old. That's not too late. But if you're going to make changes, make them soon."

"*Rachel,*" said Portia, horrified.

"It doesn't make any difference to me," said Rachel. "Marry him or don't marry him. Have kids or don't. Just don't let somebody else make these decisions for you. They're too important."

She knew right away that she was going to cry. The light was red again, and already there were two people waiting on the other side and a woman and a young boy coming up behind them on Harrison. Rachel was looking at her, not critically, not angrily. She had, instead, an expression of open curiosity on her face, as if she had finally embarked upon a long-planned experiment and now could not wait to observe the results. Portia turned away, but from the newcomers, mother and child, rather than from Rachel. She would have walked away from Rachel by now if she had really wanted to.

"Come on," Rachel said, taking her arm.

They crossed the street and turned left on Nassau. The dog strained before them, pointlessly, nose down. He stopped to sniff at a crumpled paper bag, but Rachel hauled him away. "Did I ever tell you," said Rachel, "about this couple I met up at the dog park in Rocky Hill? Both total vegans. They had a dog they raised from a puppy, and the dog was vegan, too. The couple had fed it on, I don't know, soy milk and tofu or something.

Or rice. And they were always talking about nature and nurture, and how they went to a holistic pet healer instead of the vet, because they didn't believe in vaccinations for dogs. They were, like, worse than any parent I ever had to deal with at either of my kids' schools, which is saying something, I can tell you. So one day last spring, we were all up at the dog park. I wasn't standing with them, but I saw this. There was a kid sitting on a bench eating out of a Burger King bag, and the kid dropped the bag on the ground. And the dog, the vegan dog, goes tearing over to the bag and just rips it to shreds. He ate that hamburger so fast, it was like he swallowed it whole. And the kid's screaming and the kid's parents are screaming, and this couple are just standing there, stunned. It was the funniest thing I've ever seen."

Despite herself, Portia smiled. "Nature, triumphant."

"Yeah. It was like, Folks, I'm sorry to be the one to have to tell you this, but your baby's a carnivore. Deal with it."

"What big teeth he has."

"All the better to tear great hunks of bloody flesh into little slimy bits of bloody flesh."

"What did they feed their dog after that?" said Portia.

"Oh, I have no idea. They never came back to the dog park. Too embarrassed, I'm sure."

Portia laughed. "And so they should be."

They had arrived at Maple Street. She hugged her friend and wished her a happy holiday. She and Mark would be back from Vermont on New Year's Day, just missing Rachel's family, who decamped to some family resort in the Caribbean on New Year's Eve. Then Portia walked home, slower now without the dog to set the pace. She could see Mark at the end of the street, leaning into the open trunk of the car. He mustn't have stayed long at the office.

"There's coffee," he said when she reached him.

"Thank you."

"I want to go soon. I'd rather be stuck in traffic than sit here worrying about traffic."

"Right," she said, as if this made sense. She went upstairs and took the briefest of showers, then dressed and packed the rest of her things. She had two hundred folders from the office, bundled with rubber bands, zipped into a suitcase, and a biography of Jackson Pollock for her book group, which she hadn't a prayer of getting to. When she made it downstairs, he was leaning against the car, reading today's *Times*.

"Ready, then?"

He helped her with the suitcase. She went inside and poured a travel cup of coffee for each of them. Then they locked up.

As always, when one anticipated traffic, the roads were fine. The day, sunny already, promised only clarity and bright skies as they headed north, swinging around the city, sailing up the Merritt. Mark was an intent driver, which added insult to the injurious restrictions Marcie had set for him the previous summer. He didn't have much to say, and even Portia, who had spent the preceding month arguing herself out of any real worry, began to feel uncertain. She too had been dreading this trip, and her mother at the end of it, and the pregnant teenager she was expected to be warm and generous to, and the care and placation of Mark, but most of all she had been dreading the drive and the buried worry that had been living with her and growing with her for weeks now: that she had no idea what they would say to each other when they finally had to speak, when they were trapped together in this moving car or trapped together in her mother's house, that something had shifted beneath them that he had noted and that she had noted but refused to acknowledge. And if this was true, had she caused it? Had she come back different from that trip and that night? And did he, actually, know about it? And was he ever going to tell her how he'd found out?

She had met Mark his first week in America, standing in the produce section of Hanover's then sole supermarket, looking shell-shocked. Admittedly, the Stop & Shop was poor hunting ground for fresh foods of any description, but it was also the middle of a furious winter, with power outages all that January and Interstate 91 converted to glass. Little had gotten through, and the pickings were slim. She had watched him lift and drop a couple of elderly string beans, letting them fall from his fingers like flaccid worms, and examine a yellow orange in disbelief. When he noticed her looking, he started to laugh and shake his head.

He was twenty-five then, his life defined—as it still was, to some extent—by the daughter his former girlfriend had given birth to, then withheld from him. Mark's romantic and paternal life, a marvel of bad timing, had decreed that egg fertilize sperm just as the two of them were dissolving in acrimony, and Mark's careful suggestion that Marcie consider terminating the pregnancy had the impact of an atom bomb. She would never forgive him. She would never, willingly, share the child, Cressida, and had taken every opportunity since to wage her war. Marcie, then an American postgraduate at Cambridge, had opted out of her degree course and returned home to suburban Atlanta, which was why Mark had gone on the market and taken the best American job he could get. That Hanover, New Hampshire, was some distance from Georgia posed one problem, but far more problematic was the fact that whenever Mark did make the journey south, he was met with any legal or practical obstacle Marcie could throw in his way: Cressida was ill with flu. Cressida had a school trip. Cressida had announced that she didn't want to see him. He wouldn't give up. He appealed to Marcie, to her parents (with whom she was living), to her regal, chilly attorney, and to the three attorneys he went through himself. He applied (on the advice of one) for custody, then withdrew his suit (on the advice of another). He suggested mediation. He tried sending his child support payments to escrow instead of to her. He attempted to behave as if he were not tormented.

After five years at Dartmouth, he told Portia that he needed to move south, and she agreed, though reluctantly. Emory offered Mark a job. Emory's Admissions Office offered Portia an associate's position, and so they began to detach from their lives in New England. They found an apartment near the campus, smaller than their Hanover house but just as expensive. Both gave notice. Portia told her mother. Then, only a month before their move, Marcie suddenly carried Cressida back to England, citing a teaching job. They settled in north London, with Cressida in a Montessori school. It took Mark a good two months even to find them. That was when he gave up.

She and Mark had never moved to Georgia, of course. They never considered following Marcie to England. What was the point? Keeping their daughter away from him had become Marcie's occupation. (The teaching job, nominally her excuse for leaving the country, never materialized; instead, she became a volunteer at Cressida's school.) Mark, for a time, was deeply depressed. He took a year's sabbatical and managed to bang out his Shelley book, but his life coalesced around the summer trip to see his daughter in England and the occasional visits to Atlanta, where his time with Cressida was closely controlled by Marcie and her parents. Over the years, he had managed to get his daughter to Princeton only twice, and only with Marcie ensconced in the city, an hour away and in near constant telephone contact; and though Portia had been with Mark for most of his daughter's life, she had actually met the girl only a handful of times and had never reached anything resembling intimacy with her. Cressida had been a complex child, suspicious (naturally) of her father and anyone around him, slow to show pleasure of any kind. Later, as an adolescent, she had begun to explore the forbidden fruits of her relationship with her father, taking obvious delight in the torment it caused Marcie, but with Portia she was still distant and mildly dismissive. In the last several years, and thanks to e-mail, father and daughter had forged a definite (if virtual) relationship, liberated from Marcie's control, and Mark often spoke of Cressida now, not only to Portia but to his colleagues and friends, some of whom hadn't known he had a daughter in the first place: Cressida's fondness for Wertmuller, her large and growing denim collection, the Coldplay concert at Wembley, her choice of A-level subjects.

He was, in the most essential sense, a bereaved father, a man defined by what had been taken from him, which was why it had always surprised Portia that Mark had not asked her for another child. There was no other child, she had decided. There was only the stolen one, the rightful one whom he had failed in her first, fragile moment, then spent every moment since apologizing to. And that, she certainly understood. Though she had never told him how much, or why.

Near New Haven, they stopped at a Starbucks drive-through for coffee, then turned north. She was beginning to think herself ahead, to do the necessary self-adjustment for what lay at the end of the road. Mark would find the visit difficult enough, but Portia had a special burden: to salve his dislike of Susannah even as she mustered her own affection from its hiding places. And the girl, the pregnant girl. How she would meet this absurdity, this gruesome challenge, she had no idea. They were due to spend six days, returning Sunday. An actor prepares, she thought grimly.

"I need to stop," Mark said quietly. Hartford loomed ahead, rearing up suddenly like the Emerald City. She looked at him.

"Are you okay?"

"I'm not," he confirmed. He took an exit for the city center. She turned in her seat, watching him.

"Do we need to go to a hospital?" she said, afraid. He had the look of someone barely contained: one nudge, one word, away from some terrible release. He guided the car around a one-way system of downtown streets. There was a park, a chain hotel, a pizza restaurant. He turned a corner and pulled over. "Mark," said Portia, "what can I do for you? Are you going to be sick?"

He shook his head.

"Mark?"

He was hunched forward, as far as the steering wheel would allow. She saw fingertips with bitten nails emerge from his thick, graying hair. He was making a sound she could not immediately identify, a fascination in itself. Not pain, but pain, emitted from a location so deep and so impacted that it seemed to emerge in wisps of labored breath. She put her hand on his shoulder, but he shook it away. "Don't," he said simply.

"Are you in pain? Do you need a doctor?"

"No, no," he said, but she felt for her cell phone anyway and opened it. "I said no," he said bitterly, and she stared at him.

"All right," she told him. She was amazed at how calm she sounded. She was amazed at how she knew, suddenly, what was about to happen, what was already happening and couldn't be turned back. And how drab the setting, after all: this dull little street in Hartford, a place, she realized abruptly, she had driven through hundreds of times but never actually seen. And never would again, she told herself. After this.

"I can't go any farther," said Mark. "I just can't."

"Do you want me to drive?" she asked. But she was only humoring him. She knew it had nothing at all to do with who drove.

"No." He still had his hands over his face, as if he could hide from her. "I can't go any farther. I can't go to Vermont. I can't go back to the house. I just can't do this. I'm sorry."

"Why," she said dryly, "are you sorry? If you can't, you can't."

Absurdly, she wanted to laugh. She was having a bizarre memory, of another Christmas trip, this time to Birmingham, where his parents lived. Mark's mother, a round woman with soft white hair and the bluest eyes, who taught at a local teacher-training college. Mark's father, tall like Mark and a bit stooped, in old corduroy pants and an ancient sweater. He was a university professor, an economist who taught in Sheffield. He had another flat in Sheffield and, it seemed, another family there. They all knew it, but nobody bothered to tell Portia, who made some gaffe about Christmas morning. The other family included little children, and Christmas morning was theirs. Here, sitting in the still running car on this ridiculous Hartford Street—within sight, it now occurred to her, of the train station—she was thinking of the blue bowl of satsumas on his parents' dining room table as they all looked at one another, alarmed and aggrieved, and how bright those orange fruits were, and how sharp they smelled. She hated that house in Birmingham.

"Portia," said Mark, "I need to tell you...she's pregnant."

Portia gaped at him. "Cressida?"

"What? Oh, my God, no. Helen. Helen is pregnant."

"I know that," said Portia, oddly proud of herself: an outsider with insider information. Then, in a violent, sickening moment, she understood what he was telling her. There was no whiff of smugness, no pride at all. There was no vestige of protection. He had tolerated their childlessness not only because he was not, in fact, childless himself, but because he had always held open that door—not widely enough for the both of them, but only as far as he could pass through, alone. And the car was...*still*...running.

Now she was the one who was sick. Her folded arms were pressed tightly against her abdomen, holding herself intact, and her head...it felt as if someone had taken it and shaken and shaken to empty out the blood, like a bottle with some sluggish, stubborn condiment still lurking at the bottom. What was left? She didn't know whom she was sitting beside. She didn't even know where she was.

"I can't tell you," he said, "how sorry I am. I didn't plan this. I'm not sure I even wanted it."

"But you want it now." She was amazed to hear another voice. It sounded nothing like her own.

"Yes. I'm sorry."

She began to cry. This was a lousy development. It improved nothing. It set her back. For the longest time, she kept crying. To her amazement, he offered only a hand, vaguely patting her thigh, as comfort. After a while, she took hold of it and flung it away.

"You've done nothing wrong," he told her. "I won't make any trouble for you."

"Trouble?" she screamed at him. "What the fuck are you talking about?"

"You can stay in the house as long as you need to. I mean, we'll need to talk about everything, of course."

She stared at him, blurry through her running eyes. She liked him this way, she found: indistinct, nullified. He was nearly handsome, melting into colors. Now, he wasn't Mark, only this melting thing in the driver's seat, and anyway, he was about to leave.

"I'll go now," he told her with infuriating kindness. "I don't think I should go with you. I'm sure you agree."

She didn't agree to anything. On principle. But she said nothing.

"I just...," he faltered. "I can't miss this, Portia. The first time, I made such a mistake. I can't do it. I'm sorry I..."

What? she thought wildly. "Misled me? Lied to me? Cheated on me?"

Soberly, maddeningly, he nodded.

But I, she wanted to say, *have cheated on you.* Not that it was the same thing. Not that it was, remotely, the same thing. The same thing—that was the thing she had *actually* done and hidden away. If you only knew, she thought cruelly. But she wouldn't squander it now. She wouldn't cheapen it by telling him here, in this *fetid* running car. That was for another time or, more probably, never.

"We'll talk," he said. "But now, I think I should go back. I'll move some things out. We'll both take some time."

"Speak for yourself," Portia said unkindly. "I won't need much time."

He let her have this. He was being noble, apparently.

He unfastened his seat belt and opened the car. Chilly air slipped in.

Mark unfolded his long legs and stood on the pavement. He went to the trunk and opened it, removing a small bag, and slammed the trunk shut. An instant later, he opened her door.

"I know you can't forgive me yet," he said. "One day, I hope you will. But I have to do the right thing. I have to, Portia."

"Like you had to fuck her," she said caustically. "Nothing noble about that."

He shrugged. He seemed to have tired of the conversation. "We'll talk when you get back. We'll be good to each other, I promise. I promise for myself, anyway. What you do is up to you."

He straightened up. He was so high above her. He blocked the light.

"Tell Susannah I'm sorry," he said. And he left her there.

When we approached the gate of Dachau, my grandfather stopped suddenly and broke down. He refused to go any farther, even though he and my father, sister and I had come all the way from Seattle to see the concentration camp. We stood looking at him, not sure of how to react. We understood what he was thinking and feeling, but we couldn't really understand. He had been here before, when he was exactly the age I am now. There were no Princeton applications for him, though he was (and is) a brilliant mathematician, winner of a national award for mathematics (at least, until the Nazis rescinded his prize and gave it to the competition's fourth highest scorer, and top scoring Aryan). There was no dreaming about his future, and what he might accomplish at university and beyond. There was only the terror of watching his family try and try and fail to get out of the country, first with their property intact, then with just their lives.

CHAPTER TEN

THE KNACK FOR ISOLATION

Don't wake Caitlin," Susannah said with some urgency. She was holding the door frame with one hand and pinching shut her heavy bathrobe with the other. She leaned out into the winter night, anxious and fretting, as Portia opened the car door. "Caitlin's asleep upstairs," Susannah said.

Portia was not processing very well. Coming down the long drive to the house, she had seen her mother through the living room window, her head with its long gray ponytail tipped forward as she read. She had seen the moment of awareness, the jerking of her mother's torso, the snapping turn of her neck. Susannah had leapt from the couch at the sound of the car, scurrying into the kitchen and opening the door, frantic not to embrace, it seemed, but to quiet. Now, extracting herself from the car, Portia found herself unable to look at her mother directly but saw instead the house itself, moonlit in the clear, starry night, and the field behind it, and also moonlight on the field, blue and electric bright. Out in the field, prickles of cornstalks and brush came up, spiky through the crust of old snow, and slashes of ice reflected black in that blue light, a landscape from the moon itself, or Jack London. In that same instant, she felt the vastness of the night and her own smallness and inconsequentiality, which was oddly—in the circumstances—comforting. She felt, too, an abrupt, not readily fathomable urge to walk directly into that wild and limitless place, though the wedge of dull light from the kitchen nearly reached the spot where her car had come to rest, and framed her own mother, that ultimate symbol of attachment, implying every comfort there wasn't in the snowy field. Without warning, a nimble cat darted for freedom past her mother's legs, and Portia watched it as it took flight around the side of the house and off in the direction of the field. The cat was not known to her. Her mother always seemed to have a new cat, Portia thought.

"Go in," she heard herself tell Susannah. "You'll get cold. I'm coming."

"Sh," her mother said. "She's sleeping." Then, obligingly, she stepped back into the kitchen and closed the door, waiting on the other side and peering through the window.

Portia stood for a moment, feeling the numbing cold against her face. It was punishing cold, insidious cold, the cold that dragged your body across the line. She had always had a fascination with hypothermia, it occurred to her, returning briefly to Jack London and that famous story about how the man fought and fought the cold before slipping beneath its spell. It wasn't the worst way to die, she thought, looking again at the field. Then, quite deliberately, she went to the trunk and opened it. The suitcase-shaped space where Mark's bag had been seemed miraculously intact, hours and miles later, as if he had left an intangible placeholder in its position when he extracted his things. It wasn't a large space. He hadn't brought much for a ten-day visit. Had he known? she thought, as she had occasionally thought over those hours and miles just past; but now, as then, the thought was accompanied by a blare of sharpest pain. And now, like then, she pushed it roughly away.

The trunk was packed with gifts, food, clothing. There was the suitcase of folders from the office, too many to get through, probably, but enough for a perpetual excuse to absent herself. She reached for the duffel bag of her clothes and the shopping bag of food—loaves of cranberry bread she'd baked the day before, crates of satsumas, a foil-wrapped plum pudding from Bon Appetit. She had no idea what she was doing and only intermittent memories of the road.

"Where is Mark?" Susannah said when she came into the kitchen. She had lit the stove under her kettle and had the cupboard open, revealing her vast tea collection. With surprise, Portia noted that her mother had a box of Constant Comment in her hands.

"In Princeton," she heard herself say. "He has . . . there's this crisis. With a man named Gordon Sternberg."

Susannah frowned. "But when is he coming? *Is* he coming?"

"I'm not sure," Portia said. "It's a very volatile situation. He keeps getting calls in the middle of the night and having to drive down to Philadelphia."

"Philadelphia?"

Again, she was hit by a wave of incongruity. What was she talking about? For an instant, she had to retrace the conversation, frantically rolling up its fragile string. Why on earth was she talking about Gordon Sternberg? Why was she talking about Mark?

Setting down her suitcase and the shopping bag she'd taken in, Portia watched her mother fuss with the tea. She was wondering at herself, at how—in all these hours—she hadn't once thought about what she'd say to Susannah, how she'd answer the obvious question. What had she done instead? How had she passed the grinding miles and minutes, her hands tight on the steering wheel, hunched stiffly forward and staring bleary-eyed at the road? Surely something had been accomplished, some deep thought or great problem untangled once and for all, but nothing came back, only a fuzziness and weariness.

Had she always intended to lie? She had lied to her mother for years, of course, though usually for far less consequential things: the *Ms.* subscription, a birthday gift, she had let lapse a decade earlier; the cardiologist she had promised (and failed) to see after an episode of palpitations. Lying was a well-established method of keeping Susannah away, though only one of several in her arsenal of separation: withholding of certain information, avoidance of particular hot-button issues, the expression of commonly held opinions on certain matters they could both get righteously indignant about (religious fanatics, beauty pageants, breast enlargement)—each of these was a useful means of furthering the campaign. But this particular lie had been unexpected, slipping into language without preamble and lingering afterward, like some malodorous thing. She had not intended to lead with a lie. *Mark is in Princeton.* Not technically an untruth, but not the truth. *Mark has left me. Mark is with someone else. Mark is with a woman who is pregnant with the child he never told me he wanted.* That, she thought grimly, was the inescapable, stare-you-in-the-face, invasive, pervasive, metastatic, and ultimately fatal truth.

"You didn't have to wait up for me, Mom."

"I had no idea when you'd get here."

"Ah," said Portia, though she was unsure of the connection.

"You must be tired. You must have left very late."

Portia considered this. Then, to gather information, she looked at her watch. It was nearly two-thirty in the morning, a fact that took her completely by surprise. The drive from Princeton, after all, lasted about six and a half hours, and she and Mark had left at eleven that morning. For a moment, she tried to assemble the past hours, to shuffle them into order, but they seemed to resist her. There was the walk with Rachel, the place she had stopped in Brattleboro, mainly to use the bathroom, but there was food involved, too, not that she'd eaten it. A chain restaurant with a southwestern theme. (What was happening to Vermont? she had thought, reading the menu of "sizzlin'" things, choosing at random.) There had been some time there, sitting over her "sizzlin'" plate of something, feeling ill. And a margarita, it seemed to her, though that wasn't like her at all, to drink when she was driving. But what about today was remotely like her? "Like her" was her job, and Mark, and her house on her street, and going for a walk with Rachel and the dog. "Like her" was the semiannual drive across Connecticut and up 91, past Brattleboro and Putney, and the final stretch to Hartland and her mother's house. She concentrated now on that stretch of road: white moonlight on the highway with the river to her right, dull under a sheen of ice. She did remember driving that road, and the Vermont Welcome Center, and the sick, *Blow Upon the Bruise* way she had felt passing the sign for Keene, New Hampshire, and the big A-frame house near Rockingham that for years had had an enormous stuffed animal in the window but now did not. She remembered, farther back, passing the exits for Northfield and Deerfield and Springfield in Massachusetts, but strangely couldn't say in which order they'd come. And, farther back again, to that horrible, elastic time on the street in Hartford, after Mark left, which was when her true grip on the day slipped through her fingers and was irrevocably lost. How long she had spent there, staring at the same Massachusetts plate on the same muddy green Ford Taurus on that miserable street, she had no idea at all.

It was like one of the made-for-TV movies of her youth, she thought grimly, sipping the tea Susannah had handed her. Sybil of the snows, driving their car—was it still "their" car? or had it instantly become *her* car when he left by the driver's-side door?—along that straight and narrow road, with one of her capable alternate personalities at the wheel: the girl in the steel bubble, compromised by her lack of immunity, cut off from the world. *Portia N., Portrait of a No Longer Teenage Alcoholic,* downing a mango margarita with her "sizzlin'" something or other, and then, shamefully, getting behind the wheel of the car. Who knew what damage she might have done?

"I stopped," she told Susannah. "For dinner. In Brattleboro."

Her mother frowned. "But I was going to give you dinner."

"Oh, I know, Mom. And it would have been much better than what I got. But you know how you can get so hungry, suddenly, that it actually becomes distracting? I was famished. I had to eat."

"Okay," said her mother.

"The food was awful," she assured her.

"Would you like something now?"

Portia shook her head. She hadn't, in fact, eaten much of her dinner and wasn't hungry now. To be honest, food had become inherently unappealing. Hunger would be something else to fake while she was here. Another burden. Another outright lie.

How long can I keep this up? Portia thought. The ten days of her visit? To the end of the academic year? A calendar year? Could she keep it up forever, burdening mythical Mark, her partner, with grievous workloads and familial crises?

Oh, Mom, Mark had to fill in for the dean of faculty and address the Class of '75.

Cressida's graduating from high school, and he wanted to be there.

Can you believe it? He came down with strep! He's in bed watching every episode of Six Feet Under *for the third time.*

She could draw Mark forward through an eventful, burgeoning career, pepper his health history with ailments, mine his parallel personal life for conjured experiences. Nothing too dramatic, of course. Nothing too *real*, like an affair, a pregnancy, a child. Twice a year she could come north to visit, laden with gifts and apologies from him. Susannah never came to Princeton, or hadn't for five years, at least. And now, with this pregnant teenager and—Portia could hardly bear to think of this—the baby coming, her mother would be thoroughly distracted. Sipping her tea, she tuned in sporadically to Susannah's monologue, which had pushed off from Portia's own comment about hunger into wild tales of Caitlin and the food she consumed. Bags of oranges! Half a coconut cake! The girl was struggling with her fast-food addiction, despite Susannah's own very thorough enumeration of the ecological, economical, and, yes, culinary sins of the entire industry. Susannah had found a McDonald's wrapper in the car, the incriminating crunch of environmentally indefensible Styrofoam underfoot.

How long could I keep it going? Portia wondered idly. Six months, certainly. Possibly a year. If her mother remained this distracted, it could go further. It would be like a game, she decided. A bet with herself, the reward linked to the number of years, months, days, she managed to keep her mother in the dark. Bonus points if she found herself making excuses for Mark's absence at Susannah's deathbed. *I'm so sorry, Mom. A freshman English major cut her wrists over the weekend. The whole campus is in lockdown....*

Here she stopped, stunned by her own callousness, her failure as a daughter, partner. Everything, really. She turned to her mother, really trying to focus now, full of contrition. She saw, as always, an echo of her own form in the shoulders and neck, the same hair, the same set jaw. Her mother's legs had held up—she supposed that boded well for herself—but the skin of her hands and face, skin that had rejected sunblock as some form of artifice, no better than plastic surgery or any other means of subverting the actual appearance of age, was papery and speckled with brown. Portia had used sunblock for years, ever since the first magazine articles about what it could do. Was this what she had prevented? She noted Susannah's steel gray ponytail down her back, white wisps of hair escaping around her face, and thought with some shame of the color she had begun to use, only in the last year or so, only when the gray at her temples began to colonize the rest of her head. ("This whole generation!" Susannah complained. "They've never seen a real vegetable. They don't know what a carrot is supposed to taste like! It's all processed meat and artificial flavors from some lab in New Jersey!") There were lines — new lines? old lines? — around her mother's mouth and eyes. Susannah had been for so long a local sage, matriarch to younger women, pillar of female wisdom, that her passage to real age was at once unremarkable and a jolt. But the solid, steel-haired woman across the table, waving her weathered hands over an earthenware mug of herbal tea, had plainly departed middle age. She was old, thought Portia. Pissed and old. And, oddly, looking only forward.

Caitlin was due in May and thinking of staying on, over the summer, to recover and see her baby settled. Also, said Susannah, to lose her pregnancy weight, as she intended to keep the fact of her circumstances private.

Portia, finding this conversational thread, at least, diverting, asked how this would be possible. "Don't they know why she's here?"

"They know she's here, but not why. They think it's a high school exchange. Her father phones her every Sunday to ask if she went to church."

Portia smiled.

"She did go, actually. For the first month. Not that it's easy to find the *right* kind of church. She ended up at that awful place in West Lebanon, across from the Four Aces diner. You know?"

"It used to have a sign out front that said, 'Are You on the Right Road?'" said Portia.

"It still does. They're appalling people. Terrorists, really. Of course, I took her. She's her own person, and it's not for me to decide. I just waited for her across the road in the diner. But after the first few times, she came out and said she didn't want to go back. Somebody said something to her, about her increasingly obvious 'sin,' I mean. I offered to help her find another denomination, but she hasn't mentioned it again."

Portia nodded. She still thought of the sleeping girl upstairs — in the room she typically occupied on her visits, no doubt — with some sense of unreality: a teenage incubator for her mother's absurd idea of late motherhood, a girl for whom this interlude must come wedged between obscure past and obscure future. That Susannah already spoke of the fetus as a child — known to her, dependent upon her, and even loved by her — felt so strange, so off-kilter, as if she had dressed a stone in baby clothes and held it to the breast.

Looking across the table now, she tested this image and so found herself ruminating, in turn, on the icy marble *Pietà* she had seen with Mark at St. Peter's in Rome. Their first summer together. And then, with a certain grotesque flourish, of a poster on the wall of her dermatologist's office in Princeton, which showed a buxom babe in the tiniest of bikinis on a tropical beach, luscious as a peach from the neck down, but from the neck up a withered crone. It was meant to scare you into using sunblock, and most effective.

Susannah's hopes for the child, which she was now elucidating across the table, were, naturally, beyond reproach: love and care, education and glorious self-actualization, music and art and science, organic food (lovingly prepared), and so on, all toward a far horizon of the greater good — for surely, the way her mother envisioned things, this child was born to right the wrongs of the universe. (Why, Portia thought wearily, is every unborn child the lost Einstein or Picasso? The engineer who would have reversed global warming or figured out how to run airplanes on ground-up industrial waste? Why were these aborted or miscarried fetuses never the next Dahmer or Bundy? The anonymous forty-eighth addict to overdose in 2056? The never identified participant in the gang rape? The sociopath executive who takes down an entire company and puts thousands out of work?) Listening, Portia became aware of it gradually, through the fog of her now great fatigue, and sadness, and distress at being here, and fear for the future: the full-on shocking realization that both her long-standing partner and her mother were about to become parents. Again. But not her. Not her. Soon, they would both be taking small hands into their own larger hands and walking into the future, while she . . . well, did not. While she . . . what? Began a new application season? Considered moving to a smaller house? Contemplated renewing her gym membership?

"Portia," her mother said.

She looked up. "Yuh?"

"I said, will you be able to take her?"

"Take . . . ?" said Portia.

"Caitlin," said her mother. "I need to go to Burlington on Thursday. With Frieda."

Frieda was her housemate — her only housemate since the weaver had decamped years earlier — and Burlington meant something medical.

"Is she okay?"

"Probably. They're always finding something to biopsy. If she does get cancer again, it'll be from all the radiation they've exposed her to all these years, from all the mammograms."

"Mom..." Portia sighed. "If it weren't for a mammogram, she'd already be dead."

"They don't trust us to manage our own health, with our own fingers. They don't believe we can be responsible for our own bodies. If we find it ourselves, they tell us we're hysterical. It has to come out of a machine to be real."

"*They,*" Portia commented, "are as likely to be female as male, these days."

"But the system is male."

She gave up. She was too tired and it was too pointless.

"So you can take her?"

Portia frowned. "I thought you were taking her."

"No. Not Frieda. *Caitlin.*"

"Oh. Okay. Where does she need to go?"

"As I said. To the midwife. In Hanover."

"Oh," said Portia. "Well, if you need me to. Of course. I'm sorry, Mom," she said, noting Susannah's exasperation, "I'm so tired. I think I need to go to bed."

Susannah got up. She put her mug in the sink, and Portia's, then eyed the bags by the back door

"This is food," said Portia, pointing.

"Oh, thank you."

She lifted the suitcase of files, obviously straining with the weight of it.

"That one," said Susannah, "looks suspiciously like work."

"I had to," Portia said apologetically. "We're all working over the holiday."

Her mother frowned. "What a shame. I really hoped you could relax while you were here."

She did sound aggrieved, Portia thought, but not entirely convincing.

Portia hoisted the suitcase, then the duffel of clothes, which Susannah insisted on taking from her. They went, one behind the other, into the hallway and up to the second floor, wood creaking beneath every tread on the stairs. At the closed door of the room in which she normally stayed, Susannah turned back and put her finger to her lips—mother and fetus were sleeping within—and Portia was led to the last room down the corridor. This had once been home to the weaver, and two of her works remained, pinned to the walls in dusty accusation. Now the room belonged to Frieda, who used it to write her songs and store her instruments, notebooks, and varied materials connected to her infrequent appearances as a singer-songwriter. Frieda, who had once belonged to a feminist drumming circle (the Different Drummers, they had fondly named themselves), kept her hourglass-shaped drums in one corner. These were African talking drums she had made herself in a weeklong workshop with a drum master in Boston. She had a computerized keyboard for songwriting and a trio of guitars, upright in their stands. There was a distinctly unwelcoming daybed in the corner, heaped with kilim pillows and a rough-looking African tribal cloth. Portia wondered if it had clean sheets. Or sheets at all.

"Thanks, Mom," she said, setting down her bag. "You must be tired, too."

"I have to be up early," said Susannah. "Caitlin has one more day of school before the vacation. Should I let you sleep?"

Sleep, thought Portia, nodding, as if this were an altogether new concept. For the first time, it occurred to her that she might not be able to sleep despite her exhaustion, despite her longing for the oblivion. Sleep, for the first night of her new, unpartnered life, the first night of her new reality.

Susannah stepped up close to her and, with sufficient warning, leaned forward to embrace. Portia embraced, in return, in her usual way: body moving forward, spirit pulling back. Then she was left alone.

The room had a vaguely unused air, with its yellowing music magazines stacked on a low table, and the stone cold electric typewriter clad in a film of dust. She wondered if Frieda, whose songs (she had always felt) were not terribly original or particularly melodic, had actually abandoned this career, and if that was true, why? Because her cancer had come back? Because she had begun to feel ridiculous, singing to clueless schoolchildren about the Bread and Roses campaign or serenading the like-minded with musical moralities they already shared? Perhaps she had simply moved on, from one thing to the next, one interest, one moment in her life. People did that, Portia thought wearily. They changed their minds, their lives. They changed the cast of characters or the scenery.

This wasn't the way Portia tended to think about her own life, she realized—as a progression or even a course correction. She had always considered herself fortunate, not only that she had found Mark, a compatible person who had made a home with her, but that she had found, by strange luck, a profession in which she was both competent and rewarded as such. How many people with just her qualifications and just her skills were doing time in some cubicle somewhere, moving numbers around, dying inside? Her life was a port in the storm, a craft in unpredictable waters. Her life, it occurred to her, was a careful refuge from life.

She sat on the hard daybed and nudged aside the bag of applications with her foot. There was an air mattress, she now saw, on the floor beneath the window, prepped with sheets and a quilt—an accommodation that would have ensured a sore back for herself or Mark, whoever drew it, not to mention the impossibility of sexual contact while in her mother's house. Not that they had ever had sexual contact in her mother's house. And now, she thought, trying to grasp the humor of this, they never would have sexual contact in her mother's house—by no means a terrible thing. Even this briefest levity was painful. She felt weariness in every muscle, weariness even in her skin, her hair, but she delayed lying down, afraid to find out that sleep intended to elude her. For the shortest moment she allowed herself to wonder about Mark: where he was, what, if anything, he was saying or doing. And Helen, whose face, oddly, but also mercifully, Portia could not seem to summon from memory. Was she comforting him for the loss of a sixteen-year relationship? Was she congratulating him on having finally taken action? Had they both, already, closed that very inconvenient door behind them? Thinking of Helen gave her an instant of sharpest misery and hollowed her out with loneliness. She had not felt this kind of loneliness for many, many years, an odd state of affairs, she couldn't help but think, for a person who had relatively few people of any importance in her life.

She thought suddenly about Susannah's travels, her life like a widening nautilus of contact, all of them, it seemed, perpetually in her wake or everywhere around her. She still had bosom friends from her childhood in Great Neck, most of them still living in that green and pleasant suburb. She had friends from college and even graduate school, though she had not given much of her attention to graduate school. She kept up with her co-habitants from the commune in Northern California, her neighbors from Harlem, the women she'd lived and cooked and worked with in

Baltimore, and of course the many, many neighbors and collaborators of the Northampton years. They were all in Susannah's life, all the time, it seemed, writing letters, visiting, talking ceaselessly to her, listening to her, making her evenings hum with the ringing phone. Everyone stayed with her. No one let go. Not the protégées or rivals. Not the sorority sisters from Berkeley, one of whom had later spent a year living in the womyn's collective in Baltimore. Not the long-ago boyfriend (and dope dealer), now long married and back on his fertile crescent of California soil, or even his wife, the woman he had in fact left Susannah to marry, who had also, somehow or other, become her mother's confidante.

It was a gift, thought Portia, like an ear for music or suppleness or skill with numbers, and she had not inherited it. Her gift lay elsewhere, as in the knack for isolation, the ability to make herself perfectly alone in the world—away from anyone she had harmed, and anyone else who might have cared enough to help her, and everyone who hadn't known, which was everyone.

I spent much of last year in an intensive treatment program for an eating disorder. But I don't have an eating disorder. I have never allowed others to impose their ideas of who I am on me, and I never will.

CHAPTER ELEVEN

THIS CONCERNS YOU

Caitlin, as it turned out, was a quiet girl with short brown hair and a look of perpetual diffidence. Four months along, she had reached that point in her pregnancy where a general thickness prevailed: thickness from ankle to wrist and through the middle, which had not yet morphed into the classic profile. *Pregnant?* in other words. *Or merely fat?*

Portia, who had finally fallen asleep in the still middle of the previous night, had missed the girl's departure for school in the morning, but she was alone in the house at dusk, reading folders at the kitchen table, when a school bus creaked to a halt outside and a girl in a dark blue parka descended the steps. Portia watched the girl pull tight her coat, crossing her arms over her chest. On her shoulder she carried a heavy book bag, which thumped at her hip as she came up the drive, and in one hand she held a thick roll of oversize artwork, fastened with an elastic band. When she reached the kitchen door, she stopped and stamped her feet to dislodge the snow. Portia, reflexively, shut her folder.

"You must be Caitlin," she said to the startled girl when the door was opened.

The evident Caitlin did not respond but looked perplexed.

"I'm Portia. Susannah's daughter?"

"Oh." She looked thoroughly relieved. "I forgot you were coming today."

"Yesterday, actually. I got here last night."

"I must have been sleeping," she said, noting the obvious. She took off her coat and hung it up on one of the hooks by the back door. She seemed disinclined to talk but rummaged in her backpack.

"You're on Christmas break?" Portia asked.

The girl nodded without looking up. She was wearing a zipped red sweatshirt and baggy jeans. Normal jeans, just big.

"You must be glad to get out."

Caitlin turned and looked at her. She seemed affronted. "I like school."

"Oh," said Portia. "Well, that's good."

"This school is better than my school at home. There's a decent art class. And the English teachers read the occasional book, you know?"

"They don't read books in Colorado?"

"Wyoming," Caitlin corrected her.

"Sorry."

"I guess some of them do. I had one last year, though. I swear, she didn't even read the book she was teaching us. I went on the class Web site once, to get a homework assignment. And there was this place where she wrote: 'Do not spend to much time on your rough draft.' She spelled 'too' t-o. And she was, like, the English teacher!"

Portia, who had also encountered the occasional illiterate English teacher, nodded.

"Is that normal tea?"

She frowned. "It's Constant Comment."

"Is that normal? Or herbal?"

"Oh." Portia smiled. "It's normal. I like normal tea."

"Good. I can't stand that other stuff. Can I have some?"

Portia got up and took a mug from the cupboard next to the stove.

"Where's Susannah?"

"In Hanover," said Portia. "She had a meeting. Upper Valley Women's Health."

"She has a lot of meetings," said Caitlin.

"She's a busy girl."

They experienced, over their tea, a brief moment of silent accord.

"She talks about you a lot," said Caitlin.

"Oh?" said Portia. She was torn between wanting and not wanting to hear what her mother said.

"She thinks you hate her."

Portia, looking up abruptly, was so surprised by the indelicacy of the comment that she failed to note—for a brief moment—how much it hurt her.

"That's silly," she managed to say, as if she needed to say anything at all.

"Probably normal, though. My mom thinks I hate her. She can't imagine why else I'd want to leave home in the middle of my senior year and go live with a stranger. They don't think there's anywhere better to live than Cheyenne. I kind of put it in those terms, though—that I needed some time away from them. I'd rather she think I hate her than know the real reason. I don't like it, though."

She dumped several spoons of Susannah's raw sugar into her mug and stirred. She had a broad face, with high cheekbones, hair tucked behind her ears. "Are you, like, the black sheep or something?"

Despite herself, Portia laughed. "I don't see how I could be. I mean, I'm gainfully employed. I'm a card-carrying member of NOW, and I tithe to EMILY's List. I don't harm animals or children. If I'm the family black sheep, everyone else must be a saint."

"I am," Caitlin said, deftly returning the conversation to herself, as any teenager would. She sounded more than a little smug. "I'm totally the black sheep. Though actually, my family have no idea how black I am."

"You didn't feel you could tell them what you were dealing with?" said Portia.

Caitlin gave her a look of thorough disbelief. This, Portia supposed, meant something like: *No.* Or possibly: *Duh.*

"Any special plans for your vacation?" she asked.

"I'm going to sleep. I'm tired all the time. And make *zimsterne*. We always make that at home. Cinnamon stars," she said, noting Portia's cluelessness. "My family are from Germany, originally. Well, my mother's side. My father's side goes back to Missouri, then they have no idea. We're LDS, you know."

Portia, who hadn't known, had a sudden deepening of respect for Caitlin. For a Mormon girl to leave home and lie to her family in order to first bear and then give away an illegitimate child, that took spine.

"How do you make . . . ?"

"*Zimsterne?*" Caitlin laughed. She told her, enumerating the ingredients and describing the ritual rolling out of the dough with palpable nostalgia. It was after dark now, and as Portia had been some hours at the kitchen table, no other lights were on in the house. It felt a bit primitive, a bit over the river and through the woods. She found herself toying with the notion of being alone out here, out of sight of other houses, out of earshot from the road. How long would she last, left to her own negligibly self-reliant devices? Susannah had a habit of chopping her own wood, or at least helping out when she had people (neighbors, always neighbors) over to chop it. She also planted her own vegetables and made her own bread. Frieda was in charge of repairs around the house, and she'd even rigged solar panels for the south-facing roof. The weaver ... Portia didn't know what the weaver had contributed, but then again, she'd been a weaver. Skills didn't come more elemental than that. Against such paragons of prairie womanhood, she felt a little pathetic. Portia could barely wield a plunger and was sufficiently wary of all things electrical that she called her handyman for the most minor incidents. She employed a moonlighting university janitor to clean her gutters and bought her occasionally organic food at the supermarket, like everybody else. At least she recycled the bags.

She wondered, as she listened to the girl, when Susannah was coming back and where Frieda had got to (Frieda had been sighted only briefly that morning). Susannah had not said a thing about dinner. Was Portia meant to cook? Were they going out? Restaurants were not exactly thick on the ground in Hartland, Vermont. Should she be investigating the food situation?

"Are you hungry?" she asked the girl.

"Always," Caitlin said. "I've been hungry since the test came back positive."

"No nausea, then?"

"Never. I know." She shrugged. "Supposedly I'm really lucky. But if I get out of this without four extra chins, it'll be a miracle."

Portia smiled. "Did my mom say anything to you about dinner tonight? Do you know when she's coming home?"

The girl nodded. "There's a stew. It's in the fridge. I'm supposed to put it in at six."

They both turned to look at the kitchen clock over the stove. It was nearly six.

"I'll do it," said Portia. "If you want to go rest."

"Oh yeah. I feel like I'm going to fall down. It's weird. You're fine. And then suddenly you just want to drop and sleep wherever you are. Do you have kids?"

Portia looked at her. She thought: I am the only child of the woman who says she intends to adopt your baby. Don't you know the answer to that?

Caitlin, to her credit, didn't take long to decide she'd made some sort of misstep. "Is it a personal question?" she said with real distress. "I'm sorry. I don't know if you know anyone who's LDS. Do you?"

Portia, now additionally perplexed by the non sequitur, shook her head.

"It's just, everybody has kids. Lots of kids. And they start young. So you get to assume. I apologize. It's totally different here. I never met anyone like your mom in my life."

Portia nodded and even managed to smile. "She's a force of nature."

"I probably should be looking you over or something. I mean, you're her only kid, right?"

"Far as I know," Portia said with discernible sarcasm.

"You look like you turned out okay. You're not, like, a drug addict or an ex-con, right?"

"Not yet," said Portia. "There's always time."

"And don't you work at a college?"

"I do," she said. "Is that a measure of success?"

"Beats working at Wal-Mart."

Portia heard her own laugh before she knew she was going to laugh. "That's absolutely true. Not that I've ever had to find out. I'm sure it's true."

Caitlin rolled her eyes. "Oh, it's true, you can trust me. Summer job, two years ago. So...you, like...she was a good mother, right?"

Portia made herself wait. She made herself think how important this question was, and how complex. It would not be right, for example, to tell this confused and distressed young person that it was insane to think of a sixty-eight-year-old woman—even an apparently healthy one—as an appropriate caregiver for her unborn child, or that Susannah had been making the outrageous assumption that Caitlin did not know her own mind, had not thought through her own dilemma and reached her own conclusion. But what could she get away with here? Basic big-sisterly support? A reminder that there was still plenty of time to think this through? A caution that the problem at hand concerned a few others besides herself and required, just possibly, a less spontaneous plan? But none of these came to her in time. Instead, Portia found herself making reassuring noises. Yes, Susannah had been a wonderful mother. Yes, she had had everything she needed, much of what she wanted. No, she had never been beaten or insulted. No, she had never wanted for food or shelter or been left alone with dangerous people. There had been books and ideas in the home. There had been modern dance and soccer practice and guitar lessons. There had been regular checkups and even braces when they were required. And Portia had indeed, as Caitlin had pointed out, turned out okay.

"I am sort of tired," Caitlin said. "You mind if I go upstairs?"

Portia didn't mind. She was, she discovered, a tiny bit buoyant as a result of this, their first conversation. And in fact, only now that it was over did she understand that she'd been dreading this for weeks, or ever since Susannah had announced her grand plans for the baby. Setting her mother's stew on the rack in the warming oven, listening to the girl clomp up the stairs to her bedroom, Portia found that she'd been oddly reassured by Caitlin, and in particular by her evident refusal to be cowed by what was happening to her, though why it should matter to Portia at all wasn't entirely clear. Because the baby, it now appeared, had half a chance of coming out articulate, intelligent? Because Caitlin didn't look like her idea of a knocked-up teenager, but was more like an earnest, not overly competitive Princeton applicant from a low-performing school?

She rummaged in the fridge and turned up greens of some description. These she washed and chopped while the olive oil heated. At her mother's house, she ate well by default and always had, though the purity of Susannah's larder had, when she was much younger, given her a rabid fascination with junk food—convenience store pastries, Pepperidge Farm cookies, the most secret and shameful affinity for Burger King Whoppers—so wrong, in so many ways. The discovery of SpaghettiOs (at a friend's house at the age of thirteen) had been so transformative that Portia soon developed a full-blown addiction, sneaking out to Cumberland Farms with a can opener and a spoon, downing the entire can in the bushes, and disinfecting her mouth with slugs of Listerine before returning home. During her Dartmouth years, she had been ill equipped to resist the ready availability of so many heretofore forbidden foods (the soft ice cream machine in Thayer Hall alone had dominated her diet most of freshman year), but by now Portia had more or less migrated back to the food of her childhood. It had been years since she'd tasted the high-fructose corn syrup rush of canned pasta or the oddly metallic hit of soft vanilla ice cream. Though hardly the purist her mother remained, she did her best to evade anything with a bar code. And at least she knew what to do with greens.

How this would change now, with Mark gone, was one of the ways she was beginning to test the reality of the breakup: one tiny piece at a time, rather than letting the enormity of it overwhelm her. The bed linens. The joint checking account. The friends. The annual invitation to the faculty award dinner. (This was an endowed event, prescribed in such a way that some extraordinary amount of money had to be spent each year on the food and wine—and often on use-it-up items like caviar, truffles, and excellent vintages. The dinner invitations were extended only to heads of department and their partners. It was a fabled event at the university and, according to Rachel, who had attended once when a colleague of David's was honored, completely spectacular. This year, with Mark ensconced as interim head and finally destined for an invite, they had both been looking forward to the dinner. Well, she had. And, Portia thought bitterly, chopping the greens with displaced vigor, he had, too. And what a petty thing to be fixating on, anyway, with her life in mid-upheaval.)

It was like, she thought, that fable about the blind men describing the elephant, one with his hand on the elephant's leg, another at the elephant's ear, a third at the tusk. The enormity of the elephant escaped them all in the immediate details: rough edged, smooth, and hard, flapping in the breeze. And here I am, Portia thought, worrying about dinner invitations and phone bills (because she would not, would *not*, pay for his calls to Oxford that summer, that spring, the previous winter, however long it had been going on), and the rosemary plant in their kitchen that would now obviously die, because he was the one who could keep it alive (unless it simply disappeared with him, to bloom and perfume his new kitchen and life), and their series at McCarter Theatre, the same pair of seats, row J, on the aisle, for the past four years, right next to that older couple, the great translator of Rimbaud and Hugo, and his wife, who found them so charming and young. Here I am, thought Portia, not quite divorced because I was never quite married, not a parent because I never quite had children, not even an aunt or a cousin or a sibling, not tied, not rooted, not amused, and certainly not reassured, and also far from home, because this—she glanced around at the kitchen, its severe table and stiff wooden chairs, shelves of spices in glass jars or plastic bags, stacks of remaindered Bennington Pottery plates and bowls—is certainly not my home. And yet here I am: chopping greens in Vermont while Rome burns. Or Princeton burns. Or something.

A car cruised up the drive, crunching snow as it turned before the house, sending its headlights through the window and around the room in a sweep. Susannah, thought Portia, newly irritated. At last. She opened the oven door and pulled out the rack with an oven-mitted hand, giving the stew a self-righteous stir. But when she straightened up, she saw that it wasn't her mother's Subaru at all. It was Frieda's van, a relic that refused to die, and Frieda herself reaching for the kitchen door.

"Oh, hi," said Portia. "I thought you were Mom."

"She isn't home?" said Frieda. "Meeting must be running late."

"She hasn't called."

"No."

Frieda set an armload of mail on the kitchen table, catalogs spilling over magazines: Ladyslipper, Gaia, *Alternative Medicine, Newsweek.*

"Wow," said Portia. "You guys must be on every list."

"This is all your mom," said Frieda. "I've been getting mine at a P.O. box downtown."

"Oh?"

"But you're right. There's way too much. I mean, it gets recycled, but I wish she'd cut down. Call some of these people. Tell them to stop sending. It's so excessive."

Frieda went out to the van and retrieved her guitar case and a portable amp. These she took past Portia and up the stairs, where they landed directly overhead in the room where Portia had slept. When she came back downstairs, she had changed from her gray turtleneck sweater to another sweater, light blue but otherwise identical.

"Sorry I woke you up this morning," she said, taking a seat at the table.

"Oh, that's okay," said Portia, though it had been a particularly unpleasant way to wake up, after waiting so long for sleep.

"I have to be honest, I'd completely forgotten that you were going to be in there."

Portia, who'd suspected as much at the time, said nothing.

"You always stay in the guest room. I just wasn't thinking."

Her posture, Portia saw, was peculiarly tense: fingers interwoven, arms straight. She sat so stiffly that her back did not meet the back of the chair. She was a wiry woman, thin and hard, with a lined face and darting blue eyes. Her hair, after cancer—or, more accurately, chemotherapy—had grown in steel gray, and she wore it very short, as if reluctant to become too attached to it again. She looked...not unwell, Portia thought, but not at ease. And though it was hard to tell beneath the sweater, Portia wondered if she might not be a bit too thin. More than anything, she looked like a woman with something on her mind.

"We're having...actually, I'm not sure what it is. For dinner. Something with lentils? Actually it smells pretty good. And kale. I think it's kale."

"No, I'm not staying," Frieda said shortly. "I've got plans."

"Oh." Portia frowned. "I'm sorry."

She seemed to be waiting, Portia thought.

"Something fun?"

"I'm meeting friends in Strafford. At Stone Soup."

"Oh, I love that restaurant."

Frieda's fingers, Portia noted, were drumming the tabletop. They tapped lightly, quietly, but in a rhythm.

It took a moment, but eventually she understood that she was supposed to sit down. This was important, apparently. She took the seat opposite. "How's it going?" she said.

"I've been waiting for you to come. I need to talk to you about Susannah."

Portia thought right away about Burlington, the appointment. Was it Susannah? Was Susannah sick?

"Is she okay? What is it?"

"Oh, healthwise, fine. I'm sorry if I worried you. She never gets sick at all, it's very demoralizing to the rest of us," Frieda said, making a small attempt at humor. "And her cholesterol is something disgusting, like one sixty. Without medication. But I'm worried about her because I think this thing with the girl—you know, the baby—it's just crazy. I mean, don't you think it's crazy?"

Portia, who wanted to be quite sure what they were talking about before answering such a dangerous question, said: "Which part of it, exactly?"

"Which part?" Frieda said with notable irritation. "Jesus, all of it. I mean, okay, I think it's fine that we're putting her up. Her family obviously couldn't deal with this. Did she tell you they're Mormons?"

Portia nodded.

"So I can absolutely understand that she needed to find somewhere to go. I'm totally supportive of that. And she's a nice girl. She's dealing with something really hard. You know, I actually like her. But I was barely on board with her coming here when your mother told me she might actually end up raising the baby. I mean, Jesus Christ, Portia, *she was thinking about raising the baby.*"

"I know," said Portia, motioning with her hand that the girl in question was upstairs and quite possibly within earshot. "But...she thinks Caitlin will change her mind when she sees the baby. She thinks Caitlin will end up keeping it."

"Well, that may be. God knows it wouldn't be the first time a mother has fallen in love with her child. But it's a lot to stake on a 'maybe,' and this isn't just about her. This is my life, too. And she didn't *ask* me, Portia. She *let me know.* She *kept me in the loop.*"

"Okay." She nodded.

"And she's older than I am! Portia, what the fuck is she thinking?"

This last was said softly, but with a hiss of pure vitriol. Portia was momentarily taken aback.

"I guess what you're telling me is that you don't want to do this."

Frieda sat back in her chair. She gave Portia a look of profound disgust. "I'm not doing it. And this is *my house,*" she said, visibly enraged.

"Well, Frieda, you've been here together for...what is it?"

"*My house.* I found it. I bought it. Carla and I were here since 1979, for fuck's sake. When Susannah came, we did some financial maneuvering so we each owned a third. And then Carla left, so we did another transaction, and we changed the papers again. But she has no right to do this, even if it weren't completely insane. And I've raised my kids, Portia. I have no intention of starting over again."

"Have you told her?" Portia said, struggling to stay calm.

"*Have I told her?* Every day. Every fucking day. I'm not doing it. I'm not staying for this."

"Wait," Portia said, readjusting, "you mean...are you telling me you're going to kick her out?"

"I can't," she said unhappily. "I've looked into it, believe me. Legally, it would take years for one of us to oust the other. And a fortune—which, unlike your mother," she said nastily, "I do not have. Plus I have no desire to spend however many years I have left in litigation. I'm sixty-five. There are other things I need to do. I *want* to do."

"Of course," said Portia. "You have to do what's best for you. But..."

"*What?*" Frieda said combatively.

"Well, what *are* you going to do?"

"I'm moving to Boston. Carla's been living in Somerville for the past couple of years. There's an apartment in the house. Someone's in it, but she can get them out with three months' notice. Most of my drumming circle's in Boston now." She pushed up the sleeves of her blue sweater and laced her fingers together again. Then she sat for a long moment, clearly wrestling with how indelicate she ought to be. Portia, half-curious, half-afraid, waited for her to make up her mind.

"You know," said Frieda at last, "I think...well, I've felt this for a long time, that Susannah's just at loose ends."

Portia, who had thought the same thing for most of her life, merely nodded.

"It's a quiet place, Vermont. I mean, we've got things more or less in hand here, there aren't so many battles left to fight, do you understand? It's not like when we were all in Baltimore or Susannah was in Harlem, and women couldn't get abortions or health care or child care. Even in Northampton, she was always running around, setting things up or keeping people on their toes. That clinic in Holyoke, we never would have got that moving if it wasn't for her. And when Springfield tried to get rid of that lesbian teacher, do you remember that? That was Susannah in her element."

"It was my history teacher's girlfriend," Portia said, smiling. "Of course I remember."

"I never really thought she'd be happy here," Frieda said, studying her hands. "But here we are, all these years later, and I have to be honest, it does surprise me. Not that I don't love her, of course, but for her, I'm surprised. She's a warrior, okay? I always saw her on the ramparts. And here...no ramparts. Peace has been declared. Forever." She laughed shortly. "Even a couple of years ago, with the gay marriage stuff—'Take Vermont Back' and 'Move Vermont Forward'—all it amounted to was a war of lawn signs. It's done."

"Nirvana of the Green Mountains."

"Well, we like it," Frieda sniffed. "It suits us. It suits me. But I'll leave if she goes ahead." She shook her head. "I wouldn't if I didn't have to. I love my life here. I've *built* my life here," she said with a new infusion of umbrage. "I'd like you to talk to her while you're visiting. I think she might actually listen to you. I think there's a lot going on here. Mortality. Regrets about you. All the big stuff, you know?"

"Regrets about me?" Portia said, instantly on guard.

"Oh, nothing terrible. I'm sorry, Portia, you have to forgive me. I'm very upset. I think I must be coming at this with a sledgehammer, and I don't want to. Not, you know, about you. I mean, you're great. You've become a very strong woman. You've got a great career and a solid relationship with Mark, obviously. You're a force for good in the world. She knows that. But, you know, I think she wishes you were closer."

"Physically closer?" Portia said hopefully, but she knew the answer.

"No. I mean, it was the same when you were just up the road in Hanover. She expressed the same...sadness, really. Look, it's not uncommon for mothers to feel this way. I miss the relationship I had with my boys when they were small. Of course, they call me, and we visit, but you do lose something. Well, you lose your kids, really. You get them in another form, as adult children, but you lose what you had. It's part of life, so you have to accept it, and I mean, what's the alternative? That your children never grow up? That's unacceptable. But you know, you find other things. Your grandchildren. Or other interests unrelated to children, whatever. And I've been really lucky because I have my grandkids, and my music."

Portia nodded dumbly.

"I remember, when she moved up from Northampton, you were still an undergraduate and it seemed sort of obvious that she wanted to be nearer to you. She used to talk about what it was like when you were little, how close the two of you were, but then whenever you came to visit, it was obvious to me that you needed more distance. And she just couldn't make that adjustment. I kept telling her, 'Portia can't come back until she leaves. You have to let her leave.' But she felt that something had actually happened between the two of you. There was a thing, like a rift. It was too hard for her, do you know what I'm saying?"

Portia did but couldn't respond. This was not precisely news, but it was a topic of molten heat. She looked away. They sat in silence. It was nearly six-thirty, and outside, a light snow had begun.

"Will you talk to her?" Frieda asked. "While you're here? I've never been able to change her mind about a single thing, but you might have a chance. Besides, it's your business, Portia. This concerns you, you know."

"I don't see that," Portia said, surprised. "She's of age, obviously. And generally sound mind."

"Yes, and good health. But what if that changes? What if she dies? Who gets to raise this child if she dies?"

Portia felt as if the breath were being extracted from her, slowly and carefully, almost clinically. It was suddenly plain to her that she had failed—utterly failed—to really engage with this notion of her mother's. Of course she would be responsible for the child if Caitlin did not fall in love with her baby and take it away with her, and if Susannah did indeed end up fostering or, God, even adopting this child, and then if something happened to Susannah. Of course she would have to…what? Inherit? School conferences. Roald Dahl. Legos. Swimming lessons. Driving lessons. College applications. The commandments to love and nurture and discipline and safeguard. Who else could there be? How long would she have before the torch passed? How much more of her life could she expect to live, on her own terms, before it happened? And did Susannah truly understand what she was asking of her? Or…and the new idea came to her in a powerful wave. Was this what it was ultimately about, actually for? Some disjointed, backhanded, unacknowledged effort to ensure that Portia have a child, some child, any child?

She was so full of rage that she could barely form thoughts, let alone words, but speech also required breath, and breath was still impossible to come by. She felt heat pound in her cheeks. She simply stared at Frieda, openmouthed and gasping.

"Talk to her," said Frieda. "I'm not very hopeful, but I haven't given up. You're the only person she might listen to."

Long after I have forgotten what's in the Magna Carta or the Krebs's Cycle, I will remember the lesson learned from my former best friend, Lisa, who betrayed my trust and unilaterally ended our friendship one day when we were in tenth grade.

CHAPTER TWELVE

THE DREADED THING, THE AVERAGE MAN

Susannah, however, was not interested in listening. She lasted barely five minutes the first time Portia tried to raise the matter, late that very night as Caitlin slept upstairs and Frieda, whose dinner out did not end until nearly ten, lurked in her room, undoubtedly straining herself to listen. Then she bolted from the living room, with Portia gaping after her in serious annoyance and disbelief. There was, she would later think, a definite smack of adolescence to the scene, albeit with this comical reversal of roles, though she could not remember ever participating in such a classically juvenile exit. Susannah would not be coaxed back, neither that night nor in the days that followed. She did not care to hear the myriad reasons why she should, at the very least, think again, think carefully about what she was doing. She did not want to hear Portia's areas of concern. She did not wish to consider whether the interests of a newborn baby might not, in fact, be best served by a single mother in her (almost) seventies or whether caring for an infant might not, indeed, be the best focus for her own life. Portia approached these conversations with great care, but care did not save her. Although she managed several times to lure her mother with innocuous queries and tender concerns (about Frieda's health, the state of fund-raising for the battered women's shelter in Rutland, the always damp corner of the basement), the drift of her true interests would be altogether too clear, altogether too quickly, and Susannah, aggrieved, would rise and depart. So the first days passed in anger and shared but silent meals.

Portia, who now had two very distressing things to avoid thinking about, was grateful she had brought so much work with her. She spent her days on the living room couch (her mother having laid claim to the kitchen as her own territory, and the dusty office upstairs too uncomfortable to spend any more time in than necessary), making her way through folders as Susannah prepared food for their holiday meal and Caitlin lurked in her room and Frieda made herself absent whenever she could. The atmosphere, Portia couldn't help thinking, was like that of a commune in its final days, the sum of its parts deconstructing, inexorably, into shards of individual lives, individual agendas. She had heard enough of these stories, or read them in memoirs, to imagine that this was what it must have felt like: not the impacted bitterness of an angry family, but a simple heading for the exits. Except for herself, of course, because she was more afraid to be home than she was to be here, as dispiriting as here was.

On Wednesday night, when her mother reminded her of Caitlin's appointment in Hanover the following day, she tried once again to turn the conversation—which was not, actually, a proper conversation at all—to the girl, her pregnancy, and the baby.

"Look," Susannah snapped, "can you take her? Because if you can't, I need to make arrangements."

"I can take her, of course," Portia said, straining for a conciliatory tone. "But Mom, at some point we're going to have to talk about this."

"Sure," Susannah said unkindly. "Right after we get to all the things you're never willing to talk about."

And thus ended this particular round.

The following morning, Susannah left with Frieda for Burlington, the two of them stiff and cold in each other's company. Portia waited in the kitchen for Caitlin to come downstairs. She had read the paper and did not want to start a folder, since there might not be enough time to complete it. There were no other obvious distractions. So when her eye settled on the kitchen telephone, she decided to dial her own number in Princeton, to see if she had messages. Their outgoing greeting had not been changed in years, not since the previous phone had packed it in. She had recorded it then without much care, reciting her office number and Mark's, her cell phone number and Mark's, and inviting the caller to leave a message in a tone that, she sometimes thought, sounded a bit offhand, as if she didn't much care whether they did or not. Once or twice, listening to herself as she waited on the other end of the line, impatient to retrieve the recordings, it occurred to her that she ought to do it again, to record it again, to change it in substance or at least make it a bit peppier in tone; but she had never quite gotten to it. And now, as with so many other aspects of her old life, it was too late.

She waited through the rings, three, four, five, craving, oddly, the sound of this blasé former self who had a partner and a job and a cell phone, a partner *with* a job and a cell phone, a life somewhere else, and a house in which a phone might ring long and loud through untenanted rooms, and when the phone gave its distinctive click—*Enough already! No one is here!*—she tensed, eager for her own voice. But it didn't come. Instead, a breathless Mark recited their number and thanked her for calling. "You may leave a message for Portia after the tone," Mark said. "If you are trying to reach me, please try my office or my new number." And this he gave. Local area code. Princeton prefix. The beep came, loud and sharp. Portia stared straight ahead at the kitchen phone, mounted to the wall with a long coiled cord swinging below like a lazy jump rope. It was dingy with handling, unfashionable avocado in color, and altogether unaltered since the year 1978, when it had been installed, because it would not have occurred to Susannah to fix what was not broken. Obviously, such a thought had not occurred to her, either.

Caitlin materialized, wearing layers of sweatshirts. Portia drove them both down the icy drive and onto the road, which was better, gritty with sand. The road twisted down the hill and out of the woods, into fields of snow, the highway, and the ice-packed river. Caitlin rode in silence, arms folded across her belly.

"You warm enough?" asked Portia.

"Too warm," she said. "Hot."

Portia nodded. This was the entirety of their conversation.

The midwife her mother had chosen was part of a hybrid OB-GYN practice at the south end of town: MDs and midwives, childbirth educators, even a prenatal yoga teacher. In the homey waiting room, there were framed prints of massive Native American women with their arms full of corn (they looked ready to squat and produce their offspring on the spot), fat kilim-covered pillows on the floor, and long, deep sofas. In the corner, a little fountain gurgled, the water running over polished black stones. Portia took a seat as Caitlin checked in with the receptionist, noting the range of reading material on the low table (the full ideological spectrum from *Parents* to *Mothering*, *Prevention* to *Holistic Parenting*) and the women doing the reading: an appallingly young girl in black, clutching the bony hand of her black-clad boyfriend, a woman in denim overalls and a buzz cut, a woman her own age, heavily pregnant, unwrapping a roll of Tums as she turned the pages of the *Valley Advocate*. Faculty? Faculty spouse? She wore a man's roll-necked sweater and sweatpants in the ubiquitous Dartmouth green. Caitlin sat on the opposite couch with a clipboard.

"My midwife's at the hospital," she told Portia. "I have to wait for the other midwife."

"Did they say how long?" said Portia, paying attention to a small pulse of nausea just beginning to announce itself.

"No. I'm sorry."

"It's fine," Portia told her. "I don't have any plans."

But she also had no work with her, which meant that she had no focus, no distraction from her now evident and growing discomfort. Those files that might have consumed her—and she had many, many still to read—were back at her mother's house, back in the dusty office room she'd slept in now for three fitful nights. It wasn't good practice to take files out in public. Especially in a college town. Even in an obstetrician's office. Who knew? Maybe these moms-to-be were already obsessing about college admissions.

She picked up the nearest magazine and started to read an article about a woman in Connecticut arrested for breast-feeding at a Denny's restaurant. But she didn't like the woman, who was a La Leche instructor and, Portia quickly suspected, had planned her arrest, and the civil suit that followed, well in advance. Lactation Nazis, Rachel had once called them (this after a woman in her mothers group had condemned her decision to stop nursing after six months). Portia flipped past articles on aromatherapy as a means of avoiding gestational diabetes, water birth, the dreaded cesarean, and how to outmaneuver a scalpel-happy (and, it was implicit, male) doctor. She realized that she was becoming more and more irritated with every page.

"May I see that one?" said the woman in the green sweatpants when Portia tossed the magazine back on the table.

"Oh, sure." She picked it up again and passed it down the couch. "I should warn you, it's pretty hard-core. If you're planning on taking an aspirin during labor, I wouldn't read that."

"Really?" The woman frowned. "You'd have thought the pregnancy wars would be over by now."

Caitlin, who had finished filling in her forms, was listening.

"You'd have thought." Portia halfheartedly rummaged through the other magazines. There wasn't anything she wanted to read. After a steady diet of Princeton applications for weeks, nothing felt as urgent, as vital. Nothing, she reflected, equaled the adrenaline jolt of opening the folder and meeting the person inside.

"I haven't read anything, really," the woman said. Then she sighed. "You know, I've sort of been ignoring this whole thing."

Portia heard herself laugh. But that was terrible, she thought suddenly. So she apologized. "I suppose you've had an easy pregnancy," she added. "I mean, if you've been able to ignore it."

"No, no. I mean, yes, I suppose it's been easy. I just . . . well, I've had a lot of miscarriages. A lot." The woman shrugged. She seemed embarrassed, a little out of it. "It got to the point that whenever I got pregnant I'd just start waiting for the miscarriage, because my doctor told me not to get my hopes up. So when I got pregnant, I more or less tried not to think about it. And then, last month, my husband and I kind of looked at each other one day and went, you know, 'Oh, my God, I think we're really having a baby.'"

Caitlin, beside her, said, "Oh, wow."

"I know. I mean, it's not that we're not happy, we're just in shock. And of course they're mad at me that I haven't been coming in all summer and fall, but I just couldn't put myself through all that again. So now I have to come every week, to get scans and everything. I haven't had time to think about the pregnancy wars, or the birth wars, or anything."

Portia looked at her. The woman was her own age, certainly no younger. The skin around her eyes was loose and dark. Her hair, halfhearted blond, was dark at the roots. How many miscarriages did "a lot" mean? How many years had her body been conjuring and expelling unrealized children? She felt, as she thought about this, a wave of powerful aversion — to the woman, so heavily pregnant, and then to the girl, who would soon be just as heavily pregnant.

"You okay?" said Caitlin.

"Me?" Portia asked stupidly.

"Should I go get someone?"

This was the woman, the older woman. Portia wondered what they were talking about. Then, quite suddenly, she understood that she was looking at the floor, at her two feet in the warm boots she always wore when she was in Vermont: Abominable Snowman boots, Mark called them, since they looked like the feet of the mythical Sasquatch. They had bought them one summer in the sale at the Princeton Ski Haus, though she couldn't now remember why they had gone in there, since they didn't ski. The white furry feet were planted squarely on the carpeted floor of the waiting room, and Portia, who had an excellent vantage point from between her knees, could see the tufts of synthetic hair curling around the rubber soles.

"Are you going to be sick?" she heard the woman say, but from very far away, like across the room, except that she also felt the woman's hand on her forehead, holding her forehead, just as Susannah had done years before, when she was a child and needed to throw up. It was something a mother did: holding a forehead like that. This woman, Portia thought, already knew how to do it. She was already a mother.

"You're going to be fine," the woman said in her soothing, mother voice. "They say nausea means it's a healthy pregnancy."

"Oh no," Caitlin said loudly. "She's not pregnant. I'm pregnant."

Portia shot to her feet, bashing her shins against the low table. This hurt terribly, but the pain also cleared her head. She climbed past Caitlin's knees and away from the woman, the mother. "I'm sorry," she said, not looking at either of them. "I think I need to go outside. I need some fresh air."

"Okay," Caitlin said amiably. "You don't need to wait with me."

"Can I meet you?" she asked. Her voice sounded absurdly cheery. "Do you know that café up at the top of Main Street? It's called the Dirt Cowboy?"

"Sure," said Caitlin. "I'll just walk over there when I'm done."

"Great." She took her coat from a hook near the door. "Hey, good luck with your baby," she told the woman. "I'll see you!"

And she went outside.

The day was cold and bright, a classic Hanover day. Portia walked slowly up Main Street, taking deep breaths of the hard air. She did not understand what had happened, how she had lost that time between sitting politely on the couch and eyeing the carpet between her Bigfooted feet. She had a terrible idea that there was some element to the story that eluded her, like an identity—the woman's identity—known but beyond reach, which had somehow upended her. Faculty? she thought again. Faculty spouse?

She began, without any real attentiveness, to skim her own remembered directory of Dartmouth personnel, department by department, building by building, across the campus, but it was a pointless exercise. She had been gone for years, ten years, an eternity in college time. And even when she'd been a part of this college community, she'd hardly known every face or every name. It wasn't a big school, of course, but Dartmouth's faculty were scattered far afield around the Upper Valley. They lived on winding wooded roads, out of sight of other homes, in old farmhouses in Etna or glass-and-steel boxes up in the hills with views of the Connecticut, and somehow you didn't run into them at the supermarket or the movies. She abandoned the project as she walked, giving herself over to the diversion of shopwindows. Two days before Christmas the town was empty, and this was a town unused to being empty. Dartmouth functioned year-round as a college, and the students were eternally present, trawling the few streets, queuing up at the same restaurants, trying on the same GREEN T-shirts at the Coop. In any season they dominated the sidewalks, outnumbering the grown-ups, outmaneuvering the Appalachian Trail through-hikers who stumbled out of the woods, stunned to find so many human beings in one place. Looking ahead up the hill, Portia saw no one at all, just a short man in khakis and a down jacket washing the window of Campion's.

Without really planning to, she turned down Lebanon Street, which ran behind the massive Hopkins Center, the art and performance building that doubled as Dartmouth's post office. The street, indifferently plowed, was pocked with holes and ruts and packed with dirty snow. Portia walked, her hands in the pockets of her parka, stepping with care to evade the ice, feeling the cold in her face. She supposed she was headed for the place she had once lived, her first off-campus apartment in the year after her graduation, though she knew the building was no longer there. It had risen three unlovely stories behind an excellent ice cream parlor called the Ice Cream Machine, fondly dubbed the S'Cream Machine, now similarly departed. The S'Cream Machine had been the site of many an evening run while Portia was a student, and after, ostensibly for defensible items like coffee but, inevitably, for double cones of coffee fudge. She was not yet a cook. The first few years of her so-called adult life, she ate pretty much the way she had as an undergraduate: lunches at Collis (the student center), takeout, toasted sandwiches in a grill contraption that looked like a waffle maker.

She wasn't sure when it had closed. After they'd moved to Princeton, she hadn't come back for a year or two, not until Dartmouth hosted one of the annual Ivy League conferences: minority recruitment or debates on the common application, forty or so admissions officers, newly out from under the cloud of April 15, crowded into the Hanover Inn. That first night, she had waited until after the dinner in one of the private dining rooms, then stolen out back for her fix of ice cream (the memory of which, swelled with nostalgia, had assumed ambrosial proportions), only to find a hemp and incense emporium where the S'Cream Machine had once been. Gone, very long gone, she had thought, standing in front of the Hempest, eyeing the coarse purses and dubious toiletries through the window and conjuring for some reason a title from Mark's library, of a book she had never actually taken down, let alone read. She wasn't really sure which she was thinking of: the ice cream parlor or herself. Gone from here. Long gone. And not coming back.

The Hempest, too, had moved on. The storefront now belonged to a hoagie and pizza shop, with loudly advertised free delivery on campus. The building behind it, where she had lived alone and then with Mark, was now a parking garage. Portia, idly reading the ingredients for the Big Green Special (cukes and sprouts), shivered in her parka.

She went into the Hopkins Center by the back door and was surprised to find the cafeteria open, if deserted. She bought a cup of Green Mountain Coffee to warm her hands and continued on, through the arts center and out the front door onto the college Green.

The Green, of course, was one of Dartmouth's glories. Descended, like Harvard's Yard, from the town's once communal livestock grounds, it was Hanover's historical pedigree, its link to many other New England towns of its vintage. Once, the cows and sheep of local farmers had grazed here; now, the great open space had been swallowed by the college and was ringed with its administration and classroom buildings, its library and arts center, and the Hanover Inn. It was lovely in every season (except for mud season, in which nothing could be lovely) and was today especially brilliant, glittery with snow under this bluest sky. It was the one place on campus that had never grown shabby and lost its grandeur for Portia, the place she had always paused to appreciate, even in haste, even while rushing for a class or, later, a meeting. There had been picnics here, rallies, her own graduation, outdoor classes on days too sunny to stay inside, sunbathing under the anemic New Hampshire sun, endless hanging out. In the fall of her first year, she had gathered with her classmates to build their towering bonfire of railroad ties—one for each number of their class year—just as the previous year's freshmen had gathered the October before, on the day she and Susannah arrived for an interview and a tour.

Sometimes Portia thought—and this was not an uncommon pastime for an admissions officer—of the seventeen-year-old applicant she'd been then, the shaky essays declaring an entirely artificial sense of self and an intellectual identity she had no real claim to. She had perfect recall of her SAT scores (just fine before the upward ETS "recentering" in 1994, substandard today), the English and biology teachers who had written her recommendations, the (thinly fictionalized) short story she had sent along at the last minute, about attending a pro-choice rally in Boston. Portia remembered her interview in the small office upstairs in McNutt Hall (the same small office that would, amazingly, become her own small office only a few years later), in which she had been so shy, so terrified about not being good enough, not getting this thing, this chance, which she had only just discovered she wanted very badly. She remembered—oddly, for a woman who had begun paying attention to clothing only when it had become humiliating not to—precisely what she had worn the day of her visit: a blue velour turtleneck and a pair of Levi's jeans, tan Frye boots passed down to her (about five years after they had left fashionable in their wake) by a friend of Susannah's. She remembered the simulated enthusiasm she had summoned when the interviewer asked what mattered to her.

What mattered to her? Nothing, at that time, mattered much to her, except getting into college and away from her mother. There was no passion, no dream of what she might do in the world. Certainly there was no great purpose to her life or profound imperative writ upon her soul. The truth was that Portia thought of her seventeen-year-old self with deep humility, because she had too clearly been one of those late bloomers the current system was not primed to recognize. Or perhaps, she thought now, turning at the center of the Green to set a course for McNutt itself, she had not bloomed at all, only landed where she had landed, wherever that was, through a combination of chance and passivity. It had to be said that, when she read applications for Princeton, she was not looking for students like the student she had been then, who had no clue what they might accomplish in time. Not, of course, that she would have revealed this basic truth about herself in her Dartmouth application—even then, the imperative of college admissions was to present oneself in the best possible light. She would not have actually announced that she had no particular talents, no extraordinary intelligence, no burning desire to excel in some academic field or profession, and that in the absence of a life plan or goal, her intention was to wait until something happened to her, or some opportunity presented itself, and hope that she was perceptive enough to grab it. Her deep fear of her own mediocrity was compounded, at first, by the students she would meet when she matriculated: happy, easy people, athletic and academically capable. But slowly, over the years that followed, cracks began to appear and widen. The lacrosse star who dropped out without warning. The petite girl from Georgia, last seen on a winter morning loading her family's car in front of the dorm. The plunging depressions. The pervasive smell of vomit in the women's bathroom on her floor. The alcohol—Christ, the alcohol!

Inside every one of her fellow students, she understood now, was a person who didn't live up to his or her own expectations, a person too fat, too slow, whose hair wouldn't hold a curl, who had no gift for languages, who lacked the gene for math. They were convinced they were not all they'd been cracked up to be: the track star, classicist, valedictorian, perennial leading lady, campus fixer, or teacher's favorite. The driven ones she'd known in college feared they weren't driven enough, and the slackers were sure they'd find out how deficient they were if they ever did apply themselves. Up and down the corridors of the dormitories, behind each closed door, and whether the person within was davening over organic chemistry or drinking himself into a stupor, the Dartmouth she'd attended was populated by young people who were terrified of exposure.

Twenty years later, it was worse.

By now, Portia had dwelt in the world of the college-aged, and the nearly college-aged, for a very long time. She knew these kids intimately, more intimately perhaps than when she'd been one of them. She knew that they were soft-centered, emotional beings wrapped in a terrified carapace, that even though they might appear rational and collected on paper, so focused that you wanted to marvel at their promise and maturity, they were lurch-

ing, turbulent muddles of conflict in their three-dimensional lives. She knew that they were dying to leave home and petrified to go, that they clung to their friends but knew absolutely that no one truly understood them. When she went out into their world, departing her ivory, literally ivy-clad tower to visit their schools — and it was oddly immaterial if their schools were sticky with wealth or held together by municipal duct tape and valiant teachers — she knew precisely who they were and what they were going through. She knew that their arrogance was laced with self-laceration (sometimes, in the case of the girls, literal self-laceration) and that their stated passions were, more often than not, arid things assembled in their guidance counselors' offices or at the family dinner table. She knew that the creative ones were desperately afraid they were talentless, and the intellectuals deeply suspected they weren't brilliant, and that every single one of them felt ugly and stupid and utterly fake.

This generation, raised with a mantra of self-esteem and extravagantly praised by their parents for every scribble, knew how to talk a good game. They knew how to accumulate accomplishments and present them in CV form (one infamous college counselor actually referred to such an item as a "brag sheet"), how to sell themselves to the teachers who would write their references and the alumni who would interview them. But inside they were crippled with doubt. And though there had been relatively few real scandals in recent Ivy League admissions, few cases in which applicants lied outright and gained admission as a result (any admissions officer could effortlessly cite the Harvard girl who failed to mention that she had killed her mother, the Stanford boy who'd plagiarized articles for his high school paper, and of course Princeton's own cowboy autodidact, really an ex-con in his thirties), Portia suspected that most applicants had a nagging fear that they were lying, too — or, if not actually lying, then exaggerating their interest in plant biology or modern dance, overestimating their natural aptitude for math, overstating their passion for public service. They feared that they were ordinary kids, in other words, and not the brilliant sparks they had unexpectedly persuaded the grown-ups they were. Ordinary and thoroughly average. Ordinary and undeserving.

One morning a couple of years earlier, Portia had spent a strange but fascinating hour on the filthy floor of a used-book store in Cambridge (another Ivy League admissions conference) with a pile of Harvard yearbooks, interwoven with dust, covered in flaking crimson leather. Turning the pages, she'd lost herself in the open, handsome faces of the Class of '28 and their staid, abbreviated biographies: Charles Cortez Abbott (*Lawrence, Kans., Browne & Nichols, Advocate, Hasty Pudding, Business*). Alfred Reinhart (*Lawrence, Mass., Lawrence High, Biology, Medicine*). Joseph Parkhurst (*St. Paul, Minn., Lawrenceville, Classics, Delphic, Law*). The class poem that year had been written by a man not destined to enter the pantheon of American poets, but Portia found it beguiling and terribly current. It told the story of a Harvard student who felt deflated by his college experience, having failed to letter in a sport or graduate at the top of his class, really to excel in any way at all. Determined to recapture this wasted opportunity, the student in the poem had graduated and changed his name, then re-sat the entrance exams (entrance exams! no art portfolios and viola recordings and "brag sheets" back in '28) to gain another place in the incoming Harvard freshman class, where this time around he determined to make some mark on the university. His fate, however, proved inescapable. Four years on, he found himself precisely in the same position: competent student, athlete, orator, man about town, not a star of his class, not a success in his own mind, merely the very ordinary man he ever was (though no longer quite so young). And this time he departed for good, presumably to become another nondescript alumnus in the sea of Harvard graduates. Because, the poem concluded, all of them—all of us, thought Portia, closing the yearbook in a final puff of dust—were that dreaded thing, the average man. 1928 or 2008—there was no escaping it.

The door to the Admissions Office opened as she reached the McNutt steps, and Portia found herself looking up into the florid face of Gale Eberhoff. Eberhoff, a former Dartmouth football player, oversaw recruitment for football and baseball and had done so since before Portia had set foot on campus. Winning seasons were his joy in life and losing an athlete to Yale his particular horror. He looked, for a moment, thoroughly perplexed by the sight of his former colleague. Then the synapses snapped into place.

"Well! Prodigal daughter!"

"Where's my fatted calf?" she said, giving him a hug. She had always worked well with Gale.

"Visiting your mom?"

"Yes. I had to come in on an errand. I thought I'd take a self-consciously nostalgic walk through my old haunts."

"I'm surprised you can find any," he said. "This town is turning into the Mall of America."

"We'll always have Lou's, Gale."

"And thank God for it! So tell me, how are our orange friends in the great state of New Jersey? I'm still smarting over that pitcher you stole from me last year."

She shrugged. This had been a lanky, prematurely bald boy from Rhode Island. The previous January, with applications in to Brown, Dartmouth, and Princeton, Notre Dame had offered him a full scholarship, which he'd had to accept or decline right away. Telling the three Ivies about this offer had set a flurry of events in motion, sending Portia, Gale, and presumably their Brown counterpart scrambling to process the application and make an offer of admission and financial aid—or decline him. Brown had declined. Princeton's baseball coach had wanted this boy very badly, and he was burning up the phone line to Portia's office, pleading and badgering by turns. The pitcher had come to Princeton.

"You'll get us back," she said. "You know, Jerry really wanted him. I thought he was a strong writer, too. I still remember his essay."

Gale shook his head. In the afternoon light, his cheeks seemed redder than ever. "You were always good that way. Every year in April, I feel like I'm clearing the whole cache out of my brain to make room for the next batch."

"I know what you mean," said Portia, but it wasn't true. Not that she remembered them as individuals—no one could ever do that—but she couldn't excise them, either. Instead, she sometimes felt as if she were throwing them behind her, into a great sack that grew heavier and heavier every year, and then she dragged them forward with her, all those lives.

"You ever think of coming back? Harrold is leaving, you know. And a couple of the kids, going to graduate school."

"Harrold? Really?" This was news. Harrold, Dean of Admissions for a generation, had both admitted her to Dartmouth and then hired her. "Is he going somewhere else?"

"No. He says he's done."

"College counselor?" She frowned.

"Not even that. No, he's really done. I have no idea what he's going to do. I don't think he does. Well, he does seem to mention Hawaii a lot."

"Can you blame him?" Portia smiled. "I mean, twenty-five years of Hanover winters?"

"He did say if he runs through his generous Dartmouth pension, he'll write a college admissions guidebook."

She sighed. "Well, why not? Everyone else seems to."

"I'm counting on it myself." Gale smiled, showing stained teeth. She'd forgotten he was a smoker. "Well, my wife is counting on it. That's our retirement home, she informs me."

"How is your wife?" asked Portia, and they talked about her for a bit. Gale and his wife lived in a vast colonial on Webster Terrace, down at the end of Fraternity Row. It made for a depressing walk home, she had always thought. Their daughters, Dartmouth graduates, were now lawyers in Boston. Their son (to his father's vast regret, an aesthete) was in his final year at Bard.

After she had hugged him good-bye and sent love to his wife, she went inside. The McNutt waiting room was not much changed: Windsor chairs with the college crest, coffee tables laden with yearbooks and copies of the *Dartmouth*, framed photographs of the campus on all the walls. A young woman sat at the reception desk. She looked young enough to be a student, if not an applicant.

"Can I help you?" she said brightly. The waiting room was empty.

"Oh. No," said Portia. "I'll just take an application." She took it from a pile on one of the faux Chippendale hunt cupboards.

"We have one more tour, at three-thirty."

"No thanks. I'm just passing through."

She looked around, wondering if any of her other former colleagues might show themselves. When they did not, she left.

As she stepped back outside, she saw that the light had become suddenly elusive, an early dusk settling over the snow. It was a familiar dusk, with a known glow, lavender in color, and she stood for a moment, appreciating it. There was without question an intense beauty to this place, a specific juxtaposition of white clapboard, brick, and open space ringed by winter trees. It made her think of that song they had all been taught as freshmen. Not the raucous, silly alma mater with its awful line about "the granite of New Hampshire / In their muscles and their brains" and its shifting pronouns to accommodate coeducation. But the pretty one, the one that—despite her best efforts to sing it stoically—always ended with her choking up:

By the light of many thousand sunsets,
Dartmouth Undying, like a vision starts:
Dartmouth, the gleaming, dreaming walls of Dartmouth,
Miraculously builded in our hearts . . .

It was, as someone far cleverer had once said, only a small college. And yet there were those who loved it.

Caitlin was waiting for her in the café, at a table by the window, stirring sugar into her tea.

"I'm so sorry," said Portia. "I completely lost track of the time. Is that normal tea?"

"What?" Caitlin looked up at her. She looked, suddenly, terribly young to Portia. She moved a white plastic bag from the tabletop onto one of the chairs. There was a clanking sound inside, of glass knocking together, as she set it down.

"Sneaking soda back to the house?" Portia teased.

"No. It's this stuff they gave me. I have to drink it before my next appointment. It's for a test."

"Gestational diabetes?"

"Yes." Caitlin frowned. "How did you know that?"

"There was an article in one of those magazines."

"Oh."

She went to the counter, ordered herself a coffee, and stood waiting for it, not exactly avoiding conversation with the girl, but perhaps minimizing it.

"Last time I was here it was jam-packed," Caitlin said when she returned. "There weren't any seats at all."

"Well . . ." Portia sipped her coffee, then blew on it. "That was probably in term. All the students are gone for the holidays."

"Yeah," Caitlin said, and awkward silence hung between them. "You know," she said after a minute, "sometimes I can't believe we're the same age."

"We?" Portia looked at her in alarm.

"The Dartmouth students and me. I mean, what are they, eighteen? Nineteen? I'm eighteen in June."

She nodded, waiting.

"It's just, I mean, I look at them and they're, like, having a good time, worrying about . . . I don't know, a French test or something. And I'm having a baby. It's so . . . wild. You know?"

Portia was pretty sure she did know, but she didn't say anything.

"Not...I don't want to sound like I'm not grateful. To your mom. I don't know what I would have done if I hadn't met her friend. Barbara?"

"Yes. Barb. She used to live near us when we lived in Massachusetts."

"And she had this crazy idea, to come here. But I needed a crazy idea. I needed any idea."

Portia sipped her coffee. "I think...," she said, remembering, "my mother said you wanted to go to college yourself."

To her surprise, Caitlin responded to this by laughing. She shook her head over the mug of tea, which she held between her palms. Portia looked around the room. They were indeed alone, except for the dull-looking girl who had made her coffee and a man in one of the armchairs, reading *The New Yorker*.

"Here's what's funny," Caitlin said. "Well, I think this is pretty funny. Yeah, I do want to go to college."

"There's nothing funny about that," said Portia.

"No, that's not what I mean. I realized I wanted to go to college the same day I figured out I was pregnant. It was a pretty intense day. Well," she said, eyeing Portia, "I don't know if you want to hear this."

"Of course," said Portia, surprised to discover that she did.

"I took the test in the morning. It was Labor Day weekend. I went to the drugstore and got it, then I went to the library and took the test there. I didn't want to take it home and have my mom find it."

"Okay," said Portia.

"So I'm not...I mean, it was awful. I didn't believe it at first. I couldn't believe I was pregnant."

"Were you using anything?" Portia asked, trying not to sound preemptively judgmental. Obviously she hadn't used anything.

"Anything? Like birth control?"

Portia nodded.

"My boyfriend...my *boyfriend*," she said with refreshing hostility, "told me we didn't need it. He said he wouldn't"—she took her own furtive glance around the room—"go in all the way. He said I could only get pregnant if he went in all the way. And he didn't," she finished unnecessarily.

Portia sighed. She was glad her mother wasn't here. The inevitable diatribe would not have been helpful. "If it's any comfort," she said, "you're not the first woman to get misinformation on this subject. You won't be the last, I'm sorry to say."

"Not much comfort. But thanks." She rolled her eyes.

"But what about at school? Didn't they teach you about birth control in school?"

"Oh, you're kidding." She summoned a smile. "My school? Maybe here, but not where I'm from. My school is, like, one-third LDS, one-third born again, one-third meth addicts. They taught us what your period is, and all those other fun changes that mean you're a woman now. But birth control, no way. Why would we need birth control? We're not supposed to be, you know, having sex. We were supposed to stay pure till we got married. That part of it was really clear. But, I mean, they never told us what that meant, exactly. I know girls who thought if they ever kissed someone, they weren't pure anymore. I used to think that, actually. I thought sex was kissing." She smiled and actually blushed. She looked, oddly, thoroughly innocent, circumstances notwithstanding.

"In other words, you were supposed to be the first teenagers in history not to have sex. Is that it?"

Caitlin looked suddenly delighted. "That's about it."

"Did you tell your boyfriend?"

She shook her head. "By the time I found out, he wasn't my boyfriend anymore. If I told anyone, it should have been the girl he was going out with after me. I mean, isn't he going to tell her exactly the same thing?"

"Oh, probably," Portia said. "So back to taking the test."

"Yeah. I'm in the bathroom at the library, trying not to lose it. And it was Labor Day weekend. Did I say that?"

"Yes," said Portia, sipping.

"On Labor Day weekend we always have lunch at my aunt Jane's house. All the sisters. My mom is one of six sisters and two brothers. All the sisters are married, and one of the brothers. Almost all of them have kids, so it's a ton of people. Plus my grandmother. My grandfather died a long time ago."

"Okay," Portia said, trying to follow.

"And usually I'm running around with the kids, but this time I don't feel like running around, so I'm sitting at the table with my mom and all my aunts, just, you know, trying to follow the conversation and pretend the bottom hasn't just fallen out of my life. And my aunt Susie was talking about the school her kids went to, or something about the parents at the school, and I just started looking around the table at all of them, you know?"

Of course Portia didn't know. But she nodded anyway.

"And I just . . . suddenly, I just looked at them, and I realized. Every one of them, my mom and all her sisters, they went to junior college for one or two years, and then they got married. And that was it. And then it just dawned on me, you know? That I never thought about my future, and *they* never thought about my future. They never asked me, you know, what do you want to do when you grow up? Or if I wanted to go to college. And I never asked myself. Because that part of my life was just kind of supposed to end after a year or two, and then I was supposed to get married and do what they'd done, which was have babies. And it was totally bizarre, because here I'd come to find out I was going to have a baby, and suddenly the one thing I knew was that wasn't what I wanted. Do you understand?"

Portia, dumbfounded, nodded. "That must have been very hard."

"But I love them, you know? I love all of them. I love my mom and my aunt Jane. They only want the best for me."

"Of course."

"But I couldn't tell them this. There wasn't any part of it they'd understand. My mom would have just been, you know, destroyed. And I think my dad and my brothers . . . I don't know. And that part about wanting to go to college. I mean, real college."

"Four-year college."

"Yeah. They just wouldn't have had any idea what to do with that. You know, four-year college, that means away, somewhere else. Not at home."

"Most parents," said Portia, carefully, "like to send their kids to college. Of course, they miss them, but it's an important part of their growing up and becoming independent."

Caitlin shook her head so vigorously, the thin locks of hair came out from behind her ears. "No. Not my parents. You know, all these aunts? The farthest any of them lives from each other is, like, ten miles. And it isn't just my family. It's every single person I know. Nobody ever goes away, except the boys, of course."

"Why the boys?" Portia asked suspiciously.

"Oh, they go to Brigham Young if they go to college. And they go on mission, of course. But then they come back after. But to get back to Labor

Day, I was sitting there thinking about all this and I was just, like, paralyzed, you know? And then that went on for a couple of weeks, and it was awful because I couldn't tell anybody what was happening. But finally I made myself make some kind of decision, because I wanted to be the one deciding what was going to happen. So I went to the nearest clinic, which was all the way in Casper. I mean, four hours in the car to get there. I thought I was going for an abortion, but I didn't know you couldn't just walk in and get one. They need to talk to you first and make sure you know what you're doing. I didn't expect that."

Portia nodded, waiting.

"The thing is, I wasn't really in favor of abortion. I'm pro-life. I've always been pro-life. I mean, everyone I know is pro-life. I guess I was expecting the people in the clinic would be, like, 'Step this way, lie down on the table,' you know, 'we'll get rid of it for you.' But they wanted to talk to me about how I really felt and what I really wanted to do with my life, and how I thought about the baby. Barbara was my counselor. And I kept saying, yes, I want to end it, yes, I want the abortion, but you know, she knew I couldn't do it. She made the appointment to come back and do it the next week, but when I came back I was just a wreck. I couldn't make myself do it. It just felt really wrong."

Portia drank the end of her coffee, lukewarm and grainy going down her throat. "It sounds like you were really struggling."

"Well, Barbara asked me if I'd thought about giving the baby away for adoption, and of course I thought that was a fantastic idea. I mean, right away I thought: That's it. That's my way out. But I still couldn't go home to my family and have a baby. I already looked different. I couldn't wear most of my clothes. I don't think anybody noticed yet, but I noticed."

"Then Barb mentioned my mom?"

She nodded. "Not her in particular, but she said she had some friends back east who might be able to let me live with them and I could go to school. The adoption part I could work out later, but the main thing was to get me out of the house as soon as possible. I still can't believe how fast she did it. I mean, less than a week later I was getting off the plane in Burlington." She gave a ragged sigh that spoke of barely averted tears. "I know how this sounds. I know you think I'm an idiot for getting pregnant in the first place, and then not going through with the abortion."

"I don't think that at all," Portia said, surprised.

"It's just," Caitlin continued, ignoring this, "when something like this happens, it's like, you're just knocked off your feet. I couldn't think about anything. I couldn't make any decisions, like even what to put on in the morning or which way to drive to school, let alone what to do about my life and going to college and having a baby. I think I must have gone crazy or something. I'm sure you can't imagine what I'm talking about."

"I can imagine," Portia said quietly. "I got pregnant once, a long time ago."

Caitlin snapped to attention. She looked sharply at Portia, as if Portia had just become the most fascinating thing in the universe. Portia, on the other hand, went numb. She found herself taking inventory of the palms of her hands. She had not planned to say this. She was a little bit stunned herself.

"Really?"

"Yes. Really. And I didn't even have your excuse. Susannah made sure I had a thorough sex education years before I needed it."

"So is that why you freaked out in the doctor's office?"

Portia considered this carefully. "My life is a little intense right now. I don't really want to go into the details. Look"—she straightened in her chair—"Caitlin. I'd appreciate your not mentioning what I just said to Susannah. To anyone, actually. I had a tough decision to make, just like you. I didn't share it with her at the time, and I don't particularly want to now."

"Oh." She nodded energetically. "Yeah, no problem. So...," she said carefully, unwilling to let go of this entirely, "I guess you do believe in abortion, then."

"Well, I believe in it, yes. I'm not in *favor* of it. I mean, it's not a *good* thing. But not having the option is worse. Better not to be in those circumstances in the first place."

"Totally. Hey, should we go back?"

"Oh. Yes, I think so."

Portia stood and picked up her coat. Caitlin took her parka off the back of her chair. The bottles in her plastic bag clanked together as she picked it up. "What's that?" she asked Portia as they crossed to the door. She was looking at the dark green folder Portia carried.

"It's an application to Dartmouth."

"You're applying to Dartmouth?" Caitlin laughed. "I thought you already went to Dartmouth."

"No, I just, I like to keep up with what other Ivy League schools are doing with the application format. Of course it's all online, but I just keep them in my office at school. Hey, would you like this?"

Caitlin stopped. They were outside on the pavement now, in the quickly fading light. "Really?"

"Why not? There's no harm in looking. You can apply next year if you want. You can even apply in the next few days if you get going."

"Are you kidding? They're not going to take me. I'm having a baby!"

"You're having a very unusual life experience for a teenage girl, one which is testing your character. It's already changed your life. What you have to say about that could make for a very interesting essay. Of course, I don't know what your grades were like."

Dumbfounded, Caitlin could manage only a nod. "Good. I mean, I didn't have much to work with."

"Okay, we can talk about that. Here," she said, holding out the green packet.

Caitlin took it. She stared at it. She seemed dazed. "Are you sure about this?" she said finally.

"Well, no." Portia laughed. "But stranger things have happened."

PART

II

READING SEASON

My primary extracurricular activity is reading science books.
I'm not an athlete, and I find groups a little frustrating, as it's difficult
to identify peers who are interested in the material I'm interested in,
and who are capable of discussing science and mathematics at my
level of activity.

CHAPTER THIRTEEN

INSIDE THE BOX

She came home, the day after New Year's, to take inventory.

The house, from without, was dusted with unbroken snow. Mail was heaped on the porch chair, and frustrated slips from UPS and FedEx were stuck into the outer storm door. Clearly, no one had been here for over a week, and she indulged herself in a moment of extra bitterness over the message conveyed to the neighborhood: *They're out of town, come on in and make yourself at home!* Mark's car was gone.

Portia let herself inside, wary and prepared to be bruised, but no major changes were immediately apparent. The house seemed intact, furniture and works of art in place, one early stack of mail neatly on the hall table. He had spent time here, then, closer to the beginning of her trip than to the end. He had gone about his routines, fulfilled his ordinary duties, even as he extracted himself from the premises. Perishables had been removed from the refrigerator and the breadbox, with plastic, glass, and metal rinsed out and placed in the recycling bin. A copy of *The New York Times*, dated the day before Christmas, had also been responsibly recycled. There was a local number written in pen on one corner of the front page, but Portia resisted the brief urge to dial it. Real estate agent? Moving company? Surely he knew Helen's number by heart. Oh, thought Portia, wounded by a new thought: Attorney?

Obviously, they weren't married. They had talked about it once or twice, then let the subject drift away without resolution. It seemed clear that neither needed the ceremony, but at the same time, there was a wealth of documentation between them. They shared ownership of the house and the checking account and served as primary beneficiaries of each other's wills and life insurance policies. They had been more responsible, she had sometimes thought, than many of the married couples she'd known, in which one or both partners had such anxiety or control issues about money that they couldn't meld accounts or titles, couples in which his paycheck went to him and hers to her, in which he held title to the condo while she kept the weekend place in her name. She and Mark had shaken their heads about these couples, over their shared breakfast at their shared table. They had felt superior to the husbands and wives they knew who seemed not even to like each other. She had always liked Mark. She had not, of course, always wanted to tell him everything, and she'd supposed that was all right. Was it not all right? Had he not, as she'd assumed, told everything to her, or at least everything important? He had an ex and a child and complicated relationships with both. He had a sister he did not like, who had a husband he did not like even more. He had a sense of frailty about his body (which, when they'd first met, had been a very English body, thin chested, gangly... scrawny, she supposed, though she had always found it comfortingly awkward), an atonal voice, teeth that had not benefited from fluoride, in the water or anywhere else. He had a secret appetite for whodunits and became irritated if the mysteries were too obscure or too obvious. He had a tender loyalty to the sound track of his youth, a truly shameful parade of Top of the Pops offenses: Culture Club, Spandau Ballet, Bananarama. Even, God forbid, Wham! She had been known to come home to these affronts, opening their door to George Michael, informing her (at his most repellent) that he wanted *her sex*. Mark kept this stash of small embarrassments by the CD player in the kitchen.

They were gone. She discovered this after she had stopped looking for things that were gone, things she thought he might have taken with him, that she could be angry or bereft not to find in their places, but those things were all where she had left them: the watercolor of dunes they'd bought the summer they rented a cottage in Wellfleet, the huge and heavy copper stockpot he'd found at the Lambertville flea market, an insane bargain at ten bucks, even the 1820 edition of Shelley's *Prometheus Unbound,* which Mark had bought from an Oxford bookseller with the windfall from some student prize. Portia was amazed to find this last item in its place. And when she did find it, on the bookshelf in their bedroom, she sat on the bed, stunned by an intense feeling of relief.

Past the anger at his betrayal, the humiliation of knowing he was already—or would soon be—squiring a visibly pregnant Englishwoman around campus, the as yet unexplored jealousy she had desperately been holding off, it was only at this moment clear to her that she wanted him not to have left, or at any rate to be coming back now that he had made his point. (His point? Portia thought. That he was finding her lacking in some way? That he wanted another child? Perhaps, as Clarence Porter had so succinctly put it, that she required a little "shaking up"?) She doubted very much that this would happen. Mark was nothing if not decisive. Every decision they had ever made—from their moving in together, to accepting jobs at Princeton, to far less significant things like whom to invite for dinner or what movie to see—had been made deliberately and not revisited. He wasn't leaving her, in other words. He had already left.

Portia, not surprisingly, soon discovered that she did not much like being home. The house, despite its eerie absence of absent things, was not a comfortable place, and there was nothing compelling her to be here. She had no wish to stay and face the obvious tasks: doing laundry, making shopping lists, clearing a path to the front door through settled, heavy snow. The number of messages glowing in red on the answering machine could not yet be faced, and she wondered if it wasn't possible to just start over with a new machine and a new number. (Surely the phone company was well versed in domestic upheaval. Surely the abandoned were eternally lined up at Verizon and Sprint, claiming they could never start fresh without seven altogether different digits, or at least the same digits in a different order.) Failing this, she could simply toss both and decline to replace them.

Standing in the dull silence of her foyer, Portia understood that she had no clear idea of what to do with herself, except to get away from this place. Methodically, she considered and rejected other places to be, including the gym, the supermarket at the end of her street, any public space downtown. At any of these, Mark and Helen might be lurking, ready to display their happiness and gestational glow. With each locale, indeed, came a jolt of distress, like a shot of black ink through the system, feathering out to each extremity before fading. It was the return of pain, its forces rested and restored during her short distraction and ready with a reconsidered battle plan. Considering her new circumstances, there seemed to be only one place she could retreat to, and realizing this, Portia duly began her retreat, locking the front door behind her and picking her way over the hard snow, back to her car. She had been home less than half an hour. She had been able to stand being home for only half an hour. She had the sense, suddenly, of running before a wave.

Moments later, she was cruising downtown for a parking spot. The town was wide open, and she pulled in opposite Nassau Hall, telling herself that it was really a rational, laudable thing to go to work late in the afternoon on a day when the rest of the campus was still and stony silent. This time of year, after all, was not a vacation for *her*. The application deadline had only just come and gone, and so had commenced reading season, a tunnel of stress and weighty decisions, ringing phones, an e-mail in-box that filled at a rate of four messages per minute: students terrified they had mistyped their Social Security numbers, guidance counselors duty bound to report that the applicant (along with the rest of the football team) had just been given a citation for disorderly conduct, and always—*always*—parents. Parents! Susannah had been entirely uninvolved in Portia's own college search. She remembered one heated discussion about applying to Smith—reactionary playground for future Republican wives or hotbed of radical lesbianism?—but apart from that, it had more or less been her own show. Had Susannah read her essays, checked for spelling errors? Had she offered to hunt down friends or cousins of her own friends or cousins with connections to the various admissions offices (misguided though that surely would have been, even back then)? Had she, God forbid, herself called up the offices, demanding to speak to whoever was in charge about the brilliance and promise of her daughter?

Compared with the parents Portia was dealing with now, Susannah looked like a saint.

Portia hauled her bags of folders through the FitzRandolph Gate. Nassau Hall, Princeton University's nerve center and, for a few heady months in 1777, home to the infant U.S. government, looked majestic in the failing light, with its great preening tigers and fluttering ivy, and behind it the campus unfurled, stalwart buildings linked by deserted walkways. Looking up at West College, she saw no lights at all: not Clarence's corner office (he and his partner were in New Haven with friends), not Dylan's (visiting his parents in Houston), not Corinne's (with the kids on some island).

That she was here after nightfall was not in itself unusual. In January, February, and March, as the intense period of reading gave way to the still more intense period of committee meetings, all of them frequently worked late into the night, percolating along in a fittingly collegial rhythm. She had sometimes, certainly, been the last one out the door, intent on making it through western Oregon or the Archbishop Mitty School or the imperious baseball coach's most urgent requests before allowing herself to head for home. But coming in like this, alone, in the darkness, to an empty building—in all these years, it was a first. The unbroken line of dark windows was definitely disconcerting, but at the same time she felt some relief. There would be no one up there to question her.

She opened the door with her own key and went first to the administrative warren in the back of the building, passing the abandoned receptionist's desk. She turned on the lights as she went, bathing the nondescript corridor in harsh fluorescent illumination that picked up every ding and mark on the walls, passing the silent photocopier in its alcove. Against one wall, two of the fax machines were lit and humming, neatly depositing pages and pages into their trays. In the cubicles, screen savers pulsed and danced. The smorgasbord of ill-judged baked goods had been cleared away, only a spattering of crumbs left behind. On Martha's desk, a phone purred forlornly, five times, six times, then went silent. It was all, in fact, very silent.

She hoisted her bags onto the counter below the staff mailboxes and began to lift out handfuls of files. There were a few she'd flagged to remove at this point, and she went hunting for them now, quickly locating the fluorescent pink Post-it notes on their covers. These were folders she had questions about for one reason or another, small items she might already have dealt with if Susannah were not such a Luddite, who refused to own a computer. Because she was, however, and because she did not, and because Portia had declined to drive into Hanover to undertake this sensitive business on some public terminal in Baker Library, she had merely flagged the files to come back to.

One of these was a boy from a private day school near Boston, whose guidance counselor—a woman Portia had met when she'd visited the school last spring—had declined to answer two notable questions on the secondary school report: "Has the applicant ever been found responsible for a disciplinary violation at your school, whether related to academic misconduct or behavioral misconduct, that resulted in the applicant's probation, suspension, removal, dismissal, or expulsion from your institution? To your knowledge, has the applicant ever been convicted of a misdemeanor, felony, or other crime?" Almost always, the answer to these questions was no. Sometimes it was yes, and sometimes that was not in itself the kiss of death. There were kids who'd made mistakes and grown from them. There were victims of excessive "zero tolerance" school rules, suspended for carrying a loaded water pistol or pointing a finger and declaring, "Bang." There was even the occasional Jean Valjean crime of necessity. (She had never forgotten the boy from Oregon who had shoplifted liver for his family. Liver! If only he had been a stronger student.) But she could not remember a single instance in which the guidance counselor had declined to answer the questions. It could, of course, be an oversight—a typo. But at this school? With tuition upward of twenty-five grand a year and a student parking lot crowded with Lexus coupés and BMWs? Portia suspected not.

Another worrying application was from a Rhode Island girl whose complex, mellifluous essay was somewhat at odds with her low English grades and poor score on the writing section of the SAT, not to mention the fact that the favorite book listed in the "Few Details" section was *Pride and Priviledge* by "Jane Austin." Portia, accordingly, wanted to check the girl's tribute to Fannie Lou Hamer against their data bank of essays for sale. (These were gleaned mainly from Internet sources—where they were billed as teaching tools and slathered with disclaimers—but supplemented by an Iowa entrepreneur with an essayist-for-hire business. This unpleasant individual had decided to publish his expertise in book form and closed up shop by mailing his entire backlist of custom essays to every college his clients had ever attended, plus *People* magazine.) Of course, the Rhode Island girl might simply have risen to the challenge of her essay, taking her time, thinking through her points, and checking her sentences carefully to avoid grammatical errors, but there was something in the ease of the language that worried Portia. Correctness, after all, was achievable with sweat, but in her experience it was nearly impossible to drill grace into prose.

There was also a boy from Boston Latin who had furnished a list of Princeton philosophers he wanted to work with and an essay of such dense philosophical prose that Portia had had no idea what he was talking about. (In fact, she could have sworn, when she'd read it at Susannah's kitchen table days earlier, that it had something to do with zombies. What next?

she'd thought. Mummies and vampires?) She had decided to send the essay to David and ask him to sort it out. Philosophers seemed to have a knack for recognizing their own kind as well as the impostors in their midst.

Finally, there was the Connecticut boy whose long list of school government offices, dramatic roles, community service projects, and baseball positions had ended with the words "National Judo Champion." It might, of course, be true, but in Portia's previous dealings with bona fide national judo champions (and not a few had indeed applied to Princeton), this accomplishment did tend to be noted in recommendations and to require enough practice time to preclude student government, drama, and varsity baseball. National judo champions also had a tendency to write about being national judo champions. They solicited their coaches for references and supplied newspaper reports attesting to the fact that they were...well...national judo champions. It would easily be settled by Google, Portia thought, finding the file at the very bottom of the stack and setting it aside. Why anyone would bother to lie in the age of Google was baffling.

"We are trusting skeptics," her first dean of admissions had told her years before. "We believe what they tell us, but they'd better be telling us the truth." This was Harrold McHenry, the soon-to-be former Dean of Admissions at Dartmouth, who had hauled her aboard the profession in the spring of her final Dartmouth year. Harrold's sense of fair play—fair play he sweetly assumed everyone else likewise embraced—had been one of his most endearing qualities. He had a horror of the so-called new rules of admissions, the outsmarting and end runs and decoding now rampant out there, the snake-oil salesmen promising to package and sell your kid to his or her school of choice. For as long as he could (and longer, perhaps, than he should have), Harrold stubbornly regarded each application as an open, invigorating conversation between his staff and the applicant, in which there could be no dissembling on either side. He expected total candor from each applicant and maintained that expectation even after little wildfires of scandal broke through the industry in the 1990s—kids getting other kids to take their SATs for them, applicants who wrote their own recommendations, people pretending to be Rothschilds and ranch hands. These events had been personally wounding to Harrold, but he had stayed the course, doing his best to ride the new waves, trying to maintain his personal honor code.

There was something a little haunting about this terribly ordinary room,

Portia decided. She tried, for a moment, to see it not as the generic office it absolutely was, but as the epicenter of so much fervent speculation, by students, teachers, counselors, and parents. To them, this utilitarian space was the holding pen where their child and all his or her antagonists were gathered, vetted, directed, shunted into narrower and narrower corridors leading to smaller and smaller vestibules, where they were commanded to wait in mute distress, face-to-face with their most closely matched fellow aspirants: wrestlers here, legacies there, Pakistanis to the right, woodwinds, novelists, witheringly brilliant mathematicians, faculty kids, staff kids, movie star kids, movie stars, ordinary decent kids, good debaters, great debaters, boys who wanted to be Brian Greene, girls who wanted to be Stephen Sondheim, or Meg Whitman, or Quentin Tarantino. There was, for instance, one tiny chamber in which the diver from Wisconsin sat knee to bandaged knee with the diver from Maine, the lounge where the girls from MIT's Women's Technology Program were briefly, uncomfortably, reunited, the claustrophobic cubicle where the classically trained soprano from Florida eyed the classically trained soprano from Los Angeles and the classically trained soprano from Cleveland. That it didn't actually work like this was not even relevant, because Portia understood the symbolic power of this place, banal as it was. That power was even greater, she suspected, than the symbolic power of their individual offices upstairs, the conference rooms, even Clarence's comfortable lair with its nonworking fireplace and Asher Durand.

She had been inside the machine for so long that she sometimes forgot how this—this applying to college thing—had looked from the outside, but it did come back, vividly back, when she tried to remember. It had been like watching a mass of seemingly identical sheep cram themselves into a great black building with no windows, knocking against one another, stepping on one another's hooves and over their panicked bodies when they fell. At the other end of the building, only a thin line of sheep trickled out into bountiful fields. And who were these sheep, which looked to all intents and purposes exactly like every sheep who had crowded in? What made them special? Why should they get the meadow when those others were barred? What happened inside that box was a mystery, a secret shielded from the light. She remembered how the class ahead of her in high school had been sorted, with the most cerebral Latin geek shut out from every college he'd applied to while the class's drug dealer of choice had his pick of Harvard and Brown, how the valedictorian who was also the student body president retreated in humiliation to his safety school while the dull-as-dishwater football player trotted off to Cornell. Who were these people in the admissions offices of Swarthmore and Williams, and what could they have been thinking when they accepted Camilla Weldon, Portia's soccer teammate and the most superficial girl she had ever met, but passed over Jordana Miles, who wrote her own column in the school newspaper and had actually published three short articles in *Seventeen* magazine? But there was perhaps no mystery as baffling as that of her own admission to Dartmouth.

She had been a worried high school senior lacking in...well, anything special, really. A pretty good student, pretty good soccer player, pretty good writer, and all around nice person, Portia knew exactly what would happen to her own college application if it arrived, through some warp of time and space, in this room today. With her strong GPA and merely quite good scores, busy athletic schedule, and character-building volunteer efforts, Portia Nathan's application would have left this room with a fatal designation of Academic 3/Non-Academic 4, meaning that in the real world her scholastic skills were solid, but in Princeton's supercharged applicant pool they were unremarkable, and that although she had been busy within her school community, she had not been a leader within that community (NonAc 3) or distinguished herself at the state level (NonAc 2), let alone accomplished something on a national or international scale (NonAc 1). NonAc 1's, of course, were rather thin on the ground, even in Princeton's applicant pool. They were Olympic athletes, authors of legitimately published books, Siemens prizewinners, working film or Broadway actors, International Tchaikovsky Competition violinists, and, yes, national judo champions, and they tended to be easy admits, provided they were strong students, which they usually were. But Portia's application would have landed in the great moving tide of similar applications: great kids, smart kids, hardworking kids who would certainly do great at whatever college they ended up going to, which almost certainly wasn't going to be Princeton.

The secret of her own mediocrity was quite likely similarly held by men and women all over the industry. To wade through these best and brightest seventeen-year-olds was to be, at once, deeply reassured by the goodness and potential of the American near-adult population and deeply humbled by one's own relative shortcomings. These students were absolutely going to make scientific discoveries, solve human problems, produce important works of art and scholarship, and generally—as so many of them pointed out—give back to their communities and make the world a better place. She, on the other hand, was fit only to make life-altering decisions on their behalf. And how could that make sense?

A room like this, she thought, finally gathering up her several files and the three empty canvas bags, had secrets everywhere. Every file drawer—and there were hundreds of them—was crammed with files that were crammed with secrets that were ardently protected by office protocol. (Clarence, in fact, was such a stickler for the privacy of the process that he asked admissions officers not to discuss applicants in the upstairs corridors.) But much mischief could be accomplished here, if one were so inclined, and when you thought about it—as Portia did now—wasn't it sort of surprising that mischief didn't get done all the time? This office, after all, employed a number of undergraduates at the height of the season, who sat for hours at a time in this room, slitting open the incoming envelopes and filing, filing, filing each filament of information into the thousands and thousands of separate folders. Part-time application readers from the town and university community were similarly hired during the most intense months to carefully read applications and write a first reader report. People wandered in and out, delivering food or picking up the shredded documents for recycling. Sometimes, when the receptionist was on break or in the bathroom, prospective students and their families had even stumbled inside, stopping in shock when they realized where they were and what they were seeing. Automated though it was, the system seemed rife with the potential for human influence—accidental or outright sabotage—yet you never heard of it happening. Did it happen? she wondered, closing the office door behind her and hearing the lock click. Was there some secret tradition of midnight fixing, unexplored by the ax-grinding journalists who seemed so fixated on the notion of admission for sale to big donors? Had there ever been an administrative assistant intent on sneaking in his or her cousin's child with a few covert taps of the keyboard? Or a Princeton undergraduate secretly fixing things for a friend from home? How about an idealistic admissions officer who couldn't bear to let some favorite applicant go? It was odd, Portia thought, that these questions had never occurred to her, that she had for years placed a mindless trust in the system and its practitioners, from Clarence on down to the student interns and outside readers, when any of them, probably, could find some way to tamper with the works. If they wanted. And who among them had never wanted?

She felt, when she unlocked her own office door on the second floor, an unmistakable and terribly welcome sense of tranquillity. Here, all was unaltered from the morning of her departure for Vermont, when she had stopped in briefly before meeting Rachel for their walk: her Word-a-Day calendar set to December 24 (when its word was, inauspiciously, "Inauspicious"), a scrawled note on her desk to chase down an application from a Groton student she'd read about in a *Boston Globe* piece on young environmentalists, and three bundled stacks of applications, fifty in each, which Corinne had dropped off. These folders, for which Portia was to act as second reader, hailed from her old district and were doubtless weighted with future doctors, scientists, mathematicians, and engineers from the heavily Pacific Rim immigrant applicant pool, an overendowment of abundantly overqualified kids. She sort of missed them, it occurred to her. She missed the Bay Area kids who hauled their cellos into San Francisco on the weekends, redesigned the computer systems for their schools, and interned with research scientists at Berkeley, and the Silicon Valley kids, shuttling from the tennis team to their community service duties at the tutoring center, and the Hawaiian kids with their fantastic names and intensive luau dance training. They were all in there, of course, and who else? Plus, she was anxious to see what this least favorite colleague, forced from her Mid-Atlantic comfort zone, had made of her new charges.

She stood for a long moment, merely looking.

Outside was starless night and very cold. Inside, it was also dark, and she was entirely alone, except for the kids in their thick and suppliant folders. She felt a kind of duty to them, but not only a duty. She truly preferred to be with them, these fleshless people, their best selves neatly in black-and-white on the two-dimensional paper and primly contained within each orange file. And she felt necessary to them, and she felt accountable to them, and were those really such terrible things to feel? She took off her coat and reached for the topmost folder.

My favorite saying is "no guts, no glory." I can't recall who said it first, but whenever I am in trouble or facing a big challenge, I think about this saying. What it means to me is that anything worth doing is worth doing well, not only in sports but in life. There have been times when our team is in the dumps because things are not going well, but I always draw inspiration from this saying. It has helped me to be a stronger individual everyday.

CHAPTER FOURTEEN

AREN'T THERE THINGS TO TALK ABOUT?

The kid who had written about zombies, it turned out, was the real thing. His impenetrable essay, which she had dispatched to David through the university mail, came winging back the first week in January with a cover note that read: "Definitely. Absolutely. Yes, please."

Portia found the file on the overhead shelf she used as a parking lot for applications awaiting something or other. She slipped this memo in the back and made a note in the "Department Rating" area of the reader's card, a seldom used but highly influential section on the front. Then, before she let it go, and armed with David's endorsement, she made another attempt to glean some sense from the essay:

Certain things are conscious. We may not know what it's like to be a dog, or a bat: but we know (or at least we think we know) that animals have feelings and experiences. We also know that a creature's conscious life is somehow determined by what's going on in its brain. So here's a question: What exactly is the relation between conscious experience and the brain activity that underlies it? Many philosophers—materialists—have thought that conscious experience just is brain activity, in the same sense in which heat just is the motion of molecules. The Zombie thought experiment puts pressure on this sort of view. We seem to be able to imagine or conceive a creature that is just like you in every physical respect, down to the last detail, but which is altogether unconscious. A Zombie will move and talk as if it were awake and genuinely aware of its surroundings; but its inner light is OFF. It has no subjective experience. Now the fact that we can imagine such creatures gives us some reason to believe that they are logically possible. But if it's logically possible for a creature to have a brain just like yours and no conscious experience, then consciousness is not literally identical to brain activity. Instead we should say that brain activity normally causes consciousness, in the sense in which heating up the filament in a lightbulb normally causes it to glow. On this view, the physical aspects of an organism are distinct from its subjective, mental aspects: at best there are various causal laws connecting the two domains.

She read this twice but could not follow the logic past the point about the inner light being OFF. (Did this, in fact, indicate that her own inner light was OFF?) Nonetheless, she wrote her summary and checked "High Priority—Admit" at the bottom of the card, then put the file in the pile of folders to go to Corinne for second reading.

Her colleagues were all in the early stages of their shared annual affliction. The traveling was done for the year, and what remained was this confluence of the cold and winter, and the all-in-our-hands sense of bleak responsibility: to the trustees and faculty, of course, and to the guidance counselors (who were, for better or worse, their partners in the work of getting the right students into the freshman class), and, yes, to the alumni, because Princeton honored its graduates and wished to retain their high opinion. But mainly to the applicants themselves, who collectively seemed to hover everywhere in Portia's imagination, like spectral Jude the Obscures, waiting for the verdict on their futures and—Portia very much feared—their sense of self-worth. Sometimes she imagined them, waiflike across Cannon Green and behind West College and along Nassau Street, winding their white, supplicating hands through the great iron gates. (This was not, needless to say, an image she shared with her colleagues.) No one was complaining aloud, but then again, no one had to;

the weight of the burden was intense and everywhere, and the entire crew (fighting the same cold) shuffled through the corridors with the same set of dour thoughts.

Portia, too, was well into her winter sinus misery, a malady that typically began after New Year's, did battle with a tag team of antibiotics over the winter months, and finally surrendered to modern medicine just in time for the pollen surge in April. It had begun right on schedule the week she returned from Vermont, flickering behind her cheekbones as the year turned, sneaking tendrils of pain along the facial nerves, coiling around her ears and scalp. At her appointment with the internist she got a prescription for Ceftin, the best of a bad lot, and asked for Ambien, which she'd been given but was not yet brave enough to use. Instead, she lay in bed timing the pounding in her head against the dull clicking of the bedside clock, feeling the pain across her entire face, as if the bones of her skull were contracting steadily, the flesh struggling against containment. This was not an effective sleep aid. The house would not seem to warm up, and she wondered if there was something she was supposed to have done to the boiler after her return; but the boiler was Mark's domain, and she did not want to ask him about it. She did not want to ask him about anything. She did not want her reverie that he did not exist, and that therefore nothing had happened between them, to be broken. Besides, she was hardly at home, so it hardly mattered that she was cold.

Once again, this year, the applications had jumped—up eight hundred this time—more evidence of the still swelling population bubble of teenagers and, too, perhaps, that their efforts to reach beyond the traditional applicant pool, to students who might not have thought to apply ten or even five years earlier, were proving successful. It all seemed utterly overwhelming just now, with every surface in her office piled with files and boxes more waiting downstairs in the office, but no one was panicking because they always felt this way at this particular moment in the cycle. There had never, in Portia's recollection, been any real worry that they wouldn't finish in time, though the task did have a way of expanding to fill every worker's every available hour.

This was the point in the admissions cycle when Portia became reacquainted with many of the students she'd spent the previous spring encouraging to apply to Princeton. Selling the university, of course, was not difficult, but overselling it to potential applicants sat near the top of every critic's list of complaints (the gist of this being that top-tier colleges went out of their way to get vast numbers to apply, only to admit an ever smaller percentage and earn, as a result, a higher *U.S. News & World Report* ranking). But while Portia did sometimes wish there were a way to selectively discourage the students she met while visiting high schools, she would never—and could never—do it. Not only was it the office's philosophy that every student should feel welcome to submit an application, and that equal and thorough consideration awaited everyone who did so, the fact was that you just couldn't tell, when you looked into their serious, tremulous faces at the information sessions, who was the kid who'd cheated his way through Calculus BC and who was the kid whose English teacher was going to call him "the most exciting student I've had in my thirty-year career." What if she discouraged some student who couldn't break 1200 on his SATs from applying, when he would turn out to be idio-syncratically cerebral, a true original kid whose unqualifiable abilities would lift the discourse in every class he enrolled in? How could you know that the thoroughly dull high school junior struggling to make conversation over cider and cookies would emerge as the writing program's most gifted novelist in a decade? Still, when their faces came back to her now, swimming up from the accounts of debating triumphs and stage fright at the piano recital, she sometimes wished she'd been able to say to them: *Don't. Don't try for this. Don't want this or, worse, make some terrible connection between who you are as a human being and whether or not you get in.*

The pool, once again, was absurdly strong, the applicants more driven, more packaged, more worried, even than the year before. They were decent kids who had never considered that their life experience was at all unusual, since they were like everyone else they knew, so when they set foot outside the United States, on a church home-building trip to Mexico or a visit to relatives in Bombay, they were stunned by the poverty, dumbstruck to discover how wealthy and privileged they were. They wanted to fix things, cure diseases, make it better. They wanted to turn into the amazing people their teachers swore they were and their parents had always planned for them to be. They wanted not to fall short at this finish line of their entire lives (so far) and be that kid who'd thought he was so great, who'd aimed so far above himself. Portia felt for them, of course. She wished, as she checked, again and again, the box reading "Only if room" (a euphemism for no, as there was never room), that she could reach through the folder to the kid beyond and say, *Anyone would be ecstatic to have their child turn out as great as you,* and, *Please, go and do all the things you say you intend to do.*

Few of them were eliminated easily. The campaigners, who fashioned elaborate dossiers with glossy eight-by-tens of their grinning faces and sent in reams of thick stock pages enumerating each spelling test and charity walk as far back as middle school, could not be dismissed out of hand, because you couldn't hold someone's personality against them, and besides, some idiot might have told them to do it. The student who provided an eighteenth-century family tree with the name of a distant ancestor circled in red could not be eliminated instantly, though his cover letter said he wanted to go to Princeton because his antecedent had "helped set up the place." The girl who had entered her e-mail address as HotSxxygrrrl69@yahoo.com could not be declined on the spot, because even Princeton applicants were allowed to be idiotic teenagers. The ones with low SAT scores couldn't be dispatched quickly, because some of them were superb and thoughtful writers, with recs that begged her to see past the numbers to this singular awakening mind. So when she came to an applicant who, given the benefit of every doubt, fell decisively short, she was relieved: Here was one she did not have to bring to committee, sell to her colleagues, sell to Clarence. The math geeks who hadn't done any math outside of school—"Only if room." The literary types who were poor writers—"Only if room." The faux philosophers, high on Nietzsche and Ayn Rand, who only hoped to find professors worthy of having them as a student. She had no need to trouble David with their essays:

As Sartre wrote in his play No Exit, hell is other people. This play illustrates the theory of existentialism, which is the philosophy that since God is dead, we are all ultimately responsible for everything that happens to us. This philosophy is valid in my opinion. When I first read Sartre's play, I realized that other people are cowards who hide behind religion and rules and laws. They think that their lives are not really up to them, and this makes them lazy and complacent. Since then, I have been reading the great works of philosophy on my own, starting with the Apology of Socrates which shows that it is important to stand up for what you believe in even if everyone else thinks you're wrong. After one year of intense study, I began to think of my own philosophy. I call it metaexistentialism, and it builds on the profound insights of Socrates and Sartre. My first book, Dionysus Novus: A Treatise on Agony and Ecstasy, is almost complete and I hope to publish it soon. It argues that we are most real when we experience intense emotions, and that those who are not capable of intense emotion live lives that are mediocre and sad. In college I hope to develop these ideas, and possibly teach courses in philosophy and literature to impart my philosophy to others. I have found that other people often find it hard to understand my theories. But they are not professional philosophers, and so that is to be expected. I look forward to studying with important professors who will definitely understand what I am saying.

"Only if room."

The Fannie Lou Hamer essay had not turned up in the database, but Portia, reading through it again, could not let go of her suspicions. Misspelling both the title and author of your favorite book, as this Rhode Island girl had done, was pretty close to unforgivable on a college application, but it was the disparity between this carelessness and the superbly fluid, well-constructed—and correctly spelled—essay that bothered her. There was little else noteworthy in the application. The girl was a strong student who'd taken summer classes at Brown and played squash. She did like the fact that the girl had written about Hamer, not a more obvious civil rights figure—that counted for something—but in the end she could not disentangle herself from that *Pride and Priviledge*. "Only if room." And there would not be room.

The "national judo champion" did not appear anywhere on the Web site of the United States Judo Federation. Portia looked through the application again and found nothing to outweigh this information. She marked the "Unlikely" box, effectively concluding the matter.

Which left . . . the application with the unchecked disciplinary waiver. It was three-thirty in the afternoon when she picked up the phone, summoning what she could recall of the counselor from their meeting last May. No, April, on a swing through Boston: Noble and Greenough, Milton Academy, a charter school in Roxbury run by a heroic woman in her sixties, and Porter Country Day School, Portia's final stop. The college counselor was in her late thirties, small with blond hair blown straight and an accent, Portia remembered thinking, more New York than Boston. Her name, right on the secondary school report, was Elisa Rosen. She picked up quickly, as if she'd been waiting by the phone, and if she sounded initially distracted, the utterance of the word *Princeton* made her snap to attention.

"Of course I remember," she said with great warmth. "You had a name from Shakespeare. Juliet? Helena?"

"Portia."

"Yes! The quality of mercy. Very appropriate for an admissions officer."

Portia nodded. It was not the first time she had heard this.

"How can I help?" said Elisa Rosen.

"Oh, I just had a quick question about one of your seniors."

"You've got about twenty from us this year."

"Yes. His name is Sean Aronson? I wanted—"

"Ah." The warmth in her voice had fled, quite suddenly. "And what about?"

"This may have been nothing," she said carefully. "I noticed that the disciplinary action question wasn't checked. It's not a huge deal." She listened into the silence. Which grew. "Unless," Portia said, frowning, "it is."

More silence.

"Ms. Rosen?"

"Elisa, please," the woman said. "I'm thinking about this."

Portia, now thoroughly alert, sat waiting, the application open before her, reading and rereading the question in question, as if she did not know it by heart.

"You know," Elisa said abruptly, "I think...would you mind terribly if I phoned you back in a few minutes? I'd like to phone you back."

"All right," said Portia, giving her the direct line. She hung up the phone and opened the application to the first page. Dad, an ophthalmologist, went to Brandeis. Mom, a homemaker, went to Wheaton. Two sibs, both older, one in college, one in medical school. Swimming—lots of swimming—tennis. Probable major: economics; possible career plans: law. Summers: tennis pro, work for Dad, calculus and history at Andover. One essay about his swim coach, one about tutoring a neighbor's child who had trouble with math. His favorite movie was *Donnie Darko,* the single most cited film in this year's "Few Details" section (trailed only slightly, incredibly enough, by *The Princess Bride*). She'd had the impression that *Donnie Darko* was a horror film until some boy from Maine wrote an essay about why he loved it. Now she'd concluded it was merely bizarre.

The phone rang, and Portia noted the caller ID on her phone, which was not, surprisingly, the school she had just phoned, but 617, the right area code. Tentatively, she answered. "Portia Nathan."

"It's Elisa Rosen."

"Oh yes. Hello, Elisa."

"I'm sorry I couldn't talk. I wanted to have this conversation on my cell." She laughed shortly. "I'm actually in my car right now."

By this time, Portia was paying very close attention. "I take it there's an issue here."

"Oh yes. And I decided, if any of you ever asked, I was going to answer. You're the first one to call, by the way. Congratulations," she said with deep sarcasm.

Portia found a piece of notepaper on her desk and wrote the name of the counselor and the date.

"I must ask you, please, to make this an off-the-record conversation. Can you agree to that?"

Portia considered. Sean Aronson had an Academic rating of 2 and a NonAc 3, smack in the middle of the pool. He wasn't a legacy, which vastly decreased the likelihood of a belligerent phone call if he was rejected. She could probably terminate the application without consulting Clarence. "Well, let's do this. Let's have a conversation, and if we come to something I think my boss needs to hear about, I'll stop you and you can think about it. All right?"

"Yes," she said after a minute.

"So what are we talking about here?"

"He got hold of the chemistry final in December. We have no idea how. His teacher has no idea how. Apparently, he sold it to at least two of his classmates, but we can't compel him to tell us who they were, which hasn't done wonders for our morale. Plus, when I first met with him before Christmas, he very clearly implied that he'd done it before. He wanted us to know he'd been having his way with the system for a while."

Portia, listening, turned over the pages of the file to the secondary school transcript. A's and A minuses, with, appropriately enough, a single B plus in Foundations of Ethics, junior year.

"So he was suspended, then?"

"Well, that's just it. His father told us that if we suspended him or did anything to the transcript or the recommendations, he'd sue the school. He also told our headmaster he was prepared to claim the chemistry teacher had given Sean the answers as part of an attempted seduction, and he was ready to make a sexual harassment charge. And the chemistry teacher does happen to be gay, which didn't help. So we were in meetings for days with our attorney, and we finally felt we just had to let it go. We had to," she said defensively. "We didn't want to. I mean, what I've told you, it doesn't even scratch the surface of how truly gruesome it was. And both of his references had already sent out their letters, including, I should point out, his chemistry teacher, who'd written him this glowing recommendation in November. It would have meant contacting eleven colleges with whom we've had good relationships and telling them we had a cheating scandal. But you know what? When it came time for me to fill out the SSR, I just couldn't bring myself to check that box. You know? I couldn't do it. It was my silent protest."

"I see," said Portia, writing quickly. "Well, thank you for your candor."

"I'm in my car," Elisa Rosen said again. "I feel like I'm in a spy novel. But I didn't want anyone to hear me talking about this. We kept the students from finding out, I don't know how. But if we hadn't, we'd have been overrun with parents demanding we throw him out and inform the colleges. They don't want Sean taking their kid's place, and I have to tell you, I don't really blame them. But you know what I hate most about this whole thing?"

"What?" Portia asked.

"I hate the fact that he's actually a sweet kid. Seriously, I've known Sean for years. You couldn't meet a nicer guy. Always smiling, always wants to tell you about some book he's just read or something he saw in the paper. He's very popular, but he's one of those popular kids who reaches out to the misfits, you know what I mean? And I'm not excusing what he did at all, but I gotta tell you, I don't think I'd last a week with a father like that. I mean, angry, angry man. I could hear him screaming at his son outside in the parking lot after our meeting. I wanted to call Child Protective Services."

"Okay," said Portia, frowning.

"So I'm just telling you, this is what happened. And I have no idea what he'll be like when he gets away from home. I mean, Sean is really smart, really capable. He can absolutely handle the work at Princeton, and I'm sure he'd be an asset to the university. But it's right that you have the information."

There was a light tap at her office door. Portia looked up.

"Are there any other applicants you'd like to discuss?" Elisa Rosen said hopefully.

"Oh, I'm sure your kids will do great," Portia reassured her. "This is the one I've gotten to so far. If I have any questions, I'll call. Hey, listen, Elisa, I really appreciate your talking to me. And I will keep this confidential, I promise."

"Thank you so much!"

"Okay, I've got someone in my office, so I'd better go. Come in!" she said loudly, to underscore this statement.

"I won't keep you, then," said Elisa Rosen, as if she'd initiated the conversation.

The office door opened. Rachel stood in the doorway.

"All right," Portia said, distracted. "Good-bye."

She replaced the handset and sighed.

"Muhammad comes to the mountain," said Rachel.

"Would Muhammad like to sit down?"

"Muhammad has brought you a soy latte."

"Oh. Good. Thanks." And awkwardly, she took it.

"This is what I'm resorting to," said Rachel. "You know, they stopped me at the desk. Do I look like an insane parent to you?"

"No, no," said Portia.

"I had to show my ID! It was like getting carded!"

"It's policy," Portia said, apologizing. "We had a man come up last year. He walked right into Clarence's office and said he wouldn't leave till Clarence explained in detail why his nephew hadn't been admitted."

"Really?" She seemed surprised. "I didn't know."

"Really. He was in there for fifteen minutes before anybody even knew about it. I mean, poor Clarence had no idea if the guy was dangerous or what. It's not like we have a secret panic button for campus security."

"Maybe you should," she said.

"Well, maybe we should. But we still like to operate under the delusion that everyone understands we do the best we can with a difficult situation."

Rachel set down her own coffee on Portia's desk and eyed the towering stack of folders on the spare chair.

"Let me," said Portia, moving them. "I have a system."

"I hope so," said Rachel, sounding dubious. She sat.

"Thank you," Portia said, taking the cover off her latte. "I needed this."

"Well, that's a lucky break," said Rachel, launching right in. "I wouldn't know what you need. I mean, how many messages have I left for you? I even started dropping by, but you're never home."

"It's reading season," Portia said, blowing on her coffee.

"That's bullshit. You always read at home."

"Well, this year I'm reading in the office."

"You look terrible."

"Thank you," said Portia, deeply hurt.

"Oh, shit. You don't look terrible. Well, actually, you don't look great, sweetie. But I couldn't care less how you look. I just care if you're all right."

Portia sighed. "Fine," she said dully. "Whatever."

"I'm furious at him. I told him so. I said, 'I had no idea you were such an asshole.'"

Portia searched for a response to this and couldn't locate one.

"I mean, I had her in my house! How could he do that to me? Like I would ever, *ever* have had her at my dinner table if I'd known."

"They're your colleagues, Rachel. You've got to play nice."

"Don't be ridiculous. English departments are known for internal warfare. It's our stock in trade. Jesus, Portia, I called you as soon as I heard. I'm so sorry. So sorry."

She shrugged. Again, she looked in vain for some strong emotion. But nothing. The oddness of this, she promised herself, she would turn her attention to at some—hopefully distant—point in the future.

"I was surprised," she said finally. "I didn't know. Clearly, I should have known, but I didn't. And now…" She trailed off, looking intently away from Rachel's stricken face and then drifting, drifting, searching the bulletin board behind Rachel's head to find something to hold on to. Photograph of Princeton's oldest living graduate at the head of the annual P-Rade, in a golf cart driven by someone in a tiger suit. Photograph of the baseball team, Ivy League champions, 2003, all of them graduated by now. Gym schedule for Pilates, yoga, and spinning from the previous spring. Nothing. Nothing.

"I just have so much work to do," she said, coming back to her default position.

"Are you sleeping? You don't look like you're sleeping. You certainly don't look like you're eating."

Portia looked down at herself, perplexed. What was Rachel talking about? She wore three layers at least: long-sleeved cotton shirt, turtleneck sweater, a fleece pullover with a zippered neck. The fleece had a small stain, she noticed, by the right wrist. From food? She couldn't imagine. Actually, she had only put the fleece on this morning, and she couldn't remember eating anything so far today. The shirt and sweater she had worn for a couple of days.

"Don't be silly. Just, you know, catching meals whenever I can. Do you know we have eight hundred *more* applications than last year? Do you know the median SAT is up another twenty points? It's out of control."

"I stopped at your house on the way over here. I looked through the window. Portia, I'm very concerned."

"I'm busy. Mark was the neatnik, you know."

"That's not what you always told me."

"Really? Look, Rachel, I'm dealing with things. I just have work right now. And I'm lucky nobody cares what I look like."

"It's the fact that you don't care what you look like that worries me."

"I just talked to a guidance counselor in Massachusetts. She called me from her car. She didn't want to call me from her office."

"This is a non sequitur, Portia."

"No, but it's interesting. She wanted me to know that her advisee got caught cheating on his chemistry final. They think he sold the answers to his classmates, too, but they can't prove it."

"So what's the problem?" said Rachel, humoring her. "Why even talk about it?"

"She couldn't tell us on the application because the student's father threatened to sue. So they had to, you know, sup with the devil. Can you believe it?"

"Of course I can," Rachel said, setting down her coffee. "I just can't believe we're talking about that and not about the fact that you've just split up with Mark, you look dreadful, and you haven't answered my increasingly hysterical phone messages."

"But isn't it sick that the parents have become so powerful? And she's in her car, on the phone! Like a police informant or something."

"Portia," Rachel said intently.

"The thing is," she rolled on, "I sort of understand. This kid. They must all be, just, *crazy* with this thing. It must be terrible to go through this now. The pressure from the parents and their peers, and the schools, too. Is it any wonder that some of them screw up? The real question is why more of them don't. Or maybe they do! How would we know? I mean, how do we even know they're taking their own SATs and writing their own applications? Next thing, ETS is going to ask for a fingerprint or a strand of hair before they let you have the test booklet. And the sad thing is, these applicants...they're just teenagers. And teenagers are supposed to fuck up. I mean, when else do you get to do that? But if they fuck up, or if they fuck up and they get caught, like this one, it's the end of everything."

"Fine, but that doesn't change the fact that he did fuck up," Rachel observed. "If he did that here, we'd throw him out. You know that."

"Yes, I understand that," she said, blithely deflecting the logic of this. "But what I mean is, this particular kid, who got caught, probably isn't any worse than the ones we're going to let in instead of him. Maybe he's the best of the lot and we're going to pass him over. And these parents, I know they're awful, but I feel for them, too. Because, you know what's weird? They're not older than we are anymore. All these years, I've been reading applications from high school seniors whose parents are twenty years older than me, ten years older, five years older. Now they're my age, Rachel. If I'd had a kid, like, at the end of college, he'd be this age now, in twelfth grade. He could be applying to Princeton right now. Do you see how weird that is?"

Rachel was looking steadily at her, hands in her lap, lightly holding the now empty coffee cup.

"You know," Portia heard herself say, "he hasn't called me once. He hasn't come to the house. It's like...boom! Sixteen years. I mean, doesn't he want a couch or something? Aren't there things to talk about?"

Rachel leaned forward in her chair, her calf nudging a tilting pile of folders. Instinctively, Portia reached out to shift them.

"Yes," said Rachel. "There *are* things to talk about. Even if Mark doesn't seem capable of talking about them, maybe you need to talk about them. And if not with him, and if not with me, then what about someone else?"

"Oh, Rachel..." She sighed. "I'm *fine*."

"Oh, Portia," Rachel echoed, "I do not think so."

When my church group arrived in the small Mexican town where we were to
spend a week building houses, I looked around and thought, this is a town?
I saw hovels made of cinderblocks, without windows or floors. Women and
children carrying what looked like very unclean water from a pond about half a
mile away, dogs and cats everywhere. Everyone looked hungry. I'd known there
was poverty in Mexico, of course. But I couldn't believe people were living this
way. I couldn't believe that I hadn't realized people were living this way.

CHAPTER FIFTEEN

A FEW DETAILS

In February, she came face-to-face with Jeremiah Balakian, twice in the same grim week.

First in the pile at ten on a Monday morning, three hours into her day. Her door was shut, her jeans stiff with wear, last night's snow from her trudge through town drying into white rings on her boots. The folder began, as always, with the test sheet. It showed that the applicant had taken the SATs the previous spring. Verbal was an 800—common enough in this applicant pool. The math was lower—680—but respectable. There were no SATII test results, but there were plenty of APs. Eight in all, likewise taken the previous spring. They made an unbroken line of 5's.

She turned to the second page of the application, where extracurricular, personal, and volunteer activities were listed and defined. More often than not, Princeton applicants overflowed the available seven lines with their debate teams and varsity sports, volunteer work and church activities. This applicant's was entirely blank except for a two-word notation on the top line: "Independent study." She wondered if she might be missing something.

Portia went back to the reader's card, where Martha's downstairs staff had pulled the relevant grades from the high school transcript, inserting them into a grid for each year: A's, B's, C's, D's, and F's. It was a shocker.

Mostly C's and several D's; nothing higher than a B. And no AP courses at all. But how, she wondered, given his scores on the AP exams, could that make sense? She had sometimes seen this kind of syncopation on the exams of homeschool applicants, but the applicant had clearly attended high school. She paged forward, past essays and signed forms, to the guidance counselor's portion of the paperwork and found, as she'd expected to find, an official transcript and forms. They were from Keene Central High School and were accompanied by the customary brochure about the school and its demographics, lists of clubs and teams ("Go Lions!"), and roster of colleges attended by the last five years' worth of graduates. Then, tucked behind these, she found letters related to the applicant's senior year at the Quest School. A page of densely written course evaluations from various teachers. And letters. The first letter was from John R. Halsey, humanities teacher and student adviser.

So. Yes, she nodded, shivering in her layers of dirty clothing. Here was Jeremiah.

She returned again to the front of the reader's card and looked at the Academic and Non-Academic rankings, finding herself entirely unprepared to choose one. Academic 1's were kids who had 800 SATs and job lots of AP 5's. Academic 5's were kids who had barely scraped themselves through high school. Jeremiah, apparently, was both of these. She resisted the momentary impulse to average everything out and give him a 3. Clearly, whatever he was, he was not a 3. Not that these ratings were in any way binding. They were a signpost, not an evaluation, a little shorthand to the reader as he or she embarked on a thorough consideration of everything in the folder; but setting Jeremiah up with a rating of Ac 3/NonAc 5 would only make everything an uphill battle, at least for the readers who followed her. She decided to leave the ratings aside for the moment. Instead, she began to read the application itself, slowly and with judgment suspended to the best of her ability.

Balakian, Jeremiah Vartan. She hadn't realized, when she'd met him, that he was Armenian. She didn't recall having heard his last name at all.

Home address: Keene, New Hampshire.

Possible area of academic concentration: "Humanities: art, history, languages, literature."

Possible career or professional plans. This he had left blank.

Place of birth: Lawrence, Massachusetts.

Ethnicity: Caucasian.

The address of the school she remembered all too well: One Inspiration Way, North Plain, New Hampshire.

His father was Aram Balakian, occupation retail sales, employer Stop & Shop, Keene, N.H. He had an associate's degree, Keene Community College.

His mother was Nan Balakian. The space for education was left blank. Retail sales. Stop & Shop, Keene, N.H.

No siblings.

Portia turned over the reader's card and wrote, "Mom and dad: grocery clerks. No sibs," in the "Background Information" section. Then she wrote and circled the letters *NC*, meaning that the parents had not attended college. Jeremiah, if he managed it, would be the first. She left the spaces for "Academic" and "Non-Academic" activities blank.

Under "Summers" he had written:

For the past two summers I have been employed full time at a supermarket in Keene, rotating among various positions, from stocker to warehouse to checkout, none of them particularly taxing. I wasn't very optimistic about the job at the outset, but I came to discover that examining someone's groceries is a strangely intimate and fascinating activity. When you know what people are putting in their mouths and on their bodies, you know a great deal about them: physically, emotionally, even politically. Sometimes I'd want to confront them about their choices: *Don't you know what this food is going to do to your blood pressure? Don't you know this manufacturer has one of the worst environmental records in the world? Did you know that for the same price as this fake cheese you could get real cheese?* But of course, a humble checker can't say such things. We scan and pack and take their checks or food stamps or credit cards. I learned a great deal, and I hope I'll never have to work there another day in my life.

She smiled. She flipped back in the application to check the "Work Experience" section for the name of the employer: Stop & Shop. He had worked for his parents' employer. Under "Summer" she wrote, "Grocery Clerk, FT X 2," meaning that he'd been employed for both of the past two summers, the ones Princeton cared most about. Then she turned back to the application and frowned at the "Few Details" section.

This had been a fairly recent innovation, part wink to the applicants (See? We have a sense of humor!), part palate cleanser between the nuts and bolts of the front-loaded information at the beginning of the application and the essays to come. The questions changed a little every year, but they generally asked the kids to name their favorite books, music, sources of inspiration, films, mementos, and words. (The words tended to be fairly grotesque. In the past month alone, she had come across "defenestrate" more times than she cared to remember.) This year's tweak was "Your favorite line from a movie," which had reaped hundreds of sentences Portia had never heard before and many, many citations of the classic *Godfather* line "Leave the gun. Take the cannoli."

Jeremiah's choices, to say the least, were unusual. His favorite book was Wiesenthal's *The Murderers Among Us*. His favorite source of inspiration: "Whatever book I'm reading at the time." Under favorite Web site he wrote, "I'm sorry, I don't have a computer." His favorite line from a movie? "Now tell me, do you feel anything at all?" from *Sunday Bloody Sunday*. She hadn't seen the film in a decade, at least, and yet, reading the line here, so out of context, she was amazed at how quickly and fully this opening line came back, spoken over a black screen: just that male voice — Peter Finch's voice — and then the image of a hand — Peter Finch's hand — palpating the bloated abdomen of a middle-aged man. It was a ringing, terribly bleak line, sharply foreshadowing the ninety-odd minutes of interpersonal desolation to come. The adjectives he'd chosen to describe himself were "loner (but not the scary kind)" and "fervent." Being a loner was not, she thought, something the modern teenager was often eager to admit to. "Fervent" she had never come across before.

Usually, there wasn't much to take from the "Few Details" section. Occasionally, something unusual was worth writing down. In the section of the reader's card marked "FD," she wrote: "*Sunday Bloody Sunday*," but mostly because she enjoyed thinking that Corinne would not know what it meant.

Now, and only now, it was time to read the essays.

For his longer essay, Jeremiah had chosen one of the most popular prompts, an Einstein quote: "The important thing is not to stop questioning. Curiosity has its own reason for existing. One cannot help but be in awe when one contemplates the mysteries of eternity, of life, of the marvelous structure of reality. It is enough if one tries to comprehend only a little of this mystery every day." (Albert Einstein, Princeton resident 1933–1955)

She leaned over the page, awkwardly aware of how good she wanted it to be.

I became an autodidact at eight years old, when I realized that my teachers were not going to be able to teach me. It wasn't that they were unequal to the task of teaching me—they weren't. And it wasn't that they didn't wish to teach me. I think they wished to very much. But they were busy. They needed to keep order, muster the slower ones, persuade various second graders to stop biting, pulling hair, and doing disgusting things with their body fluids. I think I spent most of that year *waiting* to learn, but I finally figured out that I could be putting that time to better use. So I set off, without much direction. I read biographies, mainly, because I had no idea how other people had lived their lives. When biographies led me into different disciplines, I followed them until my interests shifted, but I always picked up the thread with a new life story. I never bothered to devise a master plan. I had no concept of a master plan. What I was doing was almost hedonistic. It certainly was not disciplined. It has continued now for ten years.

All this time, of course, I was in school, but just barely. I'm sure it does not reflect well on me when I say that my high school classes, in the main, did not interest me, so I mostly ignored them, sometimes scraping by with passing grades, sometimes not. My high school, Keene Central, tried various methods to bring me into the fold. I was threatened with detention, which was fine with me because it was a quiet place to read, and suspension, which was even better since my parents both worked during the day, which meant that I could read in comfort, at home. I was told that I would be held back to repeat tenth grade, then eleventh grade, but to me, additional years of school meant additional years when I would not have to support myself, when I could simply continue on as I had been. Still, I believed that my guidance counselor meant well, and I regularly promised to mend my ways, but it always had to be after I finished the next book, and then the book after that.

Then, last spring I had a chance meeting with a teacher from a new private school, not far from Keene. On his advice, I registered to take AP tests in some subjects that were interesting to me. I also took the SAT a few weeks later and did all right on the verbal part, but I should have reviewed the math before I took it. Most important, though, was that I persuaded my parents to let me leave Keene Central. (It was difficult to persuade them, but not at all difficult to persuade Keene Central!) In the past few months I have spent at Quest, I have at long last learned to bend my pursuits into some thematic shape, to make links between ideas, to consider opposing ideas in a critical way. I have also developed the long overdue discipline to complete assignments, prepare for tests, and meet deadlines. For the first time, I feel an immense exhilaration about where all of this may be going, and what it has been for. Of course, it is frustrating to think about how things might have been different if I had been exposed much earlier to this kind of guidance, but it should also be said that I never thought of going to college until I began studying at Quest, so now, perhaps, my education may be extended and deepened in this new direction.

The sum total of all I've learned is that I don't know anything, really, only little pieces of things. I haven't been anywhere except for a few trips to family in Watertown, mainly because my parents aren't wealthy but also because they are settled people who don't like to travel. I haven't had any interesting jobs, but I do work during the summer at the supermarket where my parents are employed. Mostly, what I do is read. Right now, my interests are the architecture of early cities, the Ottoman Empire, George Sand, Sojourner Truth, and contemporary Japanese fiction (in translation, unfortunately; another shortcoming I would like to rectify). Earlier this fall I immersed myself in American Pop Art, with particular reference to Warhol and Lichtenstein. If I am accepted to college, I would like to delve deeper into art and architecture, European literature, Eastern religions, and the history of medicine. I would also like to continue with Latin, which was not offered at Keene Central, and which I was only able to begin this fall, and especially philosophy. I have left the question of possible future plans unanswered, because there are too many things I would need to find out first. Thank you very much for your time.

All right, she thought, relieved. So it was good. But the problems were glaring. By his own admission, he had ignored his classes, declined to follow the curriculum, and resisted guidance from teachers and administrators. Clearly, failure did not perturb him. What did? She considered for a long moment before writing, in the space allotted for Essay #1: "Autodidact since age 8. Has not done well in school but has read incessantly, esp. biographies. Clearly values education over academic 'success.' Complex picture here. Fine writer."

His second essay:

I discovered early on that I was not at all interested in the practical side of mathematics (for example, in the problem solving that anyone who wants to use math for science or engineering needs to know). What I did care about were questions like: How we can *know* that $2+2=4$? And that's not so much a mathematical question as a philosophical question. Actually, it's no different from other questions about the basic sources of our knowledge: How do we *know* that it's wrong to cause pain? How do I *know* that something I'm observing is actually happening? In all of these cases, we have knowledge of a fact that doesn't derive from ordinary sense perception. So how is that possible?

For a while, I did make an effort to follow the math curriculum in school, but I knew that I was always gravitating toward things that weren't really central to the class material. When we studied geometry, for instance, we were taught Euclid's axioms and postulates. The textbook mentioned that one of the postulates was controversial—given a line, exactly one line parallel to the original can be drawn through any given point—and that it might even be false "for our world." This was baffling to me: mathematics is supposed to be certain! If this axiom is wrong, how do we know that others aren't wrong? And if the others might be wrong, how can we claim to know anything in geometry, or in any other part of mathematics? I actually departed the curriculum completely at this point, and started reading philosophy on my own, which is exactly what I was doing when I was busy getting that D in eleventh grade math.

Since then, I've noticed that, in other classes, I tend to get stuck on questions that are raised in the very first chapter of the textbook: What is life? (in biology). What is a poem? (in English). What is the past? (in history). To be honest, I've never understood how people get beyond those questions to what comes later. It's not that I'm not interested in what comes later: I'm very interested! But I just haven't been able to get there on my own. Of course, I realize now that my unwillingness to play by the rules in my classes is going to end up hurting me, probably in ways I never considered when I was blowing off my homework. I wish I could go back and make a different decision, but if I could do that, I'd probably know so much math and physics that college would be a little redundant. So instead, I'm just going to hope it all works out for the best.

If she were in a different frame of mind, Portia thought, she might note the fact that the two essays were not very dissimilar. She liked, in general, for an applicant to take these two opportunities to show distinct facets of themselves: scholarly and personal, scholarly and musical, scholarly and socially conscious. But Jeremiah, she was getting the impression, was not particularly multifaceted. This — this avid, self-directed scholarship — was what he was, and all he was. There had been little development of a self, which was of course not all that unusual for the age group. But Jeremiah was a consumer of information and ideas. It was the most real, possibly the only real, focus in his life. This would hardly make him a hit in the eating clubs, but on the other hand, Princeton was one of the few universities where the Jeremiahs of the world could fruitfully congregate. He should be here, probably, where he could meet his peers and be properly nurtured.

In the comment space for the second essay, she wrote: "Following his own curriculum in math/philosophy. Not interested in applied math but 'gets stuck' on big questions. Reading far ahead even as he acknowledges underperforming in class. Again, strong writer."

She read what she had written and frowned. Lemonade from lemons, certainly. But lemons in abundance.

The secondary school report from Keene Central, which came next in the file, was a definite cold shower. She'd known what was coming because of the tally on the reader's card, but the transcript itself was still a blow, the very picture of a checked-out student. His highest grades, B's, had been earned in history and English; his lowest, mainly D's, in math and science. The cumulative picture of these two extremely important years of high school implied that Jeremiah didn't even belong in the pool, let alone in the class. With a sinking feeling, she turned to the brief letter by his former guidance counselor, a Burton McNulty:

> I was surprised to learn that Jeremiah had decided to go to college, because even though I tried to motivate him to do just that while he was at Keene Central, the fact is he never seemed to care about what he was going to do after high school. Jeremiah's main goal in life, in my view, was to be left alone. He hated to be reminded that he wouldn't pass English if he didn't turn in his paper, or he wouldn't pass math if he didn't sit for the final. Of course, we have had many, many students over the years who fit that description, but what was so frustrating about Jeremiah was how smart he clearly was. If only he'd applied himself, he could have been at the very top of our class, not languishing in the bottom with kids who weren't going anywhere in life. Time and again I sat him down and told him he needed to get himself together, that it would be an awful shame to waste what he had, and I thought I'd gotten through to him more than once, but then I'd get the final reports from his teachers and see he'd failed to complete assignments and skipped tests. Sometimes they really didn't want to fail him because they recognized his potential, but they were obligated to because of the missing papers and test scores. I can tell you that a couple of those D's and low C's actually should have been failing grades, but the teachers just couldn't bring themselves to do it.
>
> Jeremiah is a very nice young man, and I can't help but believe that we failed him here. I wish I had known what to say to him or how to help him, but I just came up short again and again. If the teachers at his new school were able to do something with him, then I'm very pleased. As for college, I'm a bit at a loss about what to tell you. Perhaps college will bring something out of him that high school could not. Can he do the work at a place like Princeton? Well, he's smart enough, obviously. But WILL he do the work? I just don't know. I wish only the best for him and I would love to see him succeed.

Portia, tapping her pen, read the recommendation through again, trying to spin it. This was, to say the least, an unusual letter for a Princeton applicant. Princeton applicants were typically the pride of their schools, the one in a decade for grievously overburdened counselors at massive public schools, or just the fine young men and women that private schools with long Princeton connections existed to produce. Every now and then, of course, as in the case of the morally deficient Sean Aronson, there might be a whiff of ambivalence rising from a letter of reference, a sotto voce implication that, while this was certainly a swell kid, the admissions officer reading this letter might be encouraged to look elsewhere on the list of applicants from this particular school. And though she had many times encountered students whose guidance counselors believed them to be underachievers, she could never recall a gap as big as this one. "Johnny could have been valedictorian if he had not devoted so much training time to track." "Lori might have ranked much higher if she were not so fully committed to her church activities." But Jeremiah had not thrived in high school at all, and without the excuse of extracurricular passions. He had been too busy reading. He had not cared to succeed.

She was a little surprised to find herself as engaged as she was. On the face of it, this application was not a difficult call. Was it fair, after all, to take a place from a kid who had worked his heart out—more accurately, to take it from roughly *nine* kids who had worked their hearts out—and give it to a kid who hadn't even tried to toe the line? Jeremiah, for all his potential, had not looked up from his books long enough to seek guidance that was his for the asking. There were abundant opportunities for smart kids, after all, even smart kids who happened to be poor and had parents who did not like to travel. A little research, a little initiative, and he might have found his way to CTY or one of the other academic programs with scholarships at the ready. He might have corresponded with the authors of some of the books he'd read, at least one of whom might have extended himself or herself to such a brilliant young person. Jeremiah had not availed himself of community college courses, as so many Princeton applicants did, nor had he made any effort to move himself out of a learning environment that had so obviously been inadequate to his needs. The picture he presented was immensely frustrating. But she couldn't, somehow, quell her own intrigued attention to him.

That wasn't about John Halsey, she hoped. John Halsey, whom she had almost successfully barricaded behind a wall of other thoughts. He had forgotten her, of course. Though they had not exchanged addresses, phone numbers, he obviously knew where to reach her, and he had not reached her. Perhaps she had told him not to. Perhaps she had implied, somehow, that she was in a loving, committed relationship, that the night they had passed together, asleep and awake, was something aberrant and solely carnal, and she did not wish to be reminded of it. Had she actually said that? Had she felt it? There had been times, since Christmas, when she had wiggled loose one tiny stone in the barricade and let herself peer through: Pleasure and affection were on the other side. She was always surprised to find them there. That thing had actually happened, but it wasn't happening still. It wasn't happening now. Now she had to propel herself out of bed in the morning and into her own frigid room and into clothing that was not so obviously the clothing she had worn the day before and slept in, and then she had to make her way here, to the office, where she needed to be normal in action, normal in tone, friendly to colleagues, receptive to Clarence, graciously obscure to callers ("I know I shouldn't be calling, but I just wanted you to know that my daughter just got the lead in her school play!"), and above all fast and efficient through the application in front of her, and the next one, and the one after that, and the hundreds to come, all around her in the office and more waiting downstairs. All of this took everything.

Behind Jeremiah's incriminating Keene Central documentation, his Quest material offered an oasis of text. No grades from Quest, of course, but paragraphs and paragraphs from the teachers who had begun with him only in September, praising his brilliance, his breathtaking leaps of inference and association. He was a scholar, an aesthete, a sublime intellectual. Also deeply compassionate, profoundly creative, a still forming mind that could take off in a number of directions at any time, finding ultimate expression in philosophy, history, literature, linguistics. He also painted beautifully, apparently. Portia sighed. She was steadying herself.

John Halsey's letter finished the folder:

To the Admissions Committee,

I have been a teacher for sixteen years, working in such disparate settings as a highly competitive New England prep school, a mission school in Africa, an inner city school in Boston and, now, at this new and progressive school in New Hampshire which is only just graduating its first class. I can safely say that I have never had a student who poses the challenges that Jeremiah does, nor a student so enthralling to teach, so promising, and so in need of what a great university can offer him.

I literally stumbled across Jeremiah less than a year ago, at a yard sale where he was reading his way through an encyclopedia. Even with my broad experience of teenagers, I had never seen one like him before. Our first conversation lasted about twelve hours, during which we touched upon subjects as diverse as math, poetry, aesthetics, philosophy, biology, building styles, soil content, early medical discoveries, Flemish painters and New Hampshire state politics. I will never forget it. I also discovered that he was failing eleventh grade, and had very nearly failed tenth grade. I was, to say the least, stunned.

I don't fault Jeremiah's high school. It's a big and unwieldy institution, and they do what they can to keep marginal students in school. I don't think they were unreasonable in hoping that a student of Jeremiah's abilities would make some effort of his own to excel within the framework of the school, but for reasons that are probably too complex to find their way into a letter of this type (I'm thinking about a difficult family situation and its part in forming Jeremiah's character) he just wasn't able to do so. He wanted to learn, but he resisted the structure and requirements he met with in high school.

There is good news, however. In just the few months he has spent with us at Quest, we have begun to see a real flowering in Jeremiah's scholarship. Without question, he is capable of performing academically at the highest levels. With faculty to engage with him and fellow students who can challenge and influence his ideas, his work has begun to show focus and immense depth. When I think of Jeremiah at a place like Princeton, I am elated, not just at the notion of what the university can do for him but for what he can bring to the right classroom environment. This is a remarkable, special, brilliant young man who is just coming into his own.

I am aware of the difficulties this application must pose—the transcript from Keene Central in particular. I know that Princeton applicants do not usually present transcripts full of D's and C's. I know that Princeton applicants are busy young people, with full schedules of sports and volunteer work and musical performances, whereas Jeremiah has not undertaken any extracurricular activities at all. I can certainly understand why you might be skeptical about someone with his credentials, from a brand-new school that has never sent an applicant to Princeton, let alone a matriculated student. But if my experience as a teacher means anything, and I hope it will, please understand that this is the single most extraordinary student I have ever encountered. There is such potential here.

Yours sincerely,

John R. Halsey, Humanities Teacher and Student Adviser

Ordinarily, she knew, she would have been skimming by this point in the application. After the blank extracurricular record, after the miserable transcript, she would have been turning the last pages quickly, making the briefest note on the guidance counselor's letter ("GC notes very smart kid not motivated to achieve in HS, v. frustrating student") and the references from Quest ("Sr yr tr says brilliant, self-directed, wide interests"). It was strange, she thought, how she could hear his voice in that letter—clear and sharp, striking just the right mix of reasoning and dignified supplication, gamely dodging the obstacles he knew were there. There was passion here, but held in firm check by the rules, which he clearly understood. Was he speaking to her? Did he understand the system well enough to know that she would be the one reading his letter? He had been very correct, she saw. There was no note of familiarity, certainly no outright imposition on what had passed between them, not even a reference to the fact that the applicant had met a Princeton admissions officer a few months earlier. What he'd written was thoroughly aboveboard and beyond reproach. She wanted to call him.

Surely there was some reason to call him. Surely. Some verifiable question or fact to check. The phone number was temptingly at the bottom of the sheet, so innocently there in its black on white. She might lie and say that his scores had not arrived? No, that might cause unpardonable distress. Or ask how his senior year was going? A thoroughly reasonable query for a student with a problematic record. But he would know why she was really calling.

She looked through the application one more time, more at a loss than before. The applicant was detached, unmotivated, uncooperative. The applicant was brilliant, a passionate learner. The applicant cared about nothing. The applicant cared about everything. The applicant had been thoroughly uninvolved in his school. The applicant had been thoroughly involved with his own education. He was a strange boy. He was a strange but fascinating boy who would both benefit and benefit from Princeton.

If the application had come first to anyone else, she knew, it would probably run aground at this point. Corinne would take one look at those grades and the SSR, make a brief summary note, and check "Unlikely," the 800 verbal and AP scores aside. She would discount the raves from a brand-new school with no track record, distrusting the opinions of teachers who declined to grade and test their students. She might not even be impressed by Jeremiah's obvious appetite for learning, considering it too undisciplined to translate to a challenging university curriculum that did require that deadlines be met and exams be taken.

But it had not come to Corinne. It had come to her.

She went back to the academic rating at the top of the reader's card, which she had left blank before. She was even more at a loss now. By any rational standard, Jeremiah was the very picture of a NonAc 5, but saying as much would seriously handicap him going forward. She decided once again not to choose a number. Instead, she wrote: "Complex picture—see summary." Then she turned the page over.

The summary was the most important entry on the reader's card. It was the closing argument, in which the weightiest evidence was reprised and the recommendation given. It was the place she could be openly thrilled at having found such an amazing young person to bring to Princeton, this scholar who was going to make his or her professors delighted to be teaching here, this kid whose roommates were destined to feel as if they'd won the lottery. In the applications that wowed her, the summary was the place she couldn't wait to arrive, after filling the card with the disciplined, impersonal reporting of activities and references, after the sober evaluation of the essays. This, finally, was the place where she could drop her veneer of professionalism and write, "I *love* this kid." But for most of the applications she read, it was also the place she had to write, again and again and again, that this wonderful applicant, this hardworking student, gifted musician, committed humanitarian, and talented athlete, fit comfortably in the applicant pool but, alas, did not stand out, or where she wondered aloud if the girl or boy in question had truly challenged themselves or was a strong enough writer to succeed at Princeton.

Usually she tried not to overthink her entries, but now she paused, wanting to be clear in the limited space, and persuasive, which required precise language. That language did not come quickly, but it did come at last.

"Jeremiah," wrote Portia, "is a highly unusual applicant, and requires very careful consideration. A self-proclaimed autodidact, he has essentially been a homeschooled student in a school setting, and minus an instructor. His grades are terrible—by his own admission, he has not applied himself to the school curriculum, but then again, the school he attended 9–11 did not recognize or accommodate his needs. The school he has attended since Sept. is making better progress with him. This is a brilliant student who scored 8 AP 5's without taking any AP classes. Wide range of interests, persuasive writer, no ECAs at all. I believe that this student would thrive at Princeton and adapt to its demands, and I strongly recommend admission."

At the bottom of the second page, she had to check a recommendation for the second reader, and again this most influential action posed a quandary. Checking "Unlikely" usually meant the end of any possibility of admission. Checking "Only if room" essentially accomplished the same thing, but with more regret. Neither of these was an option, as far as she was concerned. What remained were "High Priority—Admit" and "Strong Interest," the categories from which virtually all successful candidates would emerge.

"Strong Interest" was a very common recommendation in this incredible applicant pool, the likely designation for thousands and thousands of files currently undergoing first readings. "Strong Interest" applicants were phenomenal students committed to extracurricular passions, great writers, superior mathematicians, budding scientists whose names were already on published papers. But "Strong Interest" wasn't going to do it for Jeremiah. In this vast category, he would be swimming alongside students who had chewed up their high school curricula and come out begging for more, whose teachers swore they were the most gifted to emerge from their schools in years. That wasn't Jeremiah.

"High Priority—Admit," oddly enough, was slightly more idiosyncratic and hence possibly more forgiving. A Non-Academic 1, for example—a nationally placed debater with middling SATs, a working actor who wasn't perhaps such a superior student—could be a "High Priority—Admit." But Jeremiah was not a NonAc 1. Far from it. "High Priority" would require a great outlay of effort on her part in committee. She would have to argue for Jeremiah, perhaps plead for him. Undoubtedly, she would have to win over colleagues who balked at awarding a place to a kid who'd performed so poorly in high school.

She couldn't remember ever being so flummoxed by this usually straightforward act. Sometimes, by the end of a folder, she might be divided, unsure, but almost always the very act of summing things up made the appropriate designation clear. Great kid, not competitive: "Only if room." Driven kid, high achiever, great fit for Princeton: "Strong Interest." Amazing kid—one of those few applicants she would remember when this was all over, thousands of folders from now, whom she truly cared about and wanted to support: "High Priority—Admit." And that was going to be Jeremiah, she was sure.

It was a decision she would have to defend, obviously, but she would do that for him. It was right to do that for him, she thought, checking the box and closing the file.

Though just how right, she still did not understand.

That was Monday morning.

The week passed in folders, late night stops at Hoagie Haven on the frigid walk home to Maple Street, layers of clothing it was too cold to sweat in and therefore, surely, permissible to keep wearing. She had stopped cooking in her own kitchen. She had stopped looking at the mail, which she tossed into an empty box just inside the hallway. The digital number on the answering machine had climbed and climbed: 2, 11, 19, 22, little red lines rearranging themselves, until one day she came home and saw the word *Full,* which at least, and to her relief, did not change. And the house was unrelentingly cold, though she did not think of this as odd, only part of the new normal her life had become.

Still, there were irritations. The muscles of her legs, for some strange reason, had become tight and sore, as if she spent her brief periods of sleep in some strenuous, somnambulant activity. She woke to the throbbing of her calves and shrill pain in her tendons. The first few blocks of her walk to work made her wince, but then, magically, every single day, she forgot about it until the next morning. And the sinus, of course, which still tormented her and wasn't getting better but was by now so ordinary that it hardly counted as a malady. And most troubling of all, she had begun to forget things, like the name of the lawyer who had done their house sale and purchase—Mark's and hers—whom she probably ought to call, for

advice if not for the inevitable legal dissolution to come, unless Mark had already called him, which was very disagreeable to think about.

But she couldn't call him if she couldn't remember his name.

And she wouldn't have to think about it if she couldn't remember his name.

Also her growing sense that she needed to be in touch with Susannah about something, and Caitlin, who had indeed made the extraordinary decision to apply to Dartmouth, as well as UVM, reassuring Portia (to some extent) that she was giving real thought to sticking around.

But she didn't call Susannah.

And she didn't call Caitlin.

She woke before dawn every morning, sore with the cold, and then waited pointlessly to fall back to sleep. When that failed, she turned on the light and sat hunched under the coverlet to read the day's first folders against her bent knees, breathing visible breath onto the printed pages: the Vietnamese girl from Methuen who wrote about the crack house across the street; the rock climber from Choate who described hanging by his fingertips from the wall of El Capitan so vividly, she felt her own fingers throb. When the sun came up Portia put on clothes, avoiding herself in the mirror, trying to look as if she were putting some thought into it. She went downstairs to make coffee, rinsing yesterday's coffee cup, pushing aside yesterday's unread paper to make room on the table for them: the children of professors at Brown and Harvard, a corrections officer from Somers, Connecticut, a Yale microbiologist, a fast-food worker from New Bedford, and hedge fund managers from Greenwich and Darien. She knew she needed to eat breakfast, but every morning she remembered that she had forgotten to get food again, which was something she never used to forget. So she loaded up the read files in one bag and the unread files in another, zipped the bags closed, and began the walk downtown, arms and legs and back screaming in pain, and unlocked the outer door to West College, and carried them up the stairs and down the corridor, where she read and read (as the watery light filled the room and the sounds of her colleagues came into the building and up the stairs and down the corridor to their own offices): the Fairfield County kids with summer jobs in Edgartown, the strivers from Woonsocket and Bridgeport. More and more of them ran before her eyes, new immigrants and old families, brawny, brilliant kids from the great prep schools, polished and shining, kids who struggled to express themselves in the new and thorny medium of English. She had asked Clarence for them, and now she had them. She couldn't fail to see the right things, make the right decisions.

That particular week, the week that began with Jeremiah's baffling, difficult application, was the darkest, the coldest yet. She had a pair of those ugly boots everyone had worn the previous year, the soft ones that looked like overgrown bedroom slippers. Every morning they became saturated with water on her way downtown, so she took them off, and her drenched socks, and set them in the corner of the office beside the heater, where all day they dried with white lines of evaporated moisture, like tidewater marks, and the smell of damp wool filled the room. In direct contrast with her house, the office was nearly too warm, and as the day went on she would remove layers, dropping them into a pile beside her chair. Only when she got down to the clothing closest to her skin did she understand that she was not very clean and should really address that, though by the time she got home at night, it was too cold to think about being undressed, even briefly.

On Tuesday, Rachel stopped by again and tried to get Portia to go have lunch, but she had too many files to read and sent her away. On Thursday, a message appeared on her office phone from a sober-sounding male attorney whose name she didn't recognize, complaining that he had left several messages at her home and would she please call him back? She listened twice to this, if only to ascertain that he was not the lawyer who had handled their house. Had Mark, then, "given" her their lawyer? Was this a concession? Or perhaps Mark had not considered him a good enough attorney. Why were they bothering her now, at the height of reading season? Had Mark learned nothing from the sixteen years of admissions work he had at least been a close witness to? Did he not know how hard this was, how much care they needed, every single individual young person who had exactly one chance to apply to Princeton, who required her clarity, her compassion, her judgment? Why couldn't they all just leave her alone?

On Friday afternoon, she found herself, quite suddenly, without files to read. She stood for a strange, awkward moment amid the tumult of the downstairs office, looking first at the stack of files she had hoisted into Corinne's holding area and then staring blankly at her own, which was empty. It was a weightless moment, not at all pleasant. The idleness, even momentary, felt so out of synch with the tension and focus all around her, as so many thousands of pieces of paper were tracked in their journey around the maze of admissions personnel. She was not sure what to do with herself. Should she go home and try to sleep? She was tired enough, she knew, but she also knew it would be a pointless endeavor. If she could barely sleep in the deep night, how would she be able to do it in daylight? Besides, how long was this odd lacuna of inactivity going to last? The second wave of reading—in which she'd review Corinne's first pass on the applications from her former territory—had already begun, and there were still stragglers coming down the pipe, sometimes short a teacher recommendation or missing some test score.

She heard herself tapping an impatient fingertip on the countertop. In the busy room, her stillness felt unavoidably comical. Embarrassing.

"Need something?" said Martha, passing with a stack for Dylan's shelf. Portia looked at them almost enviously.

"Folders," she said.

"Are you missing some?" Martha said with alarm. Lost applications were her nightmare scenario, and rightly so.

"Oh! No. All present and accounted for. Except I have nothing to read at the moment. I don't think Corinne's ready for me yet."

"Corinne? Wouldn't think so. California had a big jump this year. You should go home!" Martha said. "I have to tell you, you're not looking very hale at the moment."

"It's the sinus," said Portia. "I get it every year."

Martha did not respond, but Portia could see that she wasn't jumping to agree with this.

"I'm going out for coffee," Portia said brightly. "I haven't been to Small World in weeks. I can't go in there with folders, and I always have folders. But look! No folders. I'm going to Small World."

"Well," Martha said dryly, "I suppose it's closer than Disney World."

"And when I come back"—she nodded at her empty shelf—"there will be folders here, waiting for me."

"It's entirely possible," Martha said merrily.

Portia looked around one last time, in case someone might be approaching with reading material bound for her holding area; but when this proved not to be the case, she returned to her office and put on her outer sweater and her coat. It felt so peculiar not to be walking with great weighty bags at the end of each arm. It felt light and unsteady, as if she had become unrooted somehow. She went outside, grateful for once for the hit of cold, which at least helped to cut through her haze. Coffee was good, she thought. It was a giver of energy without requiring digestion or even the effort of chewing. She had not done much chewing lately. She wanted to feel the heat run down her throat and settle into that hole at the core of her and take up space for a time. And she missed Small World, which was a buoyant place, full of conversation and greetings among friends, but also a place Mark frequented, which was another reason she had been avoiding it.

She was rounding the corner of Nassau Hall when she found herself shuffling past a tour group making its frigid way back to Clio and the Office of Admission welcome center. Her arms were crossed over her chest and her head was down, which was why she hadn't seen them coming, but the backward-stepping undergraduate at the head of the group caught her eye as he passed, for the unusual rhythm of his gait and the bright white of his Princeton Marching Band boater. He was telling the storied history of Nassau Hall. He was good at walking backward, she thought, shuffling forward. Was that a marching band skill? Did he really love Princeton as much as he seemed, when his mittened hand pointed out the missing blocks of sandstone, replaced by class plaques since the nineteenth century? She followed his gaze, slowing as the group stopped around her, and found herself beside a boy in an old black coat, who looked so oddly familiar that she wondered first if he might be an actor, someone whose face had flitted past on a cereal commercial or an ad for a wireless provider. His black curly hair was whipping in the wind, but he did not seem very bothered even so. Possibly he was used to the cold.

"Portia?" the boy suddenly said.

Portia thought: How strange, that there is another Portia. And apparently standing just where I am standing.

"Isn't it?"

"Portia."

This other voice was behind her. She had been swallowed up by the little crowd, nearly all of whom were paying her not the slightest attention. But this particular voice was creating a real disturbance in the field. It had spoken only one word, and she wanted it to go away.

"Hey," said the boy, "do you remember us? You came to our school. You're an admissions officer, right?"

She stared at him. The effect in the little group was seismic. Even the backward-walking guide stopped talking. The mothers and fathers were instantly alert, but no one said a word. Perhaps they couldn't believe it was true, Portia thought sourly. The way she looked, with her wet slouchy boots and multiple sweaters, the same thick braid she'd been wearing for four days or five, she couldn't remember. "It's Jeremiah," she told him, as if he had asked for clarification.

"Yes! And you're Portia. The symbol of wisdom."

"Only on my good days," she said weakly. She looked around at them all. She was tempted to reassure them: *You are not to infer, from my slovenly appearance, that your child will not be given thorough, professional evaluation by myself and my co-workers. Bye now!*

"I decided to apply to Princeton!" he said delightedly.

"That's good news," she said, careful, very careful. She could not, of course, confirm that she knew this, let alone that she had very recently read his application.

"Portia," said that voice again, and this time she really had to turn. With so many watching, and they were absolutely watching, there was really no dignified — no, *sane* — way not to. And there he was, right behind her with his dark and lanky son at his side, and a tall woman, taller than him, with long ringlets of red and gray hair. The infamous Deborah Rosengarten, no doubt.

"Hello, John," she said, her voice sounding bizarrely perky. "What a nice surprise."

"We were hoping to see you," he said. "I wrote to say we were coming."

"Wrote . . . ," she considered.

"I got your address. Through the alumni directory."

"Oh. I'm sorry. I'm a little behind on my mail." She glanced at the tour guide, trying not to make eye contact with anyone else. "Please don't let me hold you up. It's too cold to stand outside."

"Actually," he said affably, "I was just about to finish up. 'Course, you're all welcome to come back to Clio for a cup of coffee, and to pick up an application and one of our brochures if you like. Or it's all online, of course. I have a rehearsal I need to get to now, but if anyone has any more questions and you don't mind walking over to 185 Nassau, feel free to come along. Take care, folks, and I apologize for the weather."

He moved off, and several families instantly fell in behind him, one mother with a regretful glance back at Portia, who she plainly felt was a much better mark. The rest dispersed: to Nassau Street or back to Clio, presumably for the promised coffee and applications or to take the classic tourist photo beside the enormous bronze tigers next door. Portia was left standing with a new, much smaller group: John and Deborah and the children, Nelson, Jeremiah, and—now she saw, sulking off to the side—that very disagreeable girl who had been all over her about why one should even bother going to college. Simone. She hadn't seen an application from Simone, she was fairly sure. They all, with the exception of Nelson (who gazed longingly off in the direction of the Nassau Street Foot Locker), stood looking awkwardly at one another, waiting for someone to say something, to address the many permutations of discomfort among them, but the only emissions were frosty breath. Portia was painfully aware of how terrible she looked—ill rested, ill dressed, fundamentally out of sorts—while the likely Deborah Rosengarten stood tall and composed, well appointed in a hat that covered her ears, a serious parka, and warm scarves wound around her neck, willfully oblivious to the fact that she was supposed to be the stranger here. John, she could not look at. Jeremiah, too, she was having difficulty looking at. A blast of still more frigid air blew through their little congregation.

"Welcome to Princeton," she said feebly.

Hello admissions officer! I'm sure you are tired from reading all
these essays! Take a break, have some coffee. I'll be right here
when you get back.

CHAPTER SIXTEEN

SMALL WORLD

She brought them to Small World. She couldn't think of anything else
to do, and in the awkwardness, not to speak of the cold, what persisted
was a systemic craving for caffeine.

Portia led them off toward Nassau Street, and they fell in around her, as
if she had only replaced the tour guide, with Jeremiah at her side and Nelson a half step behind, his teeth chattering audibly. The girl hung back,
and the parents behind her. Portia had no idea what she could say to any
of them.

It was not pleasant to remember Princeton before Small World. There
had been a Greek luncheonette in this storefront on Witherspoon, and
the Annex, if you were really desperate, but the town, like the rest of
pre-Starbucks America, hadn't known from cappuccino. Small World, a
homegrown enterprise, had been greeted by an instantaneous and devoted
clientele and returned the favor by expanding its floor space (not too
much), menu (not too much), and palette of coffee permutations (never
enough). A decade on, the place was aptly named, a true crossroad for
nearly every stratum of local society: moms fresh from school dropoff, students, faculty, the relaxed, dressed-down men who'd made so much money
in their corporate lives that they could now run mysterious empires from
downtown Princeton. The talk was a mixture of university dross, heady
cerebral of every stripe, local fund-raising, and local boards, with scattered
scribblers trying to write their novels and the town's few social misfits, who
sometimes took a berth and stayed for hours, nursing an herbal tea. Portia had been an early patron, but it was Mark—deprived, along with the
rest of the British race, of any coffee that did not derive from dehydrated

crystals—who was the true convert. For nearly a decade, he had begun his working day here with a steaming latte and a parade of colleagues, stopping briefly at his table in the window to sort some departmental difficulty or simply vent. Often he came back later in the day for another cup, or to meet with students, or simply to be in a place where he was sure to be disturbed. It was—it had been—after home and his office in McCosh, the next place she would always have looked for him.

There was nothing to suggest he would not be at Small World at three in the afternoon, so she approached with her worrying ducklings behind, and somewhat breathless, though that might have come from any of several aspects of her predicament. Nelson informed her that he did not like coffee. There was hot chocolate, she told him. There were desserts. He seemed placated. Jeremiah was talking about a painting in the art museum, a Peaceable Kingdom. Had she seen it?

"Peaceable . . ."

"Yeah. You know, lion lies down with the lamb?"

She didn't know. She nodded.

"And it's right next to this great big blue Marilyn. It's the wildest thing."

"Blue marlon?" she asked, picturing a great mounted fish, as in someone's Florida room, circa 1955.

"Blue Marilyn. Monroe. By Warhol. Warhol was demented, but a genius. He would have *loved* seeing his Marilyn hanging right next to this Quaker utopia, don't you think? I mean, Marilyn Monroe was *his* utopia."

"Oh yes," she told him. "I forgot you were interested in pop art."

He had stepped in front of her to take the door, an uncharacteristic move, even she recognized. He looked at her intently.

"Last fall," she told him. "You were reading about Edie Sedgwick."

"Yes!" he said. He seemed disproportionally happy. "You remember."

Unexpectedly charmed, she stepped past him into the café. With her peripheral vision, even as she went to the counter and took a place at the end of the line, she was sweeping the corners, the walls, the tables. He wasn't here. He wasn't in one of the window tables he liked to read at or one of the tables in the back, hunched forward in conference. He wasn't with *her*. Portia was so relieved, she nearly forgot the myriad other reasons she had to be distressed.

Nelson wanted hot chocolate. Simone wanted espresso. John, who insisted on paying for everyone, stood with her in line while Deborah took the kids to one of the big tables in the back. The tension between them built, it seemed, exponentially. She noted and tried to ignore a building urge to bolt. She wondered if it would be different without the others, if just the two of them had run into each other somehow, unobserved. She decided it would be different but still bad. This was so much worse.

He opened his wallet and paid. The drinks began to land on the stone countertop in front of her. She couldn't seem to look at him.

"Hey," said John, so quietly that she felt herself lean closer. "Is it my imagination? Or is this just miserably awkward?"

Despite herself, she laughed. "Why, yes. Now that you mention it."

"I did write."

"I believe you." And she supposed she did, given the state of the mail at her house. She wondered idly if his letter might be in the cardboard box she'd taken to throwing her letters in, or on the floor beside it, where the mail was spilling over.

"I wanted to see you. I feel as if —"

She made him stop just by glancing at him.

Simone came. She took the tray. Portia was still waiting for her coffee and idly hoping it would never arrive.

"Look, I want to make sure you understand this. I know I said it before, but... appearances to the contrary, we're not —"

"You and Deborah," she said, to show she was keeping up.

"We're not a couple. We were. Years ago. We're not. We're friends. And I know" — he was talking softly but faster, to get this in — "you're with some-one. I'm not unclear about things."

"I'm not, actually."

"Not... unclear?" he asked.

"Not with someone. The man I was with is with someone." Oddly, she chuckled, as if this had just occurred to her. "And that someone is with someone. With child. Actually."

He looked at her with pain in his eyes. Real pain, she thought, rather surprised to see it. But then she remembered that she ought not to be look-ing at him. She took her latte, which had indeed arrived, and walked to the back of the café, summoning what remained of her professional deport-ment as she went.

"It's really nice to meet you," she told Deborah right away as she sat down. "I missed you that day at your school."

"Oh, I'm so, so sorry. It was completely ridiculous. I went over to Putney for a meeting. We're trying to get a progressive schools network started, and my co-director teaches at Putney, and it was a last minute reschedule. Of course, I'm halfway there when I remember you're coming that afternoon, but we're in deepest Vermont, you know? No signal. Nada."

"It was fine," said Portia, loosening her grip on the slightest portion of her lingering resentment. "Your staff was great."

"I know, they're spectacular. Actually, though, I don't think of them as my staff. We're trying to make an equal sharing of administrative duties and responsibilities work. It's challenging. We've been attempting to rotate the chair."

"But she can't get rid of it," John said, sitting beside Portia.

"I'm trying. One of our colleagues had it for about a week, but she had to go on bed rest for a high-risk pregnancy. Then we had one woman who held the position for about a month last spring, and that really tested our resolve."

"What do you mean?" Portia said.

John, beside her, laughed and drank his coffee.

"Well, she called a meeting over an ongoing issue. Important issue, but not, you know, critical. Not enough for an all-day thing on a Saturday, I can assure you."

"What—" Portia began, but John answered her.

"Forms of address. Yes, really. Should the students call us by our first names? Or Mr. and Ms.? That's it. I was ready to agree to whatever would get me out of the meeting."

"Which was not helpful," said Deborah. "But anyway, she's chairing this meeting, our acting head, and she says that we're going to go around in alphabetical order and say how we feel about this very important matter."

"Please note," John said, "the use of the verb *feel*."

"Okay," Portia said, actually diverted and not, she discovered, unhappy to be.

"So off we go, with Adams. Arnberg. Calder. Cisneros. Davidov. Et cetera. It's fine for him," she said, smirking at John. "He's an H. I'm an R. I'm telling you, it just dragged on and on. But this is what killed us."

Portia, noting the "us," looked at them both.

"Whenever anyone forgot themselves and said, 'I *think*...,' she would point to the ceiling and say, '*No thinking!* Today is all about *feeling*.'"

"Wait," said Simone, grasping this opportunity to diss an authority fig-ure, even a nominal authority figure. "Who is this? Are you talking about Shanta?"

"Formerly known as Linda Denise," said John. "Shanta is her spirit name."

"It means 'Peace,'" Jeremiah said affably.

"Is it her?" Simone insisted. "Because, Mom, I always said she was, like, the worst teacher. 'Cause once — I told you this! — we were supposed to be talking about 'Intimations of Immortality' and we, like, had to correct her in the middle of the discussion, because she thought the poem was 'Imita-tions of Immorality.' Remember?"

"Simone," Deborah said sharply, "you absolutely did not tell me that. And may I point out that you are hardly conveying to Portia the very seri-ous intellectual environment we are striving to create at our school!"

"No, it's okay," Portia heard herself say, but she was laughing, which was such a surprising thing that she immediately stopped doing it.

"Well, it was her. Shanta, née Linda Denise Flitterman. Who teaches English. Very capably," she said, glaring at her daughter.

"So I guess the first namers won?" said Portia. "If Simone isn't referring to her teacher as Ms. Flitterman."

"Oh. Well, consensus was reached, yes. By the time we reached the K's, we were begging for a vote."

"And shortly after," said John, "the chair rotated back to Deborah, and we chained her to it."

"My motto, as regards meetings, is: Brevity above all."

"Nasty, brutish, and short, in other words," John said, and Deborah, to Portia's unexpected dismay, swatted him.

"I am expecting to be declared 'president for life' at any moment." She laughed, this time at Portia, and Portia was even more distressed to find that she rather liked this woman, who did seem for all the world like the very significant other of the man to her right, on whom she had no claim at all but whose left leg, she now noted, was in definite contact with her own. How long had it been there?

"I'm sorry?" Portia said. She was only now realizing that they were all looking at her: five pairs of eyes. Had she said something? Or not said something when she was supposed to?

"I said, how long have you been here? It's noisy in this place, isn't it?"

"Nearly ten years," Portia said with relief. "I worked at Dartmouth before that. In admissions."

"Oh, that's right." Deborah nodded, stirring her coffee. "I forgot that. You went to Dartmouth with John."

"Well, yes and no. We were there at the same time, but—"

"She doesn't remember me," said John with a laugh. "She's too polite to say so. You see how unmemorable I was?" This last was directed to Nelson, who grinned predictably. "What a loser."

"Yeah!" his son said with palpable delight.

"I would have remembered you," said Portia, "if we'd met."

"Oh, we met," he said disconcertingly. To Deborah he said, "I knew an old flame of Portia's. She was far, far too good for him."

Portia seemed to be missing her breath. She hoped he would stop talking of his own volition.

"Isn't that always the case," said Deborah. She turned to her daughter. "They grow up eventually. Men. They get better."

"They suck," said Simone.

Once again, Portia heard herself laugh aloud. "Tell me," she said to the girl, "what changed your mind about applying to college? You seemed to feel the whole thing was a patriarchal conspiracy the last time I saw you."

Simone, unmistakably, blushed an unusual color: persimmon, magenta. But only fleetingly.

"Simone?" her mother prodded.

"It's not for everyone," she said, shrugging.

But? thought Portia.

"But?" said Deborah.

"I just don't think it's in the best interest of me as an individual to help perpetuate this bogus tradition of sitting at the feet of learned white men, getting trashed, cheering for the football team, and then collecting a piece of paper," she said with more than a hint of her former hostility.

"Simone . . ." Her mother sighed. "I don't think many American colleges are still operating on the feet-of-learned-men principle."

"I wouldn't want to get anywhere near the feet of some of the learned men around here," said Portia, and she felt—rather than heard—John laugh.

"No, but . . . I'm just saying, you can maybe figure out a way to take what you need from the experience without participating in the bullshit, you know? Maybe you can even fuck with the system from within. Wouldn't kill some of these people to learn how racist they are."

"And that's your job?" said John, but gently.

"It's *all* of our jobs," she said with passion. "Places like this need agitation. They need students who refuse to consider themselves superior to other people. I mean, what do you think is going to happen when you bring privileged people to an elitist institution? You just validate their elitism."

"Appearances to the contrary," Portia said wearily, "this is not an elitist institution. At least, not in the way you imply."

"Oh, come on."

Portia shrugged. She was not in the mood to fight with a teenage girl.

"Well," said her mother, "I'd say that about wraps up your application to Princeton, Simone."

"That's for sure," said Nelson, grinning.

"No, not at all," Portia told them. "You should absolutely apply. I'd maybe omit the word *bullshit* from your application. Just a tip."

"Simone," Deborah said, shaking her head.

"I'm not expecting to get into *Princeton,*" Simone said defensively, looking squarely at Portia. "I don't even know that I'd want to come here. I might be happier at an institution that's a bit more forward thinking. Hampshire, maybe. Or Wesleyan. Oberlin."

"Right," said Portia, losing it. "A congregation of the enlightened, where everyone in the choir gets to preach to everyone else."

John, beside her, burst out laughing.

"I think," Deborah said carefully, "there might be a middle way. Where we don't seek out people who are just like ourselves but we also refrain from attacking people who are different from ourselves."

Brava, thought Portia, again momentarily perturbed to note how much she liked Deborah.

"We like iconoclasts here," she told them. "We like young people who have a sense of mission. And we absolutely love to bring them together and watch them mess with one another's preconceptions. Inside every admissions officer is a mad scientist." She laughed.

"Well," Simone said, still petulant, "I'll think about it. I'm still looking around. I don't apply until the fall."

John said quickly, "We're going to Penn tomorrow. And Swarthmore. I think Swarthmore would be a fantastic place for Simone."

"And Bryn Mawr," said Deborah. "This summer I'm taking her out to Kenyon and Oberlin."

"Those are all great schools," said Portia. "What about you?" she asked Jeremiah.

"I want to be here," he said plainly. "This is for me."

"Jeremiah," John said uncomfortably, "you've applied to a bunch of places. We haven't seen any of the others."

"I know. But I know."

"It's a wonderful place," Portia said carefully. "But it's not the only wonderful place. A student who wants a great education can get one at almost any American college. It's a terrific time to go to college."

"Sure," he said affably. "But this. I love this. I wanted to go into every classroom we passed."

"He kept trying to sneak off the tour," John said with forced humor. "I had to restrain him."

"I wanted to disappear into that library," said Jeremiah with a motion of his head. He meant Firestone, she supposed. "I kept thinking I could run up to people and ask them what they were studying. Everything on the kiosks . . ." He looked at her. "You know? The kiosks?"

"Sure."

"Everything I saw, I wanted to do. Not the singing groups. I can't sing. Not . . . you know, I run around, but I'm not an athlete, like a team athlete. But everything else. I wish we could stay here. I don't need to see the other schools."

"Jeremiah," Deborah said tersely, "we haven't driven all this way to see one college."

"Would you like to stay?" Portia heard herself say. "I could probably arrange an overnight with an undergraduate. You could go to classes in the morning."

They all looked at her, except for Nelson, who was digging for the marshmallow in his cup.

"Really?" said Jeremiah.

"But . . . we're staying at Tara's tonight," Deborah said quietly to John.

"Deborah has a friend in Bucks County," he explained to Portia. "We were going to stop there and go on to my parents' tomorrow."

"Well, it was just a thought," Portia said. She was suddenly feeling awfully uncomfortable. She had not thought before she spoke of how it might appear to them, or what it signified for her.

"He could," said John, looking at Deborah. "The three of us could. And meet you tomorrow at my parents'."

"I don't want to stay here," Nelson said bluntly.

Silence ensued.

"Shall I just make a phone call?" Portia said, getting up. "I can see if it's even possible."

"Yes!" Jeremiah said, oblivious to the tension around the table.

"That's very kind of you," said Deborah after a moment. She looked at Simone. Portia, too, was looking at Simone, belatedly taken aback by her own rudeness. Was this offer, so suddenly formed, open to her as well? It had to be, obviously.

"Simone . . . ," she began carefully.

"Oh, no thanks. I want to go see Tara."

"And Bryn Mawr in the morning," added Deborah.

"Right. But thanks."

"Let me call," said Portia, taking out her phone. "Give me a minute."

She went outside, where the cold was now welcome, clarifying, and somewhat punitive. Her thoughts were racing. What it meant, what she had done, they must all have some grasp of it. Who first? Deborah? Or John? Simone, with her tractor-beam expression? What were they saying back there? She thought fleetingly of skin and heat. She thought of his mouth. She felt as if she had declared herself in some irreversibly public way. She felt at once excited and deeply humiliated.

Her intention was to phone Rachel, but at the last moment she reconsidered and dialed David's office. No, he assured her. She was not interrupting.

"I have a prospective student," she told him. "I was hoping you might know an undergraduate who can put him up tonight. Preferably someone with a philosophy class in the morning. He'd like to attend a class."

"Is it the zombie kid?" David said excitedly.

"What? Oh no. But interested in philosophy. Very unusual kid. Not very polished, you know? But brilliant."

"Brilliant and not very polished." David laughed. "The philosopher's coat of arms. Hang on."

She heard him speak, indecipherable. A knocking sound as he put the phone down, she supposed, and then a scrape as he took it back up.

"I've got a freshman in my office now," said David. "He has my metaphysics and epistemology seminar tomorrow at nine. Will that do?"

"Only perfectly." She smiled. "And he has room?"

"Hang on."

More indistinct sounds. She heard laughter—unmistakably David's.

"There's a bed," David said, returning. "One of his suite mates has a girlfriend in Forbes. Apparently he hasn't appeared all term."

"Fantastic." She wrote down the kid's name and arranged to bring Jeremiah to his dorm room in Mathey. Unless she called back in the next five minutes. Then she thanked David profusely and hung up.

Back at the table they were waiting for her in alert silence, like a nineteenth-century family portrait: father, mother, children, attentively seated with all hands visible. Between the two adults there was no discernible tension, which was at once perplexing and reassuring. "He can do it," she said, addressing Deborah for some reason. "If it's all right with you."

"It's fine," she said with surprising warmth. "I think it's a tremendous idea."

"This is so great," Jeremiah said, half out of his seat already.

"Shall I put him on the train to Philadelphia in the morning?" Portia asked, amazed to hear herself speak these words. She paused to admire her own ingenuous cool.

"Oh," John said, frowning. "I'm going to spend the night. I'll find a hotel in town and take him on the train tomorrow. It's all set."

She looked at Deborah. Deborah was not returning her gaze.

"And you're sure you don't want to stay yourself?" she asked Simone.

"No. Thank you. I think I should try to see as many places as possible." She said it so primly, Portia thought. This Simone was very nearly a Bryn Mawr girl of the old school: brittle, clever, imperturbable.

"Can we go?" said Jeremiah, and Nelson, who had evidently been ready to go for some time, careened to his feet, tipping the table. They put on their coats and went outside into the new dark of the afternoon, and walked back to their car in the municipal lot by the town library. John slung Jeremiah's bag over his shoulder, and his own. Portia gave directions to the highway as Nelson and Simone strapped in, and Deborah, she thought, drove off rather abruptly. She looked at John.

"Lead on," he said amiably.

Back up Witherspoon Street, back onto campus, through the arches, and across the courtyards to Mathey, its faux Gothic courtyard belying the newness of its actual construction. They climbed a staircase perfumed with stale beer to the beat of ambient rap music and found the appointed suite on the second floor, door flung open to display the universal décor of the newly emancipated Princeton male: alcoholia (on a shelf, the empty bottles of beers of many nations, all in a row), technology (an oversize television screen and snarls of wires), and Princetoniana (tigers, tigers everywhere, and in the prime position on the sitting room wall, an orange-and-black CLASS OF 2011 banner).

"Luke?" she called, knocking on the open door.

"Yes! Hey!" came a yelp from one of the bedrooms, loud over the music, which actually seemed to come from elsewhere in the building. "I'm Luke."

He was tall and reed thin, with ginger hair. He was from Albuquerque and had never been east, he informed them, until the previous fall. Winter had taken him somewhat by surprise, he admitted. He reached for Jeremiah's bag, opened the bedroom door of the absent suite mate, and tossed it on the pristine bed within. A bunch of them were planning to check out *This Is Princeton* after dinner, he told Jeremiah. Was he cool with that?

Jeremiah agreed instantly, though he couldn't have known what it was. Portia, who did know, was delighted. Someone would be back to collect him in the morning, she said. After metaphysics and epistemology. Then they left.

Now it was fully dark. Portia held her jacket at the throat and did not look at him. They took a few steps along the pathway and stopped on the same dime.

"I think," said Portia, "we did that rather well."

He took her hand.

My grandmother rolls out the dough, using a long wooden rolling pin, so faded from the imprint of her hands that the paint on the handles is barely visible. She pauses to dip her hands in the flour bowl by her elbow, then gently sprinkles flour over the perfectly flat dough as she prepares to cut out her special Italian Christmas Cookies, favorites of our family since I can recall. She checks to make sure that I am paying close attention. After all, she chides me, long after she is gone, I will one day need to recreate this exact combination of flour and water, egg and sugar, for my own child or grandchild, keeping alive this link between a girl who had barely attended school, who shared a bed with two sisters in a house without running water in a remote village in southern Italy, and her violin playing, robotics obsessed, college-bound granddaughter in Los Angeles, and on to descendents she will never know. This may be our private family tradition, but it is comes from an American story.

CHAPTER SEVENTEEN

CONTENT TO BE LED

Oh dear," he said. He was still standing behind her on the porch, though she had unlocked the door and opened it and even stepped inside. It had not occurred to her to worry about the house, and now she looked around, wary and bewildered, to see what she must have forgotten: trash? shed underwear? palpable signs of extreme loneliness and abandonment?

There was a floor lamp in the living room that she had left on all day, apparently, so the electricity was working. Light made a house look homey, didn't it? Perhaps it had been longer than all day, Portia thought, trying to remember the last time she had sat in the living room and what she might have been doing there.

"Portia," said John, who had stepped, unheard, into the room, "I think your heat might be out."

She raised her head, as if she were some animal testing the air.

"You're absolutely right," she agreed with him. She was trying for grow-ing realization but hit outrage instead, as if she were ready to murder whichever vile spirit had stolen in and shut off the furnace. "You know, I thought it was a little cold this morning, but I was running out to work. It must have happened in the night."

"Can I look at your furnace? Would you mind?"

He was almost comically gracious, and she nearly smiled. "Would you?" she asked. "I could call the oil company."

"Well, it might be necessary. In the basement?"

She showed him the door and turned on the light for him. She had not thought to look at the furnace herself.

Thirty seconds later, there was a deep rumble from below her feet and a whirring sound, and the slight vibration of the floorboards came rushing back to her, so thoroughly familiar that she wondered how she had not noticed it was gone all these weeks. The vibration meant warm air and hot water, which meant comfort. Suddenly, what she wanted most in the world was a bath.

"There's enough oil," said John, emerging from the dark corner where the furnace was ensconced. "I don't know why it went out, but it just needed to be restarted. Has it happened before?" he asked.

"No, not that I know of."

"And you think it went out in the night?"

She shifted uncomfortably, unsure of how assailable that claim might be. Would he be able to tell? From its condition? The temperature of the house? She thought of brutal parents in the emergency room, insisting the baby had only fallen from his playpen, plagiarists who swore they'd written the essay themselves. Would he know? Could he prove it?

"I really . . . I'm not sure. I've been at the office so much. It might have happened yesterday. Or before."

He was listening but not looking at her. He was looking past her, back toward the front door, where mail overflowed the open box on the floor and unopened packages were stacked like roadside cairns. She had forgotten about the packages, some of which were for Mark.

"My secretary's on strike," she said mildly.

He gave her a quizzical look.

"And my maid. And, as you already know, my handyman. Actually, I'm a little on strike myself."

"Yes," he said carefully. "I'm trying to gauge how concerned to be."

"Concerned?" Portia said. Her first impulse was offense, but this departed quickly. Instead, she had a sudden, overpowering urge to hurl herself against him and coil her hands in his light hair. She didn't do it, but the restraint cost her.

"Something is wrong," John said. He spoke softly, almost soothingly. "I don't care what your house looks like or if you turn your furnace off for the winter. I don't care how long it takes you to read your mail. I just like to know that you're all right. Are you all right?"

Portia stood looking at him. He had not unbuttoned his coat, which was slowly but perceptibly beginning not to be necessary. There was life, thin life but growing life, in the room. He was beautiful. She had forgotten how beautiful.

"Not really," she heard herself say.

He nodded soberly. "And can I do anything for you?"

Portia shrugged. "Well, you've already fixed the furnace."

"Started the furnace," he corrected. "Please don't imagine I'm one of those guys who can actually fix things."

"Then you're not out to fix me," she observed, and he looked startled.

"No. Are you broken?"

Portia sighed. "Oh, probably," she said, unbuttoning her coat. "Look, I know it's awful, but would you mind if I left you on your own for a few minutes? I just want to clean up a bit."

"You don't have to clean up." He frowned.

"Not the house. I mean me."

"Oh. Of course." He looked embarrassed.

"And when I come down, we'll see about some dinner. I won't be long,"

She dropped her coat on the back of a chair and went upstairs. Everywhere she looked, there was disorder: papers, clothing, towels, everything lying where it had fallen. The bed looked especially alarming, with files stacked along the meridian where Mark had once slept and on her own side, twisted ropes of blankets and quilts. The scene suggested tandem diagnoses of light and heavy sleeper. On the bedside table, the Pollock biography, still unfinished, for the January book group she had naturally not made it to. She couldn't even remember the bit she had managed to read.

The bathtub seemed to be filled with discarded clothing. She bent down to gather it up, armloads of jeans and tops, underpants, bras. They didn't smell, particularly, and for a moment she wondered if these were clothes she had really worn or just things from the drawers and hangers that had somehow migrated here, voyaging en masse to their winter nesting grounds. But then she found a pair of wool pants, their turned-up cuffs encrusted with dried mud, and remembered the meeting she had worn them to last month, with Clarence and the dean of the Woodrow Wilson School, and the snowstorm that afternoon through which she'd walked home. Last *month,* Portia marveled. After a moment's consideration, she carried it all to her closet and threw it in. Very little still hung on the hangers, only the good clothes, the going-out clothes from her faculty spouse life, her visiting high schools life. She could do any of those things right now, she thought, sighing. But underwear, a pair of unworn jeans, a fresh shirt—these might be difficult.

Portia ran the water, washed the tub, and put in the plug. She took off the clothes she wore and threw those, too, into the closet, then stood, naked and shivering, and contemplated the bed. To alter it in any way, she knew, was to acknowledge what might happen, but hadn't they already done that? Had he not taken her hand and walked with her, never asking where they were going, content to be led? Weren't they here now, with a functioning furnace and truly hot bathwater on the rise? She couldn't leave this, not as it was. The bed, more than anything else in the house—more than the loaded answering machine and the abandoned mail and the absent heat—was a blunt exhibition, like an art installation evoking sadness, filth, and celibacy. As the water filled the tub and the steam filled the bathroom, she carefully removed the files and ripped at the sheets. They, too, went into the closet. She put on a fresh set, then messed up the covers a bit so he wouldn't know.

She did not feel actual shame until she slid into the tub, when the hot water slid around her and her surfaces began to give up their evidence of neglect. There were streaks of old grime on her shins, rough skin on her knees, hair everywhere. She had truly not known that things had gotten this bad. She dragged a razor over every pertinent surface and rubbed her back with a wet cloth as far as she could reach. Then, pink and new from the soap and heat, she stood up and turned on the shower, letting more hot water wash everything away. Her hair, neglected for weeks, coiled in a brown rope over her shoulder, scarcely different wet than dry. Probably for the first time in her adult life, Portia lathered, rinsed, *and* repeated.

She was drying herself with a fairly clean towel when she heard the doorbell and froze, bent over. *Rachel*, was her immediate, horrified thought. Rachel had said something about stopping by, that afternoon in the office. Or Mark, here with spectacularly bad timing to have the inevitable conversation, in which everything she already knew would be painstakingly articulated. Portia went to the bedroom door and opened it, straining to hear, but the voice speaking to John at the front door was not Rachel's, or Mark's, and the only words she could make out were "Thank you" before the door clicked shut. She went to find clean clothes to put on and was only partially successful: a long-sleeved shirt but no bra, a pair of seemingly pristine jeans from the closet floor but no underpants. The jeans seemed rather large, and she wondered for a moment if they might be Mark's, but they were not Mark's. Barefoot, because the ordeal of finding clean socks felt so utterly beyond her, she went downstairs.

John was in the kitchen, surveying the open cupboards above the sink. On the kitchen table sat a takeout bag from Tiger Noodles. She could smell it from across the room and was instantly ravenous.

"Hey," he said.

"Hey." She was noncommittal.

"I wasn't honestly worried about you until I looked in the fridge," he told her.

"Ah."

"I was looking for something to cook for dinner. I wasn't snooping."

"Sure." She shrugged. "I haven't been doing much cooking."

"Yes," said John. "Or opening the fridge, I suspect."

She looked at the fridge. With its door closed, it looked perfectly normal. There was a gym class schedule from the previous summer stuck to the front with a magnet. She had no idea what was inside.

"People don't understand what reading season is like for us," she said with determined nonchalance. "It's a bunker mentality thing. We read, order in, read. Sometimes we change our clothes." Portia laughed, but even to her own ears it sounded forced. "This is perfectly normal."

"Sure." He nodded. "I hope I didn't imply otherwise. I just thought it would be quicker to order in."

She thought: Quicker than what? But she thanked him and retrieved plates and silverware. Compared with other areas of the house, the kitchen was in relatively good shape. There were dishes in the sink, of course, but didn't everyone have dishes in the sink? After a moment's pause, she hoisted open the Sub-Zero's door and found, amid the deeply suspicious perishables and desiccated remnants of former takeout meals, a pair of Corona beers, which she set on the table.

"Thanks," said John. "But I can't."

"You don't like beer?"

"It doesn't like me. I don't drink anymore."

"Oh!" she said, embarrassed. "I'm sorry."

"Don't be sorry. It's old news."

Portia put the bottles back in the fridge.

"You can," he told her. He was ladling shrimp Cantonese onto a plate. "It's not a problem for me."

"No, it's fine," she said. "I have seltzer, I think."

He brought the food to the table and sat. "One of the more valuable lessons I learned at Dartmouth. That I couldn't tolerate alcohol. It only took a year of waking up in my own vomit."

"You're precocious." She smiled. "Think how many Dartmouth men spend all four years waking up in their own vomit and never figure that out."

He laughed. "I never enjoyed it, either, that's what's truly strange about it. I didn't like the getting drunk part, or the being drunk part, any more than I liked the aftermath. So I just stopped doing it. I think I was very lucky, actually, because if I'd kept going, I know I would have ended up with a real problem. I kind of nipped it in the bud."

"I suppose it must have curbed your social life in college," she said, beginning to eat.

He shrugged. "What's social about being blitzed? When you're that far gone, it's antisocial by definition, isn't it?"

Portia nodded. "Weren't you in Tom's fraternity? I think you told me that." She said this nonchalantly, but it didn't feel nonchalant. Nothing about Tom was nonchalant, let alone this first tangible connection to him in over a decade. Suddenly, rather belatedly, the notion that John might know real things about Tom occurred to her, followed by the possibility that he was even directly in touch with Tom—e-mail, alumni association get-togethers, fall family weekends at Moosilauke, or just those annoying Christmas letters she was sure his wife inflicted on the world every December.

Portia herself, of course, had the essentials down already. She knew precisely where Tom was and whom he'd married and what he did for a living. She knew that he had donated enough to Dartmouth to merit some sort of alumni award, and that he had finished a half marathon in Wellfleet with a time of 113 minutes, and that the Boston law practice where he had interned as a college student and was now a full partner specializing in medical malpractice had recently merged with a firm in Providence. She knew from the photograph on the Web site of that law firm that his thick blond hair was now less thick and that his hairline was in retreat, but that his brilliant grin and the old raffish tilt of his head were unchanged and not the tiniest portion drained of their potency. She knew that his wife had managed a clothing store in Newton before becoming a full-time mother to their three children, and she knew those children's names: Ivy, Courtney, and Thomas III, known by his fond parents and everyone else (according to the online newsletter of the Dartmouth Class of '91) as "Trey." She declined to feel guilty about knowing these things. Every single woman on the planet with Internet access and a modicum of curiosity possessed the vital statistics of every man or woman she had loved, let go, been spurned by, come to loathe, or still longed for. Portia was not going to apologize for this, but she wasn't going to admit it, either.

"Sure. I haven't seen him for ages. But I hear from him."

"Oh?" She chewed her food with what she hoped was a thoughtful expression.

"Well, he manages a newsletter for Psi-U alums. He took all that pretty seriously."

"Yes," she said noncommittally.

"So I get the e-mails. Look," he said, sighing, "I know there's something here."

Portia looked up at him.

"It's a hot spot. I don't need to talk about it, I just don't want to pretend it isn't there, and I don't want to hurt you. From everything I know about Tom, he was probably a supreme asshole to you."

"Me among others," she said, to let him know she didn't consider herself special where Tom was concerned.

"Sure. He was very nice to me, but I wasn't a beautiful girl, which generally took me out of the danger zone."

Portia looked down at her plate, momentarily charmed by the embedded compliment. She was surprised to see that she had already eaten a good deal. It had happened quickly and without making much of an impact.

"You know that expression *coup de foudre*? French for falling madly in love with someone?"

"Thunderbolt." He nodded. "That was you and Tom?"

"Well, it was me. I can't explain it. I remember, vividly, the exact moment and the exact spot. It was on the Green. For years afterward, whenever I walked over that spot, I would feel something, physically."

He smiled. "Like hungry grass. In Ireland. You know?"

Portia didn't know.

"Wherever someone died in the Irish famine, if you walk over that spot, over the earth where they died, you feel weakness and hunger. Or so say the bards."

"Yes." She sighed. "Like that. I would be walking across the Green on my way to class, or talking with friends. Or even later, when I was supposedly a grown-up, professional woman, on my way to the Hanover Inn to talk to an alumni group, or one of our Ivy League conferences. I'd regress, totally, to that moment." She laughed. "Remember the final scene of *Carrie*? When the hand shoots out of the earth and tries to pull her down? That was me. Minus the Amy Irving curls, alas."

"And the gore, I hope." He cut the last egg roll and placed half democratically on her plate.

"Oh, there was gore," she said, sounding cryptic. "Lots and lots of gore. But not in the beginning. In the beginning it was..." She faltered. She shouldn't be able to remember how it was, so far back, through the bitter fallout and the long years with Mark, not to mention the more recent history and reverberating presence of John Halsey. Pinned to earth by the long arm of the first man she had loved, so long ago, and never able to quite get upright, let alone truly walk away. It was pathetic, she knew, but it would be more pathetic if she had not made such a facsimile of continuing her life. She sometimes tested herself by conjuring Tom — on her airplane, in her restaurant, sauntering into an information session in Clio Hall with Ivy or Courtney or Thomas-known-as-Trey. He would be frowning at her as he tried to place her features or, worse, skim past her, completely blank.

And she would always be shocked and speechless, her pulse rattling and her face shamefully wet. She was never ready for him, never once. She would never be ready.

"Hearts and flowers?" John said after a while. "Every girl's dream?"

She nodded. "Yeah. Except I wasn't supposed to be a girl. I was supposed to be a warrior. I wasn't at Dartmouth to fall in love or find a husband or any of that stuff. I wasn't there to party. I wasn't there to get good grades so I could go to law school. I was supposed to be building a postfeminist utopia on the Hanover Plain, where evolved women and men could create their highest selves in fruitful, nonsexist communion."

"Oh, wow." He laughed. "I am completely lost."

"My mother didn't want me to go to Dartmouth. She thought the college was a lost cause, and she hadn't raised me in the highest principles of gender-blind self-actualization to go off to some retro school where the women were fraternity playthings and potential future wives."

"But..." John frowned. "Dartmouth was full of amazing women."

"Which is exactly what I told her. I told her how wrong she was. And even if the men really were back in the dark ages, I told her that preaching to the choir was a waste of my talents. Like Simone at Oberlin or Antioch. What was I supposed to do on a campus where everyone already *had* a Rosie the Riveter poster and Cris Williamson in the tape deck?"

"Who?" said John.

"My point," she said, "exactly."

She got up and went to the fridge. "I think I will have that beer," she said. "If you truly don't mind."

"I truly don't," he said amiably.

She found the bottle and opened it, then sat down again.

"My mom...," Portia began. "Well, here's the thing. My mother wasn't a mom in the June Cleaver mold. That was fine. She raised me alone, for one thing, and that was also fine. But I wasn't just her child, I was her project. There was a point to me, do you see? I was supposed to make her make sense."

John was trying hard to follow. Portia saw that he couldn't quite. "You mean, she lived through your accomplishments? That's far from unusual."

"Oh, I know. In my work? Absolutely, I see that all the time. But in the case of my mother, it wasn't just that I made up for her having no traditional work. I was the work. I was what happened when you never allowed one speck of sexism or racism or homophobia into the presence of your precious child. I was supposed to be this brave new female, right? I was never supposed to know that there were people who thought I couldn't be president or cure cancer or climb Mount Everest on my hands."

"This is sounding like a Skinner box!" John said. "What did she do, raise you in a cave?"

Portia nodded. "More or less. She raised me in Northampton, Massachusetts. The Pioneer Valley. They call it 'the Happy Valley.' Remember *Heather Has Two Mommies*? We *all* had two mommies, or we had one mommy and a turkey baster. Heterosexual couples were few and far between in Northampton. *Married* heterosexual couples were almost unheard of. America was the control. We were the experiment. You see?"

He shrugged.

"And the experiment was not supposed to culminate in Thomas Wheelock Standley, the umpteenth male in his family to attend Dartmouth, captain of the rugby team, president of his fraternity, future attorney, and, incidentally, *Mayflower* descendant."

"Really?" said John. "I never knew that."

"Well, you didn't date him." She laughed. "Or you would have. It was quite the aphrodisiac for those potential future wives. And, for certain other reasons, for me."

"Okay, *now* I get it," said John. "This isn't about principles. This is about plain old rebellion. You brought home your mother's version of a Hell's Angel."

"He was *dying* to meet my mother. He was convinced she was this big, butch, man-hating dyke. I told him she wasn't."

"Wasn't what?" said John. "Big? Butch? Man hating?"

"A dyke. She was actually a failed lesbian, and that was really hard for her to accept. Of course, the women my mother tried to be with knew right away, but she absolutely believed she could will herself into homosexuality. Enough tofu, enough Meg Christian."

"Meg—?" John said, looking addled.

"Exactly." Portia drained the last of her beer. "I hope I don't seem ungrateful. Do I seem ungrateful?"

He frowned. "Why? Just because she gave you life? Scrimped and saved? Put aside her own dreams to help you achieve your own?"

"No, that would be Stella Dallas." Portia laughed. "Susannah Nathan was no Stella Dallas." She looked down at her plate. It was wiped clean. How had that happened? "Would you like some coffee? I definitely have some. I don't know about milk."

"Coffee would be nice," he said genially.

She cleared their plates and braved the fridge again to find the coffee, which she finally discovered in the freezer. There was some long abandoned vanilla ice cream, which she likewise removed to use in place of milk, necessity being the mother of invention. She felt, vaguely, good, suspiciously light, which was itself odd, given that she had just put away her most substantial meal in weeks. It might be the beer, of course, or the residual light-headedness from that transformative bath. It might be John.

With the coffee descending into its carafe, she led him to the living room and sat on the too deep couch, awkwardly folding her legs alongside her on the cushion. He sat, too. He was taller, and he did not seem to share her difficulty. He looked, actually, comfortable, with his arm along the back of the sofa, his hip disappearing into one of the cushions. The house was warm now, and though the disarray remained in the room, it also felt very nearly peaceful. She did not know what would happen or what it meant, or what she wanted it to mean. She did not know what he wanted from her, at least in the long term, or if there even was a long term. Portia had reached her present age with a list of sexual partners so abbreviated, it bordered on humiliating. Another counselor at soccer camp, the summer before college. Tom, who'd made off with some valuable thing she'd never been able to replace. Mark, her life partner, supposedly. And John. These men had nothing in common. They were not uniformly intelligent, attractive, even nice. They had not loved her. Or they had not loved her enough. From these few she had not gained the tools to understand casual sex and was ill versed in its attendant lore. And as a result, she couldn't really glean the meaning of what had happened in Keene or what might be happening now.

"What are you thinking?" said John.

"I believe that's supposed to be the woman's line," Portia said, smiling.

"And I thought we were beyond all that in the gender-blind postfeminist utopia. So what are you thinking?"

She shrugged. She had no intention of letting him know what she was thinking. "Nothing."

He shook his head. "You are a woman who's never thought nothing in her entire life."

And indeed, she thought about this and decided it was probably true, which gave her no pleasure.

"All right. I was thinking…I'm not really sure where we're going with this."

To John's credit, he did not pretend to be confused.

"Where would you like it to go?"

"I don't know."

"Is that: I really don't know? Or: I do, actually, know, but I don't want to tell you?"

"I really don't know. I'm glad you're here. I know that."

He nodded. "I want to be here. Actually, I want to be over there." He nodded at her end of the sofa.

She reached for him. His hair was soft. His mouth, on her skin, also soft. The couch, it turned out, was the perfect size after all.

When I was a child, I was given a gift of Legos. I don't remember ever playing with another toy. Over the years, I built buildings of Legos, and ships, and bridges. Then I started building robots, and helicopters that flew. When they didn't fly very well, I would pull them apart and try to figure out what was going wrong. That was actually my favorite part. By this time, my parents knew to lock up all the mechanical devices in the house, because I had a strange habit of taking them apart, too. I was in high school before I figured out that there was a name to describe the sort of thing I was so interested in doing: engineer. When I first heard that word, I thought: that is the most interesting word in the English language. And I thought: that's what I'm going to be.

CHAPTER EIGHTEEN

I'M OK, YOU'RE OK

The scar was still there, just where she had left it. It gave off an air of profound imprecision, haste, and severe pain. It had a metallic taste, too, and though this might have been her imagination, a faint but identifiable smell: yeast and seawater.

"Appendectomy," he told her, his hand on her shoulder.

"It can't be," she said, looking up at him. "Appendectomy scars don't look anything like this."

"Ah," he said sardonically. "I meant appendectomy, Ugandan style."

"Jesus."

"It could have been worse. I could have died."

"John," she said, laying her cheek against it.

"It was my own fault. I should have gone to the hospital as soon as I started feeling bad, but I honestly didn't think it was anything unusual. My gut was full of exotic flora the whole time I was in Africa. I was always getting intestinal things. So of course when I finally did drag myself into the emergency room, I played doctor and told them what was wrong with me, and they just sat me in the corner with a bucket and let me get on with it.

I was pretty checked out by then. Luckily, one of the nurses noticed the way I was holding my right side. When I woke up, I was minus an appendix. And all I got was this lousy scar. It's quite the turn-on, isn't it?"

"No," she said honestly. "But it isn't a turn-off."

"You're just being nice," he said.

"I'm not that nice." She lifted her head and looked at it carefully. The scar was not only long, it was ridged and clumsily made, asymmetrical in both width and depth, as if someone had gouged his flesh with a primitive tool and slipped in the process. She lay curled against him, one hand beneath his shoulder, the other stroking that ragged scar.

After a while, he said, "You didn't say anything about your father. Before."

"Mm-hmm," she agreed, closing her eyes.

"So...was he a turkey baster?"

Despite herself, she laughed, fluttering the hair on his chest. "No. Not at all."

"So your parents were together."

"No. I mean yes. But no. You and I have already been together longer than my father and mother were. Not," she said quickly, "that you and I are together."

"Are we not?" he said.

"I meant, in the physical sense. Together. As in, we are undoubtedly together right now."

"We are." He smiled. "Undoubtedly. Right now."

With that understood, she stopped, hoping he wouldn't pursue it.

"Then...," John said a moment later, "this was a one night sort of thing."

"Oh, not a whole night. Not a night at all, from what I've been told. And I was actually told everything there was to tell. My mother believed in being excruciatingly open about the whole thing. Lots of inappropriate details. Especially for an eight-year-old."

"Portia," said John, "you're being very obscure. I can't tell if this is a traumatic childhood experience or something you just like to joke about."

She frowned. "You know, I can't tell, either. I haven't thought about this in years."

Slowly, she extricated herself and sat up. There was, miraculously, ample room for this maneuver on the couch. Quite uncharacteristically, she found herself sort of willing to talk about this. But only if he really wanted to hear it.

"Do you really want to hear this?"

"Do you want me to hear it?"

"All right," she said, reluctantly, as if she did not. But she found that she did.

"The story of you?" he said, reaching up to touch ... his hand lingered, uncommitted, for a moment, and then landed: the hollow between her breasts. It began, lightly, to move.

"Yes. The magical story of how egg met sperm, and my perfect self was launched in the womb of my mother, on the Amtrak Montrealer."

He burst into laughter. His thin body shook, ribs and muscles and the hair that lay flat on his chest, like grass in a riverbed. He laughed and shook, and then, quite suddenly, he stopped and looked at her. "Oh shit," he said. "You're not kidding."

"No, not kidding. Why would I kid about such an important detail? And details are all I have, so if you're going to keep interrupting my flow ..."

"All right," he told her. His hand, momentarily immobilized by the laughter and then the shock, was mobile again. "I'll do my best not to interrupt."

"Good. And now a deep, cleansing breath."

"Okay," he said gamely.

"Well," said Portia. "Thirty-nine years ago, my mother, Susannah Nathan of Northampton, Massachusetts, via Long Island, Barnard, Berkeley, and cooperative living situations too numerous to list, was a divorced activist in need of a baby. The divorce isn't really relevant, actually. He was a gay man from Chile. Chile was not a great place to be a gay man in the mid-sixties, apparently, so he came to the States, but they were going to deport him, so my mother married him at the Springfield courthouse. They never lived together, and by the time my mother was looking to get with child, he'd moved out to San Francisco. He died there, actually."

"Let me guess. In the late 1980s."

"Yes, unfortunately. I did meet him once. He was a sweet guy. A musician. He probably would have made a great biological father. I might have gotten a little musical aptitude, which wouldn't have been bad, and the exotic skin tone. But he was on the other side of the country by the time my mother needed his genetic material, so that put him out of the running. My mom had another gay friend closer to home, so they tried for a couple of months, and she tried a sperm bank in Boston. Like I told you," Portia said ruefully, "she spared me none of the details."

"It's okay. I'm not eight years old."

"No. So, anyway, a couple of years went by, maybe half a dozen attempts, and nothing. But she had this fatalistic attitude. It was going to happen. She was going to be a mother, you know? And then, one day . . ."

"One perfect day!"

"On the Montrealer."

"Not the Empire Builder or the Heartland Flyer!"

"She was coming back from visiting her mother in New York, and there was a man in the seat across from her, reading a copy of *I'm OK—You're OK*."

"Oh, my God," John said, laughing again. "Please tell me you're making that part up."

"Sadly, no. If I were making it up, I'd have him reading Dostoyevsky. Though I guess Dostoyevsky wouldn't have been as much of a conversation starter. By New Haven they're rehashing their childhood angst. By Hartford, he's moved into the seat next to her."

"He'd better hurry up. Springfield is the next stop."

"Well, he did hurry up. I mean, he must have. Actually, I don't doubt my mother would happily have shared with me exactly how long he took. Like I said, she believed in total openness, but I begged her to stop. Anyway, it was truly a brief encounter."

"Well, no. *Brief Encounter* was a love story. This is more like *Strangers on a Train*."

"Which ended with murder, I seem to recall."

"Portia," said John, "are you as angry as you sound?"

She looked at him in surprise. "Do I really sound angry?"

"Vastly." His hand had now colonized her breasts and moved on to her abdomen.

"But I wouldn't be here if he hadn't. If they hadn't."

"No." He waited.

"I don't think I ever wished there'd been roses and dancing, let alone a wedding. I guess I'm not much of a romantic."

"Hey," he said, smiling, "you were conceived on a train! You have to be a romantic!"

"Well, but it wasn't romantic at all. That's sort of the key to the whole

thing. There were never any violins, for her. She was thinking sperm from
the very beginning. She was thinking, Well, why not give this way a try?
He was tall and appeared to be free of physical deformities. He looked
prosperous. He could read, obviously. She probably knew more about him
than she knew about the sperm donor she'd tried. Anyway, she got off
pregnant at Springfield and never wanted to see him again. Not even if it
worked and she did have a baby. And she never thought that this baby she
wanted so badly might want to know who its father was. I don't even have
a name. Or a destination. You know, he might have gotten off at St. Albans
or gone as far as Montreal. Maybe he was even French-Canadian, though I
suppose Susannah would have picked up the accent. I struggled horribly in
French, so probably not. Maybe he got off at White River Junction. Maybe
he was a professor at Dartmouth. Maybe he was *my* professor!"

"Not if he was reading *I'm OK—You're OK*," said John.

"Oh, don't be a snob. Lots of people read that book."

"I know. I read it."

She laughed. "Well, there you go."

"In my defense," he said, moving to her thigh, "it was in Kampala.
There was a copy in the clinic library. I was a little desperate for reading
material."

"She ought to have given me 'I'm OK' as a middle name," said Portia,
shifting for him. She closed her eyes.

"Portia I'm OK Nathan," he said dubiously. "Aren't you glad she didn't?"

Portia, who was now trying to concentrate on his hand, said nothing.

"What is your middle name, actually?"

"Mm? I don't have one. Susannah had this idea I would name myself. I
don't know, there was some tribe somewhere she'd read about, where the
girls name themselves when they reach puberty. She was all fired up to
do it. Big party, candle lighting, all her women friends in a circle, beating
crescent-shaped tambourines." She opened her eyes.

He was frowning at her.

"Crescent?" she said. "Because of the moon?"

"The moon?" He seemed still more lost.

"It's a menstrual thing," she said flatly.

"Ah."

"But I wouldn't let her do it."

"No?"

"I was embarrassed! I'd just gotten my period! I was supposed to kneel in the middle of the circle and stick a finger inside myself and show everyone the blood. Then give myself my special, secret name of womanhood."

He looked appalled. She had never told anyone about this particular idiosyncrasy, she realized. And clearly with good reason.

"I didn't want all those people looking at me. It was the most disgusting idea I'd ever heard. Besides, I didn't have a secret magical name I'd been burning to give myself. I was already Portia Nathan. That was enough of a burden. Being Susannah's daughter? Trust me. Enough of a burden."

"It certainly sounds like it."

Portia closed her eyes, the better to feel that hand, light like a feather, parting her thighs.

"You know," he said thoughtfully, "if I'd known you had this weakness for WASP men, I would have made my move in college, instead of just ogling you in Sanborn Library."

Portia wanted to laugh, but she found she didn't have the breath.

"I may not be a *Mayflower* descendant, but I did grow up on the Main Line. My family ate dinner off trays in the den, some nights."

"Well, that's . . . something." She smiled. "Not enough for a snob like me, of course. But you must be very proud."

"There are hunting prints on the staircase. We're short on emotion. Everyone knows who the alcoholics in the family are, but no one ever says anything. They just go on pouring the booze."

"Nice try," she said, sighing.

"I was hoping not to have to mention this," John said, "but I once owned a belt with whales on it."

"Oh, now you're getting me excited. If I'd known that at the time . . ."

"We have a family crest. My sister bought it from a mail-order company when she was twelve."

She opened her legs. His fingers, right away, were deep inside her.

"You're so wet," said John. All frivolity was gone; he was urgent and serious. He pulled her down beside him and kissed her closed eyelids. "Is it old wet or new wet?"

She couldn't answer right away, and when she did, the voice that emerged was far from steady. "Does it matter?"

"Not if it feels good. Does it feel good?"

"It feels . . ." She couldn't get the rest of it out.

He lifted himself up and smiled down at her. He had covered the length of her with his body: breast to breast, hip to hip, then hip to inner thigh. She was now only nominally in control of herself. His fingers, still inside her, were maddeningly controlled, regular, slick. They, and he, seemed not to care that she was moving—actually, thrashing—against him, and also, now that she could hear it, moaning some inarticulate thing. She felt the skin between them grow warm, then slippery with sweat, and a kind of ribbon of pleasure ascended inside her, circling her spine like a serpent coiling a staff. If it went on much longer, Portia thought, she would be forced to say something crude. Instead, she pulled him roughly into her and nearly cried with how sweet it was. She felt uncommonly wanton, greedy for exactly this, and now that she had it, she didn't want him to move. Luckily, he moved anyway.

It hadn't been like this with Mark at all. Mark had once joked that sexual ineptitude was his birthright as an Englishman, but, like any diligent scholar, he had set about learning her body as if she were material he knew he'd be tested on. Without doubt he'd become a technically alert and capable partner, adept at eliciting response, comforting, encouraging, safe. She had never complained about him, even to herself, but she had never thought of him as a lover, either. Partner, boyfriend, spouse in all but the fine print. Not a lover. This—above her, inside her, unalterably *with* her—was a lover, with a lover's smells and a lover's sounds, sending lover's sensations everywhere to the edges of her body. She couldn't bear to think what that made of her past.

He said, "Portia," just before he came, and then after, repeatedly, like a litany, until the word disassembled into breath and he slipped out of her with a shudder. They curled together and held fast, slowing from a run to a walk, and then a stop. When she opened her eyes, he was right there.

"Dear John." She smiled.

"Ouch."

"Your name is John. What's the problem? You used to leer at me in Sanborn."

"I didn't leer. I looked furtively. There's a difference. I wanted you. How was I to know I'd have to be a middle-aged man with thinning hair and a teenage son before you'd even look at me? When you stepped out of that car, I couldn't believe it. I couldn't believe I might get another chance."

"You act like I'm some kind of catch," said Portia, trying not to sound as if she were trawling for more compliments. "I'm just as middle-aged as you are. More, actually."

"You're lovely."

"I'm complicated."

"Your life may be complicated, but you're not. You're complex. That's not a bad thing at all."

"I'm a spinster."

"Oh, that's ridiculous."

"I live in New Jersey."

"That is a complication, but not fatal. And not a character flaw. I'm sure there are plenty of fascinating people who live in New Jersey. At least...a dozen."

"I'm a spinster who lives in New Jersey. I spend my days passing judgment on young people who are a whole lot more together than I was at their age, and probably am now. I have no children. I've obviously never had a successful relationship with a man, witness the fact that I am probably going to have to turn this house over to my partner of sixteen years, and his pregnant girlfriend. I can count my close friends on one finger. I barely tolerate having a relationship with my mother, who by the way is about to start taking care of a baby at the age of sixty-eight. I don't even have a dog."

John, who had endured this monologue with his head propped up on his hand, said, "Would you like a dog?"

Mark had been allergic. She hadn't thought about this in ages. "Yes, actually."

"Well, that takes care of that. Now you can be a childless New Jersey spinster with failed relationships, one friend, a strange mother, an unsatisfying job, a new house, and a dog. And me. If," he said, suddenly amiably, "you want me."

She touched his mouth. In the moonlight from the living room window, it had a greenish cast. After a moment, she realized that he was waiting for her, and with growing discomfort. "I didn't mean that my job was unsatisfying," she said, because she couldn't say what he wanted her to say. "I just meant, sometimes I feel as if it isn't fair that it's me making those decisions."

"Right. So the—how many years have you been doing this?"

"Sixteen."

"The sixteen years you've spent in this field, they don't count for anything. Sixteen years, hundreds of thousands of applications at two different Ivy League colleges, years of visiting schools, meeting with students, talking to counselors, administrators, alumni, colleagues, faculty...this is all bullshit, yes? I mean, anybody else could just jump in and do a better job."

She was laughing beside him. "Well, gee, if you put it that way. But you can't imagine what it's like. They're angry at you, all the time. After a while, it just grinds you down."

"Who's they? The applicants?"

"Everyone. They all have different agendas, but the one thing they have in common is that they're angry at you. I mean, me. Us. And I don't know if my colleagues feel it the way I do. Sometimes I wish I could just toughen up, you know? Not care so much."

"I'm sorry," he told her. "I still don't understand."

Portia sighed. "The applicants are angry because I can't see how special they are. Their parents are angry because I let in some other kid with a lower SAT score. The alumni are angry because they got into Princeton, but their brilliant kid got denied. The faculty's angry because we took the athlete, not the genius, but the football players know that it's easier to get in if you throw the discus, and all the violinists and pianists are pretty sure you have an edge if you play something strange, like the tuba or the harpsichord. All the New Yorkers believe that everyone applying from South Dakota gets in automatically, but out there in South Dakota they think they don't stand a chance at a place like Princeton. The working-class kids are convinced we're selling admission to the highest bidder. Simone is angry at us because we're elitist, but the elite know for sure that we're giving their places away to every black or Hispanic kid who applies. Nonlegacy kids are pissed off because they read somewhere that legacy kids are twice as likely to be admitted. But I've watched my boss get up in front of a packed house at reunions and tell all those loyal alumni that two-thirds of their kids are going to be rejected. Let me tell you, they're not thrilled about that. When I go out to visit schools, the kids are mad at me because they know I'm going to dangle this beautiful thing in front of them and encourage them to apply, and then reject their applications. The college counselors, the private ones who charge thousands of dollars, they're furious at us, because we're furious at them, and if we even smell them on an application it pisses us off, which makes it hard for them to sell their services to the parents, who are already angry at us and are now going to be angry at them, too. Should I keep going?"

"No!" he said, putting up his hands. "I get it. I get it."

"I now have a highly developed defense mechanism," she observed.

"I can feel it. It's like the walls of Troy."

Portia laughed. "I'm sorry. You wouldn't know it, but I really don't complain about this."

"No, I can tell," he said. "You have that combustible quality."

She closed her eyes. She had no idea what time it was or whether she should want to sleep. How many hours did they really have, after all, until he had to pick up Jeremiah and board a train, back to his customary life? After which she would...what? Return to the office? Clean out the refrigerator? Do her laundry?

"Are you cold?" he asked her. "Should we get a blanket?"

"I can do better than that. I can offer you a real bed. The sheets are even clean."

"That sounds like the height of luxury. I accept."

She climbed over him and reached down to pick up her clothes off the floor. John got up beside her. Sweetly, he took her hand as she led him upstairs. She took Mark's former side of the bed for herself, on purpose.

"You know," he whispered, pulling her against him, "I was just thinking, I don't know that I've ever heard the word *spinster* spoken out loud. Except in a production of *The Music Man*. I've certainly never spoken it myself."

"It's a terrifically efficient word. It says so much in two little syllables."

"Portia, you are not a spinster. Please."

She sighed.

"Listen," he said. He had curled around her, one leg between her legs, his mouth at her nape. "I had this radical idea. I know it's your bunker season, but could you come down to Wayne with us tomorrow? I promise, I'm not looking for the ride. I just wondered if you could get away for the day. I mean, it's Saturday...."

No, she started to say automatically. But even as the word formed, she found that she was turning this unexpected idea over and giving it a hard look. "For how long?" she asked.

"As long as you like. We're taking Jeremiah and Simone to Penn and Swarthmore, assuming Deborah and Simone are hitting Bryn Mawr in the morning. I'd like Nelson to have some time with his grandparents. I expect we'll head back to New Hampshire on Monday or Tuesday. Come on, come see how we really live on the Main Line." He grinned. "I'll ask Mom to throw a tailgate."

"Don't tease me," said Portia. "I'm actually thinking about it."

"Good." He kissed her neck softly. "Sleep on it. While I murmur post-somnolent suggestions into your ear. *Come with me to the land of the WASP—*"

"Are you kidding?" She laughed. "Where do you think I live?"

"I would have been down here months ago," said John. His tone had shifted, downhill, slower. "I would have come to see you. If you'd answered my letter, or contacted me. I would have been out there on the sidewalk throwing pebbles at that window."

"Well," she reminded him, "that was also my . . . someone else's window." But even as she said this, she noted something surprising: that the thought of Mark and Helen-with-child had not, for the first time, brought its customary stab of pain. She would have said something to this effect, but before she could think what it was, she had fallen deeply asleep.

*I have engaged in a myriad of activities at my school, none more
meaningful to me than accompanying the A Cappella choir.*

CHAPTER NINETEEN

THE LAND OF THE WASP

Jeremiah had seen Toni Morrison on Nassau Street, carrying a cup of coffee from Starbucks and a copy of *The New York Times*. He was beside himself, barely earthbound when they met him back at Mathey and extracted him, with difficulty, from the ersatz Gothic quadrangle. Strapped into the backseat but gripping the headrests in front, he pulled himself forward and talked incessantly as Portia drove south into Pennsylvania, his head protruding between their heads, his running commentary ricocheting among topics like a pinball: Luke's roommate from Maryland, the girl in the philosophy seminar who was "completely, completely" wrong about the Skeptics, the modern dance group last night, performing to a student quartet, *Beloved*, Professor Friedman's brown wool pants, which had a big hole in the knee (Portia was not remotely surprised to learn), and how the morning's dignified debate about Infinitism versus Foundationalism had descended into a thoroughly simplistic argument about how we could know if we were conscious beings at all and not just cells in a petri dish being manipulated by some unknown being. She was starting to feel a little light-headed, listening to him.

"Jeremiah," John said, laughing, "slow down. I beg you."

"I stayed and talked to him," Jeremiah said urgently. "We walked back to his office. He gave me a logic book and a list of stuff to read."

And he was off again: the student film they'd shown at *This Is Princeton*, and the Indian dance troupe, Luke's girlfriend, who was from Taiwan, a chemist, some kind of prodigy, the boy from upstairs who was writing a novel and taking a class from Joyce Carol Oates, the vegan burger he had eaten for dinner at Mathey, selected by mistake but actually not terrible. And *Jesus Christ, Toni Morrison!* Right there on the street!

This Is Princeton, Portia was trying to explain to John, was a sort of university variety show, comprising not only student clubs like the African drummers, Mexican dancers, a cappella groups (which were legion), improv sketch comics, rappers, ballerinas, spoken-word artists, and musicians of myriad stripes, but also the occasional faculty member or alum, who might play an instrument or sing. Portia had always liked it, because it made the applications transform to three-dimensional flesh, and she had more than once, from her seat in Richardson Auditorium, experienced a jolt of recognition: *So this is the national youth champion banjo player from Alaska* and *That must be the girl who was offered a place in the ABT corps de ballet but wanted to be a doctor instead.* To her, the annual event was a pageant of good decisions, a literal chorus of approval that she (uncharacteristically, but who would ever know?) felt entitled to take personally. "We should have gone," she said quietly to John.

"We were busy," he replied.

They were nearly passing Newtown before Jeremiah finally ran out of steam. Then he sat back and opened the book David had given him and was heard no more.

They drove south along the highway, beneath loaded winter skies. Portia had not slept particularly well, waking intermittently on the unaccustomed side of the bed, with the unaccustomed body, breathing, beside her, and lying there for long, elastic minutes, waiting for exhaustion and anxiety to battle it out. At dawn she had been woken again, this time to his hands running over her rib cage and a following jolt of desire. She marveled at how he seemed to take, at every point, the better fork in the road—soft over hard, slow over fast—until she understood that she was telling him everything he needed to know, and then she marveled at that. He pulled back the blankets and simply looked at her, and she found, to her own surprise, that she loved being frankly examined by someone who so plainly found her beautiful. They had spent the morning that way, drifting between sleep and talk and sex, but then, when it was finally time to leave the bed, they were both (as if following the same inner script) stricken with an almost comical awkwardness. Portia, when she managed to extricate herself, scurried to the bathroom, locked the door, and washed fiercely in the shower, emerging to find that there were, of course, no clean towels in evidence—no towels at all. She stuck her dripping head back into the bedroom and discovered him still under the covers, reading her Pollock biography.

"Um, see any towels?"

He did not. He offered to look in the closet, but there was four feet of dirty laundry in the closet she preferred him not to know about, so she asked for one of the blankets from the bed. He brought it to her, but not before wrapping it around his own waist, and when she came out moments later, still wrapped up in it, he was dressed. In the end, she found only a not terrible pair of brown corduroys and a shirt and sweater left behind by Mark. She looked presentable, if slightly butch. She had, quite on purpose, no real plan for later, and she was trying hard not to examine her options. Purposely, perversely, she had brought nothing with her: no change of clothes (as if she knew the whereabouts of clean clothes), no toiletries.

She knew her way around the Main Line, more or less, and had an impression of Wayne, where John had grown up, as a region straddling the border between horse country and suburbia, with serious affluence on either side. She knew that she was going to the house John had lived in from the age of four, and where his parents—following the departure of his younger sister and himself—had continued to live, with a succession of chocolate Labs. He insisted they would be happy to see her, unannounced though she might be. Not that they were easygoing people, he noted, go-with-the-flow types with extra beds at the ready and the makings to feed a crowd always on hand.

"My mom is very hospitable, but she's a planner," he explained. "You don't surprise her and expect to be welcomed. But she already knows she's getting two adults and three teenagers. Another body won't throw her. We're going to bill you as my old friend from Dartmouth who was kind enough to pull a few strings for Jeremiah."

"Oh, don't say that," she said, her voice dropping. It startled her, how instantly she was on edge. "I can't be associated with the phrase *pull a few strings*. I mean, I know I get a little paranoid about this stuff. But it's important."

"I meant because you arranged for him to go to a class, that's all."

"I know, I know," she said, feeling pretty stupid by now.

Silence ensued. It was weighted, but just this side of unpleasant.

"I wonder how Simone's liking Bryn Mawr," John said finally.

"Simone," said Portia, relieved by the segue, "is a piece of work."

"A work in progress," he chided. "She's only sixteen."

"I thought she was a senior, when I visited the school. She really took me on."

"Yes. She can't help it, you know. I mean, she has this oppositional temperament, which is innate, and if that weren't enough, she's a little bit like you were in the nurture department. Also brought up to be a warrior. But you know what? I feel like she's one of those kids who needs to crash into something before she figures out how not to do it. She's going to be great, when the smoke clears. But she'll bang herself up a lot first."

Portia sighed. "I forgot, you really know kids. All these years of teaching. You've seen everything."

"Well," he said affably, "so have you."

"No. I just see what they show me. I see the part of the iceberg that's above the waterline. Which isn't the scary part."

He turned in his seat and looked at her, his eyes boring through her peripheral vision. She pretended not to notice this, focusing instead on the road, which now twisted through tended meadows and cultivated yards, overgrown contemporary homes interspersed with older but just as expensive properties. She drove past a paddock with two roan horses grazing at the split rail fence. They were in serious tally-ho country, the horse farms and gated estates interspersed with new developments all too happy to take up the theme: Hunter's Chase, the Copse at Wyndmoor, Fox Run Estates. "You grew up here," she observed.

"Yes. Awful, isn't it? These all used to be farms. There was a farm next door to us. Now it has forty horrible homes on it, every one of them with a media center and a three-car garage." He shook his head. "But I'm just confirming all of your suspicions about the snobbery of Main Line WASPs."

"Not at all," she said, though she had been thinking exactly that. "What about your house?"

"Well, my house reflects the snobbery of an earlier time. I know that. It has every luxury on offer in the 1920s, and a bunch added on later. But maybe without this compulsion to use up every square inch of the land, just because you can. And please don't get my mother started on this. Preserving open land is one of her big things. She's gone for these long walks, for years, with the dogs. A few years ago she got hit by a golf ball off one of the courses. I don't think I've ever seen her so angry. Well, apart from the time I told her I was going to Uganda." He laughed shortly.

"Was she hurt?" Portia asked.

"Not really. Not physically. But she hasn't missed a zoning board meeting since then. We're getting close now," he said, pointing at the upcoming gap in a stone wall. The mailbox, in faded, hand-painted blue, read "Halsey."

Portia pulled off the road and drove down a long gravel track, through maple trees. The house, when it appeared, was modestly small from the front, but when John directed her past it to the detached garage, she saw that it had expanded, probably over time, in nearly a straight line, so that it resembled a classic but plainly modern version of the old New England chant: "Big house, little house, back house, barn." The long tail of the building ended before a pond, ringed by carefully placed flat stones and abutted by a garden in its winter netting.

"Oh," said John as she parked beside a blue Subaru with New Hampshire plates. Deborah's car, Portia recognized. "I thought they'd spend the afternoon at Bryn Mawr," he said, climbing out. Two great brown dogs came bounding up to him.

"Hey, guys. Samson and Delilah," he said, introducing them to Portia.

They went wild at the sound of their names.

"I love the smell of wet dog in the morning." He laughed, petting them and fending them off at the same time. And they were indeed wet, Portia noted, stepping back. And very muddy.

"Well, hi!" A woman emerged from the garage.

John pushed away the dogs and hugged her. She was short and thick through the middle, but very hale. She was dressed in the kind of clothes people wore to appear as if they relished outdoor life, but her khakis and quilted olive green jacket were the real article: streaked with brown mud, frayed at the edges. On her feet, old Wellington boots were encrusted with dirt. She looked, thought Portia, very little like John, except — she decided, eyeing the wrist protruding from that olive jacket as she hugged her son — this peculiar, embedded grace in the shoulders, arms, and hands. When they broke apart, when the wrist retreated into her coat sleeve and the hands made briefly for her coat pockets, even that small resemblance evaporated.

"This is my old friend Portia Nathan," John said, and his mother turned to her. She had a great correctness about this transition, giving him his long maternal embrace and only afterward seeming to notice Portia, and then Jeremiah, in the proper order. She extended her hand graciously, also in that order.

"Hello," said Portia, "Mrs. Halsey."

"And this is Jeremiah Balakian."

"I'm very happy to see you, Jeremiah. Portia?" she asked, though she had just heard the name.

"Yes."

"Old friend? From school?"

"Yes," said Portia.

"No," said John. "I mean, not from Lawrenceville. From Dartmouth. Portia very kindly gave us a ride down. We stayed in Princeton last night."

"I live in Princeton," she added, probably unnecessarily.

"I thought you were all coming together," his mother said. "Deborah came separately with the kids."

The kids, noted Portia, her antennae prickling. To John's mother, the former partners and their children plainly represented some flavor of family unit.

"I wasn't expecting them to show up till later," he told her. "They were supposed to go see Bryn Mawr this afternoon."

"Oh, they did," his mother said, rolling her eyes. "Only apparently Simone took one look and refused to get out of the car."

Portia laughed. "In the trade, we call that a drive-by. The kid says, 'No way am I going here.' The best option for parents is to move along."

John's mother looked keenly at Portia. She had straight hair, still somewhat blond but liberally interspersed with steely gray. "What trade is that?" she asked Portia.

"Portia is an admissions officer," John said. "At Princeton."

Those eyes, like so many eyes before them, reacted to this news.

"Well, welcome," she told them, her ingrained good manners reasserting themselves. "Come inside. I'm ready for some coffee. The dogs and I are just back from our walk. We walked all the way to Chanticleer," she told her son, who scowled.

"Mom, it's too far. Why don't you just stick with Willow Park? Isn't that enough?"

"Well, it was for me, but the dogs objected," she told her son.

"Please tell me you took a phone with you."

"Okay. I can tell you that." She held open the door for them and shut it once Jeremiah had passed inside.

Portia found herself in a warm central hall with a staircase that climbed upward to a formal landing, a round wooden table in the center of the floor, and a worn brass chandelier overhead. On the table: neatly stacked letters, the kind no one was supposed to be writing anymore, a muddle of keys in a china dish, and a photo of smiling John and his smiling female counterpart (long necked, dimpled, brandishing diploma) in a silver frame.

"I promised you hunting prints," John said puckishly, at her elbow.

"I'm sorry?" his mother asked.

Portia looked up. The prints climbed the stairs, framed in uniform cherry. She smiled.

"What about the prints?" said his mother.

"I was telling Portia about them." He set down the bags, his own and Jeremiah's.

"Do you ride?" his mother asked, looking at Portia in surprise.

"No, no. Well, once, when I was a child."

"But you're interested in hunting?" She seemed appropriately perplexed.

"No, not really."

She glanced resentfully at John, who was pretending not to enjoy himself.

Just off the staircase, a formal archway led to a living room that was itself classically formal, with long chintz sofas from which a teenager's blue-jeaned legs were just visible and a mantelpiece festooned with more silver frames. There was motion from the landing above as Deborah material-ized. Simone emerged from another doorway off the entrance hall, holding her place in a thick paperback, looking characteristically put upon. Behind her, Portia saw a dark, wood-paneled room lined with bookshelves.

"Hi," Simone managed.

"Hey, Simone," said John. "I heard you didn't see eye to eye with Bryn Mawr."

"No way," she said tersely. "Forget it."

"Some of my dearest friends went to Bryn Mawr," said John's mother. "It was always a place for smart, ambitious women."

Simone made a face. She was about to say something acerbic — even Portia could tell — but her mother cut her off.

"Just not a good fit. We decided to come visit with Eve and Robert. Save ourselves for Penn in the morning."

"How was Princeton?" Simone asked Jeremiah.

"Oh, my God." He shook his head. "Amazing."

"Portia arranged..." John glanced at her. "Portia has a friend who teaches philosophy. She asked him if Jeremiah could attend his class this morning. It was such a great opportunity for him, I thought the two of us should stay over."

"You stayed in a hotel?" his mother asked.

"I was going to," he said with what seemed like real nonchalance. "But Portia had a guest room. Jeremiah stayed with an undergraduate."

Eve Halsey looked first at Deborah, plainly trying to get a grasp on the interpersonal situation. Beneath her placid demeanor, she seemed to be genuinely puzzled: Which, if either of these women, was her son "with"? And what, to an unmarried man in his late thirties with a tall black son from the other side of the planet, did "with," after all, mean? Deborah, with admirable indifference, merely smiled and slung her arm over her daughter's thin shoulders.

"Well," John's mother finally said to Portia, "that was extremely nice of you."

"No, not at all," Portia told her. "It was nice to catch up with John. And I think it's great that Jeremiah was able to sit in on a class."

"Hey, Nelson," John said loudly. "Are you in the house?"

"Hey," came the voice from the general vicinity of those blue-jeaned legs on the living room couch.

"Could you come out and show yourself?"

"I'm on level five," he called in apparent explanation.

"Well, that is exciting," John said dryly. "But there are actual human beings here, who would like to see you. One of them is your father."

There was a grudging sigh from beyond the wall and a rustle of silk. Nelson appeared, holding an open laptop.

"You loaned him your laptop?" John asked his mother, looking as if she had let him play with her Uzi.

"Hey," Nelson said to Portia. He gave his father a brief embrace.

"Why not?" Eve Halsey said. "He promised me it wasn't one of those awful ones, with blood flying everywhere."

"Level *five*," Nelson reiterated.

"I saw the best minds of his generation gummed up with video game dreck, lost forever on *level five*," John lamented.

Deborah laughed. "Come on, John. If Allen Ginsberg were alive today, he'd probably have a huge video game collection."

"Yeah," Jeremiah said brightly. "Pong for disembodied poetics! Like, instead of the ball, it would be Corso versus Kerouac, hurling metaphors through cyberspace."

"That would be terrible, you know," Deborah said brightly. "You'd have to think while you played it."

"Pong?" said Nelson, looking at Jeremiah in clear disgust. "What are you, like, forty?"

John then leapt into the fray, elicited a grudging apology from Nelson, and instructed him to lead Jeremiah upstairs, to the room they would be sharing—his own childhood room, he informed Portia, unreconstructed for twenty years, still ornamented with the usual embarrassing teenage ephemera. Deborah and Simone were to sleep next door, in the pink princess beds that once belonged to John's sister, Diana. Portia watched the four of them climb the stairs.

"I hope you'll be able to stay for dinner, Portia," said John's mother. "I just put a roast in. John's sister is coming later, with her daughter. I know they'd love to meet you. My granddaughter, Kelsey, is in eleventh grade at Baldwin. Do you know Baldwin?"

"Of course," Portia said brightly, even as she shriveled inside. "Wonderful school."

"Then you'll stay?" John's mother said, as if the prospect of an eleventh grader from a highly competitive prep school were actually an inducement.

"Well, thank you. I'm not sure of my plans, actually. I'm kind of on the lam from work. It's our busy season. . . ."

She glanced helplessly at John, who managed to communicate sincere embarrassment while seeming fascinated by the carved banister of the staircase. Then again, if the lingering inappropriateness of her contact with Jeremiah was not enough to chase her away, she was hardly going to assign that power to a Main Line private school mom and her undoubtedly Ivy-aspiring daughter. And the truth, which was only now occurring to her, was that she wasn't ready to leave yet.

"But certainly, I'd love to stay for dinner."

"Wonderful. Well, I have to go wash the great outdoors off. John? You're downstairs." She whistled, and with a magisterial sweep of her hands, the two muddy dogs roused themselves and trotted into the kitchen, where they stayed. Then she shed her muddy boots and walked upstairs, looking purposeful. Portia could almost hear the update she was about to deliver to her daughter on the phone and the strict instructions to the surely terrific Kelsey.

John took her hand. "Come with me," he said.

He took her downstairs, past a storeroom and a wine cellar and a Ping-Pong table slightly too large for the room it was in. At the end of the corridor, the door to a small guest room had been left open. He tossed his bag on the bed beside a crisply folded towel, hand towel, and washcloth, left in a precisely stacked pile. Then he kissed her, pulling her against him. For a long moment, Portia forgot where she was.

"This is a very erotic scenario for me," he said affably, coming up for air. "You know, beautiful girl, in the basement of my own house, with my parents upstairs."

"As well as your ex," she reminded him. "And your adolescent son. And your ex's teenaged daughter. And your student."

"Killjoy," he commented, kissing her again. "Wanna sleep over?"

"Not if I have to provide free college counseling for your niece."

"Ow." He grimaced. "I'm sorry. My mom isn't really sensitive that way. You don't have to. I'm sure you're good at repelling the advances of high school juniors and their fond parents."

"Well..." She sighed. "You sort of have to be."

He smiled. "In the trade."

"In the trade."

"So, you'll sleep over?"

"I really should call my office," said Portia. "While we've been amusing ourselves, there's a stack of files with my name on it, getting taller and taller."

"Portia," he reminded her, "it's Saturday night. You're expected to work Saturday night?"

"In February? Saturday night. Friday night. All day Sunday. We get to hibernate in the summertime."

"Dad!" Nelson howled from the top of the basement stairs.

"Yes?"

"Everyone's reading, and Grandma took her laptop back. I'm bored."

"Oh no!" said John, grinning. "He's bored. Let's call the National Guard."

"Dad!" Nelson called. "Did you hear me?"

"The whole neighborhood heard you, Nel." His father laughed. "Hang on." He squeezed Portia's wrist. "If you have to leave, I do understand. But stay if you can. I'll never let my sister get you alone. I won't let any of them get you alone," he told her. "Except for me."

*Princeton has been a part of my family since I can remember. I grew
up hearing my grandfather's stories about rowing on Lake Carnegie,
and my parents' (much less dignified!) accounts of Saturday nights
on Prospect. Certainly, all three of them have enormous affection for
the institution, but they have not spared me the difficulties of being
African-American at a place like Princeton in the 1950s, and even, for
my parents, in the 1980s. In spite of this, I grew up understanding that
Princeton was a place where amazing things could be experienced,
and it has always been my passionate wish to follow my parents and
grandfather.*

CHAPTER TWENTY

FAIR IS KIND OF AN IMPRECISE CONCEPT

The family chin that John had once briefly mentioned, months earlier
in a dark hotel room in New Hampshire, materialized that evening
on the various faces of his father, sister, and niece. It was a broad chin
and quite masculine, which was somewhat less successful on the women,
but it lent John's sister, Diana, in particular, an air of command. This was
matched by a personality at once insistent and impatient, though just on
the near side of rude. Obviously tipped off, she made for Portia immediately, taking the other half of a too small sofa in the living room and leaning right in. Within moments, Portia was the possessor of Diana Halsey
Bennet's entire résumé, and John's sister was already moving on to the
unnaturally engorged résumé of her daughter, Kelsey (field hockey captain,
class secretary, treasurer of the literary magazine), who sat on the other
side of the living room, looking—to her credit—horribly embarrassed.

"I've always had a soft spot for Princeton," Diana said, sipping a glass of
white wine. "My husband went to Cornell."

Portia thought she'd better not comment on this apparent non sequitur.

"Cornell's a fantastic school," she said. "I think it's the best place in the country for some things."

"It was his safety," Diana said shortly. "He was supposed to go to Yale."

Portia wondered bleakly what "supposed to" was supposed to mean in this context. She certainly wasn't going to ask.

"Well, it's nobody's safety anymore," she responded. "Your mother is so great. I can't get over how she just handles all these people for dinner, including an unexpected guest." She hoped, perhaps not very realistically, that this would lead them to another topic or at least constitute an unignorable hint.

But Diana did not disappoint her. "That's the truth," she said with palpable distaste. "My friend Margery's daughter, Whitney, graduated last year from Baldwin. I couldn't believe it. This girl had 750s on her SATs and was in the top ten percent of her class. At Baldwin! I mean, it's not like the top ten percent at Baldwin is like the top ten percent at a public school. And Cornell turned her down. Even Tufts and Wesleyan turned her down."

"Tufts and Wesleyan are highly selective. They always have been, but now, statistically, they're as selective as the Ivies were when you and I applied to college."

Deflecting the appeal to camaraderie, Diana set her formidable jaw. For her, as for so many members of their generation, time had stood still. Obviously, the Ivies were tough, at least some of them. But other New England private colleges were supposed to catch the overflow. Wasn't that their job?

"You know," Portia said wearily, "it's just brutal for these kids. Every day I feel lucky that I'm not applying to colleges now. The field is so much bigger and so much better prepared. Which is a wonderful thing, of course. But for the kids, especially if they've gotten the idea that there are only a few places they can go and feel good about themselves, it's very difficult."

"Sure," Diana said dismissively, "but how are they supposed to feel if they can't get into their parents' colleges? I mean, what kind of message does that send, when they work hard and are so accomplished? And I can tell you, in a lot of cases I know, the kid's a much better student than the dad ever was. Some of Kevin's friends—Kevin is my husband—you know, they just trotted off to Yale and Dartmouth, and they weren't exactly intellectuals. Then along come their kids, thirty years later. And they've got straight A's, and they've dug, I don't know, sewage pits in Ecuador, and their teachers are raving about them, and they all have toll-free scores."

She stopped. She eyed Portia. "You know that expression?"

Grimly, Portia nodded. It was the highly tacky code for straight 800s.

"Right. And these kids not only are not getting into Dad's alma mater. They're not getting into Dad's safety school. They're not getting into some school Dad's never even heard of, that the guidance counselor swears is the so-called new Ivy or the Harvard of the upper plains. I think it's just a catastrophe."

Portia, by this time, was actually appalled, but she had not *quite* given up hope. "I'm sorry, I don't see that," she said carefully, "I mean, catastrophe? Maybe if the few schools you're talking about were the only places to get an education in this country. They're not. I think the landscape of higher education is pretty fantastic right now. All kinds of places are attracting great faculty and developing infrastructure. And the students are of such a high caliber that they're challenging the institutions to meet their needs. It's a great time to go to college, even at the state schools and those Harvards of the upper plains, and the little colleges that we never used to hear much about. We've got a real 'lift all boats' situation," she finished heartily. "I think, anyway."

There was more, of course. With the right audience, she would have lobbed in the old chestnut about Bill Gates dropping out of Harvard, or the recent statistic about how more CEOs had attended state universities than Ivy League schools, or even that some of the most impressive entrepreneurs these days seemed to be marching out the gates of quirky Hampshire, where the students a generation ago had been best known for on-campus farming and pharmaceuticals. But this was not the right audience, and it was frankly getting harder and harder for Portia to suppress her irritation. She shifted on the couch, letting John, seated across the room between Nelson and his niece, Kelsey, catch her eye long enough to convey his apologies. She was exhausted: the night, the drive, the bombardment of faces and surprising emotions, not to mention random desire, so inappropriate in the immediate circumstances. On another occasion, she would have been more than content to lay it all out for John's sister, and (in absentia) her bewildered friend Margery, and all the other aghast moms at the Baldwin School and every school of its ilk from wealthy suburb to wealthy suburb, from here to far Tortuga. She would have smugly, sharply, explained to Diana that the system—the much maligned system that so perplexed and offended the woman beside her—did not exist to validate her child's life, let alone her child's parents' lives. It did not exist to crown the best and the brightest, reward the hardest workers, or cast judgment on those who had not fulfilled their potential by the ripe age of eighteen. It certainly did not exist to congratulate those parents who had done the best parenting, pureed the most organic baby foods, wielded the most flash cards, hired the most tutors, or driven the greatest distances to the greatest number of field hockey games.

The system, as far as she was concerned, was not about the applicant at all. It was about the institution.

It was about delivering to the trustees, and to a lesser extent the faculty, a United Nations of scholars, an Olympiad of athletes, a conservatory of artists and musicians, a Great Society of strivers, and a treasury of riches so idiosyncratic and ill defined that the Office of Admission would not know how to go about looking for them and could not hope to find them if they suddenly stopped turning up of their own accord. So get over yourself, Portia thought through her tight, achingly tight, smile, because Diana had now moved on to last year's scholarship girl, the daughter of the school janitor, who had gone off to Harvard and was a lovely, *lovely* girl, of course, and certainly a wonderful little flute player, but had scored over one hundred points lower on the math SAT than the class salutatorian, who had been rejected not only by Harvard, but by Yale, Princeton, Brown, Dartmouth, Williams, Amherst, and—*can you believe this?*—NYU. And come on, everyone knew what that meant. And how—*how?*—could it be fair?

"Well...fair...," Portia said weakly. "Fair is kind of an imprecise concept."

"I don't think so," said Diana.

She appeared shocked. With a sinking heart, Portia could just imagine how this was going to play at Monday-morning drop-off.

"How," said Diana with great precision, "can you participate in a system you know to be unfair?"

Somewhere in the vicinity of her right ocular orbit, a whisper of pain flickered to life and persisted. How can I buy a cheap shirt at Wal-Mart knowing it's made by an illiterate ten-year-old? she wondered crossly. How can I employ an undocumented worker to mow my lawn and pretend he doesn't exist the rest of the time? What kind of life did this woman think she was living?

"Oh no," she said, in order to keep from saying any of these things. "What we do, it's very complex, but scrupulously fair. I didn't mean that. I meant...I suppose it's like building a better fruit basket." There was, she noted, a slightly absurd brightness in her voice. "You know, the apples might outshine everything else, but if you wanted a basket of apples, you'd only be considering the apples. You know?"

John's sister was looking at her intently. She wasn't giving an inch.

"You want everything in there. You want bananas and oranges and...I don't know, kiwis and mangoes. You want some exotic stuff that you've never even heard of. All kinds of fruit," she finished idiotically, "make a fruit basket."

Diana observed her coolly.

Her mother came by with a plate of Brie and crackers. "What are you two talking about?" she said, looking confident of the response.

"Fruit," Diana said dryly.

Mrs. Halsey frowned and moved on.

"Everything is read so, so carefully," Portia said, her voice low, as if this were secret, privileged information. "You can't imagine how much thought goes into these decisions. We know they're important. We know these are teenagers who've worked incredibly hard. We know that behind every one of those kids is a family and teachers and guidance counselors. We get that, don't worry."

"But I just don't see," said Diana, right back to where she had apparently departed the conversation, "how it's fair to ask kids to do great in school and score well on all these tests and then just ignore all that because they're up against..." She considered. "A more exotic fruit."

"The tests..." Portia shrugged. "You know, they're not a really good predictor of success at the college level. Only success—gradewise—for the first year of college. After that it seems to even out. And they're certainly no predictor of other things we value, like creativity and perseverance. And the grades, of course it's true that it's harder to get an A at Baldwin than in some other schools. But our mantra, really, is success within the applicant's setting. Wherever they've grown up, however they've grown up, we want them to have done everything they could with what they've had. So okay, maybe that Baldwin student had to be very bright and work very hard to do as well as she's done, but maybe she's also grown up in a household where people read books, or even just the newspaper. Lots of them don't have that, you know. How can you truly compare a kid who's been taken to the theater and art museums, or out of the country, to someone whose family couldn't afford basic nutrition and medical care, or who had to waste half his energy worrying about getting evicted? Or even just a kid who had to come up with the idea of going to college on his own, because that's far from a foregone conclusion where he comes from? We see all kinds of unfair. Morally," she concluded, but without much hope of the outcome, "the whole thing's an obstacle course."

"Oh, I'm sure your job is very hard." Diana shrugged, looking as if she were sure of no such thing. She was also looking peevishly at her daughter, as if the looming social diminishment she anticipated were all the girl's fault. "But let me ask you something. Why do you even ask, on the applications, where the parents have gone to college? I mean, if you're just going to penalize the kids for having parents who read the newspaper and take them to Europe. Isn't it better not to ask at all? I mean," she said, utterly missing the point, "the less you know, the more level the playing field. That's what I think."

Portia looked sadly at the now empty wineglass in her hand. She could not remember, really, drinking it, let alone how it had tasted, but she saw that it had been red, and she very much wanted more of it. "We ask," she said, "because it helps us create a more meaningful picture of where the kid is coming from. *And* because it matters to us if their parent went to Princeton. *And* because it matters to us if they're the first in their families to go to college. Everything matters," she finished lamely.

"Right," Diana said, looking truly indignant now. "So if my child isn't a legacy and isn't a minority either, the fat lady's basically already singing."

"No. No..." Portia looked desperately across the room, but John was now deep in conversation with his father. She was stranded on this fatal shore with no rescue in sight.

"Well, that's what I'm hearing. You're sitting pretty if your parents sneaked over the border, lack basic hygiene, pick crops for a living, are constantly threatened with eviction, and never read a newspaper. All you have to do is get the bright idea that you should go to college and the Ivy League sends you a first-class ticket. But if you have parents who truly value education and work their butts off to pay for the best schools they can afford, you're a dime a dozen."

"Diana, that's *not*—"

"But you know," she rolled on, "I don't think you people have any idea about the impact this is having. All those loyal alumni whose children aren't getting in, if you think they're going to keep on blithely writing checks to their alma mater, you're going to be very surprised. That's going to cut down on the first-class tickets, I would think."

The conversation, thought Portia, was now officially a lost cause. She looked sadly into her wineglass.

Diversion would come only with the contretemps between Deborah and Simone, audible even from upstairs, where the two had withdrawn to quarrel at full volume. The sounds were nonspecific but clearly outraged, and only Nelson and Jeremiah, playing a game of chess on the window seat, seemed genuinely unruffled. Diana, in plain discomfort, announced that she could never have gotten away with screaming at her own mother, a comment that was unheard by Mrs. Halsey (now in the kitchen) and could thus not be contradicted. Kelsey, Portia noticed, received this statement with a roll of her eyes, which made Portia smile. John got up from the opposite couch, where he had been speaking with his father, and came to get her.

"Thank you," she said when he had led her out of the room, announcing that they had volunteered to set the table.

"I wouldn't have left you, but there wasn't room on the couch. And you know, my sister wasn't going to rest until she got you to talk. Can you blame her? In her world, information is power. You've got the information."

"Everyone's got the information," Portia said, annoyed. "Every person who's ever left a job in admissions has written a book about it. Every one of them has spilled the deep, dark secrets about how to get in or shoot yourself in the foot. Anyone with twenty bucks can buy the entire codebook on Amazon. I can't tell your sister a single thing at least a dozen other people haven't published in hardcover, paperback, and assorted digital formats. Come on!"

He shrugged. "I guess she thinks there's more. Maybe you all swear a blood oath never to reveal the one crucial thing. You know, anyone who hikes the Appalachian Trail on a pogo stick automatically gets admitted. Nobody named Fred or Poindexter will ever get a place."

Despite herself, she laughed. "How did you find that out?" she said. "It had to be torture."

"Close," he said affably. "It was sex."

Simone, red in the face, came tearing down the stairs and out the front door.

"Let her go," Deborah said, following wearily. "She needs to calm down."

Portia looked after her. In a gesture that even she recognized as typical, Simone had pointedly left the door ajar, and wet snow was floating onto the foyer floor. "It's kind of cold," she noted.

"She'll come back when she's ready," said Deborah, closing the door. "I'm assuming I don't have to worry about her getting mugged in Wayne, Pennsylvania?"

This seemed not to require a response.

"What was it about?" said John.

"Oh..." Deborah shrugged. "Penn. College. Life. Me. The grand themes." She shoved her hands deep into her jeans pockets. "You know what's weird? When you're a single mom, and everybody talks about how hard it must be, what they mean is the little-kid stuff. Getting up in the middle of the night all the time because there's no one else to do it, or having to take on all the doctors' appointments and parent-teacher conferences yourself. But I'm telling you, that was nothing. This teenager stuff is hard. This is, like, crazy hard."

"It looks it," Portia said, and was quickly ashamed of having said it, as she sometimes was when called to comment on matters of parents or children. But nobody seemed to react.

John's mother called them to dinner, and the table was hurriedly set. They sat to reassuringly myriad conversations, blessedly unconnected to anything of colleges, essays, standardized tests, or the wider implications of "the application process." Portia drank more wine and ate happily, reveling in the old-fashioned staunchness of the meal: roast, salad, potatoes. She was sitting, quite deliberately, beside John, whose thigh rested against her own in a reassuring, not overtly sexual gesture. His attention, though, was dominated by the far corner of the table, where his father sat beside Nelson.

Beside, thought Portia, following his gaze. But not, somehow, interacting. Mr. Halsey, still a man of physical presence and not a little innate beauty, looked almost pained as he sat, skewed in his chair, turned definitively away from his grandson. He spoke, instead, across the granddaughter to his right, who shared his coloring and chin, to his daughter, who gestured with the long fingers of her left hand as she cut, speared, and lifted cubes of roasted potatoes with her right. They were talking about redress, a contractor who had walked off the job, something related to marble, which had arrived too veined or not veined enough. Kelsey, the field hockey captain, sat stiffly, eating in silence, and Nelson, who seemed not to have noticed that he was being ignored, watched the exchange, frowning occasionally at the indecipherable parts.

"I'm telling you," said Diana, "it's a good thing I didn't listen to Kevin and give him the rest of the money up front. He wanted it, you know."

"I hope you know what you're doing," said Mrs. Halsey. "You put one glass or one plate down a tiny bit too hard and it smashes to little pieces. I think you're much better off with Corian. Ours looks exactly the way it looked when it went in."

Her husband nodded. "Can't destroy it."

"Mom," John said suddenly, "did I tell you that Nelson wrote an essay for a state competition?"

"Black History Month," Nelson said affably.

"He's a finalist," John went on. "We're going to Manchester next week for a ceremony with the governor."

"Well," said his mother. "Nelson, congratulations."

"What's your essay about?" Portia asked.

"Buck Jordan," said Nelson. "And the Negro Leagues."

"Baseball," John said helpfully.

"Yes, of course," his father said. "Eve, is there any more of the wine?"

"I can open another bottle," she said, rising.

Portia felt an unmistakable chill settle over the table, or at least their end of it.

After a moment, John's father turned to Deborah. "Sure you shouldn't go after her?" he said.

"I'm thinking about it," she said uncomfortably. But even as she said it, they all heard the front door click heavily open. There was a conspiracy of silence as Simone stalked in, surveyed the table and its open setting, and sat down heavily. Without a word, Jeremiah passed her the roasted potatoes. John's mother returned and handed the open bottle to her husband.

"Portia," she said with a deliberate brightness, "can I ask you, how did you get into admissions work? Is it something you go to school for?"

"Oh...no. Well, some people get degrees in education. I haven't done that. I just fell into it, actually."

Portia felt Diana's disapproval all the way across the table. "Fell into it," she repeated.

"I worked at the Admissions Office at Dartmouth when I was an undergraduate. I gave tours, and then I worked the desk in the office. They offered me a job just before graduation. I really had no idea what I was going to do after graduation. I wish I'd been like John," she said, happy to imply that she and John were in fact old friends, old comrades, that her being here was not the bizarrely sudden event that it actually was. "I'd say most of us had figured things out by senior year. But I wasn't one of them. I thought I'd stay on and work for the college, and maybe lightning would strike. So I said yes."

"Well, that was good luck," Diana observed.

"Yes," said Portia, willfully ignoring the implications.

"And lightning never struck?"

"It turned out I liked the work," she said evenly. "I had an aptitude for it. I liked the mix of solid guidelines and creativity. And I loved the kids."

"That's funny," said Simone, the first time she had spoken since her return. "I mean, you don't have any kids of your own, right?"

Deborah looked at her daughter in horror. Then, to Portia's great dismay, she apologized on her behalf.

"What?" said Simone, all innocence. "She doesn't, right?"

"That's right," Portia said, sounding unnaturally bright. "Maybe that's the reason I can enjoy keeping company with thousands of teenagers a year. Because none of them are mine."

"Touché," Deborah said under her breath and with the faintest of smiles.

"You must get bombarded wherever you go," said John's father. "Everybody wants to know the magic formula."

"If only there were one." She laughed with forced mirth. "We'd just set the computer to make all the decisions, then we'd go off to Bora-Bora with a nice beach book."

"Where's Bora-Bora?" said Nelson.

"French Polynesia," said Jeremiah.

"But I'm sure you get tired of answering questions," John said pointedly.

"The same questions," Portia said. "Over and over. Yes. Sometimes I think I should have cards printed up, with my answers, and just hand them out."

"Like what?" said Diana.

"Like...'What's the SAT cutoff for Princeton?' Answer: There isn't one. Which nobody believes. No cutoffs. No limits. No quotas. Or, 'How many hours of community service does Princeton require?' Answer: None. Not one hour. Not that we don't think it's great to serve the community. But when you make it a requirement, and that's just what's happened in so many schools, it does undercut the impact. How could it not?"

"Baldwin has a community service requirement," Diana said defensively. "We feel it's important for our students to give back."

"It *is* important," Portia assured her. "But it's not a requirement. For admission. We don't penalize kids if they don't do it. We're mainly interested in what they've done in the classroom."

"But I imagine the lion's share of your applicants have done just great in the classroom," said John's father. "Then what do you do? Do you have some kind of points formula to compare an A from Andover to an A from...I don't know, a public high school in Mississippi?"

"You don't have to answer that," said John, glaring at his father.

"No, it's okay. We have a big staff, Mr. Halsey. And we're each assigned to a different part of the country. My colleague in charge of the South has been able to get to know the schools in her region very well. She knows exactly what an A from a public high school in Mississippi means. She also knows how many applicants we have from schools in Mississippi, how many have come to Princeton in the past, and how they've done at Princeton. A student from Mississippi has a lot to offer a northern school."

"As opposed to those Andover students," Diana said tersely. "Who are a dime a dozen."

"And fantastically prepared," said John. "I'm sure."

"Yes. And wonderful kids. From all over the world, you know. The prep schools have changed, too. They're hardly the all-white, all-Christian, even all-American bastions they were. Today, a prep school student could be from any kind of background at all. For that matter, so could a legacy. We've had coeducation and diversity long enough to produce legacy applicants of all different ethnicities. It always surprises me when people assume legacies are always white. Do they think our black and Asian and

Hispanic graduates aren't having children? And the kids themselves are great applicants, because they come from families that value education very highly."

"But," said Mr. Halsey, "you have to forgive me, I still don't understand how this works. If you're not going to use the SAT and if you don't set some kind of standard that ranks an Andover A against an A from an underserved school, then it's hard for an outsider to figure out what goes on behind the curtain. There must be a formula."

"There isn't," she said, beyond joking.

"But —"

"My dad," said John, "is an engineer. Can you tell?"

"Oh." He looked chagrined. "Am I being rude?"

"Only slightly," said John.

"No, not at all," Portia said quickly. "I know it looks mysterious from the outside, and it's definitely more art than science. But that's the way it should be, because if we made it just about one standard — any standard, like a GPA or a test — we'd have a very different campus environment. From our perspective, what we're doing works beautifully. What we're doing produces spectacular undergraduate classes, and a very vibrant campus environment. For us, that's the most important thing — and the academics, of course. Which is not to say that we're complacent about it. The whole thing is like an animal that's constantly evolving. I mean, we just got rid of Early Decision — that was a course correction. In a few years, it might have changed again."

"Can I be excused?" said Nelson.

His grandmother said, "Yes," and his father said, "No," simultaneously. Nelson, weighing his options, stayed put.

"Okay," Diana said. "I don't want to be the heavy here, but can I just say, as the mother of a prospective applicant — I mean, to places like Princeton, if not Princeton itself — that it's very frustrating. We're all trying to figure out what you want. And it feels like every time we figure out the rules, you just change them. One year it's 'well-rounded students.' The next it's minorities who play the flute," she said bitterly. Then, as if remembering that it wasn't supposed to be about her, she rephrased her conclusion. "These kids want to be able to give you what you *want*."

And therein, thought Portia with a regretful look at her cooling dinner, resided the problem. Or one of the problems. She took a sip of her wine and decided she might as well say it, pearls before swine though it almost certainly was. But there was always a chance that Jeremiah, Kelsey, Simone, or even Nelson might hear it and take it to heart.

"We're very much aware of that," she told them. "We understand the frustration. And I don't think there's anyone in my field right now who isn't worried about what this is doing to the kids. And I don't just mean the competition, though that's bad enough. I mean what the process is doing to them psychologically."

"Psychologically," said John's mother, as if she were unsure of the word's meaning.

"We've got twenty-five percent of all college applications in this country going to one percent of the schools. And that one percent includes the only fifteen American colleges who accept less than twenty percent of their applicants. We know there are parents who are doing everything they can to game the system. They're having their kids diagnosed ADHD or learning disabled so they can get extra time on the SAT. Now that ETS has stopped denoting which students have been given extra time, there's no reason not to. But the *message*. To the *kids*," she said, looking at them. "They've been tutored in everything, for years, whether they need it or not. So what they come to understand is: I'm not good enough to do it on my own. I need help to be successful."

"That's terrible," Deborah said emotionally.

"Yes. And how can that not carry forward into their adult lives? I think it already impacts their experience as college students. We have students who freak out when they no longer have that support. They're e-mailing their tutors and sending them their papers for review. They feel fraudulent."

"What do you mean, fraudulent?" said Diana.

Portia sighed. "I had a pretty scary conversation last year with one of my friend Rachel's babysitters. She's a senior at Princeton now. She told me a lot of her friends have a kind of disassociation. They've spent years assembling this perfect self to display to us—to people who are going to make these important decisions about them. But sometimes they don't feel they're that person at all. They don't feel smart or capable in the least, and of course when they get to Princeton they're surrounded by their peers, who have done just as good a job of assembling this competent veneer, so then they feel as if they're the only fake in the bunch. This girl, Samantha, was telling me there's so much self-doubt. When I heard that, I suddenly felt as if I've been doing these kids a disservice."

"They expect a lot from themselves," John said.

"Oh, my God. So much. I honestly wonder if we're not creating, or at least abetting, this surge of anxiety and depression in college-aged kids. And then there's the other side of the coin, which the babysitter also pointed out to me. Which is that some of them get to college and they just let all those balls they've been juggling for years fall out of their hands. They've worked themselves into the ground to get in. They feel like they missed out on slacking off. So now that they're in, they're going to have that lazy teenager thing they never had in high school. Seriously, the whole system. I wonder about it sometimes. But this is where we are. In a few years, it will probably look different."

John smiled. "Maybe you should evolve in the direction of taking slackers," he suggested. "Video game players."

"Yeah!" Nelson grinned.

"Comic book readers. Recreational shoppers," said John.

"Facebook addicts," said Kelsey.

"They're *all* Facebook addicts," said Diana, sounding almost likable.

"We call these people 'late bloomers,'" Portia said, smiling.

"I was a late bloomer," Deborah announced. "I didn't know what I was supposed to do with myself when I graduated from college. I sort of let myself get recruited by Procter and Gamble. I spent two years in Cincinnati working on Cascade detergent."

"This is a little-known fact about Deborah," John said fondly. "She is directly responsible for the fact that the background color on the Cascade box is green."

"That's true," Deborah said. "It was a remarkable accomplishment. I had to fight off the blue and orange factions. But strangely, even such a compelling victory was not enough to keep me in product management. I decided I wanted to teach."

"I think it doesn't matter how you get there," John said. "Just that you get there. If you get to the right place, you're lucky."

"Which means," said Simone, who had made a meal entirely of potatoes, "that you suppose you are."

"Good God, I hope so." John's mother laughed. "We had to sit through Africa and inner-city Boston. I was terrified about where he'd be going next."

"Gaza!" his father said grimly. "Sierra Leone."

John shrugged. "Don't they need teachers in Sierra Leone?"

"But not you," his mother said, alarmed.

"No." He sighed. "Not me. I like where I am. And I'm not taking Nelson to Sierra Leone."

His mother and father both looked at Nelson.

"No way," said Nelson. "Can I be excused now?"

The stage creaked under my feet as I strode across the wooden boards. I had prepared for this moment my whole life, from the first scales my little fingers were drilled to make, to the trembling solo pieces, the Etudes, Nocturnes, Marches, Minuets and finally the very difficult piece, Liszt's Waldesrauschen, that I was about to play. I could see my parents and grandmother in the front row of the theater, and my teacher and his wife beside them. If I succeeded, I would win the concerto competition of the New England Piano Teachers' Association. But my fingers wouldn't move.

CHAPTER TWENTY-ONE

ONCE THERE WAS AND WAS NOT

This time, all pertinent parties agreed that he could go, so he left, followed directly by Jeremiah, Simone, and then Deborah. Soon after, Kelsey and Diana went home. Kelsey stopped at the door to say that Portia had given her a lot to think about (which Portia found oddly touching), and Diana actually hugged her and said she hoped they'd meet again. In an official context? Portia thought automatically and cynically, but there was something in the warmth of that hug she hadn't expected. Approval, it occurred to her. Of her appearance at the family table and in her brother's life? Clearly, even Diana had a grasp of the Deborah dynamic that eluded her. But all seemed, if not overtly well, then at least well-ish, and Portia was surprised, as she watched Diana's SUV take off into the winter night, to find that she was feeling strangely content.

The rest of the evening slipped away from her. She seemed to lack the will to make any kind of decision. Every time she thought she must leave, or at least think about leaving, she let herself be deterred: clearing the table, a game of chess with Jeremiah (actually three, so quickly was he able to dispatch her), and even an awkward but at least basically good-natured conversation with Simone about her current obsession with Simone Weil (of whom — happily — Portia knew nothing, which set the stage for Simone to be strident, which seemed to please her very much). Once, months ear-lier, she'd imagined Simone to be named in honor of Simone de Beauvoir, and this turned out to be true. But Simone, contrary soul that she was, had recently ferreted out an amusing little factoid about her namesake and took a certain pleasure in publishing it: that de Beauvoir had scored second highest on the French university entrance exams of 1928, the year of her application. Weil, her classmate, had come in first.

All roads, thought Portia, listening and nodding as Simone talked on, lead to admissions. Or was that so only in her own mired life? How was it that she had come to stand at this one specific portal and all the world had serendipitously lined up to gain entry? It was a narcissistic way of see-ing things, she knew, and that was odd, because she was not a very good narcissist and had no great need to place herself at the center of the uni-verse. She believed, absolutely, that if she were to abandon her post, her profession, and turn what talents she had to something else—anything else—the loss of stature would not really diminish her. She had never, for example, had much relish for the moment of panic-laced fascination that usually occurred when someone learned her job title. She had never taken pleasure in the undeniable power intrinsic to her work, except where it gave her the chance to extract some young, gifted person from an environ-ment of limitations. (And who would not take pleasure in that?) All of it was the job and not her. And the job was so interesting, did it really matter that she herself was not?

By the end of the evening, Simone had started to warm to the idea of Penn, and even more to Swarthmore, which Portia happened to think would be an excellent place for her. She was a smart girl with her own ideas, prickly in some of the good ways and certainly promising. Portia thought she would thrive away from home and away from her mother, though her mother had done a formidable job raising her. She might do anything with herself, as long as it involved advocacy and perseverance, both clear strengths. Portia did not say so, but she also hoped Simone would think about Princeton, where she would certainly be challenged and where opinionated women would always be welcome, and she invited the girl to get in touch with her if she wanted any guidance along the way. This alone, it occurred to her, made her glad she had come home with John and stayed this long. And the realization that Deborah was someone she might truly like, and that John (if he aged as his father had) would likely be handsome until the end of his life, and that, in a very general way, it was good to move among people who were basically nice and interested and welcoming and did not know her very well, and who seemed to at least entertain the idea of her being with him, with John, without obvious horror.

With John, she thought, reflexively shaking her head at the oddity of this preposition. Two months ago, she'd been intractably partnered with another man. Two days ago, she'd been adrift in a freezing house with an untended fridge and, to put it kindly, distracted personal hygiene. She resisted the notion of rescue. She was not particularly interested in rescue. Since the age of twenty she had supported herself, financially, emotionally. It was one of the few things she was actually proud of, though she understood it had come at some cost. Like, she thought, the cost of being *with* another person. Surely she was not really capable of being *with* anyone, even this passionate, tender, settled man, at once so solid and so miraculously permeable. She also doubted very much that she deserved him.

Simone and her mother drifted upstairs, not far behind John's parents, who said a brisk good night in the living room doorway, each clutching a matching black mug of tea. John took Nelson up, but Jeremiah lingered to swiftly demolish Portia at chess one last time. He had grown almost mellow by the end of the day, a different animal from the wired Toni Morrison fan in the car that morning, and she felt as if she were getting perhaps her first good look at him here, bent over the chess board, chewing the soft part of his thumb but not, oddly, the nail. She wanted suddenly to last a little longer in the game, not really to prolong it or even to salve her ego, but to get more time with this Jeremiah. His hair, in the light from matching chinoiserie lamps, glowed black in glossy, looping curls. That was an Armenian thing, she supposed. Where the almost feminine mouth, pale skin, and extra-long arms came from had to be closer to home: mom or dad, or grandparents. He was closing in on her king, tightening the vise, wrapping things up. She resisted where she could, but it was pointless to do more than cast distractions in his path. Besides, her attention was not on the board. And there were things she wished she could talk to him about that were ethically out of bounds.

Why had he stayed so long in a school that must have frustrated and disappointed him on a daily basis? Was there not one teacher he could have gone to for help, one mentor willing to take up a brilliant misfit? Why had his parents not done what they could to see him accommodated academically? Deerfield and Northfield were not far from Keene, and a school like St. Paul's might have found scholarship money for a brilliant New Hampshire student. Why had he not looked ahead to college, at least, as a goal? Why, overall, did he not seem more...well, ambitious? Surely it was not enough to sit reading forever. Surely he felt some compulsion to get up and do something with what he'd learned or add to the body of learning in some way. There were plenty of applicants to places like Princeton who wanted no more than that: a chance to add to the sum total of what was known. And that was fine. But nowhere in Jeremiah's application had he indicated such a wish. What did he want? From the university? From himself?

In a few more moves, he had her king pinned behind a useless pawn. She declined to play again and was just thinking how she might bring up some of these questions when he looked up at her, disarmingly frank, and with no trace of awkwardness at all said that he wanted to thank her very, very much for what she'd done for him.

"What have I done?" Portia said.

"Well, a few things, actually. Finding a way for me to stay on campus last night. I can't tell you how fantastic it was. And being able to go to Professor Friedman's class. Thank you for setting that up for me. I'm not sure why you did it, to tell you the truth."

Why she had done it was hardly something she intended to share with Jeremiah.

"It's my pleasure."

"And, also for coming to my school. I mean, John and Deborah were both talking to me about college. I never thought about that before. I just thought I'd get a job, you know, and sort of keep on going by myself. I knew there was a job for me where my parents work. But after you came I asked John if I could go to Princeton. He made me apply to a lot of places. We know it's a long shot."

Less long by the minute, Portia thought.

"I think college is absolutely the right place for you," she told him. "I think you'd get to meet people more like you. Kids who felt like they never really got with the program in high school. A lot of those kids meet up at places like Princeton. Or wherever you go."

"You mean"—he smiled, showing white, slightly protruding teeth—"the geeks all unite."

"Everybody unites," she said, smiling, too. "The geeks, the theater kids, the poets, the military history enthusiasts. That whole first semester, it's 'Where've you been all my life?' all over campus. It's kind of fun."

"Yeah," said Jeremiah. "Like a big dating service for nerds."

She laughed.

And then Jeremiah got to his feet and went away up the stairs, and she stayed behind, resetting the chess pieces. By the time John came down, having settled his son and student in the bunk beds still ensconced in his childhood room, she had figured out what to say in order to make plausible her departure. *I wish I could stay,* she would tell him. *Even though I haven't taken a day off for weeks. Yes, even though today was Saturday and tomorrow is Sunday.* And then she would hug him and kiss him and tell him that she would call soon, and she would ask him to thank his parents and Deborah and even his sister. And then she would leave and let whatever was going to happen, whatever was already happening, keep on happening, only more slowly.

But when he came into the room, he hugged *her* and kissed *her*. And she forgot the perfectly reasonable things she was going to say to him. She went downstairs with him and let him pull her down next to him on the inelegant guest bed, where he curled around her.

"I should go," she said, though she was feeling slightly less urgency about the idea than she had felt upstairs.

"Yes, so you said. Are you cold? I'm cold."

She was cold. He reached down to the foot of the bed and pulled a heavy quilt over them both. "That's better." They were both still fully clothed.

"Personally," said John, "I think you should stay. I think you should stay here in this extremely uncomfortable bed, with me, and go back first thing in the morning. What's the point of going now?"

She thought about it. She supposed there must be a point.

"And I'm going to be very cold down here without you."

"Selfish," she murmured.

"Did Jeremiah speak to you?" John said, shifting against her under the quilt. "I know he wanted to. He's so grateful for what you did."

"It's my job," Portia said carefully.

"Yes, of course. But to him, you're someone who doesn't see him as a discipline problem or an underachiever. He's still not used to adults who recognize his gifts. It's as if his whole life has jumped the track in the last year. He was on his way to living one kind of life story. Now he has a whole new life story to think about."

"Well," she said, sighing, "that's a nice metaphor. And fitting, for an Armenian. Storytelling's a big thing in the culture, isn't it?"

"Yes," John said yawning audibly. "But of course he's not really an Armenian."

She frowned. "Jeremiah Vartan Balakian is not Armenian?" she said. "On what planet?"

"Yes, sure. But he's adopted," John said. "You know that."

She shook her head, which was as good as saying no, she had no idea.

"First thing last fall, I had my class write thousand-word autobiographies. Jeremiah's ... Jesus, it was brilliant," he said sleepily, at her ear. "It started, 'Once there was and was not, a boy named Jeremiah Vartan Balakian.' Which is the traditional opening of an Armenian story. I mean, the 'Once there was and was not.' I could have given him an A just for the first sentence. But it was very tender, actually. When he discovered he was adopted, he felt such relief. He forgave his parents immediately. Not for adopting him, of course. For just having no idea what to do with him. And it explains so much about the way he grew up. Socially." He yawned again. "You're staying, right?"

"I don't know," said Portia, who didn't.

"But you need to sleep."

"Yes," agreed Portia, who suddenly, and to her own surprise, was already drifting in that direction: suffused with heat, increasingly addled. She felt as if her hands were holding so tightly to a rope slicked with something wet, something slippery, like algae or long strands of seaweed moving in a current, so that she was constantly slipping and slipping, but her hands were throbbing and tight in spite of this. And it was warm underwater, and she wanted to let go, but every time she was nearly there some urgent spasm made her grip the rope anew, and it would start again. The wine and the heat and the breath at the nape of her neck, which was also hot, and she began to feel the general goodness of things, quite apart from the nagging pain in her fingers, clutching, and that she might as well give up on that, too, except that there was something, something, warm and amorphous in this otherwise pleasant underwater place that was not good. And that something kept disturbing her, irritating her, reminding her of something she could not quite place but knew was not good and not going away.

And this went on, who knew how long? But when she woke it was in an acrid, jerking way, clawing for air. She thought: Now I know exactly what it feels like to choke to death, or be willfully choked, which even in that distant way she recognized as illogical, because she would hardly choke herself, and John, she could feel, had turned in sleep behind her and curled away from her, spine to spine. And still, she hurtled awake with one hand protectively at her own throat and the other over her eyes, as if the notion of looking into the darkness were something she wished to protect herself from, too, though when she did open her eyes, it was so black in the room that there was nothing to see. Nothing to need protecting from, she thought erratically. Except...*something*.

Portia sat up. John moved behind her, and she automatically pulled back the quilt around him, so he wouldn't wake from cold. She did not want him to be awake with her just now. She perched, stiff and tense, at the edge of the bed, her aching hands on her knees, staring into the darkness, willing the obscure thing to come to light, and fearing that, and willing it again, if only to be done with the fear of not knowing what it was. It was, whatever it was, a thing of substantial proportions, of unignorable heft. It was something she had not known before she'd slept, but something she would, once she discovered it, never be able to not know again. And it was so close, so almost actual.

She got to her feet, feeling the strain in her calves and shoulders. She picked up her bag from a chair in the corner, declining to consider what this meant, and stepped out into the basement corridor. There was a small bathroom down the hall, and she went in and turned on the switch and stared at herself in the garish fluorescent light, while a green-hued, terrified woman stared back: dark brown hair, blue circles under each brown eye. It was not a very lovely face, because it was Susannah's face, with its strong nose and wide, high cheekbones and thick wavy hair, and she had never thought of Susannah as lovely. For years, growing up especially, she had examined herself this way, looking not for similarities but for differences, an element or trait that could not be assigned to her mother but had to be some wild card entry of her unknown father: the man on the train, the man of the unknown embarkation and the unknown destination, to whom she was—whatever her mother thought—as closely linked as to Susannah. She had never found it. On the contrary, and against her will, she had grown physically more and more like Susannah, as if to prove her mother's argument that the man had been no more than a means to an end, a catalyst without any contribution of its own. So she had stopped looking, and she had put the idea of him away with other things she could not bear to think of.

Upstairs she went, quietly, so quietly that she could not even hear herself. Through the basement door and up the grand staircase, lined by the promised hunting prints, footfalls disappearing into the carpeted runner. On one end of the landing, a formidable door that seemed to promise a master suite. On the other, a longer corridor with doors on either side, close together. She went to the first of these, holding her breath as she turned the knob, pushing the door inside. Two beds on a faded pink carpet, two bodies under two pink coverlets: Deborah and Simone. Portia stepped back. She was in control of each finger, the angle of her head and neck, but not of herself. She closed the door.

The next door was to a bathroom, with an automatic light that flickered horribly overhead when she nudged it open. She was amazed that no one had stopped her yet.

The next door opened to sleeping boys. Nelson, in the bottom bunk, snoring gently into his pillow, one arm flung overboard so the knuckles brushed the bare wooden floor. She was not yet ready to look up. Later, she would not be able to say how long it had taken her to look up.

She understood what it was to have a blank for a parent. Did that mean she understood precisely half of what it was like for Jeremiah, who had been transplanted into foreign soil, roots excised from the earth and swaddled into an antiseptic ball? One-half of a mystery was still a mystery. She knew, looking at him, that she could not have defended her certainty in any convincing way. But she was: riveted, calm, flushed with horror, and utterly certain.

Afterward, driving back, she would think very carefully, very clinically, about how long she had spent in the room, looking and looking at the boy in the top bunk. Of course, she did not like to think what would have happened if he had woken up, or if Deborah or Simone had needed the bathroom. There was no possible justification, no rational explanation to alleviate the vision of herself, her middle-aged, acerbic, strange, and hysterical self, standing in a nighttime room of sleeping teenage boys who barely knew her, and whom she barely knew, looking and—after the first few minutes, when she began to be certain of what she was seeing—weeping. Later, driving north on 95, crossing the Delaware back to New Jersey, she let them appear before her, one by one, and conjured the disgust and loathing on their incredulous faces: Mrs. Halsey, Mr. Halsey, Deborah, Simone, Nelson . . . John. "I don't understand," John would say, aghast at her. "Why were you there? What were you doing?"

Why am I here? she thought. And what—exactly what—am I doing? All these years, her sole objective had been to keep still and hope no one would ever know. She had been a mistress of stillness. She had mastered the simulation of peace without a wisp of real peace, like a nun from a silent order who was screaming inside her head, or a yogi racked with pain. How she had managed to fool anyone, let alone everyone, mystified her (how obtuse people were!) and, oddly, made her extraordinarily bitter. Because the price of her gift for evasion was to have no one, not one person, who understood how horrible she felt. All the time. Absolutely all the time.

The boys breathed and breathed. They were beautiful: Nelson with his obsidian skin shining in the light from the hallway. Jeremiah's black curls against the pillow, one sinewy arm thrown up over his head. She had a terrible idea that she might not be able to leave this spot, that the first sleepy risers would find her here, rooted, frozen, staring into the room, floundering for some shred of an explanation. It was the horror of this scenario that finally extracted her, breaking the suction of her feet to the carpeted floor, ripping away her gaze. There was a window at the end of the hallway, admitting—she noted with dismay—the first shards of morning light. Portia turned and walked quickly away from it, and down the stairs, and out the front door. She got into her car, scrambled fearfully for the key in her purse (terrified that she might have to go back to the basement room, where John still slept) and finally found it, then slapped it into the ignition. The car, starting up, seemed the loudest thing in the universe.

She drove away down the lane and then, by instinct, to wider and wider roads, aiming vaguely east into the dawn and then vaguely north, until she hit the unmistakable artery of Route 95 and understood that she was no longer driving away but going home. Of course, the going home did not seem tolerable, either, except . . . it came to her slowly . . . for the one sliver of relief that she might possibly find there, one tiny fact that might dismantle the wonderful, dreadful conviction she had conjured in that hallway. For that slim chance, she thought, it was worth going back. Already she had a craving to find it and so relieve herself, to once again not know what she was sure that she knew, and go back to feeling the nothing she had felt for seventeen years. How soft and quiet that familiar nothing was, and how she craved it again.

Across the Delaware, she found herself slowed by roadwork ahead, surrounded by drivers who clearly neither expected nor accepted traffic on a Sunday morning. For herself, Portia was surprised to discover that she was not impatient. Now that she understood what she needed to find out, and how she was going to do that, the frantic part of her circumstances was tamped, and a kind of grim resolve had taken its place. What she needed to know, she would certainly know in due course, whether in ten minutes or two hours, and there would be either relief or the greatest dismay. She could wait for that. The cars inched north to her exit. And when she exited, the road was clear into Princeton.

There was a space on Witherspoon, miraculous, in front of Small World, but the whiff of satisfaction was short-lived. Even as Portia twisted to unbuckle her seat belt, she caught the shape, and then the eye, of Mark, emerging from the coffee shop, followed by the protruding midsection of a similarly recognizable woman. It was too late to pretend she hadn't seen or wasn't there. He looked, to his credit, similarly appalled, but Helen went on, impervious, her brittle little mouth moving, though mercifully silent through the car window. Mark stood frozen, half looking at Portia, half listening to Helen, who waved about one bony hand. A left hand, Portia noted. That wore a glittering ring.

Portia threw herself out of the car and scurried up the street side of the parked cars, annoying drivers. There was slush on the ground and on the stone path crossing in front of Nassau Hall, the very place she had stopped, only two days before, when somebody called her name: before pregnant Helen and frozen Mark, and the night, and the drive, and the dinner party and the story of the train and the unexpected grace of the lovemaking. Before the possibility of Jeremiah, who now that the fact of him was only steps ahead seemed almost material beside her, silently keeping pace with her along the walkway.

She pushed open the door to West College and shed her coat as she took the stairs, wet boots slapping the steps. There were others here, behind their closed or ajar doors, who registered her passing but did not exactly look up. She went first to the pending files on the shelf over her desk, but she knew perfectly well it wasn't there. It wasn't anywhere in her office. It was already gone, in that last group sent to Corinne for a second reading.

Portia sat at her desk and stared ahead, at the outdated gym schedule and the Oldest Living Graduate. Also, the poem by Sylvia Plath that Rachel had given her once, years before, as a joke, she supposed.

"The Applicant"

First, are you our sort of a person?
Do you wear
A glass eye, false teeth or a crutch,
A brace or a hook,
Rubber breasts or a rubber crotch,

Stitches to show something's missing? No, no? Then
How can we give you a thing?
Stop crying.
Open your hand.
Empty? Empty.

Portia looked, illogically, at her own hands. *Empty? Empty.* Then, taken by a new idea, she got to her feet and rushed out into the corridor and downstairs, passing through the small lobby to the office, normally a hive at eight a.m., but not on a Sunday. Martha, though, was at her desk, wielding her signature letter opener — a brass instrument with a sharp point at the business end — against a stack of bulky mailers: CDs and art portfolios from applicants, research papers, novels in progress, unsolicited letters from classmates, congressmen, coaches, friends of the family who had once attended Princeton. Even this late.

Martha looked up and waved. "You're here early."

"Not earlier than you. Are we getting mail on Sunday now?"

"Oh." She shook her head. "I never finished yesterday's. Do you think they really believe we can read an entire novel? Or are we just supposed to weigh it?"

"I don't know," said Portia.

"It kind of gets to me," said Martha. "Tell me something. Do they really look at this stuff? In creative writing?"

"Of course," said Portia. "They may not read every word of a five-hundred-page manuscript, but they do look. Usually, a look is enough."

Martha nodded. "So if one of these is actually hundreds of pages of 'All work and no play makes Jack a dull boy,' you'd know about it?"

"Yeah," said Portia. "I don't think you need to worry about Jack Nicholson coming through the door with an ax."

"I'm not worried," Martha said, brandishing her miniature brass sword. "Why do you think I'm never without my letter opener? You okay? You look awful."

The shift was so abrupt that Portia lost the wherewithal to take offense. "Do I? I'm sorry."

"What are you apologizing for?" said Martha, looking actually more concerned. "I told Clarence to hire more readers this year. He said he would, but somewhere between the mouth and the brain...you know what he's like."

No, she realized suddenly. She didn't know what he was like. This thought alarmed her. "I'm not behind," she said, which she hoped was the point.

"No, I'm not suggesting. And it's fine for the younger ones. They just drink more of those Bull drinks, with the caffeine. Dylan's going through them by the case. But for you, and Clarence, and Corinne."

"Oh, I'm fine," she said, relieved. Concerns for her physical state were almost a welcome distraction. That Martha remained so wonderfully ignorant of her actual condition came as an unexpected boon. "In fact, I got away a bit over the weekend. So actually, if anything, I've been kind of slacking off."

Martha, for her part, looked unconvinced. "Well, Portia, I'm sorry to have to say this, but you don't seem very rested to me. If you take my advice, which of course you won't, you'll reconsider spending the day in the office and go home and sleep."

Portia fought a brief wave of irritation. Martha had worked here for years, since before she herself had joined the office. They had always been at least cordial and at most actually affectionate. Probably, they had had conversations just like this in the past, perhaps many of them. But today, and despite the clear accuracy of Martha's observations and the suitability of her advice, Portia wanted to hit her, or at least walk away. Instead, and after the briefest possible interlude, she gathered herself, produced a facsimile of a smile, and said: "God, I would love that. But you know, I'm really okay. I'm going to work this morning, then I'll go home. But this is the deal I made with myself, you know, for taking yesterday off. So," she went on, attempting to block whatever Martha's next objection might be, "I'm looking for that batch I left Corinne on Thursday."

"Thursday . . . ," Martha considered.

"It's just," she said, utterly unnecessarily, "I wanted to check something."

"Thursday . . ." Martha frowned. "She took a lot home with her for the weekend. I don't know if they were yours or first reads. Want me to call her?"

"No," Portia said a bit too shortly. "No, it can wait. She's a quick read."

Though she wasn't, really. Not quick enough.

"Anything I can help you with?"

Portia shook her head. She was entertaining a pointless fantasy, in which despite the very conversation that had just taken place, she would walk calmly to her box and find the single folder she wanted to find, miraculously separated from the multitudes of superficially identical folders, and placidly open it to find the reader's card, marked with her own blue ballpoint print, and now, beside that, with Corinne's favorite brown felt-tip and tight little script: "Agree with first reader? Disagree?" She often disagreed. She would disagree now, Portia was certain. What would she do when Corinne disagreed?

"If you're determined to work . . . ," Martha said helpfully. She nodded at the table where the ill-conceived brownies, cakes, and vegan power bars had earlier been displayed. It was now a groaning board of files, stacked in uniform heights, bound by rubber bands, decorated by Post-it notes. "This is you," she said, gesturing at the nearest pile. It was Corinne's. Ready for second reads. "She left it off before she went home on Friday."

"Ah. Good," said Portia with disproportionate heartiness. She scooped up the stack. "Well, if I don't come out by tomorrow, send the sniffer dogs."

"I'll send Jack Nicholson," said Martha, returning to her mailers.

Portia trudged upstairs with the folders. Her arms ached from them, and her legs and back, and she felt, as she rose and rose, the profound physical impact of her two nights of lost sleep and all that had taken place between them. In her office, she let them drop heavily on the desktop, sat down, and simply stared at them, bleary-eyed and depleted. She thought of nothing, and then of random, disconnected things: the Edie Sedgwick biography, and Deborah's curling red hair, and Jeremiah's long arms, and

Rachel's dog, increasingly arthritic and—even she could tell—addled in mind. She thought of Helen's convex belly and Mark's look of great discomfort, and the furnace John had reset so easily, and the tall notched stones she had once seen in Ireland years ago, on vacation with Mark, and realized for the first time that she had stored this particular little memory because the stones—ogham stones, they were called—were so very like the tall stacks of files that filled and marked her life. She remembered the field, but not where in Ireland it was, and their rental car pulled not far enough off the road, so that the drivers of two passing cars, forced to carve a semicircle around it, had sent vaguely hostile grunts in their direction—tourists, obviously. Who else would trudge up an incline, evading scattered sheep shit, to look at rocks some long-gone person had chipped into some lost meaning? The ogham cuts were an ancient, ritualistic language from the Celts, the notches meaning numbers or letters, perhaps a calendar. Like a bar code, it suddenly occurred to her. Or the data of thousands of seventeen-year-olds, compacted to a language of bytes.

She sat up straight in her chair and touched the space bar of her computer. The university screen saver evaporated, and she was offered the usual log-in box. She typed her password and entered the system, evading the ninety-four messages accrued since Friday, wonderfully impervious to everything else, because the distance between not knowing and knowing was contracting and the answer drawing nearer with each stroke of her fingertips. Of course, she might have had this information days ago, luxuriously alone, with the application itself in her very hands, but she hadn't known to look, and how could that be her fault? She might have done what she was doing now much earlier, the very moment she arrived this morning, saving herself the all too accurate scrutiny of Martha, who now knew there was something very wrong with her. She might have gone home and done it there, from her home computer, in even greater privacy. That none of these possibilities had occurred to her made her irritated and then a little giddy, because she was flying through the system now, and her hands were moving rapidly on the keys, and rapidly through the vast orbit of letters and numbers, and the software that sorted, codified, and clamped them together. She wanted only a few of these letters and numbers.

"Balakian," she wrote, but in her haste misspelled the name. She typed, "Jeremiah," and there were many. First names, middle names, even last names. "Balakian, Jeremiah Vartan." She opened the data file and made herself read by internal metronome and in rigid order: "Name." "Address." "School." She knew this already. "Place of Birth." She knew this, too. She had seen it before, but it had made no impact. Why, she railed at herself, had it made no impact? "Date of Birth."

She closed the data file. Then she closed her eyes.

First, are you our sort of a person? She had to wonder if she herself even *was* a sort of person, and *had* a sort of person, and if so, what they would be. Dishonest? Obscure? Defined by missing things? But I love him, she thought now, as if this were the most important point to be making. *Surely there has never been a question of that.* Because he was the single real thing in her life, and it was everything else that felt finally ill defined. And her own life had gathered itself around this empty space, which had finally found itself an occupant, with heft and color and texture. Of course, that occupant was him: the applicant who both was and absolutely was not Jeremiah Vartan Balakian.

VOX CLAMANTIS
IN DESERTO

I don't remember a time when my father was not living under the cloud of cancer. Diagnosed when I was in kindergarten, he has battled his way through surgeries, radiation therapies, and increasingly experimental chemotherapies. There are times when I feel very privileged, because I know that he is in the care of excellent doctors at a cutting edge cancer center, and I know that no one on earth is getting better treatment than he is today. But I also feel terrible frustration that, despite so much effort and funding, we have still not cracked the problem of a single little cell growing out of control.

CHAPTER TWENTY-TWO

A THING FOR JEWISH GIRLS

One October evening, on the precise patch of the Dartmouth College Green that John Halsey would years later compare, in its lasting effect, to Irish hungry grass, Portia Nathan was hit by a rogue lacrosse ball and swiftly knocked out. Afterward, she would regret that the scenario had not been a bit more elegant. All of the right elements were there: innocent girl, athletic (presumably attractive) boy, graceful loss of consciousness segueing to graceful reestablishment of consciousness. It didn't happen that way. True, the night was clear and crisp, and she was wearing a floaty Indian shirt that had (until that night, when it was more or less destroyed) been one of her favorites, and her hair that fall had never been longer, straighter, shinier. True, she was about to gain the uninterrupted attention of the person she would spend the next several years hoping to attract, and then retain, and then reattract. But the actual event was humiliatingly coarse.

The lacrosse ball did not, for one thing, hit her in some delicate location—the back of the head, perhaps, or the shoulder—but square in the eye. And her unconsciousness ended not with a Sleeping Beauty–like stretch and purr, but with an upright jolt and a hearty spasm of vomit, hitting directly the boy who leaned over her, a dark head in a halo of moonlight.

The Greek chorus of her classmates, who rushed to gather around her, produced involuntary sounds of disgust and then, like the well-brought-up citizens they were, withdrew to a more circumspect distance. Only the boy himself and his two fellow lacrosse players stayed with her, and the girl Portia happened to have been standing beside when the fateful ball made contact. By the time the paramedics arrived, she was more or less upright, sticky with blood, vomit, and the fluid from her wildly painful right eye, which she instinctively kept covered with her hand. The other eye, which mercilessly recorded her attentive audience of fascinated classmates and her own very disagreeable physical disarray (not the least part of which was the fact that she had come to a sitting position with her legs splayed far apart and couldn't seem to figure out how to bring them together), took refuge in the strangely calming vision of a monogram on the boy's white shirt — TSW — etched in dignified maroon and only a little spattered with the recent contents of her stomach.

This occasion was — so ironically — the very one that had formed her initial attachment to Dartmouth: the annual building of the class bonfire, an autumn ritual for the freshmen to bond and socialize and display their superiority to all previous classes by making their chimney of railroad ties one tier higher than the year before. The lumber had been dropped off days earlier near the center of the Green, and a small group of planners and worker bees had taken charge of it, mapping out the structure and directing the labor, doing the actual work while others gathered round, chatting and socializing as the tower rose. All week the class had filtered through, climbing the ladder of wood to hoist a tie or two or remaining earthbound to hoist a beer. Groups sat on the grass during the day and shivered in standing groups at night, exchanging that basic information they had been exchanging now, for weeks, and were all growing sick of but somehow still fixated upon: *What's your name? Where are you from? What dorm are you in? Where else did you apply?* Portia herself had done her part a few days earlier, when the bonfire was only as high as her head and the freshman girls on her floor had gone as a group. Since then, she had passed through once or twice a day, sometimes at night, amused and a tiny bit proud to find herself within the very tableau that had brought her here in the first place.

It was not, of course, a noble business to throw up in front of an audience, but even so, the reaction was surprisingly visceral. Hypocritical, too, given the drunken desecrations of Fraternity Row and the omnipresent odors in the bathrooms of her all-female dormitory. Even so, Portia and her involuntary emission that night would attain the status of minor legend within their class, and largely because just about everyone got to witness the outcome (the vomit, in other words) while few had witnessed the mitigating fact of the lacrosse ball hitting her in the eye and knocking her out. She would, she suspected even then, adding tears of shame to the other bodily fluids in play, forever be that girl who passed out beside the bonfire and blew chunks over everyone, a cautionary tale, surely, of a young innocent away from home and meeting the scarlet A-for-Alcohol for the first time. She would share her sad lot with the girl who never washed her hair through the fall term, wore shorts through the snow all winter, and disappeared in the spring, never to be seen again, and the first boy to drink himself sick in Fayerweather Hall during Freshman Week, who happily accepted the honorary lifetime nickname of "Boot" as a result (that scarlet A-for-Alcohol having not quite the negative quality for men that it had for women).

Still, the news wasn't all bleak. Portia had a couple of things going for her that night, first and foremost the darkness (since what man-made illumination there was at the center of the college Green was focused on the rising tower of railroad ties and not on her). Afterward, there wouldn't be many of the hundred or so witnesses who could have picked her out of a crowd without the helpful additions of tears and vomit. Also fortunate was the fact that Portia had not, until that moment, made much of an impression on her classmates, and therefore few already knew who the effluent-covered freshman actually was. Once the incident had been mined for socialization value (*Omigod, that's so disgusting! So, what's your name? Where are you from?* etc., etc.), the assembled did tend to move on to other topics.

The paramedics brought her to Dick's House, the campus infirmary, and only when they left her there in the care of the nurses did she realize that the cloth she had for some time been holding against her eye was actually the once white shirt of the boy who had stood over her. How it had come into her hand was a mystery, but there was no doubt of what it was, not with its monogram—*TSW*—disconcertingly pristine. She groggily refused to give it up to the nurses.

The eye was not seriously damaged, thankfully. With a patch, a single stitch in her right brow, and an astoundingly effective analgesic, she floated away from all remaining pain and mortification and woke up many hours later to bright sunlight, still clutching the shirt.

Over the following week, her eye healed, her bruise faded, her single stitch dissolved, and on the eve of homecoming the bonfire went up in its usual conflagration, sealing the unity of their class for all time. She washed the shirt, intending (hoping!) to return it to its owner, and it was only when the fabric had been finally fully liberated from its stains and then ironed in the damp little laundry room in the basement that she realized she did not know to whom it belonged. That boy, its owner — so real to her in his solid silhouette — had no actual name and no clear face, and as the fall progressed and the accident slipped mercifully into the past, Portia was increasingly reluctant to bring it up.

Unfortunately, as her chances for resolution waned, her eagerness only seemed to build. She looked for the shape of him constantly as she moved around the campus, scrutinizing boys as she brushed past them in the hallways of classroom buildings, and at the dining room tables in Thayer, and at parties in dormitory rooms and the sticky basements of fraternities. And always as she crossed the Green, as if she might most likely find him here, at the scene of the crime. She tried to remember the specific backlit outlines of his shoulders and head, and strained to recall whether he had spoken, and if so, what he had said. Obviously, he had removed his shirt — this shirt — and given it to her. How had she managed to miss this very interesting transaction and all the information that might have come with it? Because there was little information to be had. He was tall and broad, with hair more flat than thick and curling. There had been a shirt beneath the shirt with the monogram, but it had been too dark to see the collar or the pattern. Mostly, she remembered the lacrosse stick, and she even went along to one of the home games that fall (Dartmouth versus Princeton, as it happened), to try to pick him out among the hurling players. But he could have been any of half a dozen or so, or none of them, and she went home feeling slightly sullied from the whole thing.

She was (and how Susannah would have raged at this, if she'd known) very much like a reverse Cinderella looking for her prince, with only the clue of the monogram to fit his symbolic foot. In fact, it occurred to her more than once that the monogram itself was taking the brunt of her fixation, that the identity of the man who had hit her — maybe — and felt bad enough about that to remove and pass along to her his clothing, was actually no more and no less than a monogram, and so it was the monogram, and not the man it belonged to, that truly held her.

Unfortunately, given the circumstances, Portia had had little experience with monograms. Susannah had not seen fit to monogram a single sheet, towel, washcloth, napkin, picture frame, slipper, item of stationery, or article of clothing. Susannah's friends and their children also lived monogram-free lives, so Portia had no way of knowing that a monogram reading say, *T S W*—with its central *S* ever so slightly larger than the *T* and *W* that flanked it — represented a person whose initials were actually *T W S*. And so, when Portia had the bright idea to consult her freshman book, the directory of her class, she had looked long and hard at every boy with a last name starting in *W* and a first name starting in *T*. There she discovered Teddy Washington of Columbia, South Carolina (a reedy African-American who had coincidentally been on Portia's freshman trip), and Theo Westerboerk of the Netherlands (stout and already balding), and Travis Wall of Hanover, New Hampshire (son of a math professor), none of them remotely like the former owner of the monogram. To be even more thorough, she found and searched the freshman books of the sophomore, junior, and senior classes, but the dozen or so TWs that emerged from those were likewise wrong.

By winter, Portia had let this particular preoccupation recede. She was happy with her classes that term and attempting to write a play for the annual student one-act competition (she never finished this), and she had taken up with the astounding Marrow siblings, who had evidently brought with them to college the boisterous intellectual ambience of their family's apartment on the Upper West Side. The freshman class had three sets of twins, two of them disconcertingly identical, and Rebecca and Daniel Marrow. The Marrows were, individually and collectively, extraordinary. Rebecca (already a novelist) and Daniel (a Westinghouse finalist for his work on staphylococcus) had followed their brother Jonathan (chess champion) to Dartmouth. (Another super-high-achieving brother, Benjamin, was cooling his heels elsewhere in the Ivy League.)

Rebecca was a force of nature, a flower of Ashkenazi frizz in a sea of limp WASP coiffure, a vintage double-breasted men's herringbone tweed in a crowd of down jackets and vests. Only a few months into their college career, Rebecca had established herself as the nexus of creative people on campus. At her self-termed salons, salmon (shipped, from Zabar's, by Mom) was served on black bread and sprinkled with red onion, and wine was dispensed from bottles with French labels and actual corks. Most of the poets and writers dropped by at least once (the more sensitive flowers among them put off by the din), as well as the Latinists and the theater crowd, and all seemed more than relieved to have found one another, even in a charmless cinder-block room with a view of an access road. Portia had blundered into the scene, falsely declaring (falsely believing) that she would be doing something theatrical at some point in her Dartmouth career.

One Sunday afternoon in February, as the campus nursed a collective hangover from the exertions of fraternity and sorority rush, Rebecca announced that she had invited Tom Standley, from her seven a.m. French drill, over for coffee, and would Portia please come, too, because she didn't want him thinking that she, you know, liked him, and he kind of had this thing for Jewish girls.

What did that mean? Portia had asked, a little alarmed.

It meant that he had already taken two home to Mom, who was apparently quite the anti-Semite, which was apparently quite the point.

Rebecca, who knew every Israelite on campus, including faculty and staff, and seemed to assume that Portia did as well, was acquainted with both of these girls from Shabbat dinners at the student center. One, she reported, had gone to visit the Standley family over Christmas break and returned to campus reeling, half with the hilarity of it, half in horror. The parents, she reported, had been under the impression that her surname—Applebaum—was Appleton, and all had been well until all had been revealed.

"Obviously, he told them that was her name," Portia said to Rebecca, defending the Jewish honor of this unknown girl.

"Ya think?" Rebecca laughed. "But like I said, he's a sweet guy. I just don't want him getting the wrong idea."

That this would be accomplished by shoving another Jewish girl in his face was a notion that did not occur to her until later, but by then, of course, she was well over the cliff and unlikely to think rationally about much of anything.

When he arrived, knocking on the open door and cradling a tired cactus by way of a hostess gift, she recognized him right away, the blank outline filled in, and the colors, shading, texture, voice, in a brilliant, almost violent moment. By the time he crossed the threshold, he had been transformed from that dark, backlit body to something complex and whole, a fully assembled eighteen-year-old male who could hit a stranger with a lacrosse ball and then strip off his own expensive shirt to wipe away the various aftereffects, a careless person who had taken care of her. That he did not experience the same rush of recognition was actually a boon, Portia felt, because she needed time to recover from the fact of him, appearing, entering, taking the armchair behind her after giving Rebecca a generous embrace. In just that tiny passage of time, she had found herself cataclysmically in love, a state she was surprised to recognize so easily, given that she had never inhabited it before. The ground untrustworthy, the surface of her skin burning for contact, she needed all available restraint to keep from saying things, touching things, simply flinging herself against him.

By then, others had arrived: theater types, who erroneously (as it would turn out) considered Portia one of their tribe. Conversation was puttering along, lubricated by wine and a certain jovial superiority, which stemmed from the assumption that all present had shunned the absurd and anti-intellectual ritual of fraternity rush.

"Those pathetic drones," said someone, a Thespian from—he had earlier noted—Meryl Streep's New Jersey hometown. "Trotting off down the Row with their plastic cups, ready to waste the next four years on beer pong."

"At least it gets them out of the way," said someone else, a girl who practically lived at Sanborn, the English Department library, surrounded by her journals and poems in progress. "I'd rather they barfed on one another instead of on me."

This comment produced no spark of recognition in Tom Standley, to Portia's relief.

"Well, I rushed a fraternity," he said instead, not smugly so much as perplexed. "I'm excited, actually."

They all looked at him in mild shock, as if he were a newly declared atheist at Bible study. This changed the entire chemistry in the room.

"Yeah?" said Rebecca. "Which one?"

Again, with no sense at all of its significance, he named the WASPiest, wealthiest, and most thoroughly Republican house on campus.

"Ugh," said one of the girls, extravagantly repelled.

"All those *Dartmouth Review* guys are in there," said another, as if this were likely to dissuade him.

"Yeah," said Tom. "But you know, they don't push it on you. They're good guys."

"Hitler was very fond of his dog, I believe," Daniel said in a treacly voice. "And of course, he was an artist, too."

"Daniel," Rebecca scolded.

"I look at it like this," said Tom. "The next couple of years, we're all going to be running around like crazy. I'm going to France sometime. Next year or junior year. And I want to do an internship at this law firm in Boston. I keep thinking, when I come back here, half my friends are going to be away off campus. And it'll be nice to have a smaller group of guys to hang out with. You know, not as impersonal as a dorm."

Unfortunately for the assembled, this was a difficult argument to dismiss out of hand. Many of the campus's social woes stemmed from the scheme known as the Dartmouth Plan, which required students to spend a portion of their time off campus, studying, working, or interning, shuttling back and forth from Hanover like a continually shuffled deck of cards. Portia and her classmates were newly immersed in this reality, having returned from Christmas break only weeks earlier to find replacement casts of dorm mates. The fact that rush took place at precisely this point in the year was not, she supposed, arbitrary, and while Daniel and the others continued to assail the conformist in their midst, she suspected she was not the only one who empathized with his sentiments. She sat silently, in any case, measuring in millimeters the distance between her hand and his, while they asserted their moral and intellectual superiority.

"I already know half the guys in the frat," Tom said. "I went to school with some of them, and I played lacrosse against a bunch of the others. I went to camp in Vermont with two of them." He shrugged. "It's like moving off campus with your friends, only the house is a frat house."

"What's your last name again?" said Daniel.

"Standley," Tom said affably.

"Oh. *Well*," said Daniel.

"Thomas W. Standley," Rebecca chortled. "Ask him what the *W* stands for."

"Nah," said Tom, grinning. "It's not a big deal."

"No, no," Rebecca said. "Of course not."

"What?" said one of the Latinists. "Winthrop? Wigglesworth?"

"Wharton?" said Daniel.

"Winslow?" said a girl.

"Wheelock!" Rebecca crowed, unable to contain herself.

There was a stunned silence.

"As in . . . ?" said the girl, meaning the Reverend Eleazar Wheelock, sent north from Yale two centuries earlier to educate (that is, convert) the Indians of New Hampshire, founder of Moor's Indian Charity School (later Dartmouth College) in Dresden (later Hanover), New Hampshire.

"Wow," said Daniel. "No kidding?"

"No, actually," Tom said. "Not Eleazar. His cousin, also named Wheelock, but far less distinguished. Hey," he said, "did you choose your middle name?"

"What, Irwin?" Rebecca laughed. "What makes you think he didn't?"

The party, having soured irrevocably, broke up soon after, though Tom seemed not to take offense. He gave Rebecca a big hug, waved affably at the boys, and turned a luminous face to Portia, who still had not spoken in his presence. After he was gone, she helped Rebecca rinse the glasses in the chilly kitchenette at the end of the corridor, then went to Sanborn to stare pointlessly at her notes for a paper on *The Winter's Tale*. Five months after arriving on campus, she felt, for the first time, that there was a cohesion to the experience, more than just a jerking along to class, parties, activities in which she could not find traction. Already, just in her first term, she had tasted and spat out too many potential selves, learning only what she was not and did not want, but never what she was or did. As an exercise in least resistance, she had tried out for the soccer team, only to discover, among her potential teammates, women who cared passionately about the sport, which — she simultaneously discovered — she did not, nor ever had. Someone on her floor had suggested she come along to crew tryouts, and that she had loved for the river at dawn and the rhythm of the boat and the magic of the balance and glide, which were so much more difficult to attain than they appeared, until she noted the broad, muscular back of the team goddess, a senior girl trying for the Olympics, and superficially decided that she had no desire to look like that. Afterward, she had cast herself as a playwright and a literary type, though already these selves were beginning to chafe. But now, brilliantly, suddenly, Portia had the rushing, thrilling sense that her life was migrating into order, forming around a point, starting to make, if not actual sense, then at least a point of embarkation. She had fallen in love, and that was the fact of her.

Portia had graduated high school a virgin, despite Susannah's best efforts to instill in her a joyful ownership of her sexuality. This comprised frank and open conversation from an early age, an arsenal of what-a-girl-should-know information on matters of contraception, disease, and the somewhat more elemental emotional composition of heterosexual teenage boys. It also featured a series of concerned interventions as Portia's high school years began to pass without her having begun (or, at any rate, told her mother she'd begun) her wondrous personal sexual journey. Portia, who by then had years of experience deflecting Susannah's interest, did not find it hard to fend off her mother on this matter, but she was becoming concerned herself. To be a virgin in high school wasn't, even in the omnisexual milieu of the Pioneer Valley, such a social black spot. But leaving for college that way seemed downright negligent, sort of like going off without being able to write a critical paper or operate a washer-dryer. She chose well—a fellow counselor at the summer camp UMass ran for soccer players—and had a reasonably good experience. At the end of August the boy decamped to Reed, which was comfortably far away, and they petered out after only a letter or two.

But this was what the entire exercise had been for, thought Portia that night, uselessly shuffling the pages of her sorry *Winter's Tale* paper. She was ready for it, she crowed to herself, her heart pounding. She had made herself ready. And while she had never before had cause to see herself as a passionate woman, it was wondrous, shimmering, to find that she actually was. Obviously, she was! Every nerve ending seemed to be singing, every synapse firing simultaneously. She had an object and a clear goal, and from that night, all that mattered was to summon him.

Wistful leaves fluttered over me as I sat overlooking the azure Pacific ocean and pondered the great gift I had been given the first time I was inspired to write a poem. In fourth grade I wrote my first poem, and ever since I have journaled everyday, filling countless journals with my stories and verses. My goal is to one day publish a book of my writings, and last spring I took a step toward that goal when my poem "Vortex" was selected for publication by the League of American Poets for an anthology of the best poetry by American teens.

CHAPTER TWENTY-THREE

THE LOW DOOR IN THE WALL

Nearly a year of this would follow, a year in which Portia could do nothing without looking first for Tom (at the student center, and the library, and for one precious term in the immense geology class she had taken to fulfill a science requirement), and then, if he was miraculously, luminously, present, choosing carefully where and how to position herself, always weighing the angle at which his gaze might fall on her. If it ever fell. Which it never seemed to do. A year in which she could not bring herself to actually approach him, but attended every party at Tom's socially unassailable fraternity (where, nonetheless, the beer was just as stale as it was everywhere else on Fraternity Row, the furniture just as shabby, the basement floor just as sticky, the boys just as single-minded, and the drinking games on continual loop in the bar just as inane). A year of lying-awake torment in which imagined touching alternated with imagined conversation, invented smells and tastes, and great insights, reached with the catalyst of his undoubted brilliance. But nothing actually happened, and none of this brought her any closer to Tom than the outer periphery of his orbit, which was itself many light-years from the source of her designated light.

It might have been easier to bear had he remained as high-minded (read: celibate) as she, but this appeared not to be the case. Whenever Tom was not surrounded by his fraternity-brothers-slash-rugby-teammates (despite the incident that had, in her view, brought them together, he had actually abandoned lacrosse for the even less restrictive mores of the rugby team), he was in the unwelcome company of girls. And far from those Jewish girls of his supposed preference, these girls always seemed to be blond, stick-figured specimens, clad in Fair Isle sweaters and white turtlenecks with patterns of tiny frogs or hearts or strawberries. Indeed, there was such a sameness to them that only a very, very close observer (like Portia) could detect the small discrepancies that meant there was not, in fact, one particular well-groomed and springy female in Tom's life, but multiple, sequential girlfriends. They were uniformly pale, straight of spine, short, and giggly, but one had blond hair to her shoulders, another to her chin, another to a clavicle protruding from anorexia, and a fourth was short enough to fit comfortably—wrenchingly—beneath Tom's sinewy arm.

Portia might have been raised in the nurturing bubble of the Happy Valley, fed on the I-have-a-dream-of-a-common-language utterances of poets and sages, but she knew right away what she was dealing with here. She was not quite a dolt who supposed there was no such thing as class in America, but the few WASPs she had actually contended with were those who had—like her mother—renounced privilege and resolved to tend their own gardens, whether on or off the commune. Amherst and Northampton and the even more hippie-infested hill towns to the north and west were one great muddle of altered surnames and handmade musical instruments, reused plastic bags from the Co-Op, and clothing made on someone's loom. For her, students of other races and nationalities did not offer the much vaunted collegiate experience of "diversity"; for her, diversity came personified by a boy with whales imprinted on his salmon-colored slacks and a girl with a hairband carefully, precisely holding back her rigorously straight blond hair. People like Tom and the little girls under his arm were exotic fauna to her. How had they evolved? What did they eat? Why did they dress like that? And how could she be more . . . well, like them?

Individually, she had found, the females of the species were affable, sweet, fun, and rigorously polite when you mixed with them in the classroom or the dorm. In groups of two or more, however, they seemed to undergo a metamorphosis, shifting into a dialect she could grasp only the edges of, and becoming mysteriously intertwined, like a grove of slender, rustling aspen trees with a single root system underground. Even so, and not unreasonably, Portia tried cultivating friendships with some of these girls and, when that failed, with some of the boys, but she never seemed to pass through their collective membrane of well-mannered exclusion. She fell in with them as they walked out of class and nonchalantly sat at their tables in Thayer, from which (unlike those queen bees of the seventh grade) they were far too polite to exclude her. She collected their names — Peyton, Avery, Perry, Winkie — but they never seemed to take in hers. At the very nadir of her subjugation, she went down the street to Campion's, which carried ample stock of anything a Dartmouth preppy might require, and spent good money on a turtleneck adorned with little shamrocks. (Portia's roommate, an intense Chinese pianist, would memorably say of this item: "Oh? Are we Irish now?") Sitting at their tables, wearing their clothes, falling into step beside them…these things did not bring her joy. They made her feel, instead, bizarrely earthy, hairy, vaguely unclean, and in her shamrock-imprinted turtleneck, which (in spite of her skeptical roommate) she had begun to wear constantly, just a tiny bit ridiculous.

Also gargantuan.

In the real world, she wasn't fat, but she did have substance: thighs and breasts, wide shoulders and hips, and long, skinny feet. Her body was Susannah's body, made for fieldwork on the Russian steppes and lots of childbearing (because you had to assume the Cossacks were going to kill a few). The little blond girls — she towered above them. The sleeveless Lilly Pulitzer dresses she tried on at Campion's were always tight across the back. She had to suck in her breath to button the high-wasted khaki pants she'd ordered from L.L.Bean, and that stupid turtleneck stretched so much across her chest that the shamrocks looked distorted.

Susannah, of course, considered dieting to be the fruit of the poisoned tree that was male chauvinist society. Portia, who was, after all, an athlete for most of her adolescence, had never seen the point of restricting her food intake, but then again, she'd never had to size herself up against girls who could have shopped in the boys' department. Now, she embarked upon the usual sorry voyage of self-loathing and well-meaning starvation, getting a late start on calories versus carbs, Tarnower versus Atkins. She had been raised too well to resort to finger-pointing — down-the-throat finger-pointing — which was the second most popular leisure-time activity in her all-women's dormitory (the first being late night gorging on peanut butter and Mallomars), but she was out for bones: hips, knees, even the jutting clavicle of that anorexic girl who obviously had the strength of character to starve herself. Which Portia did not. At least, not for more than a day or two, after which she would succumb to a base urge to feed herself.

Still, she beat on. Tom was her green light, her low door in the wall. (She was actually encouraged, rather than deterred, by Evelyn Waugh's *Brideshead Revisited,* which she read that freshman spring in her course on British fiction with no self-awareness whatsoever.) She could never get close enough, or lovely enough, or interesting enough, to catch his attention. And nothing else had caught her own.

Since quitting the crew team, Portia had not had a regular crowd and in time had drifted from Rebecca and her salon of thinkers and artists. Her roommate, with whom she'd been randomly paired, was an odd, driven girl, increasingly obscure as the months passed and by the end of the spring term barely speaking to Portia or anyone else. (Two years on, she would be expelled for plagiarizing a paper on Rosie the Riveter, evaporate from the roster of alumni, and never be heard from again.) All through the bitter New Hampshire winter, Portia battled serial sinus infections. When spring came and the campus softened into mud, she declared a halfhearted major in art history, then switched (hardly more enthusiastically) to English, organizing her projected Dartmouth Plan around a study abroad program in Edinburgh, the fall of her junior year. She finished out the semester with indifferent grades and returned that summer to the soccer camp (out of shape from her own abandonment of the game, not to mention her loss of muscle from erratic nourishment, but at least relieved that her beau of the previous summer had stayed on the West Coast), and so endured what would be her final months under Susannah's roof. At the time, it did not occur to her that she was depressed, and had been for a while, but later she would wonder at Susannah's obtuseness on the matter. Susannah, whose microattentions had been the burden of her life, who had borne down on her relentlessly to discover what she was thinking, what she was feeling, what concerned and obsessed and riled and devastated her, had seemed to achieve this long desired distance just at the moment a bit of attention might have served them both. Portia would spend many evenings that summer on the fetid living room couch, watching Ben Johnson first win and then lose his gold medal at Seoul and listening to her mother rage beside her as Bush wiped the floor with Dukakis; and years later, these—rather than the very worrying state of her emotions, not to speak of her grades, plans, and actual (rather than imaginary) relationships — were her clearest memories of those months.

And then, astoundingly, like a lacrosse ball out of the darkness, it all changed again.

On an afternoon in late October, Thomas Wheelock Standley came and sat next to her in the student center, taking the empty seat so quietly that she had no time to react. There was no obvious reason for this. The place was far from full, and she had commandeered a choice table at a window overlooking the Green, complete with its view of the new freshmen struggling to build their own bonfire. There was, unfurled before her on the table, a copy of the *Dartmouth,* containing a passionate but inelegantly written editorial objecting to the *Dartmouth Review*'s most recent outrage, and this Portia had been reading, dully, feeling the familiar mixture of accord and resignation she always felt when the subject came up. The struggle between the two publications had become slightly epic, one hoisting a totem of Woodward and Bernstein, the other a totem of William F. Buckley (a substantial contributor, as it happened), and clashing at every opportunity. Ideologically, the thing was a no-brainer. The *Review* had patronized blacks and women on campus, infiltrated the gay and lesbian student association with a hidden tape recorder (and published transcripts), and staged a lobster feast in response to a campuswide fast sponsored by the Third World Association. They were, without question, a repellent lot. But they seemed, like any other class of vermin, ineradicable, and she had seen enough of her mother's various agitations to question the point of protest.

When he began to speak to her, she failed at first to truly process the words. It seemed to her that this must be only another of the countless imaginary conversations they had had, on subjects too numerous to count, and this one simply following on from the last or the one before. He asked about the editorial, and gave his opinion of the bonfire being assembled outside, and asked what classes she was taking this term.

Portia gaped. For one thing, she looked not terribly well and was wearing not her khaki-and-shamrock ensemble of the previous spring, but old jeans and a purple Amherst sweatshirt that had not seen the inside of a washing machine in some time. Her hair, likewise neglected, fell in heavy waves down her back, curling in places when it wanted to curl, and she had, she realized, and with horror, been actually chewing the thumbnail of her left hand when he sat down, and possibly for a minute or so after.

"I'm sorry," she said at last, when there was a break in the conversation, "but do we know each other?"

"Of course!" he said brightly. "Remember, at Rebecca's? Last winter?"

She nodded, thoroughly numb.

"I'm Tom," he said. "Remember?"

Portia eventually indicated that she did.

"And you're Portia," he added. "You're Jewish, right?"

She stared at him, turning this question in her addled brain.

Jewish was a door that opened onto many rooms. *Jewish,* meaning of the faith, worshipping that long-ago God of the desert who had singled you—or at least your ancestor—out for special treatment (how "special" could itself be endlessly debated). Portia was a stalwart atheist, believing no more in the baffling desert God than the equally baffling Gods of Joseph Smith or Mother Ann Lee. Or *Jewish,* meaning of the tribe, marked and endlessly victimized, blown across the planet for generations but inextricably tied to one another and their shared past, like the Celts or the Mongols or the Africans. But here, too, she felt unqualified to stake much of a claim, given that she was, as far as she knew, only half Jewish (albeit the half that counted) and had no idea what the other half was and whether it might actually cancel out Susannah's half. She had sometimes explained that she had not been "raised" Jewish, could not speak Hebrew or dance the hora, had never read from the Torah or Talmud or attended synagogue or—God forbid!—been bat mitzvahed. Her religious upbringing was limited to the brass menorah Susannah had produced one year when she was small, lit two nights running, and abandoned (for years!) on the mantelpiece in the living room, and also to Susannah's brief flirtation with Feminist Seders, a women-only Passover assembly with an orange on the seder plate and a Haggadah full of solidarity with oppressed women across the globe. But that, too, had abated after a year or two.

She looked at him carefully. She had not been this close to him for many months, not since that day in February in Rebecca's crowded cinder-block room, except for the one giddy morning last spring when she had taken the seat behind him in geology and was able to spend the entire class period examining the geological strata of his blond hair. *He has this thing for Jewish girls,* she remembered, then, dredging the extraordinary phrase from her memory, shaking it off, holding it up to the light, then letting it fill her with the strangest happiness. He seemed not at all concerned to be waiting this long for an answer.

"Yes," she told him, smiling. "Yes, I am."

I would like to share with you something about my current medical situation. Last month, I consulted with my doctor because of a digestive problem. He performed tests and I was given a diagnosis of Irritable Bowel Syndrome (IBS). There is no cure for IBS, and I do not know what the future will hold for me, but I am determined to face this challenge with the same determination I have faced every other challenge in my life.

CHAPTER TWENTY-FOUR

The Destination Board

A little over a year later, in a grubby café not far from the Gare du Nord, with a plate of highly suspect celeriac before her and a very heavy backpack at her feet and a heart — not to put too fine a point on it — newly rent to howling shreds, Portia realized that she was pregnant.

The celeriac was not something she had ordered on purpose. She wasn't entirely sure what it was, for one thing, and — speaking no French — was not in a position to ask. But of the various cold items in bowls on the counter, it actually looked the least dangerous, if not the most appetizing, and she was too bereft to walk any farther, so she went inside the café and nodded and pointed at the bowl, thinking vaguely that it might be a kind of pasta and unlikely to hurt her stomach, which had been bothering her. But then the small plate of the stuff materialized before her, and she was able to give it a good look and a good sniff. A thin tendril of nausea began to waft up from the plate and coil around her throat, and Portia, who without entirely realizing it had already begun to cry, suddenly understood — irrevocably, precisely, horribly — just what that nausea meant.

She was not supposed to be alone in the café, in Paris, on the eve of the Christmas holiday. She was supposed to be with Tom, toasting the end of the term and the start of their great, defiantly unstructured European adventure, anticipated for giddy months, refined by postcard (from Edinburgh to the small town near Toulouse where Tom had spent the fall, and back). They had met only once during that time, in London, for a weekend of well-worn tourist exercises and a room in a Bloomsbury hotel. The hotel was called the Ivanhoe, but the garish mural in the basement bar portrayed an Antarctic scene, with penguins and sleds. ("Wrong Scott," the manager had said mirthlessly when asked.) When she thought of the weekend later, especially in the queasy misery of that unlovely Paris café, she thought only—with sharp, wounding jolts of pain—of the elation that had wound through it and of one moment in particular: walking through Berkeley Square on the damp Saturday afternoon, destination Knightsbridge, especially Harrods, especially the food hall where Tom's mother had once taken him to tea when he was very young and his father was working at the London office of Morgan Stanley. Tom had made a fetish of this memory, as he had of certain iconic moments in his life: the note his father had left hidden beneath his pillow on the day he left for boarding school, the jumping trophy won at a horse show and then taken away when another rider objected to the height of his pony (half a hand too tall, it turned out), the southern gothic horror show of a family reunion (South Carolina, his mother's side), when the weekend was crashed by self-termed relations who had not really been invited. And tea at Harrods with his mother and brother, stirring pebbles of hard sugar into their cups. Taking her there seemed to Portia like an act of union, even an end run around the mother in question, who had been far from welcoming in the flesh. And walking there across the city, into the building darkness, with Portia's waving hair (which he loved) escaping from its enclosures (in the way that he loved), and feeling still the physical prickle of his hands on her body, and passing through Berkeley Square, Tom had started to sing, not unreasonably and not—it had to be said—particularly well, that old song about nightingales in Berkeley Square, and she had thought: This can only be the sweetest moment of my life.

Had it happened that day? That afternoon? Later that night, after the play they had gone to with good intentions but then left in the intermission, because, all things considered, they would rather be back at the Ivanhoe, back in bed? Or the next morning, before he had left for the ferry and she for King's Cross and Edinburgh, for the interminable final weeks of their separation? She hadn't felt anything physical. She had been far more attuned to her general anticipation for their reunion and the effort of late-in-the-day scholarship to redeem her (thus far) undistinguished school-work. But nothing of the body. Nothing...clinical. Moving a fork through those repellent white, soupy strings of celeriac, she could not remember when she had last had her period. Then she could not remember when she had last thought about it.

Tom had come to Paris, as planned. And the train station, as planned. But he had left her there to go be with some other woman, and that had certainly not been planned, at least not by her. The woman, who apparently waited discreetly outside (in a café probably far more picturesque than the one she herself was sitting in), was a Dartmouth sophomore from his language program, with a name Portia had immediately repressed, so that even years later she found herself making it up with the aid of an imaginary WASP rhyming dictionary: *Twinky? Blinky? Stinky?* This person would prove to be athletic and flat and asexual and blond, not—in other words—outwardly distinguishable from the women who had preceded Portia's tenure in Tom's life (minus, of course, the Jewish girls), but—cruelly—she would be the one he married.

Yet Rebecca had also been far from mistaken about the Jewish girls.

From the moment he'd sat beside her in the student center and non-chalantly reminded her of who he was and where they'd met to that final night in the Wrong Scott hotel, Tom had thrown himself headlong into her assorted relative abundances: flesh and hair, emotion, eccentricity. He had adored the extravagance of Susannah, who was a screamer, a gesturer, a sensualist, whose disapproval (even) had passion and extravagance. He had adored Susannah so much that he had been impervious to the fact that Susannah had not adored him back, not the littlest bit. Portia, fearing the worst—expecting the worst—had first taken him home over the winter break, for three days of brittle tension that culminated in an outburst even Tom could absolutely not miss, in which her mother had dragged her from the dinner table (Tom had been explaining that his work covering sports for the *Dartmouth Review* was not political—it was sports, after all!), secured her behind the insubstantial door of the sitting room, and demanded to know what the *fuck* she thought she was doing with this reactionary, boorish, chauvinistic son of privilege.

She loved him, that's what she was doing. She loved him, thrilled to him, hummed to the music of him. Because his arm around her shoulders was weighted with joy and her body raced and soared under his hands. Because she believed him when he said that she was beautiful, and he said so all the time. Because he had picked her—amazing, amazing, amazing—and every day picked her again and would certainly pick her forever.

Though he hadn't actually told her that, of course.

Portia had a single room in the dormitory all that year but barely used it except to change clothes, drag herself through a series of sinus infections, and fanatically shave her legs (lest a single dark hair mar her perceived loveliness). She lived mainly in Tom's room at the fraternity, careful never to impose more than the absolutely required personal items and textbooks, careful to maintain, always, the lightness of the visitor. In fact, when she was not with him, she had not even the strength to mimic lightness but craved only the next time and the next talk and the next touch.

Susannah, she was sure, had never felt a thing like this. Certainly, in a lifetime of far too intimate confessions to her daughter, she had described nothing remotely similar, only the husband of convenience, and the men who were evolved enough to be wonderful lovers and responsible partners, and the genetic providers from the laboratory or the train. Nothing like this. Nothing like this. Which was the reason, Portia told herself, that Susannah was so out of her mind with resentment, wild at the sight of her sated, admired, cherished, and elevated daughter. "Don't bring him back," she had even said, that awful winter break, "and don't come back yourself until you've figured out why you have to act this way. I didn't raise you for the Junior League."

So she had taken him away the day before Christmas, and off they had gone down the MassPike, east to the rolling exurbs of Boston and the impeccably groomed home of Tom's mother, father, brother, and horses. Mrs. Standley—"Caroline. *Please.*"—was a transplanted southerner who looked as if she were perpetually freezing. She wore her hair in a girlish pigtail, but brutally slicked back and bound by an enamel clasp. She looked emaciated, swallowed by corduroys and L.L.Bean sweaters many sizes too large, and a pair of green Wellington boots like the ones the new English princess had worn on her honeymoon. These were taken out daily for rambles with the dogs or schooling one of the horses over jumps in the field next door, an activity Caroline approached with a grimness that seemed inappropriate for a leisure-time pursuit. She was, to Portia, the picture of hospitality: hand extended at the door, towels folded at the foot of the guest bed. There was even a gift for Portia under the fragrant tree, a silver necklace of irreproachable taste in the box of a jeweler on Main Street—a Main Street clad in seasonal finery and olde tyme American splendor. Tom, who had recovered quickly from their Amherst misadventure, loved being home. He loved introducing her to family friends and the kids he had grown up with, and watching the flicker of confusion on their faces. *Where was Portia from?* She was from Northampton. *Northampton? Lot of strange people in Northampton. Communists and lesbians, wasn't that right?* Portia supposed. *What did her parents do?* Her mother was an organizer. *Oh? What did she organize?* (In time, Portia amended this to "volunteer," a much simpler concept for them to grasp.) *And her father?* "I was raised by a single mom," she would say, eyes downcast, hoping against hope that from this display of regret, they would conclude her father was dead. Dead father. Volunteer mother. Tragic but familiar. And noble! And at least the father had been fiscally responsible, so the widow hadn't had to work.

But she wasn't one of them. Clearly. At Christmas Eve services, she betrayed a certain awkwardness, knew none of the hymns, and seemed underdressed. For the Boxing Day party they attended every year, she was loaned an unobjectionable dress by Tom's mother, but it had been too tight to zip up completely, and she had made the fatal error of wearing a Dartmouth sweatshirt over it. Why hadn't Tom stopped her? She'd brought no gifts for the family and had been forced to forage in town at the last minute, finding only impersonal things with a whiff of desperation about them. Why hadn't Tom warned her? By the end of their stay she was frantic, trying to make up for her shortcomings or else to distract them with those attributes she did possess: good brain, good grasp of world affairs, good powers of argument. These, however, had no worth in the Standley home, and she left having won over only one family member, Tom's brother, who had suffered a breakdown in law school and was (in his parents' euphemism) working independently on a project related to international copyrights until the following fall.

The decline in her fortunes could be traced in the brittle features of Caroline Standley, who might have met her son's new girlfriend at the door with a rigorously correct embrace, but whose fear and disappointment built and built over the ensuing days. She was never less than scrupulously polite to Portia and full of terribly interested queries about her life at college and before, but the strain she was under became more and more evident, spreading like a pool of insidious fluid under the very, very taut skin of her face. Portia, growing frantic as the days passed, lingered in bed in the morning, retired early in the evening, and took every opportunity to lead Tom off for walks in the fields or visits to the local haunts of his youth. She generally kept herself out of sight as much as she could, and when she could not she made it her business to seem light, kind, and irreproachable. To this growing strain between his girlfriend and mother, Tom seemed oddly impervious. He touched Portia whenever he wanted, on the forearm, the shoulder, the back of the neck, crossing the invisible lines between neighbors at the dinner table or on the couch or in the car. He padded down the hall to the guest room in the middle of the night for very hushed bouts of lovemaking, then rose early to help his mother exercise the horses, generally behaving as if all were well—which perhaps, to him, was the case. Portia, of course, never said a word to Tom about the silent but acrid force field between herself and Caroline. What good could come of it? Why burden him? Tom's mother, clearly, had recognized the aberration of this slovenly Jewish girl of dubious parentage for what it was—rebellion, pure and simple—and opted to wait out her son's bizarre fascination, which surely couldn't last much longer, an opinion that Portia, very fearfully, shared. (Between the two women, in fact, there was a perfect, if silent, meeting of the minds on this point.)

Both, however, were wrong, to Portia's great amazement and Caroline's infinite distress. Through the winter, and Tom's ten-week internship at the Boston law firm (he visited often), and the spring, when Portia, putting the nail in the coffin of her theater interests, spent three months working for the Bread and Puppet group up in Glover, Vermont (she visited often), and on into a halcyon summer term, in which their sophomore class reunited, more or less, from wherever (to quote the college's regretted alma mater) across "the girdled Earth" they'd roamed in their disparate Dartmouth Plans. It was a sweet summer, clear and warm, with the doors of Sanborn Library thrown open onto a dappled Baker Lawn. Portia wandered inside and outside as the afternoons passed, out when she wanted the air, inside when the sun began to withdraw its heat, always nearby when tea was rolled out at four and the business of studying paused, by common agreement. All of her courses were guts, or felt like guts, since who could take seriously the novels of Jean Rhys (Modern British Fiction) or even the thorny notion of theodicy (Judeo-Christianity and the Problem of Evil) when the class was held beneath one of the few surviving elm trees at the edge of the Green? Through the long summer days, her path and Tom's interwove, like a minuet in an Austen novel, bringing them again and again face-to-face. Whenever the appearance of a couple was indicated, they were there together, someone's hand in someone else's: fraternity parties down the Row, the summer formal at the Woodstock Inn, the Summer Carnival variety show in Webster Hall. Sometimes, after dinner, she went with him and others down the hill to the river and out onto the dock where she had once helped hoist her crew shell, to swim in the brilliant Connecticut and sit and laugh with her new friends, who were, of course, Tom's friends. At night, she and Tom slept in the same bed.

At first, she nursed a powerful if not wholly rational resentment against her mother for neglecting—in all of the assorted warnings and war cries since (it seemed) the moment of her birth—the fact of romantic love, let alone its legitimacy. For Portia, this was akin to discovering a new sense, which society had perversely elected to suppress, holding it to be—perhaps—downright incendiary in comparison with the unobjectionable touch, taste, smell, feel, and sight. Susannah might never have felt the passion, the gut-twisting adoration, her daughter was then feeling (and how different she might have been, as a mother—as a human being!—if she had), but was that cause to deny to her own child the wondrous thing in which Portia had dwelt, now, for nearly a year? Her relations with her mother were strained for a time, with outright silence following their holiday expulsion from Northampton and lasting several months. But they thawed in June when Susannah announced her imminent and quite surprising move north to Vermont that summer. To keep tabs on me? Portia thought selfishly, but when the air cleared she was actually happy for her mother and helped her sort through the Augean stable their Northampton house had become. With Susannah ensconced in Hartland with her chums, and Portia's own worldly possessions reduced to a single stack of cartons in the new basement, she felt nearly adult, brave, flush with love, and eager for the fall in Edinburgh and the torrid, wondrous winter and spring to follow, when she would wander around Europe with Tom.

An adventure that was not to include grimy cafés like the one she found herself in, or—when you came right down to it—things to eat that seemed likely to make her ill.

She wasted no time in wondering whether she were truly pregnant: She knew that she was. Her body, now that she was paying the slightest attention to it, seemed to be screaming at her from all corners: sore and suddenly pendulous breasts, a sour taste in her mouth, a gag reflex wound up so tight that even a passing breeze made her want to vomit. And the fact—which ought to have been obvious—that she had skipped a period. That she had missed this, above all, appalled her.

Screaming pain had taken up residence in her head, pounding like an Athena who would never, for her own part, do something as idiotic as falling in love. She sat, masochistically hunched over the nauseating celeriac, eyes full, battling to keep herself from exploding. She found herself thinking of the two very different forms of Parkinson's disease—one freezing the features, the other causing uncontrollable movement—and how the most unfortunate sufferers had both at the same time. That was how she felt: vibrating, maniacal, but grim and unmoving, too. Suspended in motion, at the apex of misery. I will be here in an hour's time, she thought dully. And tomorrow. And next week. And in six months. And forever. Never feeling better or getting over it.

Though he—Tom—was already gone, off on a train somewhere, with Winky or Stinky. Probably raising a glass of red wine to toast the adventure under way. It made her sick.

This gave her an idea. She went down an alarmingly narrow stairway to the bathroom, tiny and unclean, and efficiently threw up. Then she came back to the table and ordered tea. *"Thé,"* she said hoarsely. *"Por favor."*

Not right. It would occur to her about two minutes too late.

When her tea arrived, she downed it, scalding her mouth. Now that felt horrible, too.

Common sense, of course, should have dictated that it would end this way, give or take a location and what was on the plate. Tom was always going to be heading off with a Winky or a Stinky, bound for the future he—to his credit—had never once told Portia he didn't want, a future of law firms and the lonely fellowship of Massachusetts Republicans and the tailgate martinis when Dartmouth played Harvard or Brown, the athletic children and beach stickers from the Vineyard on the back of his car. Their time together, she now understood, had been exotica for him, perhaps a defiant gesture that he was so much more than the stock character from the stock prep school novel that he appeared to be, he was a complex man who chose whom to love and cared not a whit for the trappings of American class, which anyway everyone knew did not exist. For a blessed year, he had brandished Portia at fraternity events and family gatherings, daring his friends and relations to sputter their approval for his choice and their admiration for his independent spirit. Here was Portia, child of a self-declared feminist and rabble-rouser, born without a discernible father, rocked in a cradle of hemp, nourished by herbs and yogurt. Here was the product of no family in particular, from no particular place, and anyone who even thought about questioning the wisdom of this pairing would find him selectively deaf and entirely silent, for he was far, far superior to such base notions. His parents and brother and cousins and schoolmates, the people he had known forever and would always know, whose children would play with his children and go to school with his children, who years from now would still be around him and alongside him—Tom owed them nothing. He made his own choices. He was a modern man living a modern life.

And he had been very understanding to Portia, there, under the colossal destination board at the Gare du Nord. Very solicitous for her well-being. And full of suggestions for what she might do next. Could he buy her a coffee? Take her to speak with the train clerk? His French, he noted proudly, was now nearly fluent. Would he like her to look into flights home for that day? Or the next? Did she need help finding a hotel?

No. And no. She actually let him pat her on the shoulder. She actually hugged him back when he hugged her warmly. To her horror, she realized that she was declining his aid not because she didn't need it, but because she seemed intent upon making this nicer for him. The impulse, moreover, felt disturbingly natural, as if she had done it before—many, many times before. Easier for Tom, who seemed impervious to the fact that the woman within his warm embrace was disassembling: synapse from synapse, sinew from sinew, muscle from muscle, held together (she greatly feared) only by those strong encircling arms. Impervious . . . just as he was to the fact that his mother hated Portia, or that Portia's mother hated him, and the fact that he had dominated Portia's social life (did he never wonder why she had made no other friends?) and that they had never once slept in the various dormitory rooms she had been assigned, which were more private than his room on the loud (and smelly) upstairs corridor of his fraternity house, or the fact that, more than halfway through her time at college, she seemed to have formed no real academic purpose and certainly no vision of a gratifying career. He had missed many things, it seemed clear to her now, but by the same token he had never actually been dishonest. There had been, certainly, attestations of love, but love of the moment, not—and this was a fine distinction—lasting love. Certainly there had been no offer of permanence, no talk of marriage or even a vague future together. She must have inferred these things, conjuring them out of sensual happiness and what still felt like clear affection, mindlessly assembling a prospect of shared time, shared contentment. For the first time in her life, she felt brutally stupid.

And so, in the great tradition of ill-treated women everywhere, she decided to blame herself.

Astoundingly, both earlier on the echoing floor of the train station and now, who knew how long after in the awful café, what she found herself thinking of most was not his cruelty or even his prior affection, but the outer edges of his body, the planes and depths of him, the variant textures. Scenes and sounds assailed her, rattling through her head without stopping, as if some part of her brain were trying to flush the information and another part barring the door, desperately storing the data where it could not be dislodged. She longed, with an addict's longing, for numbness, would have given anything for numbness, but was too afraid to be drunk in a foreign country where she was alone, and despite an upbringing that was close to reprobate as far as others were concerned, she had never ingested a drug stronger than marijuana, which in any case had made her only paranoid and very hungry. She was on her own. With her tearing pain and surging nausea. And she hadn't the first idea what to do with herself.

She paid by putting her largest bill on the table, watching the waiter reject it (too big to make change for—she got that), and substituting another, which was grudgingly taken. With this transaction complete, she gathered her things and left the café, walking back in the direction of the train station, if only because that felt familiar. It was getting dark quickly now, and there was a quickening along the streets, converging on the Gare du Nord. Portia joined in, letting the herd carry her back into the station. She set down her backpack in the middle of the crowd and, like everyone else, looked up at the immense destination board. Around her, people arrived, paused, departed. She peered at the lines of text on the board overhead, trying to figure out which words went together and what they meant. This seemed like more of an intellectual exercise than a practical one, which was just fine, since she wasn't really thinking about getting on one of the trains.

"Orry Chantilly Creil Clermont St. Just," read the first line. And the next: "Dammartin Crépy Soissons Anizy Laon." And the next: "Orry-La-Wille Chantilly Gouvieux Creil." And then: "Compiegne Saint-Quentin Aulnoye Maubeuge." The only destination she recognized was "London Waterloo," but something in her recoiled at going back on the very train that had brought her here only a few hours before, so happy and excited to begin. Then, near the end of the list, she found another line of names she could decipher: "Bruxelles Berchem Rotterdam Amsterdam." A woman with a large suitcase jostled her and moved off without apology. Or perhaps, thought Portia, watching her go, that mumble she'd made had been an apology, and that tiny fact, that there might be some comfort available to her that would miss its mark simply because she wasn't capable of receiving it, made her suddenly angry. She looked up at the board again, alighting on the few words she could understand, and decided on the spot to go to Amsterdam, where—while English was hardly the official language—at least no one would be surprised, let alone offended, that she spoke no Dutch. It was, besides, a four-hour journey, which meant four hours of being able to sit, staring at nothing out a dark train window, with no one wondering if there was something seriously wrong with her. That the train would deposit her alone in a strange city late that night did not trouble her, given the general precariousness of her situation: Surely four hours would be enough time to figure out how to fix the mess her life had suddenly become.

At the last stop before Amsterdam, a tall Dutch man with stud earrings and a pink Mohawk got on the train and began passing out flyers to anyone who looked like a tourist on a budget. Portia got one of these: an ad for a youth hostel not far from the station, in a barge on one of the canals, no less. When they arrived in the city, she followed the man, along with a trio of American boys from the Midwest, to this marvel of hospitality, paid her nominal fee, and picked out a top bunk, where she fell mercifully asleep. In the morning she began walking the city, hunched against bitter winds in her red down jacket, hands clenched in her pockets. She went to the Van Gogh Museum and Anne Frank House, numb to both in her private misery, and ate dry sandwiches in a café near the Rijksmuseum. That night, she went with the midwestern boys to a club in an old warehouse, where multiple stages showcased a variety of terrible techno-bands, cafés, lounges heady with cannabis, even a movie theater where some Dutch documentary about tanks rolling into a gray Eastern European city seemed to play on continuous loop. "This is stupid," said one of the boys, whose name was Dan, or Ben. They got up and left, but Portia stayed, watching the tanks roll on and on through the gray winter streets. In the morning, she went back to the train station and took a train to Munich.

Later, it was clear to her that any sensible person would have headed south to someplace warm, parked herself in a pleasant spot, and taken a couple of weeks to figure things out; but she was hardly sensible just then. The trains themselves, she discovered, were where she wanted most to be, not the destinations, always in transit and never arriving. On the trains, it wasn't noteworthy that she was by herself, sitting silently, staring forlornly out the window. That was how people were on trains — all people, not just abandoned American girls who had just realized they were pregnant. At first she worried over her destinations, not because of money (the Eurail Passes she and Tom had bought were good for any train in the network), but because she didn't want to get to a city in the middle of the night. In Berlin, however, she found the station at two a.m. comfortingly busy, with young people sleeping in alcoves and blearily drinking coffee in the station cafés, and she stopped worrying about this, too. Through the holiday season she took the trains, duly walking the cities, respectfully viewing the landmarks, eating — when she could eat — the culinary highlights of wherever she happened to be, and then moving on, speaking only to fellow travelers and guides, waiters, and hotel or hostel employees. She was not very responsible about addressing the considerable problem she faced, but she did, as the days and then weeks passed, discover that the very fact of the problem was gradually muting the blow of Tom's desertion, deflecting her pain into the worry about her situation.

She had never questioned the right of women to terminate their pregnancies, and she certainly did not question it now. With Susannah, she had boarded the middle-of-the-night buses at the gates of Smith College for the long, long drives to Washington to march for the right to keep abortion safe and legal. Not in denial of the life it terminated — like most sane advocates of abortion rights, Portia certainly acknowledged that there was another life involved — but because a woman's ownership of her own body trumped that incipient (not yet viable) life. She had always taken it for granted that were she ever to find herself in precisely these circumstances, abortion was the option she would choose. Not — certainly — without regret, but with sober acknowledgment that termination was the right decision in some cases. That it had happened to her, that there was actual life inside her, did not compel a sudden reversal of her convictions, but she wasn't stupid. She was only a little pregnant, despite what anyone said. She had some time. And she had no wish to experience an abortion in a foreign country where she might not have the language to ask—for example—for more pain relief or an extra blanket. And she was far from ready to face Susannah and hear what Susannah had to say about all this, to defend her scrupulous use of the diaphragm and her alliance with Tom, who was far, far from the reactionary dolt he—all right—appeared to be, but a real, complex man who, just like her, struggled with the transition from who he was raised to be to who he wanted to be. A few more weeks, she could stay away from her mother, away from the inevitable clinic and table and stirrups. A few more weeks of her now almost cherished trains and blurry landscapes of farmland and dreary cities, the screeching of steel on steel as they slowed into a terminal, the echoing loudspeaker voices in French or Dutch or German and then in languages she couldn't immediately name. She spent Christmas in a hotel room in a nondescript town on the French-German border and New Year's in the restaurant of an inn near Prague, fending off the attentions of two drunken Italians. She dragged herself through Mozart's Salzburg birthplace and inspected the carefully worded memorial stone before Hitler's childhood home in Linz: *Für Frieden, Freiheit und Demokratie nie Wieder Faschismus Millionen Tote Mahnen*. Finally, in Vienna, she bought a ticket to an afternoon demonstration at the Spanish Riding School and sat in her chilly seat, watching the great white horses parade and pirouette beneath their grim-faced Napoleonic riders, leaping like frogs in their jangling tack. This is stupid, Portia thought.

And then she went home.

CHAPTER TWENTY-FIVE

I'M NOT HERE NOW

At the bus station in Boston, Portia was about to buy herself a ticket to Northampton when she suddenly realized that she didn't live there anymore. Only a few months earlier, she had helped her mother pack up the house and ferry her belongings up 91 to Hartland, where she then spent a couple of days repainting Susannah's bedroom lavender with white trim. And all of this, she now understood, had simply slipped her mind as she had numbly made her way across the ocean, unthinkingly imagining herself back in the house and on the street where she'd grown up. She stood at the ticket window with two shuffling bodies behind her, waiting for this curiously elongated transaction to conclude so they could get wherever they were going, but Portia had abruptly found herself without a destination and taken on the general demeanor of a pillar of salt. There was no longer any reason to be in Northampton. She felt no desire at all to go back to Dartmouth, where she wasn't supposed to be now and wasn't at all sure she'd ever want to be again. And something in her quailed at the idea of going to Hartland, presenting herself to the three of them—Susannah, Frieda, and Carla—a wayward young lady indeed. Those women, veterans of protests and marches, strikes, actions, sit-ins, initiatives, drives, and boycotts—they would encircle her with comfort and affirmation, assure her that she had been horrendously victimized, shelter her from the wackos at the clinic (if the state of Vermont had managed to produce any), and make sure she got all the pain pills she was entitled to. They would do this out of love and also pride, because wasn't this precisely what they had worked and petitioned and agitated for? So that she, a young flowering woman who had every right to determine what was best in these unfortunate circumstances, would not have to put herself in the hands of some slimy practitioner or stick a wire hanger up inside herself and bleed to death?

And she did want to be taken care of, didn't she?

And she did want that clinic, and the pain pills, and for it all to be over. Didn't she?

Apart from the nausea, Portia had done a pretty good job of repressing the whole thing. Her clothes still fit, though admittedly she hadn't worn anything very form-fitting in her tramp around Europe. It was true that she had avoided the mirror, unwilling to confront the more subtle changes under way, but that was very deliberate on her part, as she had no wish to subject herself to more distress. Now the termination couldn't be more than a few days away, and she might come out the other side without ever having seen herself pregnant. But when she tried to imagine where this liberation would take place, she found her head spinning. The line behind her grew longer and more impatient. There were too many options and nothing she could hold on to. Boston itself, of course. Portland. Providence. Burlington. New England must be jammed with politically evolved places for a girl to get out of trouble. There were hotels everywhere. There were pharmacies and hospitals. Did it even matter where she went? Just as long as Susannah wasn't there, she thought suddenly. And this thought was so alarming that she quickly stepped out of line and let the person behind her move up to the window.

It made no sense, thought Portia, shouldering her backpack again and walking across the room to an empty bench. Why should she do this without Susannah? Her mother would want to help, to support her and be of use. And Portia obviously needed the help; no one should have to go through an abortion alone — she knew that much. A few minutes ago, she'd been so intent on finding her way home to the nest that she'd forgotten the nest wasn't there anymore. Now she was prepared to go anywhere her mother wasn't. Because, she thought, beginning to prod this paradox, I don't want her to know that I was dumb enough to get pregnant? Because I don't need to hear her opinion of Tom, thanks very much? How about, she thought, moving closer to it, because I don't want her to know what I am going to do, in case she tries to stop me?

She smiled at this initially absurd notion.

Susannah, who had once claimed to have written the slogan "If you're against abortion, don't have one"? Susannah, who had been a volunteer at the clinic in Springfield, holding a blanket over the scared girls as she led them inside, taking the brunt of the curses herself?

And of course, I believe in it, too, thought Portia.

She just didn't want to.

She began to sweat, still in her warm winter coat, clutching her backpack against her belly.

Because it was murder to kill it? she thought very, very carefully.

It was not murder.

Because I want to have a baby? I want to be a mother?

She did not want to have a baby or be a mother. It was absurd to think of doing that—that was for later, when she was no longer a child herself. When she was with someone. She didn't want to do it the way Susannah had done it. She wanted the normal things: love, partnership, hearth, and home. Of course she wanted children. She just had never thought about it before.

By then it was early evening, raining faintly. She had slept a little on the plane, but she was still tired and very dirty, with rapidly diminishing reserves. She felt, more than anything, the need for a decision, even a working plan to get her to some place of rest, where the next decisions could at least be made in some comfort. Portia got to her feet and went back to the ticket booth, taking her new place in line. She looked at the destination board and read down the list: "Worcester, Albany, Providence, Hartford, Lawrence." She had been to all of these places, except for Lawrence. She knew no one who lived in Lawrence or who had ever lived there, and not much about the place at all except that it was not so small that a pregnant stranger would be noted. That realization was suddenly thrilling, because it meant that she could be invisible in Lawrence. Full of purpose, she bought a one-way ticket, a transaction that felt otherworldly, magical. No one would find her in Lawrence, she thought, climbing aboard the bus and making her way to the back. She had not realized until that moment that she had been trying to disappear.

That night, she stayed in a motor lodge near the Lawrence bus station. It was not a restful place. Down the corridor, a couple fought with drunken abandon, but she was irrationally pleased to see American television again and fell asleep to Johnny Carson interviewing a celebrity she did not recognize. She spent the next day in bed, too, except for a midday meal at the IHOP across the road, writing lists of things to take care of on the back of her place mat: place to live, something to do (job? volunteer?), Susannah, school, doctor. Doctor? thought Portia. The word had the impact of a needle, breaking into her reverie of independence. It was not that she had decided to ignore the fact of her pregnancy, only repress it for a little while longer. She had also decided to believe that a college-educated woman who'd possessed her own copy of *Our Bodies, Ourselves* since the age of thirteen must be capable, on her own, of being responsibly pregnant, not like some seduced and abandoned cheerleader who wasn't even sure how she'd gotten that way. Obviously, Portia had taken a pass on any tests and medications recommended for the first trimester, but she couldn't have missed anything too important. Women, after all, had been having healthy babies even before Hippocrates, let alone *What to Expect*. Her European sojourn had featured lots of walking, often with the backpack, so she felt generally well, apart from the daily puking, but that was starting to fade, too—first one fairly good day per week, then three, then five. She had money—that was one thing she didn't have to wring her hands over. She was supposed to be traveling in Europe, staying in hotels, and eating in restaurants. It couldn't cost more to stay in one faded mill town, rent an apartment, and keep still. She was not expected home for two months and at Dartmouth for three. These were problems to be addressed, surely. But she had time.

The next day, restored by more sleep and more showers, she went out and found a furnished apartment to rent, in one of the old textile mills that were being converted to residences. The agent was eager to get bodies in while the construction continued, then out before she hoped (insanely, Portia thought) to sell the units as condos, probably by the fall. Did Portia have pets? Did she smoke? No and no. Was she employed? the woman asked worriedly.

"I'm a writer," said Portia. "I'm working on a book."

She was, in fact, working on a book. She was working on *The Pickwick Papers,* which she borrowed from the Lawrence City Library, checking it out instead of the mindless fare she'd originally gone in for. Reading her way through Dickens—*Pickwick* to *Edwin Drood*—seemed like a serious project for an English major who had never taken on anything but *A Christmas Carol,* and that mainly in the form of Albert Finney's *Scrooge.* In her apartment, which had been furnished in nouveau mismatched cast-off, she lay on the faintly malodorous couch and began the picaresque, finishing it three days later. Then she took it back and exchanged it for *Oliver Twist*.

Portia had called her mother on Christmas Day and New Year's, both times from chilly pay phones located on broad central European boulevards. She called now from the public phone in the library and spoke of thick hot chocolate in the cafés and the smell of chestnuts cooking over coals in the vendors' carts, the boorish American boys who had tagged along with them for a few days, from Paris to Brussels and then on to Munich... details she pulled from the bulletin board in the library basement, events and fund-raisers and church sales, promising her mother that she felt fine, felt safe, was happy, would call again soon. She was reasonably assured that the old-fashioned rotary phones in the Hartland house would not betray her secret. She was thinking, she might say, of writing to Dartmouth, delaying her return until the summer term or perhaps even the fall. Dartmouth wouldn't care if she moved things around or even—if it came to that—whether or not she graduated with her class. That was the point of the Dartmouth Plan, to let her education alter with new interests and circumstances and be personal and idiosyncratic. It was a great thing, actually. And did she mention how educational it all was? The Mozart museum? The villa where the Wannsee Conference had been held?

It shocked her, how convincing she was, how pleased with herself she sounded. It shocked her how easily she parried Susannah's objections, which were first resentful of the added time away (from school? from her?) and the apparent longevity of Tom's affections, then increasingly resigned to the distance, both physical (away from her) and emotional (between the two of them).

Portia finished *Oliver Twist* and moved on to *The Life and Adventures of Nicholas Nickleby*.

She needed bigger clothes. A book in the library said she ought to be taking folic acid, so she took it.

A woman and her sister moved in next door. The sister had Down syndrome and liked to play checkers. Portia, after a game or two, figured out how to lose stealthily.

She finished *Nicholas Nickleby* and started *The Old Curiosity Shop*.

In March, she found a doctor in an old Victorian on Haverill Street with a downright Dickensian sign out front: SMITHFIELD, BEERKIN, AND NOGGS, INFERTILITY AND OBSTETRICS.

Hers was Beerkin, and he saw her first in an office that had once been the house's front parlor, complete with fireplace and window seat. "Who have you been seeing up until now?" he asked her, noting that she was probably at sixteen weeks.

Portia explained that she had recently returned from Europe. "I've sort of been doing it on my own," she said to his obvious disapproval.

He examined her, made notes, pronounced her healthy, gave her proper vitamins and a test for gestational diabetes. When they returned to his consulting room, Portia told him that she wanted to discuss adoption with someone.

He looked at her blankly. "Discuss?"

"Adoption."

"You mean, you're giving up this child?"

Now the disapproval was palpable.

"I'd like to consider it."

"May I ask why?" he said.

She looked at him in complete disbelief. "No," Portia said. "You can't."

After a minute, he said: "I know a group here in town that takes in young women in your situation."

"I don't need to be taken in," she said unkindly. "I just want to talk to someone who can explain the options."

He frowned at her. "I don't know if you really understand the trauma of giving your baby away," he said with highly disingenuous concern.

"I don't either," Portia said deliberately, as if to a child. "That is why I would like to discuss it with someone." She got up. "Do you have a name for me?"

He held her gaze for a long moment. He must not, it occurred to her, be used to single pregnant girls who gave him a hard time.

"The nurse has a list," he said finally.

Portia collected the list and took it home with her. Catholic Adoption Services. Lutheran Services. LDS Family Services. New Hope Christian. The idea of the people who would call these agencies, people who only wanted a baby sanctioned by their own faith, appalled her. At the bottom of the page, in a different typewriter font—as if it were a grudging afterthought—was the state agency number for adoptive services. They could see her the following week.

She paid her rent in traveler's checks. When those ran out, she drew on her bank account in Hanover. One of the librarians who saw her every day asked if she would tutor a couple of seventh graders who were failing English. Their names were Milagro and Gloria, and they were cousins. Portia had never taught anything except soccer, but the girls tried hard and got a little better. She was in the library study room with them when the baby kicked for the first time. Squealing, they put their hands on her belly.

Portia finished *The Old Curiosity Shop* on the morning of her appointment with the social worker, a transplanted Californian who asked to be called Lisa and whose husband taught Latin just over the hill at Andover. To Portia's disappointment, Lisa, too, seemed quite taken with the idea that Portia couldn't know what was best for her, that she must be unaware there was support, in the state of Massachusetts, for single mothers.

"I get calls every day," she explained patiently to Portia. "Women who gave up their babies in the fifties and sixties. They've never gotten over it. It ruined their lives."

"My life will not be ruined," Portia said firmly.

"Back then," the social worker went on, "the idea was that the baby would get a family that could give it what a single mother couldn't, and the birth mother would just magically forget that she had ever given birth. She was supposed to go back to school, meet somebody, get married, and have her real babies. But you couldn't become a mother and then sign a piece of paper that said you weren't a mother. Biology is a little tougher than that. And today there isn't the stigma of a single parent."

"I'm aware of that," said Portia, who was, after all, the daughter of a militant single mother.

"You're clearly an intelligent woman. You can go to college, and the college might well have day care facilities. You'd be eligible for medical coverage and other benefits. You think you can't do this, but you can."

"I don't *want* to do it," said Portia, losing her temper. "*That's* the reason. Would you be happier if I had an abortion?"

"You can't," said Lisa. "It's too late."

"I know it's too late!" Portia told her. She was just barely in control by this point. "I mean, if I'd *had* one. Listen, I'm pro-choice, and this is my choice, okay? And please don't tell me there won't be families willing to adopt a white newborn."

Lisa sighed. "No, I wouldn't tell you that."

"Because you can't have that many white newborns coming down the pike, I'm guessing."

The woman shrugged. Portia almost felt sorry for her. But not sorry enough to stop making her perfectly valid point.

"How many? I'm just curious."

"What?" said Lisa, though she probably knew exactly what she was being asked.

"White newborns. Available for adoption in this state. Last year, say."

She waited.

"Oh...well, I'd have to look it up."

"Ballpark." Portia folded her arms.

Lisa sighed. "I do remember one, last year. I don't think there were others."

"And how many families willing to adopt that one white newborn?"

The social worker looked at her. She was no longer trying to be nurturing or even polite. "Quite a number," she said at last. "As I'm sure there will be quite a number hoping to adopt your child. If you continue to make that decision."

"Past tense," Portia said unkindly. "I've made it."

"But you don't have to make it yet. You can wait. You can see how you feel once your baby is born. I can promise you, there will still be families then."

"No," Portia said icily. "Look, it's my life and my decision. I'm trying to do the right thing, for both of us. Can you just explain to me, what is the problem here?"

But she was the problem. In the silence that followed, Portia understood this very clearly. There was something off about her, a woman who clearly could raise her own child and bafflingly didn't want to. It had not occurred to her that she would run into this difficulty. Honed as she was on the brutality of the clinic bomber, the "pro-life" assassin, and the prayerful protesters helpfully pointing out that young girls terminating their pregnancies had the agonies of hell to look forward to, she'd naively assumed that choosing to carry and give birth to her child would have everybody standing up and applauding. Not so.

The social worker leaned forward and spoke softly. "Can I ask you, is this pregnancy the result of a rape or an incestuous relationship?"

Disgusted, Portia shook her head.

"Is there something you'd like the police to know about?"

Yeah, she thought fiercely. I'd like the police to know that I'm asking for an entirely reasonable and not to mention perfectly legal form of help and not getting it.

"No. Look, are you going to be able to handle this adoption? Should I go to New Hampshire or Vermont?"

Lisa looked sharply at her. "That's not necessary. I just wanted to be sure you had adequate counseling. In fact, I'd like to refer you to one of our staff therapists. It's part of our service package," she said.

Portia looked down, intensely irritated. Then she agreed, made another appointment for the following month, and left. She had given them the very least amount of information she legally could: a name, a Social Security number, birth date, level of education. She'd said nothing about Tom except that he, like her, was Caucasian and college educated. No, she did not wish to give his name.

"Has he been notified of the pregnancy?"

Portia hesitated. "Yes," she said.

"And you have discussed this decision with him?"

What did they want from her? thought Portia, struggling to contain herself. "Yes. Sure."

"All right," Lisa said sadly. "I'll get the paperwork started."

There was no master plan. Portia did not intend to micromanage the adoption, choose the family, name her baby. She had no wish to present Tom with the fact of what had happened, torment her mother, explain herself to Dartmouth College, or do any single thing that might bring any other human being into her confidence. She barely wanted to be in her own confidence. She would be writing no letters, contacting no registry, doing no search for the child she was determined to relinquish. What she wanted—the only thing she truly wanted—was to place her healthy baby in good, responsible hands and then do the very thing Lisa had declared to be impossible: magically forget that she had ever given birth. She refused to believe it would not be possible. Those women, the ones whose lives had been destroyed, they weren't like her. They'd been forced and pressured and abandoned. Of course they'd felt violated. Of course they'd been distraught and enraged. But this was different. Not because she was a better person. There was nothing to be proud of. She had been born later and given choices. She felt for those women, of course, but she would be able to do what they could not do: become a mother and then sign a piece of paper that said she wasn't one.

By the time all this was over, she would have been in Lawrence for seven months and three seasons. She would have read thirteen Dickens novels, with only *Edwin Drood* left to finish (she would somehow never, in the ensuing eighteen years, find time to finish it), and coached Milagro and Gloria to final grades of B and B plus, respectively. She would have paid rent for the first time and interviewed doctors for the first time (after the unsavory encounter with Dr. Beerkin, she shopped around until she found a grandmotherly OB-GYN in an office at the hospital). She would have lost upward of fifty games of checkers to the woman with Down syndrome next door, whose delight at winning never seemed to diminish.

It hadn't even been especially hard, she would think years later. Ever since she could remember, she had fretted about the idea of growing up, always somehow worried that she would not be able to actually achieve adulthood when the time came. Since freshman year, she had watched women about to graduate go sloping off to interviews at Career and Employment Services, unsteady in unfamiliar heels, their customary sweats and jeans replaced with broad-shouldered suits. Sometimes they would fly off to Cleveland or Chicago or New York for further interviews and return with incredible stories of hotel rooms with concierge service and in-room movies—everything on the corporate tab. After commence-ment, off they would go to their tiny apartments and the late night car ser-vice home (again, on the company) when the account or the deal required them to stay late. They came back to visit and brought new tales of their new lives in the great world. To the college girls still in their nightgowns with their open chem or econ textbooks and powdered cocoa, they spoke of group runs with the Roadrunners Club in the park, summer shares on Fire Island, credit cards, dry cleaning, and wine tastings. Somehow, Portia had allowed herself to believe that this—this package of employee perks and health club memberships—represented adult life, not just because the former rowers and field hockey players and sorority treasurers had trans-formed themselves into businesswomen, speed-walking to work in their Lady Foot Locker sneakers, but because their lives didn't look remotely like Susannah's life. That part of it was a good thing. That part of it, Por-tia thought she might like very much. But in the end, she didn't think she could ever pull off such a transformation.

Yet in the seven months she'd spent in Lawrence, it hadn't been at all difficult to assemble the trappings of adulthood, the accumulation of objects, the rituals, the paper trail of bills and checks. Not every twenty-year-old woman was a junior in college, it seemed; some were living on their own in places like Lawrence, paying their rent, making small talk with the bored teenager in the checkout line, taking care that there was enough toilet paper. It was, she would think perversely, a thing to be sort of proud of, perhaps not on the scale of bringing a human being into the world, but unlike the human being in question, a thing she would certainly be taking away with her. And when she went back to Dartmouth, and when she saw Tom again, she would not be the same childish person she had been, but a placid, seasoned woman, moving forward, unencumbered and unafraid, and above all else, contained. No one would ever know what had happened here. Portia would barely know, herself.

She clung stubbornly to this idea.

Through the summer, which was very hot, she grew ponderous and breathless. The sisters next door moved on, complaining of the construction dust, and a man Portia didn't like the look of took the apartment. The counselor she'd been coerced into seeing tried to get her to talk about the adoption. She did not want to talk about the adoption. Portia did not even want to approve the family. She didn't want to know anything about where the baby was, only that it would be safe, as if they could promise that. She let them tell her only that the couple were from Watertown, in their thirties, and married for a decade. They were, according to Lisa, "ecstatic."

All right.

And so she went home and tried to settle into *The Mystery of Edwin Drood* and waited for it to begin.

On the ponderously hot morning of Sunday, August 19, her water broke as she was walking home along the Merrimack River with a bag of the few things she could still stand to eat: Triscuit crackers, peanut butter, carrots, and cranberry juice. At first, she thought she had somehow broken the juice and irrationally looked for the red liquid on the ground. When it wasn't there, it took her a long, addled moment to realize what was happening. She stood where she was, deliberately considering her options, stunned by how quickly her world had just contracted to a few mundane decisions.

Get home, put the food in the kitchen, call the taxi?

Set down the bag, ask a passerby to phone the doctor?

Stand very still until someone noticed that she was having a baby and took care of her?

She went on home, stopping twice to fully appreciate the earliest (and, sadly, mildest) contractions, and when she arrived, she carefully placed the plastic bag on the kitchen table. Of course, she would not be eating this food now, but wouldn't she want it when she came home? After? Or would these always be the foods of her pregnancy, things she would never want to see again, like the vast dresses she'd been wearing for the past two months and the dirty Keds her swollen feet had come to rely on, and the 1960s television shows that seemed to dominate the local channels? She was trying to think past the elephant, which was not just in the room but squarely in her path. She did not want to go to the hospital too soon and be sent home, multiplying what she imagined would be, at the very least, an uncomfortable journey, but after only another ninety minutes she decided to move while she was still competent to manage the trip. She called the taxi company, and while she waited for it to arrive, she called Lisa and told her what was happening. The social worker at the hospital would be informed, Lisa said, and she would call the parents now and tell them what was happening. "Good luck," she told Portia, who was momentarily stymied by the use of the word *parents*.

She had not attended Lamaze classes, not because she objected to the idea of it, but because she couldn't face not having a partner. She had, however, dutifully read a book about the method, which — sadly — she had to jettison entirely once the contractions hit their stride. Within minutes of changing into a gown she was gasping for relief, which they seemed happy enough to give her, and with the lower half of her body mercifully numb, she fell almost peacefully asleep and awoke four hours later, nearly fully dilated. The room's other bed had acquired an occupant, a sleeping woman with straw yellow hair and a ruddy complexion. She was immense, her midsection so large but so ill defined that Portia couldn't tell whether she had had her baby yet or not, and she never found out, because as soon as her lower abdomen came jolting back to life, they moved her down the corridor to an antiseptic little chamber.

The grandmotherly OB-GYN was away on the Cape with her actual grandchildren for the weekend. Her replacement was called "Dr. B." He came in clapping his hands but never actually looked up from the end of

the table, and he never asked her name. She tried not to take this personally, as he wasn't much of a conversationalist in general and made use of
a single abbreviated word, one size fits all, to conduct the labor. "'Kay,"
he said at the end of each contraction. "'Kay," he said when the next one
began. "'Kay" meant whatever it had to mean: *Good job. Try harder. Stop
pushing. Push harder.* It was extraordinary how quickly she deciphered all
this. She wanted to laugh at him, but by the time she caught her breath, it
didn't seem funny anymore. "'Kay," he said, "next one."

It occurred to her that she didn't know what the *B* stood for or if it represented his first name or his last, and then it occurred to her that that was
something to add to the blessedly long list of things she did not know and
would not know, like her baby's name, and what he — or she — would turn
out to be, and who would love him. She did not believe that she could love
him. Susannah, whatever else was wrong with her, had thrown herself into
maternal love, and Portia felt, again, that she must be very unnatural, and
it did pain her that she did not already love her baby, did not believe she
would eventually love her baby, would wish her baby away in a breath if she
could catch her breath, especially if the pain went, too. But she couldn't do
anything if she couldn't breathe. She couldn't be expected to produce the
baby, or whatever raging thing had gotten itself trapped deep inside her, not
if every time she tried to gather her strength, the deep pain of it came soaring through her body, leaving no appendage unturned, making every part
of her crackle horribly. She remembered now that she had asked for the
version of labor without pain, but when she tried to bring this up, it came
out sounding sort of vague, as if she were still in Europe and attempting to
accomplish the task at hand in some unfamiliar language, managing only
to state the obvious: "Hurts, hurts, stop."

"'Kay," said Dr. B. "Third time's the charm."

Was he trying to be funny? Portia thought.

Then, in her acrid fog, she thought: I have to do this three times?

"You got anyone here, sweetheart?" said the nurse at her ear.

Portia turned vaguely in her direction. "What?"

"Your mama? Boyfriend?"

"No," she panted.

"Well," the woman said comfortingly, "that's okay. One good parent's
one more than a lotta kids get."

"No," said Portia. "It'll have two. It's being adopted."

Her hand, on Portia's shoulder, seemed to turn instantly cool and even slightly clammy.

"You giving your baby away?" she said in a whisper.

Portia, in the grip of a contraction, with no breath to spare, only nodded.

"Why you wanna do that?" said the nurse. "It's your baby."

Astoundingly, no one in the room seemed to react to this. Perhaps they couldn't hear it. Perhaps, thought Portia, it had not actually been said aloud.

"I have to," she said, or possibly said.

"'Kay," said Dr. B. "This is it."

A hand—that same hand?—patted her shoulder.

"I *have* to," she possibly said again, but louder this time. She had to say it louder, over the din of the pain.

"You gonna see your baby now," the nurse said matter-of-factly, and Portia waved her hand to say no, she didn't want to see the baby. Nobody had said anything about having to see the baby. Wasn't that optional? They couldn't make her, she thought, and shut her eyes, idiotically, like a five-year-old.

But she could hear it, crying even louder than she was crying, bitter wailing that ricocheted against the bones and the walls and the tiles. Portia pressed her hands against her ears. "Little boy," said the most deafening voice in the world. The physical pain was suddenly gone, lifted from her like a sodden tablecloth, and now there was only the other thing: the tearing, searing agony that had irreversibly replaced it.

I don't want to, thought Portia. She shook her head, eyes squeezed shut, hands over ears. "Please," she told the nurse, whose hand had left her shoulder, giving way to a blast of frigid air.

They had taken him to the far corner of the room, where three nurses who had come from nowhere attended him, rubbing, cutting, wrapping, lifting. The soreness was her legs, coming together. I don't want to, she thought again.

"Would you like to hold your baby?" said a man, and it took Portia too long to realize that this was Dr. B., who could say other things aside from "'kay" after all, and that he was standing close, just past the hands covering her ears, and already holding the baby, who was also, as a result, close.

Very close. She shook her head, bereft and also enraged, because hadn't she already said no? Hadn't she said no? Had she said no?

"I don't want to," Portia said to the insides of her eyelids and the insides of her hands, because if they took him now, before she truly looked and truly heard him, then she could still retain this delicate skein of not knowing. It was possible. People did it. They did it for things even worse than this, far worse than this: affairs and diseases and men who fell out of love. She remembered, quite suddenly, the man her mother had married, who had died a long and terrifying death from a disease no one understood. The Chilean musician who might have been her father but wasn't, she thought, curling up tight on the hospital bed, kicking away the nurse at the foot of the bed who was trying to clean her and dry her. He had died childless in a hospital bed like this one, surrounded by his friends and lovers, half of whom would die soon after of the same baffling thing. His name had been Renaldo. Portia and Susannah had visited during his illness, Portia just old enough to recoil from the sores in his mouth, the furious dark patches on his arms, legs, and chest. He was a very sick man, but not a mournful man. He had swung her hand from his hospital bed. He had told her: "I wake up every morning and pretend I'm not dying."

He could do it, and he was covered with stigmata—the world knew what he refused to acknowledge. Perhaps there was a life in that, she thought. Perhaps it will be possible to wake up every morning and pretend there was never a baby. *I've never been here. I'm not here now. I never even opened my eyes.*

"'Kay," the man said softly. He took a step back and turned to carry the baby away. She took her hands away from her ears, and white noise came pouring in. She opened her eyes and saw white light. Of course she did not intend to look after him as he left the room. She was so close to escaping, sight unseen, but some rigid claw turned her head and held her there, insisting that she witness this tiny shock of the new: protruding from the striped hospital blanket, a head of darkest hair and a nose momentarily flattened by birth. That hair took hold of something inside her and wrung it wildly. Portia tried to sit up and made a sound she couldn't really decipher. They had all finished with her. There was no one left in the room, even to vaguely pat her shoulder, even to disapprove.

It was just—she would later think—that she had not been expecting what she saw. Tom's hair was blond, like his parents' and brother's hair.

Her own hair was the same as Susannah's: dark brown, stubbornly wavy. The meaning of this would not be immediately clear, but in the years that followed—years and months and weeks and days—she would come to understand, and with devastating impact, just what it signified. The black-haired child they took away was not only a child, but one of the very few people in the world she knew for a fact was related to her. And the only chance she would ever have to see her father's face.

PART
IV

———❧❧———

DECISIONS

For as long as I can remember, my most important goal has been to make my way to a great university, where I could spread my academic wings and engage in intellectual exchanges with my peers. I have been thinking about this, dreaming about this and, yes, also worrying about this since I first discovered what the acronym SAT stood for. Now, all these years later, I look at what I've accomplished and discover, to my great concern, that I am only one of thousands just like me, ambitious and well-prepared for college, but not particularly outstanding in the context of your applicant pool. Of course, I wish that I had written a novel or won a Grammy or modeled for Vogue, but to be totally honest, I just don't understand the necessity of completing or even beginning my life's work by the age of seventeen. And the fact is, I was really busy with Honors Calculus.

CHAPTER TWENTY-SIX

WHO AMONG US HAS DIED?

For the first time in weeks (and thanks to John), there was heat in the house, but Portia still could not seem to get warm. She lay beneath all available blankets, quilts, the duvet from her own bed and the one from the guest bed, clenched like a fist and wild for relief. She was discovering, first, that she had somehow known this would happen, that the baby she had once refused to see would one day materialize before her and force her to look at him. And also that the act of excising those nine months from her memory, and the life she had after all saved by carrying to life, and the phantom child growing without her in some unknown place with some unknown woman pretending to be her and some unknown man pretending to be Tom, was a fearful, constant presence. It was the rasping monster resurrected by the monkey's paw, drawing closer and closer to home. It was the silent corpse of Eurydice, always a half step behind every step she had taken since Lawrence, Massachusetts. She did not remember ever actually deciding to tell no one, but she had never told, never even considered telling. Instead, she had filled the place her son might have occupied with shame. Shame: like poured cement, assuming exactly the dimensions of the missing child.

But shame about what, exactly? Portia refused, then as now, to feel disgrace at having become pregnant at the age of twenty. She declined to apologize for not choosing to terminate, bizarrely old-fashioned as that was. Even now, she wasn't completely sure why she had done it. She hadn't, after all, been shunned by her family, thrown out of school, church, community, dumped in one of those terrible places for bad girls to be warehoused until she could produce an infant for some superior woman to raise. Her mother would have embraced her, certainly would have enabled her to continue school. And Dartmouth, despite its macho bluster, would not have blinked an eye — or not much of an eye — at a single mom finishing up her degree, commuting to campus from Hartland.

But she had never thought of keeping him, and the shame of that had become the body within her body. She was suffused with shame, drenched with it, riddled with it like something metastasized. Her bones kept it erect and her muscles made it move and her skin contained it, and everything she had ever felt or thought or done since that morning seventeen years before, when the baby had left her body and the room and — she believed — her life, had been felt in shame, thought in shame, and done in shame.

Now it felt as if that shame were leaking from every pore of her, leaking and leaking as the first day passed, and then the next, and then the next. The bed was soaked with it, and the blankets and duvets made a damp tent to huddle beneath. It was, she would later think, a kind of an afterbirth, seventeen years in the making, and she wondered how long this was going to take, how long until, finally, she was dry and done. Her body claimed not to understand the logic of this. There was, it seemed to her, no end to the backlog of weeping.

It had never occurred to her to tell Tom. Not senior year, when she'd had to turn away her face at the sight of him. Not when she read about his marriage to the very Winky or Stinky (*all right, all right,* in fact Binty, née Elizabeth) Caldwell Hemming, who had waltzed away with him that day in Paris, or the births of his other children in the alumni magazine. She knew this was wrong. She knew that he had the right to know there was a child, to be a father if he chose it, not that she believed for a minute that he would actually have chosen it. But it was still wrong, even increasingly wrong, she supposed, after he'd had other children and perhaps understood the enormity of what had been kept from him. He didn't deserve that baby, was what she told herself, not after the way he had left her, not after failing to know—magically, she supposed—that they had conceived a child. Coming and leaving, impervious and nonchalant, where she, at least, had endured the variant pains of carrying the baby and giving birth to the baby and hardening herself against the baby, an effort that had now lasted for many years and blasted every other part of her life out of its way, while he had married and made a family and gone on to lead the life he was always going to lead. How must he remember her? The exotic Jewish girl who had his mother so riled up, who seemed to understand that it couldn't be a lasting thing, a *real* thing, they were too differently wired, and who had become, of all things, a Dartmouth admissions officer—I mean, who could have seen that one coming?

The truth was that she had long ago consigned Tom to his own life, with his family and unsurprising career path, in the very Boston suburb from which he had sprung. Once a year, on average, she did dream of him, but the Tom in her dreams did not confront or condemn her. He didn't cry or wring his hands. On the contrary, he did mindless things with her, mundane things. Married things, it occurred to Portia now, like going to a movie and walking out because it was boring, or kissing her on the cheek, or watching children in a Christmas pageant. It was hardly passionate (even the kissing) and never emotionally fraught, except for one time many years ago, when her dream self had stood in Tom's (imagined) tasteful kitchen, with hands on hips, and reminded him (reminded him?) that he had another child, and what kind of father did he think he was? She had woken from that dream in a motel on the Oregon coast, heart pounding, the waves outside pounding, sweaty and cold and unable to calm herself. But only that one time. And when it happened next, a year or more later, they were back in the school auditorium or at the movies.

Away downstairs, the phone was ringing again, its tinny, accompanying voice a half step behind:

"Call from ... Princeton ... Univ. ... Call from ... Princeton ... Univ. ..."

Surely the office. Clarence or Corinne or possibly Martha, checking to see when she would be back. That was a relief. Yesterday there had been several, presumably from John:

"Call from ... cell phone ... NH. ... Call from ... cell phone ... NH."

Which she, of course, had not answered either. John, she could not face. She couldn't stand to think of him waking up (in the morning? in the middle of the night?) to wonder what had happened to her (bathroom? kitchen? insomniac nighttime jog through the muddy Pennsylvania countryside?) or, worse, somehow intuit everything, know everything. Perhaps by now they had all gleaned the meaning of her abrupt departure, or perhaps she had been seen, frozen in place in the upstairs hallway like Lot's too curious wife, punished forever for what she had done.

Once, in the application essay of a young scientist, she had read a graphic description of latent tuberculosis: deactivated infections walled off behind a casement of immune cells in the lung. They could stay that way for years, the boy had written, silently ticking, doing no outward harm, and then, without warning, burst open to flood the body with what he had memorably termed an "untidy" form of death. But that's me, Portia had thought, fighting off a wave of dread as she checked "High Priority—Admit" at the bottom of that page, how many years ago? Her latent disease, outwardly doing no harm, inwardly building to a slaughter: necrotic, poisonous, infectious, terminal. In August, it would be eighteen years. Eighteen years a-growing, like the child himself. Eighteen years of searching faces on the street and in the crowds. Eighteen years of declining to hold other women's babies or play with their children. Years of walled-off longing. Of letting her few friends know that they should not ask about this, of letting Mark believe that they had actually decided not to have children, of telling herself that if she were meant to be a mother, deserved to be a mother, she would now have a one-year-old child, or a seven-year-old child, or a thirteen-year-old child, or an eighteen-year-old child, but she didn't deserve it because she had failed that child in the very first moment of his life, and wouldn't she just do the same thing to another child?

Merely adequate mothers, mothers harmed by their own terrible mothers, rotten mothers who destroyed their children in manners too numerous to conceive—they didn't give their children away. They held them and brought them home and took care of them—sometimes poorly, sometimes wrongly, but as well as they could. Those lousy parents, at least, had tried. Portia hadn't even tried. She had done what none of them had done, refusing even to look at the baby who moments before had been inside—*inside*—her own body. She hadn't touched him or carried him. She hadn't named him, even to herself. There weren't words for the terrible thing she had done, the terrible thing she was. Her only hope had been to keep it from herself and thus from anyone else who might have some misconceived inclination to think well of her—to love her.

She had phoned in some fraudulent malady to the office and also fraudulently claimed to be working at home, and ordinarily this would have been true, but in fact she had not been able to face a single one of the files Martha had pressed on her. Without them, there was no buffer, no distracting wedge to place between herself and herself, as she had—she now understood—been doing for years. In the great annual bombardment of lives—little lives, lives unmarred by the kind of gruesome and incapacitating flaw in her own life—there had lain the means of constant evasion, and now it occurred to her that this might be the very reason she had thrown herself back into it, year after year, to wade among the hundreds and thousands and ultimately hundreds of thousands of seventeen-year-olds, all fresh and new, none of whom could possibly be the one she had been looking for all along.

Now, that was finished. Now—this year—all of the names and aspirations and batting statistics and Latin citations and FFA honors and part-time jobs tutoring the neighbors' children in math belonged to seventeen-year-olds who might just possibly know her son. They might have run cross-country alongside her son or smoked cigarettes behind the maintenance shed with him. They were the cohorts her son might have had and the girls he might have once been in love with or the kids on his language immersion program in Barcelona. They were the classmates who might have beaten him in the student body president election or fouled him on the basketball court. They were the possible deadweight on his biology lab team, the cheerleaders who perhaps bounced alongside his football games, the buddies he theoretically passed time with in the inane way teenage boys passed time. Maybe they knew him. Maybe they could tell her what he was like.

Or maybe they could, actually, be him. Her own son. Born Lawrence, Massachusetts, August 19, 1990. Name unknown. Parents unknown. Address unknown. Interests unknown. Talents unknown. Future plans unknown. Thoughts about her, the person who had sent him out into the world without seeming to care in the slightest, never to answer the questions he must have had or offer him the smallest comfort, never to come after him—unknown.

And the worst of it was that none of this was new. She thought, bizarrely, of an old ghost story she had long ago loved in a shivery, prickly way, about a woman who dreams the same dream every night: old road winding through woodland, house glimpsed in the distance (on a cliff above the sea, of course), and how she walks up the long, long drive and knocks on the door to ask the old man inside if the house is for sale.

"Oh, you wouldn't want it," he tells her with a curious expression. "It's haunted."

"Haunted?" the woman asks. "By whom?"

"By you," says the man, closing the door in her ghostly face.

All ghost stories come to this, she understood. All ghost stories end in one of these two ways: *You are dead* or *I am dead*. If people only understood this, Portia thought, they would never be frightened, they would only need to ask themselves, *Who among us has died?*

And then it occurred to her that she was the ghost in her story. She had spent years haunting her own life, without ever noticing.

Downstairs, the phone clicked alive in the empty rooms.

"Call from . . . Princeton . . . Univ. . . . Call from . . . Princeton . . . Univ. . . ."

Once, long ago, this would almost certainly have been Mark, phoning as he walked home to see if he needed to stop at the store, or checking in on his way to whoever's house they were meeting at for dinner, to ask her to bring a bottle of wine from the cool corner of the basement, their most unscientifically maintained "cellar." Neither of them cared overly much about wine. When they found something that seemed good to them, they tried to remember the name, but if the wine store on Hullfish Street didn't have the exact bottle, they were soon once again in the morass of lyrical names and vibrant labels, as likely to vastly overspend as they were to buy something everyone else seemed to know was dreadful. She hadn't set foot in the cellar since January, when she'd made one pointless visit to the chilly furnace, and took a moment to congratulate herself on at least not having drowned their breakup in whatever Shiraz or Merlot or, she supposed, unredeemable plonk might be down there. She wondered if Helen had been drinking wine or anything else as she slouched toward delivery. Europeans, Portia had noted, maintained a disdainful skepticism about the proscription against alcohol in pregnancy, citing various intellectuals whose mothers had apparently drowned themselves in Bordeaux; but Portia had once taken a class with Michael Dorris at Dartmouth and had seen, many times, the professor with his adopted son, an addled, vacant boy destroyed by his mother's alcoholism before he could escape her by being born. When Dorris wrote his book about fetal alcohol syndrome the following year, she hadn't even needed to read it to know the connection was true.

When it happened to her, she drank nothing. She had done that much for him.

And he was brilliant. Eccentric, of course, but brilliant. Where had that come from? Not Tom, surely, who was smart in a plodding, capable way. Not from her. Susannah was bright but scattered, Tom's parents had been so closed off to her that she had no sense of what they thought, let alone how. The person she had always thought of as *I'm OK — You're OK* couldn't have had that much to contribute to Jeremiah, could he? Unless . . . what if he had been some sociologist or critic, preparing a blistering lecture on pop psychology for the idiot masses? For the first time in days, Portia felt her face contract in a strained approximation of a smile. Was it not the height of narcissism to suggest that of the hundreds of thousands of vapid Americans who read that very book that very year, her biological father was the only one to read it for the purposes of scholarly vivisection?

Perhaps she was getting a little better.

To test this theory, Portia sat up in bed, clutching her own knees, which, she observed, were still clad in the jeans she had worn to Pennsylvania. They were slack with wear, undeniably grimy, and it occurred to her that it must be strange that she was wearing them at all, and also strange that she hadn't noticed the strangeness before. This is how depressed people behave, she suddenly thought, taking a mental step back to scrutinize the cross-legged person in the center of her slovenly nest. But the thought of being depressed made her smile again. She had never thought of herself as a depressive person. Depressive people rent their garments and howled in grief and took to their beds . . . well, like this. But had she ever felt, actually, depressed? She was a contained person, that was all. Even-keeled. Perhaps a little judgmental, but who could fault her for that? She judged for a living, didn't she, and it was ingrained, and she was a responsible representative of whatever it was she represented. She wasn't like Mark, who had had low periods, usually related to Cressida and the spiteful whims of his ex. Or her mother — Portia could see now that those last years in Northampton, Susannah had not been her habitual steamroller self, that something had left her household and her life when Portia departed for college, a slowly deflating balloon where the familiar person had once been. Susannah had indeed been depressed, Portia supposed. Maybe for a long time. Maybe until that phone call only a few months earlier and her crazy idea about taking in this mother and baby and just possibly starting the whole thing over again. I'm not like that, Portia thought fiercely, even as a fresh reminder of grief came rolling through her. She meant, she wasn't like that in life—her real, actual life. She wasn't a whiner or a self-flagellant or given to dramatic plunges like...well, again, like this one. The tearful thing she might be now, the thing made up of useless limbs and a brain that refused to make thoughts—it wasn't really her. It wasn't going to be her—please, please—for much longer, let alone forever.

She decided, in a very clinical way—as you might prescribe a course of supplements for some detected deficiency—to think of the last time she had felt happy, and she found, to ever growing distress, that she was feeling her way further and further back. Past the years with Mark and the various contentments therein, and the walks with Rachel, and the visits home to Susannah, always careful not to show her hand, holding back, always holding back, and the pleasure of doing her job well, and how she liked her house, or would surely like her house when it transmogrified, at some unknowable point in the future, into a home. She thought of endorphin highs, the heady combinations of good talk and good food at the tables of their friends—tables, she could not help but notice, that she had not seen since Mark's departure. She thought of how good it felt when they—when the admissions officers from the Ivy League and the other most selective colleges—had their meetings, nominally to build the fences that kept things neighborly, but somehow also to fan their mutual flame: find the great kids, the ones who dreamed and toiled and took nothing for granted, and bring them here, and give them what they need, and watch them change the world. Mark, when she had brought him along to one of these conferences (only once, and many years before), had shaken his head as they drove back to Hanover and said, "You're all such do-gooders."

And she had laughed, unsure of whether to take offense or be flattered. This was not news to her, of course. The newest admissions officers spoke only of what they dreamed of unearthing in some inner-city school or depressed, abandoned town. The older guard grew filmy eyed recounting the young doctors and engineers and novelists whose Cornell or Yale education had changed—no, *made*—their lives. That this rosy-hued altruism existed in direct contrast with the public face of the Ivy League admissions officer—which was something akin to the Witch in *Snow White* or the pompous and dismissive Professor Charles Kingsfield of *The Paper Chase*—only added to the perverse satisfaction of the matter. Portia actually knew several colleagues who had indeed chosen college admissions instead of the Peace Corps or VISTA or, more recently, Teach for America (itself a product of Princeton, or at least one Princeton student's senior thesis). Make the world better: her mother's never actually articulated life philosophy. And Portia had done that, she had, though Susannah herself had never gleaned or at least never acknowledged the connection. She had been stuck, eternally stuck, on the notion that Portia toiled in service to elitism and exclusivity, that her work was to preserve some antiquated ideal of American success as the exclusive property of already privileged white men. Susannah had been addled by the undeniable wealth of first Dartmouth and then Princeton, as if it were shameful for an educational institution to have too much money. She had convinced herself that her daughter, raised so carefully to make everything right with the world, was in thrall to some imagined power trip of saying no and no and no and no, over and over again, all the while unclipping the velvet rope to motion inside the sons and daughters of suburban stockbrokers and generous alumni. At first, Portia had done her best to persuade her mother that admissions work was part of the solution, not a shoring up of the system itself. She'd explained to Susannah that elite universities were hot spots of social mobility, that admission to a Dartmouth or a Princeton could provide in four years what might have required generations a century before, and that the beneficiaries of these shining opportunities had every intention of aiding their communities, using their intellectual abilities to fix the problems that affected everyone, and serving as role models for others who followed. Where, exactly, was the problem in all this? But Susannah had clung to her own barricades, and after the first few years, Portia had surrendered: *Fine, fine. I'm a maidservant to the patriarchy, a hapless flunky for the myopic American aristocracy, fanning the flames of its elitist institutions so that future slacker generations can raise their kids in a gated community or play a round at the Maidstone Club, just as they've been doing since the first Pilgrim bottom landed smack on Plymouth Rock.*

And yet. And yet. It might just possibly be time to cede the moral high ground, Portia thought dimly, observing the white knuckles of her oddly bony hands, which were indeed offputtingly spectral. I have been as stubborn as she was. And besides, there wasn't much to be proud of in the scene she currently set: woman alone, in the middle of her bed, in the middle of the day, in the middle of her life. Or perhaps not quite alone, as someone was apparently downstairs, alternately knocking at the front door and pushing the doorbell, which had long emitted a weakened chime.

Portia looked resentfully in this general direction.

Alone, moreover, had not been thrust upon her, but chosen—she saw this now so clearly, she wondered that it had never occurred to her before—within her relationship with Mark and beyond, in the people she had firmly pushed away, beginning with her own child and following on with friends, colleagues, and now with the man who had miraculously emerged, long past the time she deserved love, offering what felt astoundingly like love. All of that energy, she shook her head, spent keeping people out, just so that she could maintain this enviable solitude.

The person downstairs seemed disinclined to leave. The doorbell rang again, and the knocking continued. They must be thick, she thought irritably. She had half a mind to leave her bed and go downstairs and tell them, whoever they were, how thick they were, or if not thick, then rude, because wasn't this a clarion-clear *no*? And did they not understand the meaning of *no*?

Then, to her great surprise, she heard a key roll in the lock and the door swing open.

"Portia?... Portia?" The voice was shrill and laced with fear.

It was Rachel.

"I'm upstairs," said Portia, but the sound barely emerged.

"Portia?"

"Here!" she managed, like child answering attendance.

"I'm coming up."

A moment later she appeared in the doorway, breathing hard, anger rapidly replacing relief. "I've been calling for days," said Rachel. "Portia, do you have any idea how worried I was?"

Obviously no, thought Portia, but it seemed rude to say this.

"We're starting committee," she said, suddenly realizing that this was, in fact, the case. But when? Tomorrow? Today? Had she already missed a meeting?

"Oh, bullshit. Look at yourself. You look like fucking Howard Hughes."

Despite herself, Portia laughed. "Thanks."

"And this house."

"I've gotten a little behind in my cleaning routine."

Rachel glared at her.

"You have a key to my house," Portia observed.

"No. But I know where you hide your spare. And I was worried enough to use it. Clarence Porter called me this morning."

She was suddenly very, very alert. "Oh?"

"He wanted to know if I'd heard from you. He said you weren't respond-ing to e-mails and calls. Are you trying to get fired?"

Was she? Portia thought. And the answer surprised her: *Not yet.*

"No, I just . . . I've been down with the flu. As you see," she said, sound-ing slightly accusatory. "And I went to Pennsylvania."

Rachel stared at her. She was well dressed for a rescue mission: neat black pantsuit, leather boots with a modest heel. She looked as if she were going to an office or coming from an office, if it was that day of the week and that time of the day. What time was it? What day was it?

She was about to ask what day it was when it came to her that she really could not do that and maintain the illusion of well-being.

"I've been sleeping," she said instead.

"Portia, I don't know how much of this you've heard. I know you're upset. You don't have to do this alone, you know. You have friends."

What? She frowned. There was a "this"? "I'm not sure," she said carefully.

"Of course you do. My relationship with Mark will never be the same, but I do have to deal with him. And I have to deal with Helen, which kills me, because she's a royal bitch. And I think they've both behaved terribly, but you know? It's done. And you couldn't possibly want him back."

"Back?" Portia stared at her. "I don't want him back."

Rachel sat on the edge of the bed. "Good. I know I'm not supposed to be glad about the wedding, but I am. I was dreading it."

This statement was so baffling that Portia found she had to replay it in her brain before responding, but to no avail.

"I thought you didn't like them," she told Rachel. "Why are you glad about the wedding?"

"Canceling the wedding," said Rachel, twisting a long lock of curling brown hair around her finger. "I thought I was going to have to put Sea-

Bands on my wrists, like when I was pregnant, to keep from getting nauseous in the church."

"Rachel," said Portia, almost unkindly, "I don't know what you're talking about."

Rachel eyed her. "No?"

"No."

"Which part?" she asked.

"Which *part*?" said Portia, completely lost.

"You knew they were getting married, right?"

Did she? Portia thought distractedly. She supposed she did. Though she hadn't known about an actual wedding. Who would tell her?

"I guess."

"It was supposed to be last weekend. Saturday morning," said Rachel. "In the chapel, reception at Prospect. But Gordon Sternberg died."

"He did?" said Portia.

"I guess you missed that, too. They found him on the street in Philadelphia. One of the great scholars of his generation. Author of fourteen major works of criticism on English literature. In a doorway in Kensington, holding a bottle of Canadian Club whiskey. It's incredible. I mean, how did it happen? He supervised my dissertation, you know."

"Yes, of course," said Portia. "I'm very sorry."

She waved her thin hand vaguely in the air. "No. I don't deserve condolences. None of us do. Gordon went down in flames, and we couldn't help him, but we should all have kept trying. And Mark—you know, they called him Thursday night to come down and identify the body. I guess he just felt it wasn't right to go ahead with a wedding. Gordon actually had his funeral there, when the wedding was supposed to take place. At the chapel."

Portia nodded. On Saturday morning, when Mark, unbeknownst to her, was to have been married, and Gordon Sternberg, unbeknownst to her, had instead been eulogized, she had been driving south with her lover and her son. Isn't it crazy? she thought. That I have a lover? That I have a son? She almost asked this out loud.

"That was good of Mark," she said instead. "To cancel. It was the right thing to do."

"I know," Rachel said gruffly. "Though I'm still too angry at him to want to think well of him."

"Don't be angry," Portia heard herself say. "I don't think things were really right between us. I kept things from him. I shouldn't have. I'm responsible, too."

Rachel said nothing, and Portia was forced to look up at her. She rested on her hip, braced by one hand on the mattress. She was waiting for Portia to say more. *What things had she kept from him?* for example. *What things weren't right?* But Portia, having given so much away, felt suddenly very, very exhausted.

"They're still getting married, though," she observed. "I assume?"

"Yes. Sure. They went down to Trenton yesterday morning and did it there. Thank goodness I wasn't invited to that. Nobody was, I think. Just as well. I get that they need to do it. Legally, for immigration and the baby. But if it's any comfort to you, I don't think he's particularly happy."

"That's not a comfort," said Portia, laughing awkwardly. She was trying to absorb the fact that Mark was married. Finally married. He had not married Marcie, the mother of Cressida, the woman who had spent the past sixteen years punishing him — perhaps for that very thing. He had not married Portia. He had married Helen.

But the clerk's office in Trenton would not have been open on a Sunday, which meant that yesterday must have been a Monday. Which meant that she had been here, in this bed, for nearly three days. No wonder the office was coming for her.

"What did Clarence say?" she asked Rachel.

"Only had I been in touch with you, because you hadn't come into the office and you weren't answering the home phone. So then I got scared because you weren't answering my calls, either. I thought maybe you were really down about the wedding. So I came rushing over here as soon as my class was over."

Class, thought Portia. The mystery of her friend's professional attire was laid to rest. It meant that while she had lain here, life had continued, work had continued, weddings and funerals had taken place. Only she had stood still.

She swung her legs over the side of the bed. "I have to go in to work," she said sharply.

"But you're sick," said Rachel, reaching for her shoulder.

"But I'm going to be fine," said Portia, because she was.

My biggest inspiration is my little cousin Sandra, who is afflicted with Down Syndrome. Sandra has a sunny disposition and loves to be silly. When I babysit for her, we can spend hours making cookies or playing Old Maid, and she is wonderful company. But sometimes I look at her not as a loving cousin but as a future biology major and physician. In my life as a doctor, I will work to find a cure for Down Syndrome, so that other children will not be held back the way she has been. If I can't find a way to use my talents to give back to my community, then I will feel that I have failed.

CHAPTER TWENTY-SEVEN

SHORT STORIES

At some point, while she'd been away, the administrative assistants had performed their annual veiling of the downstairs conference room, a ritual that oddly involved not a curtain to cover the glass separating the room from the corridor, but a mosaic of white copy paper, each individual page affixed with a piece of tape. This act, which signaled the onset of committee meetings and the massing wave of decisions to come, had long mystified Portia, who wondered why, if privacy was so important — and of course it was — the office had not seen fit to build an actual wall, or at least to invest in some sort of fabric sheeting that could be drawn whenever the committee got down to work. That would have to be a bit more soothing to any anxious parents, stopping in to hand-deliver a last minute CD of their child performing Bach on the cello or a testimonial from the coach. Not that anything could really buffer the stress on either side of the glass.

Statistically, she was ready for committee. She had already read more applications this year than last and had finished her entire district except for the fifty or so still missing pieces. (Though applications, from first arrivals to in-under-the-wires, were given equal weight, there was a certain undeniable quality of diminishment in the folders as they reached the far end of the punctuality bell curve. The early filers were organized, type

A, staggeringly accomplished; the latecomers were a bit more relaxed, a bit less coiled to chase down their guidance counselors and teachers and make sure they'd sent in their forms, perhaps even a bit more inclined to just throw a Princeton application at the wall and see if, by some quirk of fortune, it stuck.) Portia, in spite of everything that reading season had wrought in her life, had nonetheless made her way, folder by folder, through every corner of her region, completing a symbolic pilgrimage from school to school. The backward view from West College included miles of coastline and chains of mountain ranges—Greens, Whites, Presidentials—from Vermont to Maine. She could see old towns and towns so new that the gates of their gated communities had barely been hung, the great boarding prep schools, creaking in amber tradition, and the suburban public schools around Boston (which seemed no less infused with competitive mania than the Grotons and Choates), and the great academies of Boston itself, from which Brahmin sons, born into the expectation of Harvard (and all it then represented), had once crossed the river to Cambridge en masse, and now the children of immigrants, drawn to this country by a vision of Harvard (and all it now represented), still crossed the river to Cambridge en masse.

Then, too, Portia had served as second reader to Corinne's files, revisiting the schools, teachers, and even a few families she had dwelt among for the past five years and finding again the intense, driven musicians and biologists, the offspring of new (and vast) Silicon wealth, the striving children of parents who worked in fields, construction, and even sweatshops, who were sometimes the only English speakers in their families and who wrote of mothers and fathers so dependent on them that Portia wondered how they would cope when these burdened sons and daughters flew away to meet their dizzying futures.

Over and over and over, even as she read these still forming lives as distinct, individual things, they braided themselves together into the same American story: *My family came after the famine, after the Armenian Genocide, after the Shoah, after the Cambodian refugee camp. My family came last year, with nothing, and we still have nothing except for my 4.6 GPA and my National Merit semifinalist citation and my reference from the Chief of Oncology, who calls my work on cancerous skin cells "uniquely promising," and my chance to attend Princeton. We came here so my parents could take the invisible, uniformed, dangerous jobs, so the next generation could be doc-*

tors and engineers, so the generation after that could be environmentalists, poets, directors of nonprofit organizations. Almost every applicant seemed at home in this most American of equations, Portia thought. Their voices strained to merge, and she had to hold them back, pick them laboriously apart until they resumed their separate selves, some of whom would be admitted, most of whom would not. It felt wrong, given the chorus they so effortlessly made. Why should one American dream be more valid than another? Why should one family saga weigh more than the next?

Corinne's appraisals, Portia admitted grudgingly, were largely on target. She had a scrupulous fairness, a rigid bar that refused to patronize — which was a good thing, Portia instructed herself. She had, also, a discernible fondness for classicists and a just detectable distaste for athletes who insisted the joy of competing was enough, who bravely declared that they were as proud of their hard-won last-place finish as they would have been of a victory. She could not resist noting grammatical errors ("Grm Ers") and flaws in spelling ("Spl Ers") and had, in her reader's card summaries, a penchant for the words *lukewarm* ("LW") and *boilerplate* ("BP"); but on the whole, Portia found that she rarely disagreed with her colleague.

Except, of course, about Jeremiah.

Corinne had, as promised, been fast, and his application was waiting for her on her return, shuffled in among its seventy-four fellow travelers. Each of these now bore her trademark brown felt-tip script on the flip side of the reader's card, a space about half as large as that assigned to the first reader — in this case, Portia — enough to agree or disagree and say why. As in: "Agree w/PN, Joseph has been a credit to his school, gifted linguist and debater, but middling writer and LW recs. Not seeing strong intellectual curiosity here, plus notably weak senior yr." Or: "Second PN's opinion of Jenny, fantastic student, v strong writer/mathematician, CW program says one of strongest fiction samples they've seen this year. Would love to see her @ PU."

Portia moved quickly through the pile, affirming and affirming. It wasn't unheard of to have disagreement, but it wasn't the norm. They were all, after all, looking for the same things, or at least the same array of different things, and while the sheer weight of the numbers meant that many of the students they loved could not be offered admission, it wouldn't be for lack of approbation. This would not be the situation with Jeremiah. And while disagreement between first and second readers made for lively discussion in committee—which was not a bad thing—the curt assessment Portia read and reread on Jeremiah's reader's card meant rough seas ahead.

"Afraid I must disagree w/PN," Corinne had written. "Clearly, Jeremiah was not well served by his public school, and his later success at the new school implies that he might have done better with good guidance. However, I don't see that we can ignore the appalling grades he seems to have been contented with grades 9–11, or his own lack of initiative in finding a solution for himself. This student may not be disciplined enough to thrive @ PU academically, and I see no signif non-acs to mitigate. Sorry not to be able to support this AP."

Portia returned the card to its folder and tried to calm herself. Calm was desirable. She knew what she had to do, and it wouldn't be furthered by losing control. She had made up her mind about this sometime in the lost few days she'd spent away from the office, at the end of some cul-de-sac of twisted meditation and justification and regret, and it had (somewhat surprisingly) stayed with her. After a moment, she closed the folder and got to her feet, assembled a cheery expression, and went to rap smartly on Clarence's door.

"It's me!" she said brightly, leaning in. "Back from the dead."

"Well," he said kindly, palms flat on his desktop, "I'm relieved."

"Sometimes I push myself too hard," she told him. "Then I crash. I do apologize."

"Not at all," he said. "It's only that I was worried. We couldn't reach you. And I know it had to be a difficult weekend."

It took her a moment to realize that he was talking about Mark. About Mark's wedding to someone who wasn't her. It should not have surprised her that he knew, but it did, as if her own decision not to speak about it had been somehow binding for everyone. This was ridiculously naive, of course. A move like Mark's, played out within the university community, involving infidelities and pregnancies and retroactively suspicious hirings, must have prime real estate on the local grapevine. All of her colleagues undoubtedly knew, had known for months. Even Dylan and Martha. Even Corinne. Especially Corinne.

"That's kind of you," she said carefully. "But I'm really all right. I do want a quick word, though, if you have time."

"All the time in the world," he said affably, pushing back in his chair. "Until that phone rings. I'm waiting on a conference call with Gwendolyn and Kate." Gwendolyn was the president of Princeton; Kate was the dean of students.

"Okay…" She took the chair opposite his desk. "I'll be quick. Do you remember that school in New Hampshire I visited in October? The new one."

He nodded. "Quest," he said, which was impressive. Clarence could be extraordinarily impressive. Beyond his veneer of fine suits and fine manners, past the ambient fog of cologne, lay rooms of mental cabinetry in which masses of information were neatly filed. "You were intrigued."

"I was. By one student in particular. Different-drummer kid, very brilliant. He'd done horribly in public school. I was hoping he'd apply."

"And I suppose he did." Clarence smiled, his fingertips softly drumming the desktop in an absentminded accompaniment. "Or we would not be discussing him."

"Yes, he did. And the application is unconventional, to say the least. He was adopted, and his parents didn't attend college. I think it's possible they didn't see what he was or what he needed. He wasn't on any kind of a college track until last fall, and his transcript is a mess, but I'm very excited by this kid. I think he's amazing."

Clarence pursed his lips, already a step ahead. "Corinne disagrees, I take it?"

"Yes. Very much so. I just wanted to tell you, I know it doesn't look good, but I've talked to this kid, and I believe in him. I wondered if you'd look over the folder before we met on him."

On his desk, the phone began to purr. "Of course. Leave it with me," he said, reaching out one perfectly manicured hand.

"Thank you, Clarence," said Portia, backing out.

She closed the door as he rolled out his silken baritone: "Kate, yes, I have it here.…"

He was her third boss in admissions, her second at Princeton, when he'd replaced the towering and kindly Martin Quilty. Quilty, a passionate advocate for affirmative action, had wrested the university from its racial monochrome over twenty years of service, but more than any admissions officer Portia had ever known, he had carried the weight of the job with him and suffered from it. Over the years, his handsome face had creased and fallen, and he looked more than anything like a man of constant sorrow. He was a graduate of Princeton with a deep love for the university, but he also had a determination to make it a better place, and—most important—a *fairer* place than when he himself had been an undergraduate. Then, he had been a white man among white men, an undistinguished scholar among many undistinguished scholars.

Ten years earlier, in her get-acquainted lunch with Martin in the old Annex (the setting for generations of Princetonian lunches and genteel debauchery, since depressingly replaced by a very ordinary Italian restaurant), he had told her that he liked to consider each application a short story, revealing itself—revealing the applicant—at its own pace and on its own terms, and Portia had been unexpectedly charmed. (How sweetly old-fashioned, she had thought. A little bit like Martin himself.) But was it practical? Short stories aside, the university was still going to need tuba players and Pacific Islanders and a good shortstop every year, and also, what if an applicant just didn't have much of a story yet? What if he was kind of a great, normal kid who drove the family car to his lifeguard job at the lake every summer and wanted to be a doctor? What if there was no terminal illness or piano championship, no classic immigrant saga or "Amazing Grace"–like moment of awe at the power of language, or numbers, or space? It seemed absolutely crazy, she had thought at the time (though nodding avidly to impress her new boss), to expect these seventeen-year-old lives to have much in the way of a narrative arc. American lives, despite what a famous Princetonian had once said, were entitled to second acts.

Martin Quilty's office now belonged to Clarence, but back then it had been dominated by framed color photos of ancestral lands in County Mayo, and endemic disarray. It had been a mess, but it had also been the kind of place she'd felt able to wander through and linger in. She missed that. At the end of the day, however, and in spite of the fact that Martin had welcomed input, advice, and debate from his staff, he still made each and every admissions decision on his own. When Clarence came from Yale to replace him, he had brought with him that office's more democratic—if surely more arduous—tradition of committee for all, or at least for most. Applicants whose first and second (and often third) readers had concluded they were not realistic admits might be stockpiled downstairs in the office, awaiting a final just-to-be-sure going-over, but the thousands of bright, accomplished applicants who remained would all have their chance in committee, each of them summarized by his or her region team leader much as a wigged and robed barrister might present a case in Chancery: *My lords and ladies, Tiffany is the likely valedictorian of her class of five hundred and fifty, captain of the softball team, a passionate artist whose portfolio, regrettably, did not wow our Art Department. Her history teacher says she is a joy in class who often asks for extra reading. The guidance counselor is new this year and does not know her well. The school has had twenty-three applicants to Princeton over the past five years, two admits, one attending. Her mother had some college but didn't graduate. Dad is a city sanitation employee in Portland, Maine—no college. Tiffany is the eldest of five children, two of them autistic. One of her essays concerns growing up with this challenge, feeling guilty about wanting to be away from her brothers, but loving them and being defensive of them. This is a strong candidate, though perhaps not a clear admit. Thank you, my lords and ladies.*

It was at once the most satisfying and most frustrating part of the admissions cycle. By the time they left the conference room, the mass of fantastic kids—kids she had known for months through their written words and the words written about them, and whom she had sometimes met in person—would have been sorted and penned, irrevocably separated from one another. Like fish, Portia persisted in thinking, borrowing the office metaphor created years earlier by Martin Quilty and still in use. The thousands of application folders were the "pool," and a viable applicant was "swimming." Sometimes, in the dark winter months of reading period, in her office or at home, she thought of them all as muscular, frantic salmon fighting their way from ocean to river to stream, leaping and leaping upward toward their mutual goal. She still felt a wave of satisfaction when an applicant who'd moved or wowed her was affirmed and admitted by her colleagues. She still felt a pang of deep loss when she had to say good-bye to them and even today remembered more than a few of the ones that got away: good kids who'd worked hard, accomplished athletes and students, talented writers and musicians, just wonderful young people. They had, of course, gone to other great colleges and done superbly well—Portia knew they had, they must have—but she had always felt, in some indelible way, that she had failed them.

She couldn't do that now, she thought, coming back to her little office and shutting the door.

It felt very strange, at first. It was almost an unknown sensation, like a moment of miraculous understanding about something you've always only pretended to understand. For the first time in a very long time, there was a thing Portia wanted—desperately. There was an aim, a prize, and something she would gladly give anything she had to possess. Her adult life—the life she had lived since the moment she shut her eyes to not see the face of her baby—had been marked by no purpose at all, not monetary gain or career ascension, not love, not spiritual progress, not travel or variety of experience, not the alleviation of suffering, not the exploration of some passionate interest, not other children. What motivates a person without a goal? she wondered with nearly clinical curiosity. And she thought almost immediately of how the cycle of her admissions life had always drawn her back for the next year and the next, how every summer she recovered from the loss of so many great kids and how gradually her sense of having failed them dulled and faded. Then, when autumn came, her appetite would sharpen and her curiosity build. Once again, she wanted to know who waited in the folders. She wanted to meet them and find out about their lives, learn about what mattered to them, what they'd done and what they wanted from life, hear the passion in their voices when they told her what they dreamed of achieving. That passion was infectious, addictive, and she had spent her working life riding the slipstream of so many hopeful, determined young people, thoughtlessly hitching along on the draft of their greater energy, their extraordinary goals. It felt like a kind of addiction, or at least an unauthorized use of something that was not hers to use, and thinking about it, she was ashamed of herself in a new way.

But now there wasn't time to indulge in new shame or anything else that could distract her. She needed her wits and her energy, every force at her disposal, because she had a goal of her own. Finally. She had a thing she wanted desperately, powerfully, like the kids in the folders who wished so hard and asked so eloquently. The thing she wanted couldn't give her peace or make right the things she had done. It would not mitigate the harm. But it would be something: a gift for Jeremiah. Long overdue, perhaps, but also perhaps just in time.

"Make sure your essay stands out," my college advisor told me. "It doesn't have to be about your philosophy of life. One of the best essays I ever read was about cutting up a fish." But I've never cut up a fish. And if I did, I can't imagine how to make that interesting.

CHAPTER TWENTY-EIGHT

THE AMAZING AND THE EXTRAORDINARY

Portia's first rule of committee preparation had nothing to do with public speaking and nothing to do with strategizing. It was: *Don't drink too much before the meeting.* This applied especially to coffee, even if you have been up for hours, getting ready to face your colleagues in this most secret, fraught, satisfying, and, yes, irritating of arenas, and a few good mugs of caffeine-enriched coffee might have made the whole process go a little more smoothly. But Clarence had brought with him most of the rituals of the Yale department from which he'd sprung (and been sprung), and one of them was: If you left the conference room to use the facilities, you sat out the vote for the applicant on the table, no matter how little of the conversation you'd missed.

It was fair, Portia thought, and it did keep things moving (which became more paramount with each year that passed, as the pool grew and grew), but it added yet another layer of fretting to an already stressful process. In addition to worrying about how to wield her own votes, how and when to show goodwill to her colleagues and curry it in return, she had to frequently ask herself where her vote might be less valuable to an applicant and so plan to pee accordingly. For a kid whose application she'd read and intended to fight for, she couldn't afford to be absent, but for a kid who, from the very top of the discussion, was going to be an easy call—Siemens winner, published author, Olympic hopeful—she could safely slip out, as long as she did it fast.

Murmuring apologies, Portia entered the committee room behind Robin

Hindery (one of Clarence's most recent hires and less than a year out of Princeton herself) and took the last open seat at the far end of the long table from Clarence. There were bottles of water (from which she automatically averted her eyes) in the center of the table. It was nearly nine-thirty. A late start. A bad sign.

"Is that everyone?" said Corinne, pointedly not looking in Portia's direction. She was, also pointedly, sitting at Clarence's right hand and dressed for battle in a severe gray jacket (so unadorned with detail that it could only be expensive) and her ill-advisedly jet black hair ramrod straight and lacquered into place behind her ears.

"I'm sorry," Portia said again, disliking herself for saying it.

"Me too," said Robin.

Clarence was looking over his legal pad. Beside him, his assistant, Abby, regarded them all above the screen of her open laptop, her hands poised over the keys like a court reporter, which was more or less the function she served here. They were all assembled, except for Victoria (who handled the overseas applicants and was returning from a recruiting trip to India today) and Jordan (like Robin, a new Princeton graduate, called home to Virginia over the weekend for a family emergency). Which left them with seven on this particular committee, some colleagues Portia had worked with for years, some she barely knew, some she liked and admired, others she would have been thrilled never to make small talk—let alone life-altering decisions—with again.

"First," said Clarence, interlacing his fingers over the stack of folders before him, "the good news. Our numbers, as you know, are up another nine percent from last year, and we're seeing spectacular applicants, as you also know. I couldn't be more pleased with where we are at the outset. I'm saying this now," he added, chuckling, "before things get ugly."

Portia made a point of smiling at Robin, who was looking just slightly terrified.

"And so, to the bad news, which is a lot like the good news. Up nine percent. Spectacular kids. That means hard decisions. And of course, we get attached to these applicants. I'm saying this especially to you, Robin," said Clarence, "and I'll say it to Jordan when she gets back tomorrow, because it's your first time through. Some of them are not going to get in. Actually, a lot of them aren't, and we can't help that. But these are great kids and they're going to end up at great colleges and they're going to be fine. We do not imagine that the only path to their success goes through us. We have far more respect for them than that."

He looked down at the printout before him. "We will move quickly and carefully. We will ask and answer questions respectfully. And then we will vote. We no longer have time to defer decisions. He picked up a yellow Post-it from the cover of his uppermost folder and gave it a dubious look, as if he expected whatever it contained to suddenly alter. "One note, if I may, before we get started. I am urged, in yet another phone call from my good friend Mr. Salter, to impress upon you all the gravity of his circumstances, by which he means that the Jazz Ensemble is about to graduate its entire complement of saxophone players." Clarence raised an eyebrow at Jordan, who had himself wielded a trombone for the irascible Mr. Salter only a few years earlier. Jordan shook his head and laughed.

"Poor Mr. S."

"Indeed," said Clarence. "But this being the case, I have promised to keep an eye out for saxophone players. If he does not get them, he is going to be very unhappy, as a result of which he has vowed to make me very unhappy. Unfortunately, he knows that I am a purist about jazz, so please. For him. For me," Clarence said, woefully, "bring me saxophone players."

Around the table, everyone relaxed. With a dramatic flourish, Clarence crumpled the Post-it and dropped it on the table beside him.

"Ladies and gentlemen? Deepa? Are you ready?"

Deepa nodded. She looked exhausted, Portia saw, and a little unkempt, which was unlike her. She unfolded her glasses and gently shook them open, then she put them on and solemnly opened the first folder in her substantial pile. "Yulia Karasov," said Deepa. "Class rank two of four hundred and fifty, magnet school in a suburb of Atlanta, five-year count eighty-three applications, fourteen admits, eleven attends. Family emigrated from Russia ten years ago. Yulia is the youngest of three, older sibs are at Yale and Emory. Dad is a radiologist. Mom is a lab technician. Russian and English spoken at home. Yulia is captain of the cross-country team, sports editor on the school paper. One summer at CTY, one on a language program in France. Math 760, verbal 710, AP fives in chemistry, history, biology. Helen writes that she has known she wanted to be a doctor since the age of five, but a CTY teacher moved her in the direction of research, and it was a struggle to let go of the image of herself as a doctor. Good writer.

Recs all mention her extreme work ethic. She'll rewrite a paper even after it's been graded, not for credit."

"Very driven," said Dylan, who had been second reader for the applications from the South. "But I loved what she wrote about giving up being a doctor. It felt very honest."

"This transcript is loaded," said Deepa, gazing down at it. "She's done everything she could here, but the recs aren't special. They admire her, but they don't love her."

"Is this a kid who's going to contribute?" asked Corinne. "Will she write for the *Prince*?"

"It's hard to say," Deepa said. "The only passion in the application was for something she was giving up. Obviously, she'll be fine academically...."

Deepa's voice trailed off, but her point was made. Yulia Karasov, accomplished and dedicated as she was, would not be offered admission. Clarence called for a show of hands. It was swift.

Abby entered the information in her laptop. The folder was closed and the box marked "Deny" was checked on its cover in Clarence's fat red pen. And then they were on to the next.

Andrew Powers. Beloved at his private school outside of Memphis, the kind of student any teacher would be grateful to have, the kind of son any parent would be proud of. There were letters from his father's partner, Princeton '64, and his mother's cousin, Princeton '78, praising his character and skills on the lacrosse field. He had taken the SATs four times, topping out at 700 math, 690 verbal. His essay of praise for his grandfather's war service felt stretched to fit the most general of prompts. The alum who'd interviewed him noted that he had few questions about Princeton and didn't seem to know much about the place. "Why are you applying?" she had asked him. "To see if I could get in," replied Andrew Powers. The vote to decline was unanimous.

Mary McCoy, Columbia, South Carolina, first in her class of thirty, the first violinist in the state youth orchestra, first in her family to attend college. "Students like Mary are the reason I wanted to be a teacher," said the woman who taught her multivariable calculus. "Students like Mary make me a better teacher." Ten students from her Catholic girls' school had applied to Princeton over the past five years, with none admitted. Mary would be the first.

All that morning they moved through the southern states, painfully, student by student. Portia sat very still, willing herself to be like a wind chime, letting the information move over her, raising her arm when the moment called for it. She asked few questions. She was afraid of showing her hand, which had only one thing in it. Every young man and young woman, every flutist and chemist and dancer and track star, every tempered plea, was an opportunity to lose the sole thing that mattered to her, every blossoming young person a young person who might take his place and her own chance to make restitution. This girl who dreamed of bringing technology to rural Africa. This boy who lived for political commentary. The girl who had fallen in love with Italian cinema. The boy who designed and built a waste management system for an off-the-grid community in Alabama. If she said yes to them, would there still be room for Jeremiah?

Of course she said yes to them. She had to say yes. She wanted to say yes. But every time she did, it took something out of her.

She looked around the table. Corinne had a husband and her two children. Deepa, a widow, had remarried the year before in a West Windsor temple, a ceremony Portia had attended. Robin, less than a year out of Princeton, had a boyfriend in the Music Department. Clarence's partner had come with him from Yale, a slender, bespectacled man, every bit as well dressed as Clarence, who wrote political biographies and seldom came to campus. Portia doubted he would know her if they met, say, at McCaffrey's or Small World. But she knew him.

Todd Simmonds of Louisville was the nephew of a Princeton trustee. Dad: attorney. Mom: homemaker. Good student, not great. Football player, but obviously not a recruit. He wrote about his love of southern history. He had done a summer internship for Morris Dees. There was a letter from Morris Dees, faint of praise, probably written by someone else, Portia thought. They put him on the wait list.

Portia, giving in to her thirst, opened a bottle of water and drank.

There was a lively discussion about Joanna White, African-American, mother a dean at Rollins College, father deceased. Joanna had attended an invitational humanities program for high school juniors the previous summer at Princeton, and there was a letter in her file from Mark, which Deepa read aloud, saying what a fine contributor she had been to the class. Portia, listening, was struck by the kindness in the letter and thought how strange it was that the writer might have been as removed from her as any of the other hundreds and hundreds of Princeton professors, but was instead the man she had lived with for many years. Sometimes, exhausted, he had said to her, "You have no idea what I do all day," and she would roll her eyes and pretend to be sympathetic about his workload, as if her own were not just as intense. But the goodness in the letter affected her now, and it occurred to her, not for the first time, that Mark had always saved the best of himself for the people he dealt with in his professional life, though perhaps—and this did strike her for the first time—she had done that as well.

Joanna White was the kind of humanities student the summer program had been designed to find, something akin to the magnet programs for science and math that effectively pinpointed great students in those fields. But Joanna's grades beyond the humanities were dreadful and her SATs a lopsided 610/780.

"I met with her last summer," said Deepa, speaking in her typically soft voice. "During the program. She asked Professor Telford if she could speak to an admissions officer, and he called me. She's very focused and very brilliant. She knows there's a problem with her transcript, but she said to me, 'I can do so much here.' And I have to say, Mark Telford agreed. He said he was more impressed by her than by any other student who'd come through the program."

"Mom's a dean?" Corinne asked.

"Yes. Father died in Iraq."

This had an instant impact.

"Let's vote," said Clarence.

A boy from West Virginia wrote that even his application to Princeton broke a three-generation tradition for the men in his family, all of whom had attended the Citadel. But he was a painter, and the slides he'd sent had been viewed with great excitement by the Art Department. "If you give us one artist this year, give us this one," Deepa read from the evaluation form.

"Never been north of the Mason-Dixon." Clarence smiled, looking down at the folder.

He was first in his class of over two hundred, only 22 percent of whom attended four-year colleges, and the first ever to apply to Princeton. They voted and moved on.

Lunch was sandwiches from Cox's, brought in precisely at noon. Portia took hers up to her office and sat at her desk, reading Mark's eulogy for Gordon Sternberg, which had been posted on the English Department Web site. It was dignified and diplomatic, full of praise for the astounding reach of Gordon's written work. It cited his humor, his forty years of devoted students, the sometimes grudging high opinion of his colleagues around the world, not a few of whom had feuded with him very publicly and for years. It seemed to imply that his life had ended not in a filthy Philadelphia alley, but at some undefined moment of triumph, as if he had suddenly succumbed to a painless death while holding forth to an immense lecture hall packed with former students, admiring members of the department, respectful rivals, adoring children, and a devoted wife. It was, thought Portia, a masterwork of tenderness and tact. And sitting at her desk with a barely touched tuna-fish sandwich in her hands, she was proud of Mark for writing it and an instant later terribly sad that she had not been there to hear him deliver it.

And then it was time to go back.

There were lots of Princeton families in the South. Princeton had once had the reputation of being the most southern of Ivy League colleges, not geographically but in temperament. It was well-known, though hardly a matter of pride, that students had once brought their own servants with them from home, housing them off campus in a neighborhood of town that was still, a century later, predominantly black; but the Princeton of 2008 was a very different construct. Through the afternoon, tie after tie was unceremoniously severed, with young men and women cast adrift from family tradition to find other places to be educated. Portia, still trying to bend and not break, could not help but be sad for these, too. She shrank from imagining the stunning impact of that slender envelope, arriving in homes where devotion to alma mater was entwined with family lore, where alumni wrote checks and attended reunions, perhaps imagining that their sons and daughters might one day live in the new dorm or take a class from a professor in the newly endowed chair. In a few weeks' time, this group, more than any other, would flood the office with letters and calls, angry and shocked and heartbroken, but that was Clarence's cross to bear, and he seemed to manage it well.

On and on they flew. She craved the easy ones, the slam dunks: Math Olympiad finalists, congressional interns, the winner of Princeton's international high school poetry prize (this year, a girl from North Carolina), the banjo player who'd taken a year off after high school to busk his way around Europe, the amputee who'd won the grand slalom at the Turin Winter Paralympics. It felt wonderful to gather these people together, imagine them convening at the lab bench or the cafeteria table. It felt amazing to wonder whether the soprano from Savannah, Georgia, would meet the tenor from Baton Rouge in their freshman seminar on Wagner and fall in love, or whether the fiery (but, she had to admit, articulate and persuasive) neocon from Charleston would have his worldview altered, ever so slightly, by the Chilean boy whose two fathers had adopted him at birth, brought him home to Atlanta, and raised him to reimagine the world.

There was, around the table, a calibration taking place, similar to the one Portia always felt at the very start of the reading season, when the first and then the second and then the third applicant seemed equally impressive, equally compelling, and then the fourth and the fifth, and so on until you came to that one who was so amazing, so extraordinary, that the landscape suddenly snapped to clarity: *Oh yes, now I understand. These impressive, compelling kids, enormously likable kids—they're the ones we* don't *take. This amazing, extraordinary kid, that's the kid we take.* A class of the amazing and the extraordinary. A class of working actors and winning athletes and protoliterary scholars who had so impressed Mark Telford that he'd asked for their admission, and protophilosophers already capable of discussing zombie theory with David Friedman, and the boy whose memoir was about to be published, and the girl from Richmond who had spent the previous year in Gabon establishing a sanctuary for young women who had been expelled from their families or had no families in the first place, as well as a charitable foundation to support its operation, and the young researchers already attached to major studies, and the QuestBridge scholars, and the boy from Thailand who had made his way through every math class the country's best university could offer him, even though he wasn't yet seventeen, and the ones who were choosing between college and the careers they had already begun, as dancers and models and gymnasts and ice skaters—careers that might not wait four years for them to return—and the violinists and oboists and trombonists and already accomplished composers the Music Department requested, calling them "simply brilliant" and "rare." They were breathtaking. And they would come here and fight among themselves and make things and learn from one another and break one another's hearts and push their professors to rise to their own level of curiosity and effort and come out of the closet and get engaged and get religion and change their religion and lose their religion and make the university better, and then make the world better. It gave her a sensation of almost calm, almost happiness. *All things shall be well. . . . All manner of things shall be well.*

But only if Jeremiah could be here with them.

"You have an aggressive tumor in your leg," said my doctor. I was twelve years old and baseball was my whole life. To be completely honest, I cared less about having the lower half of my right leg removed than I cared about whether I'd be able to play in next Saturday's game against Freeport.

CHAPTER TWENTY-NINE

A HIGHLY UNUSUAL APPLICANT

She knew better than to hound him. He did not like to be hounded. He was a very organized man, very composed. Every day he appeared in committee with a new shirt, a new bow tie, and a suit that might have been new or just identical to the one he had worn the day before: crisp and fresh and dark blue with the faintest stripes.

The days went by and he gave no sign that he had read Jeremiah's file: no comment, no note, no e-mail. In the committee room, hundreds and then thousands of seventeen-year-olds were passing before them, their names one by one assigned to their final Princeton destinations: Deny, Admit, Wait List. First the South and then the Northwest, California, the Plains, the Midwest, foreign applications, country by country, and the Mid-Atlantic. New York and its suburbs would take nearly a week. Finally, only her own folders remained.

Still, he said nothing to her. There was no reassurance, no "I haven't forgotten," and every day she had to ask herself, again, if she ought to be doing something: reminding him, nudging him, pleading with him.

They were moving well. Last year, Clarence had hired Robin Hindery and Jordan Cobb precisely because he had expected this jump in the numbers; the rise of the common application, the decline of Early Decision, and the peaking children-of-baby-boomers population had made for indelible writing on the wall. The tone in the committee room was elevated, generally. Portia tried to hold her tongue. She had not asked to be last at bat, but she didn't want to get there with anyone mad at her. So Deepa had argued passionately for an academically undistinguished boy whose severe stutter (he had written) had formed his character and unlocked his love for music. Dylan had gone to bat for a girl at the Native American school who Portia was not at all certain would be able to handle the workload. Corinne seemed to have found a number of Latinists she could not live without, and Jordan pleaded for so many kids who'd had miserable lives that Clarence had had to take her aside and remind her that it was not the university's place to compensate every young person for every terrible thing that had happened to them. Kids whose parents had died, whose siblings had died, whose friends had died, whose teachers had died. Kids who'd battled cancer and depression and the aftereffects of car accidents. Kids who lived in communities without hope, who had somehow nonetheless acquired hope for themselves. Kids who gave the school's address instead of a home address, because there wasn't really what you might call a permanent home address, whose twenty-five-hour-a-week job at McDonald's or ShopRite was essential to the family income. Kids who had somehow dodged abusive fathers, schizophrenic mothers, violent neighborhoods. Kids who had kids and were desperate to make a better life for them.

Portia wanted to give every one of her colleagues whatever it was — whoever it was — they wanted. Although technically there was no such thing as quid pro quo in committee, no tacit understanding that she would give Robin the girl whose sisters and mother lived in hiding (who had possibly the lowest academic profile to have reached the committee room all these weeks, who wrote clearly and unsentimentally about the toll of violence in her family) and Robin, when the time came, would let her have Jeremiah. She did not allow herself to appear sycophantic. She gave herself a stern expression, as if she were dubious of everyone's motives, everyone's claims, but in the end she voted to admit whenever she sensed an urgency that was somehow personal, because Jeremiah would also be one of these applicants, she knew: divisive, a little worrying. And as the folders and the names and the accomplishments flew by, and as it looked more and more as if they would come last to her own geographic area, the Northeast, she knew that every one of her colleagues was running short of expansiveness. It was one thing, at the outset of committee meetings, to acquiesce against your better judgment when the class felt wide open, with places to spare and room to make, just possibly, a bit of a mistake. But now, with thousands of such high-achieving kids already slated for denial, it was going to be harder to get a Jeremiah past. She would need all of her passion and all of her persuasiveness and all of their goodwill.

Then, toward the end of the third week, when they had dealt with nearly everyone but the nearly two thousand students from her own district who were, in Martin Quilty's oddly endearing phrase, still "swimming," she entered her office after a grueling day to find Jeremiah's folder in the center of her desk, an orange Post-it note stuck to the cover. "Let's discuss in committee," it said.

Portia sat down heavily. It was not the response she had hoped for. She had hoped for some indication that Clarence concurred, or at least for a chance to talk to him again before having to strut and fret her moment upon the committee stage. At Dartmouth, there had long been an unwritten rule that each admissions officer got one free pass, one applicant they could bring to the dean once the decisions had all been made, and have that student's wait list designation altered to acceptance. It had been a genteel sort of tradition, and they had not abused it, because it spread a kind of goodness through the office and the enterprise itself. Because you might have a gut feeling about some kid, whose transcript was, say, somewhat under par, because his essay was the one you remembered out of thousands, and you just knew he would go on to do something amazing with his life, and you could—personally, single-handedly—make it happen for that kid. But only once a year, and only after the files had all been closed, and only for the wait list (it didn't work if the applicant had been denied outright), and only very quietly, strictly between the officer and the dean.

Not at Princeton. Not under Martin Quilty, who had turned her away when she'd tried it the first year, smiling his customary sad smile and letting her know never to attempt it again; and certainly not under Clarence, who would think she was mad.

Jeremiah was going to get one chance, and one chance only, in the last days of committee meetings, with an incoming split opinion between his first and second readers and without a gesture of encouragement from Clarence. Portia closed her eyes.

At least, it occurred to her, she could give some thought to where in the order he might fall. First folder of the day was not the place for Jeremiah, but neither was last. She went through them, one by one, reminding herself who each applicant was and what they'd done, what mattered to them, what she'd had to say about them, and what Corinne had written in response. They were all deflatingly superior, cerebral, engaged, ready to hit some college campus running and take off into their avidly anticipated futures. Each of them had earned either a "High Priority—Admit" or a "Strong Interest" designation from her. Nearly all of them had been just as lauded by Corinne. Against their backdrop, Jeremiah was an undisciplined smart kid, flailing against authority, beating his own different drum with merry abandon. It was going to be a slaughter.

She went back to the top of the pile and began again, skimming: crew champions, choreographers, fencers, editors of the literary magazine (*Expressions*), kids cheered by their counselors as the soul of the school or cited by their teachers as the best they had ever taught. This time, she was not looking for weakness, but willing the best among them to make themselves known, and slowly they did. There were many of the best of them. Most of them, by any standard, were the best of them. And when those best pulled away and were placed one by one into a stack of their own, there were only about twenty left.

The ordinarily qualified.

The usually brilliant.

The expectedly talented.

Portia took a deep breath. She would begin with one of these. Then, one from the larger pile. Then, seven...no, eight of the ones everyone would see were not incredible enough. And then...Jeremiah. Her colleagues would be ready to listen by then. They would have begun to wonder: Where were the great applicants from the Northeast? They would want to say yes to someone, or at least be willing to say it, though it would still be very hard to push Jeremiah through.

She didn't sleep well that night and was up early, putting unprecedented thought into what she wore and how she arranged her hair. She worried especially about Corinne, who had made it through almost three weeks of twelve-hour committees without, it seemed, putting a hair out of place, while all around her the rest of them—and even, a bit, Clarence—wilted and sweated and, as the day wore on, took on a washed-out, acrid cast. Corinne brought from home clear glass bottles of water infused with some rosy liquid, and this she poured out, bit by bit, into a matching tumbler, sipping through the hours until the drink, whatever it was, was all gone. No one ever asked. When she was hungry she eschewed, of course, the Dunkin' Donuts Abby sometimes brought and the bowls of M&M's Deepa liked to set down in the middle of the long table but withdrew from her black leather bag a container of Greek yogurt or a package of rye thins or a perfect blushing pear. She never raised her voice but managed to communicate disapproval with a flickering glance, and Portia was never once surprised to see how she voted.

She chose, finally, a brown dress she had bought at Ann Taylor in Palmer Square, an item so plain that it was above reproach and, since it had never been worn, as unsullied as the day she'd acquired it. She wore stockings and black leather loafers because she did not have brown, but Rachel (who followed things like this) had once told her that black and brown were considered chic when mixed. Portia decided to put her faith in this, though she knew that Corinne would never go so far as to think her chic. She pulled her hair off her face and pinned it into a bun and then, after considering the finished effect in the mirror, cinched the billowing midsection of the dress with a black belt. It was meant to be belted, she remembered now. The saleswoman had said so, though perhaps she had only been trying to sell a belt.

Portia badly wanted coffee, but she resisted. She wanted a script she could memorize, but there were too many unknowns, too many factors, so she walked along Nassau Street with her hands clenched in the pockets of her overcoat, trying to think of nothing but the breath she made, visible before each step. She fell in with Jordan, crossing before Nassau Hall, and gave her a comradely grin. "End's in sight," she said brightly.

"Oh, my God. I had no idea anyone could get this tired."

"Don't worry. They bring in a team of massage therapists on the last day of committee."

"They do?" said Jordan. She was a tiny girl with a white blond pageboy.

"Sadly, I jest," said Portia. "I wish it were true. But we do get to go home and take a bath and order a pizza."

"Well," Jordan said, laughing, "I guess that's something."

How was her father? Portia asked as they passed the Henry Moore sculpture beside their building. (It looked like a lethal and deformed doughnut.) Her father's heart attack had been the family emergency.

"Quitting smoking," Jordan said wryly. "About twenty years too late, but I'm glad he's doing it now. Of course, I'm also glad I don't have to be within a mile of him when he does it."

They opened the door to West College and went inside. Corinne was standing in the hall outside the conference room, towering over Deepa, who held a ceramic mug of tea. Deepa was nodding distractedly, but she was glad to focus on Portia.

"Well, you look nice," said Corinne, but she sounded very surprised about it, which rather offset the compliment.

"Thanks," Portia said. "Don't want to lose any of my kids because I've got ring around the collar."

"Please!" Deepa laughed. "If it were up to that, there'd be no southern students in the Class of 2012."

"Portia," said Corinne, "did you get the note I sent you about the Loomis Chaffee girl?"

Portia, who had seen but not read the e-mail, took a guess. "The one with the suspension sophomore year?"

Corinne nodded. Her black hair shone fiercely in the overhead fluorescent light. "I have a close friend at Loomis, so I asked about it. It was just a smoking infraction."

Portia took a steadying breath and smiled carefully. Boarding school suspensions were tricky things, as often to do with smoking and dormitory rule breaking as with far more serious (from an admissions perspective) honor code violations or outright crimes. But looking into applicants from her area was not Corinne's concern. Talking to anyone at Loomis, even a "close friend"—*especially* a "close friend"—about anything admissions related was a serious overstep, an act of aggression. She felt herself nodding like an idiot, even as a variety of caustic statements hammered at her to be spoken. But this was not the time for them. Instead, she summoned every ounce of grace she possessed and said, "Thank you. I ought to have done it myself. I'm going to make a note."

And she walked swiftly upstairs, as if intent on doing just that.

In the office, she threw her coat over the chair in the corner and just breathed deeply for a moment. There was nothing surprising in this, Portia told herself. Corinne had never pretended not to be enraged about having been moved to California, and more than likely she had had her own eye on the New England district. But with her children now ensconced at Andover, even she must recognize at least the appearance of impropriety in that. Or did Corinne imagine she could evaluate her own children's classmates? Was she that myopic?

Breathe, Portia told herself. *Not now. You don't have time for this now.*

She gathered up the stack of folders on her desk, flipping through one final time to confirm the order, then she went back down.

This time, she helped herself to coffee. With her own geographic area on the table, they could hardly go on without her, and she took an absurd amount of pleasure in the caffeine buzz that went directly to her head.

"Howdy," Dylan said from across the table. He looked upbeat, as if, with only the Northeast to go, he had allowed himself to believe that the hardest part of the admissions cycle was nearly done; but that was like coming to a final leg of the triathlon and realizing you still had a marathon to run. There were more applications from the Northeast than from any other part of the country. They hailed from the lousiest underfunded and overcrowded public high schools and the greatest private schools in the land and everything in between. Princeton could pretty much fill its class from this district alone and had once done precisely that. There would be thousands of them, and she felt responsible for them all. But she cared about only one.

"Good morning," said Clarence, taking his customary seat. He appeared, as usual, as if he had just been released by his valet, and the still pleasant smell of lavender he wore settled over the room. Portia found that she was trying not to look at him.

Instead, she looked down at her pile. Last night, when she had not been sleeping, she had been imagining this, wondering if, at the last moment, she would find herself shuffling the folders into random order, denying Jeremiah even this illusion of an advantage. But she did not. And then, at last, it was time to begin.

"Leah Felder," she read, reciting the student's identifying number for Martha. "Darien High School. We have fourteen applications from this school, and Leah's GPA ranks twelfth out of two-fifty. Dad a broker, mom a professional fund-raiser, younger of two siblings. Leah wrote a very moving essay about her brother, who survived cancer. She plays soccer and swims on varsity squads. Summers: part-time job, language program at Dartmouth, trips with family. She is hardworking and active in her school community. Her recs convey how very likable she is, but don't single her out for academic promise. First reader marked 'Only if room' with an arrow up. Second reader agreed." She looked around the table. "Are there questions?"

"Anything that stands out in the athletics?" asked Deepa.

Portia pretended to look, but she didn't have to look. "No."

"Okay."

They voted.

"Sarah Lenaghan," read Portia from the next folder. She had chosen Sarah very carefully. They were going to love Sarah. Sarah was going to put them all in a good mood. "Second in a class of forty-two at Winsor School, five-year count: ninety-eight applied, fifteen accepts, nine attends. Dad's an attorney employed by MIT, mom is a homemaker. Sarah has run the Boston Marathon every year since the age of fifteen. She is a poet who edits her school literary magazine. Winner of the Bennington Young Writers Competition last fall, also an honorable mention in the Princeton competition. SATs 800 verbal, 720 math, AP fives in English, French, History and Latin. Summers, she is part of a tutoring program in Roxbury, Harvard Summer School, and her teacher there said she was one of the best young poets he'd ever taught. Raves from GC and her English teacher. I'd like to say that these were two of the best essays I read this year. And her mom's PU Class of '89."

Portia looked up. She noted, with satisfaction, the effect of this. Legacy status was never a reason for admission, but it could be a tipping point. Not that Sarah was going to need a tipping point.

"Did she send in any work for evaluation?" asked Corinne.

"No," Portia said.

"I wonder why not," said Corinne.

"Well, the creative writing faculty judge the poetry competition. I think that's an endorsement."

Corinne nodded almost grudgingly.

"She also loves Princeton. She said she wishes she could have applied ED, but since she can't, she'd like us to know that she would definitely attend if admitted."

Portia picked up the reader's card and read aloud from her summary. "Sarah is going to be somebody's great roommate, fun to be around but also cerebral and involved. Recs love her, gifted poet. Would be great here." She had checked "High Priority—Admit," and she told them that, too. "Second reader concurred. She wrote: 'Fantastic kid.'"

Portia smiled at Corinne.

"Yes," said Corinne. "I remember her."

"Okay," said Clarence. "Let's vote."

And Sarah Paley Lenaghan was admitted to Princeton.

And then there were eight in a row. Members of the team. Participants in the club. Pretty good writers with pretty good scores. Wonderful kids who made up the chorus, voices indistinguishable from one another. Portia paced herself. She read each summary slowly, as if she didn't know they weren't going to get in. They were students with kind but vague recommendations, "a pleasure to have in class." They were the backbone of the woodwinds section, active in the church youth group, the kind of student you could always call upon to help with the Martin Luther King Day activities. And one after another they were turned away.

Around the table, there was the faintest sense of unease. It was not, of course, that eight in a row would be denied, but eight such easy calls — no debate to speak of, no real questioning. Corinne was frowning into her pink-tinged water. Clarence, as was his habit, tapped his fingertips together, and Portia could make out the gleam of his well-tended fingernails as they caught the overhead light. Even Dylan was avoiding her eyes, intent on some doodle he was grinding into his legal pad.

She placed the last of them in the pile and opened Jeremiah's folder.

"Jeremiah Balakian. This is our first applicant from Quest, a new school in rural New Hampshire which I visited last fall, so no available statistics on college attendance and no admit rates. Quest is an extremely interesting school. I would call it experimental, but academically rigorous. The founders have come from other prep schools, and they've brought with them the most successful elements of their former schools. I was really impressed with the students I met there, and with this applicant in particular."

She focused on the reader's card, summarizing its contents to the group: Jeremiah was an only child. Parents both worked in a supermarket, and neither attended college. This was apparently not a family in which academic success was stressed. His first three years of high school at the local public school in Keene were a disaster. He seemed to have been unable to adapt to a school environment, and his grades certainly reflected that. Frequently, he was in danger of failing individual courses.

"Now," she said, looking up at them, "just in case you're wondering why you're listening to this, Jeremiah is also a self-described autodidact since the age of eight. He is widely read, in texts far beyond what his classes were doing. He had no plan to attend college until this past fall, when he switched schools and came into contact with teachers who were willing to teach him the way he needed to be taught. He took the SATs and eight AP subject tests last spring."

"Wait, so he did have AP classes?" Dylan asked.

"No. None. He scored an 800 verbal and eight AP fives."

"Whoa," Dylan said, but under his breath.

"Math was significantly lower, I think," said Corinne.

"Yes," Portia said tersely. "This, of course, is a highly unusual applicant. This is a kid who had zero guidance. Nothing. Not at home and not at school. But he was brilliant. And I don't think it occurred to him that there was a community of scholarship—of his kind of scholarship—available to him. I think he believed he would get some kind of blue-collar job somewhere and spend his life reading books and thinking about them. Then he lucked out. He met someone who recognized his potential. So he comes to us with a pretty bizarre track record. No extracurriculars. A miserable transcript, nine through eleven. And these tests he just sat down and took."

"And absolutely no guarantee that he'd put in any more effort here than he did in his high school," Corinne reminded them all.

"How were the essays?" said Clarence. "Can he write?"

She told them yes. Then she read to them from Jeremiah's essay:

Since then, I've noticed that, in other classes, I tend to get stuck on questions that are raised in the very first chapter of the textbook: What is life? (in biology). What is a poem? (in English). What is the past? (in history). To be honest, I've never understood how people get beyond those questions to what comes later. It's not that I'm not interested in what comes later: I'm very interested! But I just haven't been able to get there on my own. Of course, I realize now that my unwillingness to play by the rules in my classes is going to end up hurting me, probably in ways I never considered when I was blowing off my homework. I wish I could go back and make a different decision, but if I could do that, I'd probably know so much math and physics that college would be a little redundant.

When she looked up, Dylan was grinning. "Love this kid," he said.

Yes, please, she thought.

"I'm sorry," Corinne said. "I'm not disputing his intelligence, but we're all highly aware of what's available for kids like this. There are organizations with searchlights, looking for these kids. At the very least, these students know that they can get quality teaching in college. I mean, how many of our applicants actually start community college while they're still in high school? Couldn't he have taken some courses outside of school if he wasn't getting what he needed? Couldn't he get on the computer?"

"He doesn't have a computer," Portia said archly.

"Well, at the library, then. I just don't see how we could take a student like this, who for all we know isn't going to be able to handle an intense academic community. I seem to remember the guidance counselor at his old school saying he couldn't grasp that if he didn't do the paper or sit the exam, he was going to fail. He can't get away with that here, no matter how brilliant he is."

"The teacher at his new school doesn't think that will be a problem. Listen," she said, sounding—to herself, at least—as if she were just slightly losing them. "Let me find this," she said, noting the breathlessness. She paged through the folder. "Here. 'Without question, he is capable of performing academically at the highest levels. With faculty to engage with him and fellow students to challenge and influence his ideas, his work has begun to show focus and immense depth. When I think of Jeremiah at a place like Princeton, I am elated, not just at the notion of what the university can do for him but for what he can bring to the right classroom environment. This is a remarkable, special, brilliant young man who is just coming into his own.'"

"Too many unknowns." Corinne shook her head. "We don't know this school at all. We have no idea how their idea of a well-qualified student is going to do here."

"It's a chance," Portia admitted, looking not at Corinne but at Clarence. "I mean, is he going to be on the football team and sing in the glee club? No. Is he a campus leader? I would say not. But this is the kind of student our faculty love. Maybe, from our perspective, he could have done more, he could have made himself more of a résumé and a paper trail, but he got himself from nowhere to where he is now."

"I hope you're not implying that he gets special credit because he's poor," said Corinne.

"No, of course not. What I mean is that even the idea of academic success was just...not there in his life. Not in his family and not at school.

He educated himself, purely by instinct. I think, of all the students I've read this year, maybe all the students I've ever read, he's the one who will get the most out of his education here. I really, really..." Portia looked at them. They looked disengaged. They were waiting for her to finish. "I believe in him," she said. "I want him here."

It couldn't have been plainer. It was tantamount to saying, *Give me this one. I've been good. I've worked hard. Give him to me.*

But they didn't. The vote was 5–2. Only Dylan had voted for Jeremiah.

"I'm sorry," said Dylan.

And then they went on to the next.

Every sacrifice of my parents has been for my brother and me. When we came here, my father could not use his university qualification from Beijing University for engineering work. He became a waiter in a restaurant owned by someone his cousin knew, and we lived in a room over the restaurant. My brother was born here. I have tried to make the best use of my education, not only because it is my dream to be a doctor, but to show my parents, my father especially, that I know what he did for me and I will forever be grateful for that.

CHAPTER THIRTY

A FOR ADMISSION

One afternoon at the beginning of April, with the earliest of new green things fighting their way through well-tended flower beds all over campus, Portia found herself once again taking a hushed and tentative call from Elisa Rosen.

It had been, at least until the phone rang, a moment of near immobility throughout the office, an annual point of dead calm before the storm—the storm now carefully apportioned into nineteen thousand separate parts, all stacked up and waiting downstairs. Committee was over and the letters would shortly be printed and sent, setting off the climactic act of this annual drama. Portia and the others had reached the final stragglers only the afternoon before, most of these in files still incomplete, as if the applicants within had been abandoned on a battlefield, missing body parts or given up for dead, and indeed nearly all of them would be declined. The meetings, begun weeks earlier in angst and frenzy, had ended thus with a whimper, not a bang. Now, in their aftermath, the weight of so many separate decisions settled over everything—barely noticeable individually but cumulatively ponderous.

Portia was, in fact, sitting quite still when the call came. She was looking over, in an idle way, the roster of admitted students who, while not expressly recruited for baseball, were strong players hoping to play for

Princeton. The coach would do his own outreach to these boys, making phone calls after the letters went out, encouraging them to attend the hosting weekend for admitted students to be held later in April. He had been happy with his recruits, especially a pitcher from Arizona who had also been assiduously courted by Yale and Cornell, and a Mississippi outfielder who possessed some batting statistic Portia didn't quite comprehend but which had made this normally stoic man seem to go limp with excitement. Barring some moral outrage, these players and the others Princeton had chosen were set to choose Princeton in return, and this list of twenty-three players from around the country (and Japan!) was looking like an enviable backup roster. Some of these kids, of course, would choose other colleges, but many would come here, and once here they would shore up the team for the next four years and help to keep everyone who cared about these things a little happier than they would otherwise have been. She was just making a note next to the name of a Cincinnati player who was also, she recalled, the winner of his regional Math Olympiad, when the phone purred to life. She reached for it without looking and spoke.

"Oh, Portia. Hi!" It was a woman's voice. She sounded surprised, as if she were the one receiving the call. "It's Elisa Rosen? The college counselor at Porter Country Day? In Massachusetts?"

"Hello, Elisa," Portia said. "Not calling from your car again, I hope."

"What?" Elisa said. "Oh! No." She gave a nervous laugh. "I do have my door closed, though. My office door."

Portia sighed. The conversation was rapidly living down to expectations.

"Listen, I decided . . . I thought long and hard about this, before I called."

Portia nodded. Now there was a "this." Another "this." "I hope it isn't about Mr. Aronson again," she said. She was about to tell her that they were done for the year, that whatever "this" was, it wouldn't make any difference now. But Elisa had launched into a kind of litany of self-doubt and personal struggle.

"I thought . . . well, I was kind of expecting to hear from you sometime around now. You know . . . because when I took over this job? From Astrid Davis? Did you work with Astrid?"

Portia said she had not and reminded Elisa that she was new to the region this year.

"Oh, well, she retired. Well, not retired, actually, she opened up a consulting business for applicants. She keeps in touch with me, which has been great. You know, when I have a question about something. And she told me you'd probably be calling a few days before the letters go out? Like, sort of a heads-up about who you're taking, so we can counsel them about their decisions after they've heard from the colleges? And I did hear from . . . uh . . . one or two other Ivies, but not you guys, so I started to think about calling you myself. Because I . . . well, I thought it might make a difference if you knew this. If it's not too late."

It's too late, she nearly said. And even if it weren't too late, whatever Elisa wanted to tell her would be irrelevant, especially if it had anything to do with Sean Aronson. Surely Elisa didn't think they would take Sean Aronson over the fourteen other applicants from Porter Day who had *not* stolen and sold the chemistry final last fall.

As for those phone calls, Elisa had not been delusional to expect a very confidential heads-up around this time. Calls of that nature had once been a courtesy extended to schools that had always sent and would always send their graduates to Princeton. They were not entirely a one-sided gesture, since guidance counselors (or, at most of the prep schools, entire departments of college counselors) were the ones who would encourage the best students to apply to Princeton and might even push a student accepted at other top-tier schools to choose them instead. Goodwill at this point in the application cycle was greatly important for all concerned, because when the letters went out and the Web site concurrently released the admissions decisions to every applicant, it was the guidance counselors who often found themselves on the front lines of parental rage and grief. Often enough, these people would end up taking the bullet (not literally—at least, not so far) for Portia and her colleagues.

Those phone calls, however, were an unwelcome reminder of how the process was perceived as advantaging the advantaged, and though most guidance counselors had strictly withheld the information from students until the notification date arrived, it still felt wrong that the college-counseling department at Choate knew the fate of its applicants before the grievously overburdened guidance counselor at an underfunded school received the same information. Accordingly, the calls had become another casualty of changing admissions practices, and so out they had gone, landing in the Dumpster beside Early Decision and minority quotas, and leaving not a few of the counselors with whom they'd worked for years feeling not a tiny bit chagrined. "We used to have such a nice, open exchange of information," the head of college counseling at the Bishop's School had told her the year before, on Portia's final swing through Southern California before taking up her new post. "Now I'm happy when you tell me how the weather is in New Jersey."

"Why don't we schedule a call for next week?" Portia said, trying for a middle path. "You know, it's not really our practice anymore to have these conversations before the letters go out. Of course, I'd love to have your input after the students have been notified."

"Oh!" Elisa said. "No! I'm not calling you to find out. I wanted to tell you something. I know how huge your field is. I mean, it's crazy, I know that. But I thought, well, one of our applicants . . . of course I don't know if you've decided to take him or not, but he's not in a position to attend Princeton. It's just . . . I'm sure what I'm calling to tell you is totally not kosher, but I thought, if you knew it, there might be another one of our kids you could take a closer look at."

Portia frowned at her list of baseball players. "So . . . this is about Sean Aronson?"

"Sean?" Elisa sounded surprised. "Oh, Sean is . . . well, he's . . . technically he's on leave from Porter since the beginning of the term. He was arrested, actually. It's a very sad situation, for all of us."

Portia was restraining herself, but just barely. More academic infractions? That wouldn't involve the police. DUI? Breaking and entering? Was it even worse?

"I'm sorry," she told Elisa, meaning it. "That's a shame. I remember you told me he was a really good kid. But, Elisa, even if he couldn't accept an offer from Princeton, that doesn't really affect your other—"

"No!" Elisa cut her off. "This has nothing to do with Sean Aronson. I'm calling about a kid named Jesse Bolton. He's going to Yale. I don't know if you'll recall him. He's our newspaper editor. He works for *The Boston Globe* in the summers?"

Absently, Portia nodded. She did not need reminding about who Jesse Bolton was. Jesse Bolton, indeed, was one of the only two from Porter Country Day's fifteen applicants to be admitted to Princeton, the other being a girl named Cassandra Wiley, a dancer who commuted into the city every afternoon to take class at the Boston Ballet. That these two had come before the committee less than an hour after Jeremiah's application had been rejected gave their admits a glow of reflected pain, but Portia would be the first to say that they were extraordinary young people. Jesse in particular had won a national award for high school journalists from the Scripps Foundation and submitted some very impressive clips from the *Globe*. He had also written a razor-sharp essay about the day laborers who tended the lawns and commercial plantings in his wealthy community. His description of a grim Latino man using a leaf blower to blow leaves against the natural surge of a windstorm, the futility of that effort and the negating of that labor, was one of the most searing images she had encountered in the thousands of essays she had read this year.

"I see," she said carefully, giving nothing away.

"He got in early," Elisa said, sounding furtive again. "He pulled all of his regular decision applications, but his dad went to Princeton. Of course, you know. And Dr. Bolton insisted Jesse keep that one in. Jesse stopped in to see me yesterday, though. He's definitely going to Yale."

Portia sat back in her chair and looked up at the bulletin board over her desk. She found the photograph of the 2003 Princeton baseball team and thought how the boys on the list in her lap, or some of them, at least, would be in a picture like that. The 2009 Princeton baseball team. The 2010 Princeton baseball team. She had never seen any of the students in the photograph play, it occurred to her. She had never gone to see a single baseball game at Princeton, though she had helped admit most of the team members. She had never liked baseball, really.

"That's too bad," she heard herself say, and it really was. Too bad that they had blown an admit on a kid they'd never had a chance at. Too bad there was a Princeton dad out there who wanted his kid here more than he wanted his kid happy. Of course, there were students who had done far worse, like received an early admit and then trophy-hunted the rest of the Ivy League, only to accept the original offer. It was poor form, but it wasn't illegal when Yale's offer wasn't binding. And it did sound as if Jesse had wanted to do the right thing.

"I know. What a waste." And she could hear Elisa Rosen's thoughts, as clearly as if they'd been spoken aloud: *Since Jesse's out of the picture, would you take another of our kids?* "Anyway," said Elisa, "as I said, I really thought about whether you ought to know this. And I decided . . . I just couldn't see a downside, you know? To keeping the communication going."

And Portia, very suddenly, wanted very much not to keep the communication going, not with Elisa Rosen or any of the others at any of the other handsome, moneyed schools populated by Seans and Jesses and their thoroughly entitled parents. She felt her empathy for the college counselor leave her in a rush. She pictured Elisa Rosen walking a plank over snapping, hungry, angry parents, each one brandishing their broken contract: *You said if I paid the tuition, you said if he got a rave from his biology teacher, you said if he got 750 or above on the math SAT, dug a ditch in Costa Rica, lettered in swimming, wrote about the brace he wore for scoliosis in the eighth grade, the most gruesome, painful, crushing personal experience of his life, he would get in. You said. And I wrote those checks. And he did those things. And they turned him down. And I will never forgive you for lying to me.*

With whatever strength she could muster, she thanked Elisa Rosen for her time and said good-bye. Then she got up out of her chair and went to the window.

That morning, for the first time since fall, she had opened the window, and now the remarkably mild air was moving through her little office, smelling rich and damp. There was only the briefest season of ugliness in this town, and it was over now for another year, with the mud sinking back into the earth and the black squirrels starting to wake up. Outside, the mostly buried armament poked its end out of Cannon Green, and a couple walked behind it, their winter coats unzipped and lifting behind them in the breeze. These two, like every one of them, every one of the thousands in their rooms, or eating dinner, or going to rehearsal or practice right now, all over campus, had been weighed and measured and talked through and voted on, then they had disappeared into the maw of anonymous data in the registrar's computer. And unless something happened—unless one of them plagiarized or got a Rhodes or picked up a bullhorn and led a rally out on Cannon Green—neither Portia nor her colleagues ever thought of them again. They were simply gone from the collective ken of admissions, their files unceremoniously transferred to the registrar's suite of offices in a caravan of file boxes, their names replaced by thousands of other names, with their thousands of other needs and wishes and difficulties, when the fall rolled around again. As for the other folders, the deny folders, they were shredded.

That was probably the moment when she understood what she was going to do.

Already, the office felt empty. It was a rare lull in the admissions year. It was the perfect time to do this one small thing. Many of her colleagues, in fact, had dispersed. Deepa was in Georgia, visiting schools and speaking to parents' groups in Atlanta and Athens. Dylan had gone to see the University of Texas, where he'd been admitted to a graduate program in Latin. Jordan had gone back to Virginia for the weekend, to be with her mother while her father had bypass surgery. Corinne had decamped for Andover to watch her daughter in a cross-country meet. Clarence was around, of course, but he had left for the day, brandishing tickets to the Met.

Portia returned to her chair and sat, very still, listening to the quiet, trying to think it through. Of course she would be found out. That was not in question. But if she could do it well enough, she would not be found out right away. Four days, five days...that was all it would take, long enough for the letters to go out, because once they were out, Clarence would have to stand by the offer. If she could do it well enough, she might have that long, and although she could not bring herself to believe in fate, which was no better than religion, which was itself a kind of religion, she knew a gift when she saw one. Jesse Bolton, bound for Yale, was a gift.

Hours went by. She didn't move or make noise. She wasn't here. Occasionally, the entrance door downstairs gave a faint creak as the few others, and Martha and her staff, departed for the day.

Still, Portia could not seem to get herself out of the chair. She had never, to her knowledge, cheated or stolen. In fact, she possessed, like far better Jews than herself, a surfeit of guilt, and it took very little to set that off. Once, in the seventh grade, she had pretended to be ill in order to get out of an algebra test, then was so overwhelmed by remorse that she had confessed and forced her mother to take her in anyway, even though Susannah had been happy enough to let her have the day off. Among her high school friends, swiping candy bars from Cumberland Farms was so common as to be unremarkable, but Portia could never bring herself to do it. She had never bought a copy of CliffsNotes or even allowed herself to ask a classmate for help when she was stuck, not that she condemned those things. But she'd had to do everything alone for it to be real: mediocre and real versus superlative and false. Good for you, she thought sourly. And look where it's got you.

What time it was when she finally got to her feet she didn't know, and that was strangely encouraging. Some black hour in the shifting middle of the night, silence in the building, silence even on the campus: It must be very late or very early. She put on her coat, opened her office door, and shut it quietly behind her.

Admissions officers had access to the data files, of course, but they were not empowered to register decisions in the system. Only one person could register an admit, and that wasn't Martha, who had perhaps the farthest-reaching overview of what was happening. It wasn't even Clarence. It was Abby, the assistant who sat in the antechamber outside his office.

As it happened, Portia knew Abby's password for access to the system, but even if she hadn't, it wouldn't have been difficult to guess. Abby's daughter, Louisa, had gone to Russia as a Bear Stearns analyst ten years before, met a Muscovite doctor named Grisha, and moved there permanently. Two years later, she had given birth to a wide-eyed boy named Aleksei, whose image (dipping his toes into the Baltic Sea, grinning before St. Basil's) papered the cubicle of his adoring grandmother. One day the previous year, when Abby was home sick with flu, she had asked Portia to help Clarence extract some bit of data he needed, and Portia had not been at all surprised to learn that her password was Aleksei.

When she got to the desk, she sat quietly in Abby's seat and turned on the monitor. The screen flickered alarmingly to life, banishing its vaguely psychedelic screen saver and replacing it with yet another photograph of the blissfully smiling boy, this time on the first day of school, holding the traditional bouquet for his teacher. With a fingernail, she carefully entered the letters, and the system welcomed her.

It was not difficult. She went first to Jesse Bolton's entry, overwriting the A beside his name with a D and hitting Return.

D, she thought, for *Don't even think about it*.

Then she found Jeremiah and did the same thing, in reverse. *A for Admission*. Also: *Amoral*. Also: *Absolutely against the rules*.

She exited Abby's account and put the terminal back to sleep, watching little Aleksei's face disappear behind coiling, swirling comets of purple.

Breathing, Portia got to her feet.

She walked softly, rubber soles on carpeting, down the hall and then the staircase, closing the doors carefully behind her so they didn't click, as if there were anyone there to hear it. Then she made her way to the ground-floor office and, solely by the glow of the emergency light, entered the office security code and went inside.

The deny files were stacked in a room off the office, awaiting shredding. It was a room without windows, but when Portia switched on the light the blare of it unnerved her even so. She started to look around quickly. There were thousands here, of course, about seventeen thousand, and the folders nearly filled the space, covering two long tables and lining a bookcase against one wall; but they turned out to be neatly sorted, state by state and school by school where there were multiple applicants. New Hampshire — St. Paul's and Exeter aside — was not exactly a breeding ground for Princeton applicants. Portia had little difficulty locating the file. She extracted it and nudged the pile it had come from into place. Then she went back into the main room.

The admit files were arranged alphabetically in file boxes on the same table where those appalling vegan "health bars" had once resided, waiting for someone brave enough to eat them. There were, naturally, far fewer of these, and she had no difficulty finding Jesse Bolton: Princeton legacy, future journalist, future Yalie. Portia went to the supply cupboard past Martha's desk and took out two unused orange folders. Then she carefully peeled back the color-coded stickers from Jeremiah's and Jesse's and affixed them to the new folders. She slid the contents of each — reader's card, application, transcript, school report, and recs — into the new folders and clumsily folded and stuffed the old folders into her coat pocket. Then she took a red pen from Martha's desk, checked "Admit" on the front of Jeremiah's refashioned folder, and slid it into place, snug between Babbitt, Christopher, and Balthazar, Henri-Paul. *Babbitt, Balakian, Balthazar.* Portia shook her head. Then, quickly, she checked "Deny" on Jesse Bolton's new file, slipped back into the adjacent room, and placed it with the files of his rejected schoolmates, just behind the appropriately declined application of Sam Aronson. *I'm sorry,* she told it, and she found that she truly was, because Jesse Bolton had deserved to know that the admissions officers at Princeton thought he was wonderful and hoped that he would choose them, bring his undeniable gifts to the *Prince,* carry on his father's valued tradition. One application among these thousands, multiplied by seventeen years. Could it really be as wrong as it felt?

When she let herself outside, the air felt clammy and unexpectedly cold. She turned up her collar and walked through the campus, past the art museum and the mansion that had once been home to the university president, then out through the arches to Prospect Avenue, where the eating clubs faced off in a row. They were larger than the fraternities at Dartmouth and looked considerably more solid—less Animal House, in other words, than Animal Mansion—but Portia often wondered how Princeton managed to retain its reputation of gentility when Saturday nights on Prospect rivaled any debauchery she had ever seen in Hanover. Tonight, however, no one stirred, and she walked quickly down the moonlit street, leaving the clubs behind and beginning to pass the neat, pleasant homes of faculty members and university administrators. One bore the after-effects of an Easter egg hunt the previous weekend, with discarded plastic eggs and hastily removed bits of foil soggily embedded in the lawn; another was lined with little plastic flags bearing the logo of an electric-dog-containment company and the words *Puppy in Training*. Finally, at the end of the avenue, she came to Gordon Sternberg's home and stopped for a moment to look. Perhaps it was not as abandoned as it appeared, she thought. Perhaps some of those dark windows had sleeping Sternbergs in them, Gordon's wife or kids returned to sort through his things or start the wrenching process of moving out. She had met the kids, she was fairly sure, at some of the parties, but she doubted she would know them now, nor would they know her. Gordon himself had barely registered her. She had only been Mark's not-even-wife, not pretty enough to be noticed, not clever enough to talk to about his work, which was the only thing he truly liked to talk about. Whenever she reminded him, as she often did, that she worked at the Office of Admission, he lurched into cruel discourses on the doltish students who had dared to attend his classes, charity cases, he supposed, or the opposite: children of too much wealth and too little brain, who had obviously bought their way in.

Another expert with an opinion about admissions.

Another authority who was sure he could do it better.

Now she saw that it was no longer entirely dark, that the first intimation of morning had crept overhead, casting the Sternbergs' stucco house, which was actually white, with a faintly rosy tint. And she was suddenly exhausted—all the adrenaline of subterfuge bled out of her in a rush, and she thought she could sleep now, if only she could get herself home.

Portia turned the corner and headed west on Harrison, thinking of sheets and the weight of her quilt, the bed where she could stop, if not actually rest, the place where she might be comfortable, if not actually safe, while she waited for the ax to fall.

Since my mother's death, I have watched my father make a valiant
effort to do the things she would have done for my sister and me. This
has been amusing at times, like when he tried to explain menstruation
to my very embarrassed sister, but for the most part he has risen to every
occasion. My mother used to attend every one of my diving meets, and
now it is my father I can see from the uppermost board, looking up at
me with a big grin on his face. I miss my mother every day, but I know
how fortunate I am to have my father. Without him, I don't think I
would have come through the last couple of years.

CHAPTER THIRTY-ONE

99 PERCENT PURE

It didn't fall, or not at first. The next day, she stayed fretfully at home, not trusting herself to go back. She made coffee and drank it and paced, waiting for the phone to ring, the police to arrive, something irrevocable, but no one even asked after her. By midday, she decided to start cleaning the house, just to take her mind off of what might be happening at the office; but in fact, not much was happening at the office, at least upstairs. Downstairs, in Martha's domain, eighteen hundred letters of acceptance began to emerge from a wall of printers, and the seventeen thousand folders in the small adjacent room waited to be fed to the shredders.

By late afternoon, Portia had bundled months' worth of recyclable papers and stacked them by the curb. She had done half a dozen loads of laundry and folded Mark's clothes into a cardboard box, flipped the mattress, and remade the bed. She had sorted the mail to glean an amount of actual correspondence that was at once depressing and illuminating. This handful of significant stuff included several recent letters from Mark's attorney, some personal notes from university friends she'd assumed had abandoned her, and the letter to which John had alluded several weeks back. She put these aside to deal with later and tackled her fridge, throwing away various putrid items with satisfying abandon, after which she drove to McCaffrey's and stocked up, filling her cart with all kinds of things she had forgotten she liked to eat. Back at the house, she opened up some of the windows and let the spring air inside.

Then, with no reasonable excuses to keep her away from her office, Portia went back and began to do her waiting there.

She set about, as if everything were normal, to lay some groundwork for the next admissions cycle, thinking about which schools she wanted to visit and putting them together in theoretical trips. Maine and northern New Hampshire. Hotchkiss and Taft. Boston Latin and the magnet school in New Bedford. She found excuses—not too many, not too obvious—to go downstairs so she could check on the notification letters, which were still being prepped, still clearly in residence, and then climbed the stairs back to her office, heart thudding, head racing.

Then, quite suddenly a few days later, those thousands of letters were gone: dozens of plastic bins of them loaded onto a line of U.S. mail trucks that backed up to the front door of West College. Portia watched from her window as the trucks wound around the campus drive and disappeared from sight. Now, she thought, sinking into her chair and laying her head down on the desktop, she was safe, or Jeremiah, at least, was safe. Five months from now, he would come with his strange ideas and meandering imagination, and he would meet other teachers like John Halsey and other oddball kids like himself, who had blundered through high school like bats in the light, addled by the unfathomable rules of social conduct and the indelible judgments of teenagers. She actually fell asleep that way, waking only when one of the financial aid officers knocked on her door to check a detail. And then she went home and slept again.

A couple of days were allowed to pass. All over the world, the blows were absorbed. Portia and the others prepared to woo the admitted students, if necessary. There was a meeting to plan the hosting weekend. She sat in her office, watching the in-box on her computer, listening for the deceptive purr of the phone, heralding vitriol at the other end of the line. Those calls were coming, she knew.

But the first one had nothing to do with Princeton.

Caitlin had given birth to her baby on the day she received her own notification from Dartmouth. These two events, it transpired, were not unrelated.

"I was jumping up and down," she told Portia, phoning from her hospital room at Mary Hitchcock. "In the hallway? Just inside the front door, you know? And all of a sudden I went, 'Wow, I think I peed my pants.' So we both started screaming and Susannah drove me over. I'm so happy!" she crowed, though she didn't really specify about what. Caitlin claimed that she had seriously considered naming the baby Eleazar if it had turned out to be a boy, but thankfully it was not a boy. The baby was to be named Alice, after both an ancestor who had emigrated from Germany to Utah in the 1850s and one of Caitlin's aunts, who had assumed Caitlin would attend a two-year college and then marry.

"Thank you," she told Portia, who had really not done so much, only reviewed Caitlin's application and advised against an early essay about singing in her high school choir.

"Don't be silly. You were a great applicant. You're going to have a fantastic experience."

"Oh, my God, I know," said Caitlin. She sounded a little out of it, actually. A little blissed out, a little drugged. Portia let her go, promising to call the next day, then she hung up with a smile.

Then it started slowly. A happy call from a coach in Maine. A tearful call from the principal of the charter school in Roxbury, where a remarkable young man named DeShahn Mellings, trumpet virtuoso and gifted debater, had just received the best news of his life. And then the pace began to pick up. It was like kernels of corn beginning to pop, first slowly, with lacunae, and then in a solid mass. And some of them were brutal, but they were not the one Portia was waiting for.

She accepted the bittersweet thanks of Sarah Lenaghan's college counselor, who was consoling eight of Sarah's classmates, and the assurances of Milton Academy's head of counseling that Carter Ralston, in whom the development office had expressed such interest, was very fired up to attend Princeton. (Ralston had been a strong applicant, it turned out, with an 800 verbal, a beautiful essay about traveling in South America, and a New England Prep School Athletic Conference record for the high jump.) She had spent a scant fifteen minutes (not a single moment more than she could bear) talking to her old colleague Rand Cumming, who seemed astounded that some number less than twenty-seven of his twenty-seven applicants had been admitted, and an hour on the phone with William Roden at Deerfield, moving at his insistence through the list of more than forty applicants, about a quarter of whom had been either admitted or wait-listed. Sadly, Matt Boyce, once wrapped in an orange swaddling cloth, was not one of them. But Deerfield had sent them wonderful applicants, as always, Portia reminded him. Kids from Europe and Asia as well, all of them wonderfully prepared and immensely likable.

"I hope you'll encourage them to come to our hosting weekend," she told them. "And let me know if you want me to set up any meetings for them while they're here. I can get the rowers out on the water, if they'd like. And the Music Department is very eager to meet Sandra Lu."

He promised he would.

On the fourth day, she began to be surprised that nothing had happened to her. The fifth day passed. The ecstatic calls waned; she and all of her colleagues were now soothing and placating, getting yelled at or wept at, begged and cursed, in the annual ritual of response: usually parental, occasionally from the guidance counselors and coaches, often enough from the applicants themselves. This year, one of the worst calls would be from Matt Boyce's mother, who'd struggled to maintain her composure through the conversation. "Can't you put him on the waiting list?" she'd asked, her voice barely above a whisper. "It's so heartbreaking for him. It's all he's ever wanted."

And when Portia had said, with genuine regret, that this would not be possible, the woman had turned on a dime and announced that her next call was to the president's office, then the development office, and then to alumni affairs, where it was to be firmly understood that no one in her family of Princetonians would ever give another penny to the school.

"It's so difficult," said Portia, illogically hoping that Matt Boyce's mother would suddenly understand the reality of the numbers, the complexity of the problem. But the woman told her to go fuck herself and hung up.

Portia hung up, too, then stared at the phone, wondering who'd be next. The boy whose eighteenth-century antecedent had "helped set up the place"? The guidance counselor from the private school in Connecticut who seemed to feel, each year, that the decisions contained in his advisees' letters were just a preliminary suggestion, like the first step in a drawn-out negotiation? Some devastated kid insisting that her future had been destroyed? She did not doubt their disappointment and frustration. These applicants had done nothing wrong. They had not "deserved" the slender envelopes any more than the others had "deserved" the thick packets of welcome, glossy look books and invitations to hosting weekend. Still, it was fair. Scrupulously fair, if not entirely fair. It was, as Martin Quilty had once memorably put it, making his case to an alumni group, "like Ivory Snow. Ninety-nine percent pure."

Clarence emerged occasionally to knock on someone's door and go over some point before he phoned back an irate alum, but it was all routine. It was like last year and the year before. It was incredible. It was passing. Already, she wondered if the calls weren't tapering off.

And then the weekend came. There were no phone calls over the weekend.

By Monday, she had begun to test the idea that nothing was going to happen to her. This was a riveting thought and came with a retinue of attendant thoughts, which were also riveting: that she might spend the next four years being close to Jeremiah, perhaps getting to know him. She could offer him a place to stay over the school breaks—surely he would rather stay in Princeton than go home to his parents, his vacation job at the market. Over time, they would grow close, like great friends who sense some deeper bond they can't articulate. She would make sure he received every single thing the university was able to give him, not just the education and financial support, but the travel, work experience, the cultural smorgasbord undreamed of by a boy from working-class New Hampshire, and the guidance of mentors who understood his complexity and promise and truly wanted him to succeed. It was a soaring feeling. It was a feeling of sweetness and deep resolve. It was, for her, for probably the first time—peace.

And then it happened: without real warning and brutishly quick.

First, Abby came, knocking on her door and leaning in. "Oh, good. I thought you might have left," she said. "Clarence wants to see you."

Portia went numb. She nodded. "What about, do you know?"

"No idea," said Abby. "Hey, did you decide if you're going to the NACAC this year? I'm booking travel."

Irrationally, Portia decided the question was a good omen. "I think so. I love Seattle."

She got to her feet and followed Abby, who returned to her desk. Portia went in alone.

"Hello," she said tentatively.

He said nothing but nodded at the seat opposite his own. Then he sat, fingertips touching, two lonely files on the desk before him. For a long moment, she pretended that she knew nothing and asked herself what could this mean—this strange, charged silence? This rigid expression and bald stare? She told herself that she did not recognize this assemblage of features, which were not charming Clarence or proper Clarence or Clarence-the-leader-of-the-team or Clarence off guard, laughing at the joke, or the Clarence who might disarm the most conservative of alumni men, those Class of '40-somethings and '50-somethings and even '60-somethings, not a few of whom were actually, secretly, *appalled* that the gates to Princeton were now being guarded by a black man, a gay man, a man from Yale (which was possibly the worst of the three). This, Portia realized with a start, was a Clarence she had never once seen before. This was Clarence enraged. And her career, which had so very recently felt uncurtailed, a string of unknown length stretched vaguely forward to retirement, now had precious minutes to run.

"I had a call," he said. His voice was quiet but packed with bitterness.

Portia looked past him, to the Asher Durand behind his desk. Did he ever look at it? she wondered. She always did whenever she was here in the office. This would almost certainly be the last time.

"Oh yes?"

"From Richard Bolton, class of '81. Father of Jesse Bolton. Are you familiar with Jesse Bolton?"

Portia, glumly, nodded.

"I was not. So I asked Martha to pull the file before I called him back." He flipped open the cover. "Budding journalist. Writes for *The Boston Globe*. National award from Scripps. Is this coming back?"

She was tempted to tell him that he didn't have to be a jerk about it.

"I remember this kid. We loved this kid." Portia looked at her hands. *"We admitted this kid,"* he said through gritted teeth. "And yet..." He held up the file, pointing out, with one of his long, elegant fingers, the "Deny" box checked in red pen. "Are you ready to explain this to me?"

What good would that do? she wanted to say.

After a very uncomfortable pause, he went on.

"And so I asked for the admit list. I looked for Bolton, Jesse. No Bolton, Jesse. But I did find Balakian, Jeremiah."

He held up the other file. "Mr. Balakian has accepted our offer of admission," he said with barely contained vitriol. "I don't remember making him an offer of admission, Portia. Now, I'd like to ask you again. Why did you do this? Why would you throw away your career and your reputation? And, what's far more important to me, *our* reputation? On this?"

"He isn't a 'this,'" Portia said lamely.

Clarence leaned forward. He was halfway across the desk. For a man of such refined tastes, he had a very muscular build, she observed. His neck, within the collar of his elegant pink shirt, was defined by muscles and sinews. She took an almost clinical interest in this and wondered how he had achieved so much definition in such an odd area.

"You," he rasped at her, "have exposed this office and the university to a completely undeserved scandal. What you have done is unconscionable. How dare you be so cavalier with this institution? If word were to get out about this, the damage would be irreparable."

Portia sat up, newly alert. "Well, I won't tell anyone," she said brightly.

"No," Clarence said tightly. "You won't. And I won't either. What you will do is submit your resignation. I don't care what excuse you use, but I never want to see you in this building again. I will keep this matter between ourselves. Not for your sake, I can assure you. But if I ever hear that you've gone to work for another admissions department, I will be on the phone to your dean before they nail your name to the door. Is that understood?"

"Well," she said, "let me take a moment to think it over."

Clarence actually banged his fist on the desk. The ink blotter muffled the blow.

"You have no choice. This career is over. I can't tell you how thoroughly disappointed I am."

Portia shrugged. She was finding a distinct lack of outrage in all this. And it wasn't just because none of it was a surprise. She was ready to go. She was ready for something else. On the spot, she decided she also wanted to live somewhere else.

She got to her feet. "He's going to Yale," she said. "Jesse Bolton. The guidance counselor told me. We never had a chance at him."

Clarence reacted to this, but then he remembered himself. "That's not the point," he said fiercely. "As you know. I only wish you'd tell me why."

And she actually considered doing that. It might have surprised him to know how far such an uncomplicated request finally traveled: ahead to an idea of her own future, behind to the college student she had once been, running a ring about herself in the names of men he barely knew or had never even heard of: Tom and John and Mark and Jeremiah. How strange that she had come to be defined by so many men. What would Susannah have to say about that? She could imagine what Susannah would have to say about that. And no one had ever asked her why before, because no one had ever known there was a why. And she found, very much to her own surprise, that she did want to talk about it. She did want to tell somebody why she had done this strange and unchangeable and thoroughly uncharacteristic thing. And there were people who ought to be told, because what she had done — not just now, but then — had actually hurt those people, and they deserved to know why. But Clarence wasn't one of them.

"Would it make any difference?" she asked him, looking up. "About the job, I mean."

"It would not," Clarence huffed.

"Then I won't, if you don't mind. I assume you'll be standing by the offer."

"To Balakian? I don't see how we can rescind it without the whole thing blowing up in our faces."

Out of common courtesy, Portia tried to banish any outward sign of smugness. "Well, I'll be going, then," she said. "I've learned so much working with you, Clarence."

He glared at her. Apparently, he considered her praise offensive.

"I'm sorry to have disappointed you," she told him. "I'm going to write you a fantastic letter of resignation."

He gathered up the two folders on his desk and slapped one — which one? — briskly on top of the other. Then he pointedly looked away from her.

Portia left the room. She stood for a stunned moment outside his door.

"You heading home?" said Abby. She didn't look up from her computer screen. There was a new grinning Aleksei on the desktop.

"Yes," said Portia. "Good-bye."

"Bye, then."

Portia turned and walked off down the corridor. Everyone seemed to have gone for the day, infected by the warm spring weather, taking cover from the vitriol on the phones and in the computer in-boxes. She walked slowly to her office and went inside, wondering what belonged to her and what did not: yearbooks, manuals, sheaves of printer paper, her sizable collection of what she'd always called "admissions lit," books touting surefire strategies to get into college, ways to "package" yourself and be your own college consultant. Books that hurled ridiculous solutions at a problem they never actually stated: that there were simply too many qualified applicants for each available spot, and there always would be, and no amount of strategizing, "brag sheet" construction, or SAT prep was ever going to circumvent that bald little fact. She was fairly sure she owned those books, but not at all sure she wanted to take them with her into whatever her new life was going to be.

In the end, she could find only a single thing she wanted: the Plath poem Rachel had given her, the one that began, "First, are you our sort of a person?" She reached across her desk and plucked it from the bulletin board and folded it carefully and slipped it into the pocket of her jeans. Travel light, Portia told herself. She left the building by the front door.

*Of course, I was disappointed not to be able to accept an unpaid
summer internship at a marketing firm, but after a few weeks in my
not terribly exciting retail job in an outlet mall, I started to realize that
I was learning a lot about the very subject I'd hoped to learn about at
my internship. After ten weeks of watching people purchase items they
didn't need and, in some cases, didn't even like, I believe I know far
more now about human psychology and behavior than I did before I
first pinned on my Land's End name tag.*

CHAPTER THIRTY-TWO

PROMETHEUS UNBOUND

Mark turned up at seven that evening, right on time, and Portia let
him in with a smile that felt surprisingly genuine. It was a comfort
that she had decided not to hate Mark. If Portia could have hated him and
still done what she was about to do, then she might have indulged herself,
but that wasn't going to be possible. And in fact, the more she probed her
own current distress, the more she discovered that it was mainly illusory.
On the contrary, she felt not terrible. She felt bizarrely settled, in spite of
how precarious her situation actually was. And when this was over, she
told herself, she might be permitted to feel better than she had in many
years.

Mark was thin. He looked drawn, and he wore a wedding ring, and Portia found that she had to avert her eyes from it, if only to retain focus. He
gave her an awkward hug, looking fairly surprised to find himself making
the gesture. "You look very well," he told her.

Portia laughed. "I doubt that. But thanks."

"You finished for the year?"

"All over but the shouting."

He looked perplexed.

"You know, the letters go out, the calls come in. 'How could you reject my son? You took the kid who got a B plus in chemistry and he got an A minus.'"

"Oh, right." He shrugged. "I forgot."

"Most people are fine, but the unhappy people take up most of your time." She looked directly at him. "Let's not talk about work. I talk about work too much. I've made some tea."

He seemed relieved. "I'm really glad you called, Portia."

"Yes. I'm sorry, I should have done it months ago. I just wasn't ready."

The teapot was already on the kitchen table. Portia led the way and poured for them both. She had always shared his taste in tea: the more English and staid, the better. The day PG Tips had appeared in the tea aisle at McCaffrey's had been a good day for their household.

"Thanks," he said when she passed him the milk.

"I had a baby," said Portia. Then, amazed at herself, she burst out laughing. It was not happy laughter, particularly.

"You . . . what?" He stared at her.

"I never said those words out loud. Never once. 'I had a baby.' You know, it's easier the second time."

"When?" Mark looked stricken. "Before you met me, I'm assuming."

"Yes. A year before. He was adopted." Her face was streaming with tears, she was surprised to note. That seemed to have happened very quickly.

"Portia," said Mark, "I'm so sorry." He actually reached for her hand, and she let him take it.

"You know why I never went into therapy?" she said brightly. "Because someone once told me that what happens in therapy is, they help you figure out who to blame, and then they get you to blame them, and then you feel better. So I thought, Well, I don't need that. I already know who to blame."

"You must have been very confused," Mark told her.

"Oh, I should have been more confused. If I'd been more confused, I might have made another decision. I might have let someone actually talk to me about it. I don't know why I thought I had to do it all by myself." She wiped her face with the back of her hand. "I'm quite the chatterbox tonight."

"Why didn't you tell me?" he asked, looking finally, appropriately pained.

"I should have. More than anyone else, I should have told you, because it changed things for us, and you had no idea why. I'm sure you were telling me you wanted kids, but I pretended not to know. I couldn't...I didn't think I could go back there. I'm so sorry."

"But...why couldn't we? You were, what, twenty-one when we got together? It's not exactly past childbearing age."

"No, no." She shook her head. This was the part he wouldn't understand, she thought, and she took a moment to say it as well as she could. "It's...*that* was my child. When I couldn't even do that, I couldn't get near it again. I just wanted to get as far away from it as I could. And you had Cressida, and that was such a terrible thing for you...."

He looked alarmed. "I love Cressida. I've never regretted having her."

"No, of course. But I always thought, Well, he already has a child...."

Mark stirred his tea but didn't drink it. "I should have insisted we talk it through. I should never have let it go."

They sat in charged silence. Portia looked at her hands.

"Who was the father?" he said quietly.

"Tom Standley. My boyfriend in college."

Mark nodded. "You've mentioned him."

"I never told him. It was very wrong of me."

He didn't disagree with her. "I'm surprised your mother didn't commandeer the entire situation."

"She didn't know. I didn't tell her, either. I didn't tell anyone, Mark. It took me all these years to tell you."

He stared at her. It seemed to be finally sinking in. "Portia," he said, shaking his head. "This must have been so hard for you."

She was crying again, not in a violent way, but steadily, like a pipe that couldn't be twisted entirely closed. It made her think of that character in the *Iliad,* with the wound that wouldn't heal. The stench of it was so unbearable that his compatriots—supposedly his friends—had left him alone on an island. What tormented her most, she thought, was how many things would have been more or less the same if she had indeed told her mother, who would indeed have commandeered the situation. Portia could have finished school, taken her job at the Admissions Office, met Mark, moved to Princeton...everything the same but everything better. And now she would have a seventeen-year-old son.

"The strange thing is," she said, "that I kept waiting to feel better about it. I knew it would be hard at the beginning, but I thought, you know, in time I'd feel better. Even a tiny bit better, even very gradually. But it never happened. I think it went the other direction, actually. I had to work harder and harder just to not think about what I'd done. And the baby, of course. And I live in this world of seventeen-year-old kids, you know? Every year, they're always seventeen years old. And then one year he was seventeen, too. It just...it made it very hard."

"Yes," Mark said. "Losing a child is the hardest thing."

"But what happened to you is different. Everyone who knows what happened to you feels compassion for you. *I* feel compassion for you. She was taken from you against your will. If you'd had a child who died, there would have been compassion, of course. But there's no compassion for a mother who gives up her child. We're on our own. We can't even feel compassion for ourselves."

She was, by the end of this, speaking through her hands. Her fingers smelled faintly of bleach from the laundry. Her voice came in jolts, every word produced only with effort. All this time, she realized, she had thought vaguely of the two of them as equally pained. Now she understood that she had been jealous for years: *Poor Mark, deprived of his child by her lunatic mother, prevented from being the father he was born to be.*

"I've wronged a lot of people," she said, as if she were just now reviewing the lists. "But mostly you."

"Well, I doubt that," he told her. "But I accept the apology. I only wish you'd felt you could share it with me."

"You had enough on your plate." Portia sighed. "The whole Cressida situation was just tearing you up."

He smiled suddenly. "Cressida is coming to spend her gap year with me. Marcie is beside herself. She applied to Newnham for law but didn't get a place. I'm hoping, if she likes it here, maybe she'll want to stay for university in the States."

Portia nodded. "That would be nice."

"Maybe you'd help her with her applications," Mark said, suddenly a tiny bit shy.

She laughed. "I'd be glad to. If I'm still here."

Mark looked at her sharply. "You're leaving Princeton?"

"I don't know. Maybe. I don't know."

"Is it work? Or"—he gestured vaguely at the kitchen—"this?"

"I don't know. Neither. Or both. It's just something I'm thinking about." Portia got up and went to the sink. She splashed water on her face and dried it off. She noted that she was no longer crying. "I suppose I'll need to get out of this house, at any rate."

He looked astonished. "Well, we ought to come to some kind of agreement," he said carefully. "You've been getting our letters, of course."

She shrugged. "I'm sorry. I haven't read them. I'll listen now if you want to make a proposal."

Mark ran a hand through his graying hair. The ring caught the overhead light and winked gold. He seemed to be thinking something through, and it occurred to Portia that the proposal he was now assembling might not be the same one as in his attorney's letters.

They talked until late, and through another pot of PG Tips. After the first hour, she went to find a legal pad, and they made the necessary decisions.

"How's Helen?" she asked as he was getting ready to leave. She felt quite brave, saying this.

"Okay. Very crabby, actually. She's on bed rest."

"Oh?"

"Preterm labor. She had lofty goals of finishing her Woolf book, but she can't concentrate. So she's ended up watching a gruesome amount of daytime television, which sends her blood pressure shooting up and makes the whole situation worse." He smiled at this. To her own surprise, Portia smiled, too.

"You're going to be all right," he told her, picking up his 1820 *Prometheus Unbound,* which Portia had retrieved for him from upstairs. "I'm not sure how I know that, but I know it."

"Thanks," she said, smiling awkwardly. "I actually think so, too."

"And we'll . . . I mean, I would like for us to still . . . you know, be in touch. Be friends."

For the first time that evening, she lied to him. "Of course."

He looked relieved.

"I really am glad about Cressida," Portia said.

"Yes." Mark shook his head. "But you know, you always told me it would work out eventually. You said if I waited long enough, she would come to me. Remember?"

"I said that?" said Portia, stunned.

"You did. You said it for years. And you see, it was true." He reached out and pulled her against him, a tight but thoroughly unromantic hug. She could smell the old-book smell of the Shelley close to her cheek. "Maybe yours will, too," he said quietly.

"Maybe," she said. But that was a lie as well.

*"Do you know what it means to leave a thing unfinished?" This is
the question pondered by the title character of my favorite novel, MY
NAME IS ASHER LEV. Like Lev, I have given much thought to
this question, which is at once a universal question and, I believe, an
inherently Jewish one. For Jews, after all, the world is broken, and
hence imperfect. Part of our mission as human beings who love and
believe in our G-d is to act in accordance with tikkun ha-olam, to
repair and restore the broken world with goodness and decency. This
should be the mission of every life, Jewish or not.*

CHAPTER THIRTY-THREE

A SENSE OF BEING DRAWN IN

As far as Greenfield, Massachusetts, she had no real intention of making the detour, but there was something about the Vermont border, drawing closer, that got her thinking. She wasn't in a hurry, now. She had taken a calm, measured leave, signing papers in an impersonal legal office on Alexander Road, depositing the check they gave her (drawn, it pained her to note, on the joint account of Mark Telford and Helen Garrett) in a new account of her own. In the end, she had been the one to relinquish the house, taking away her things, finally pulling out of the drive in her over-stuffed Toyota. She had allowed herself to be feted by her colleagues at a dinner in Lahiere's, to which even Corinne had come, and even Clarence, though he was very careful, very, very careful, to be vague in his good wishes. As far as she could tell, the stated reason for her departure—that she had decided to return to New England, spend quality time with her mother, and help care for a newborn who had, somewhat mysteriously, joined the household—was not being challenged. Clarence, it seemed, had indeed contained the truth.

VERMONT WELCOME CENTER, read the sign just past the border. Portia knew exactly what was in there: maple syrup, cheese, photographs of cows, cows, cows. Get used to it, she thought, suppressing a smile. It amazed her to be back, and not just visiting. Susannah was amazed about it, too, but she was also overwhelmed, caring for Alice and caring for Caitlin, who was also caring for Alice. Only a month earlier, Frieda had made good on her promise to move out, and Portia's mother wasn't going to decline the help.

There wasn't, quite, a plan, only a semiprecise intention for the future, which included Caitlin commuting to Hanover and Susannah and Portia taking care of the baby. Susannah hadn't really engaged with the longer implications of this, but Portia certainly had: Caitlin, she was sure, might be happy to share the care of her child, share even Alice's affections — but she would not give her up. And, of course, she should not give her up. She was going to graduate with a Dartmouth degree and a four-year-old daughter, and off she would go to live and work and raise her child, and that was as it should be. And Susannah would have to find, at last, some real thing of her own. And Portia, also, some real thing of her own. But not today.

Today she had driven north on the well-remembered road, passing all the well-remembered landmarks, but by the time she crossed the border she had begun to feel a distinct gravitational pull: east, across the river and the state line, past a red barn and a hex sign, into the woods, and on down a dirt road absurdly named Inspiration Way. She drove without a real — or at least an examined — objective, only a gradual and building sense of being drawn in. But as Portia actually passed the homemade sign for the Quest School she suddenly remembered to be several things at once: embarrassed, for one, and of course guilty, and not a little worried about how she would be received.

To her surprise, there were other cars on the dirt road, three of them backed up and waiting where the drive ended at the small parking lot. This was not unrelated to the fact that something seemed to be happening at the school. Cars were being directed into a field and parking in an obedient line along the ground. Beyond the barn, an open-sided tent fluttered over rows of folding chairs. Portia would have liked to turn around, but there was no way to do it until she reached the head of the line, and when she did, she saw to her chagrin that John was stationed there, greeting the drivers. He looked entirely shocked to see her, and she decided she had to say something first.

"I think I've come at a bad time," said Portia. "I had no idea you had an event. I'm going to come back."

"It's our graduation," he said, frowning.

"I'll come back," she said again.

"No, stay. If Jeremiah knew you were here, he'd want you to stay. I mean, if you can stay."

There were two cars behind her now. She pulled her own out of the way and cut the ignition. When she got out, he was already beside her.

"I don't want to take you away from your post," she said awkwardly.

"No, it's all right. I have great faith that our guests will be able to figure out where to park. I'm amazed to see you, you know."

"Oh?" said Portia, as if this were not entirely clear.

"Well, I just thought, you know, that was that."

"I'm sure you were angry," Portia told him. "And entitled to be."

"Yes, a little," he admitted. "But mostly at myself. I mean, disappear on me once, shame on you. Disappear on me twice, shame on me. I have no idea what's going on with you. I guess I felt, if you wanted something from me, you know where I am."

"I do know where you are." She laughed and held up her hands. "As you see."

He smiled, too. He was a little slow on the uptake, it seemed. He said: "I see."

John looked at the car. It was jammed within an inch of its life.

"You always pack this light for a visit?"

"I'm moving to Hartland for a bit, to stay with my mother. Remember that baby she was talking about adopting? She was born two months ago. She's called Alice. I'm looking forward to meeting her."

"How long is 'a bit'?" asked John. "Like, the summer?"

"Like, indefinitely. I've left Princeton."

He looked at her intently. "The university? Or the town?"

"Both. Don't look so surprised." She couldn't help laughing. "It's not the end of the world. I needed a little shaking up, that's all."

"But . . . what are you going to do? Will you work at Dartmouth?"

"No. I don't think so."

"Well," John said, considering, "you could always write a book. Doesn't everyone who leaves Ivy League admissions write a 'how to get into college' book?"

She laughed. "I guess. But does the world really need another one?"

"You could help us," he said, suddenly very serious. "We have twelve kids who are going to be seniors in . . ." He checked his watch. "About an hour and ten minutes. We have no idea what we're doing. They could use a little guidance."

Cars were rolling past them, Volvos and hybrids, some of them gently rusting, their backseats full of kids and coolers. They reminded Portia of the families she had grown up with: women alone with Asian daughters, women in pairs, an "It's a Small World After All" of ethnicities. In the field beside the great barn, kids were running and screaming. The chairs in the open tent were in neat rows, but no one was sitting down yet. In and around the barn, students and adults and children were everywhere, drinking cider and setting up picnic tables, playing volleyball over a sagging net. She saw Deborah, talking intently with a couple of parents, gesturing so hard with her glass of cider that it sloshed dangerously around the rim. Then she noticed that Jeremiah was one of the volleyball players, leaping and slapping next to Nelson, who had—as Jeremiah did not—the grace of a natural athlete. They high-fived each other after every spike.

Portia could feel the late afternoon sun, dry and hot. She tipped up her face and closed her eyes and smiled. She was letting herself consider what John had said. She was letting herself consider a few things, actually.

"Why don't you stay?" he asked her. "Come to graduation. Stay for dinner. We have a potluck. We have a band coming later. You can see Jeremiah. I know he wants to thank you for what you did."

Portia looked at him, newly alert. "What do you mean?" she said, barely audibly.

"Well, I'm sure you had to argue for him. I know he couldn't have been an easy kid to say yes to. I'm very grateful, too. I was going to write to you," he said, looking away. "I really was."

"It's okay," she told him. "You gave me some good chances, and I really blew them."

He looked at her carefully. He took a long time. She was, she realized, inviting him to make his own conclusions, and when he did, she let him know that they were her conclusions, too.

"Hartland, Vermont?" he said, looking pleased with himself. "That's courtin' distance in New England, you know."

"I beg your pardon?" Portia said.

"Up here in the mountains, courtin' distance is . . . let me see, as far as a cow can travel between milkings."

"Well, I don't know very much about cows, but that does sound unlikely.

I mean, it's got to be fifty miles from here to Hartland. You can't expect a cow to walk that far."

"Did I say walk?" he said archly. "You're totally allowed to load the cow in a truck. Absolutely. It's the twenty-first century!"

Portia laughed. "And you are the authority on this? Do I need to remind you that you grew up on the Main Line?"

"No, please don't. They say it takes three New Hampshire generations before you're not a Flatlander. I'm trying to pass here. If you blow my cover, I'm going to look very uncool."

"Oh yes, I can see you're trying to pass," Portia told him, fingering the sleeve of his blue button-down shirt. "You look quite the native in this fine Brooks Brothers ensemble."

"I am attempting to put the 'gentleman' back in 'gentleman farmer,'" he informed her.

"Well, good luck with that."

He smiled at her. He had, she now recalled, a beautiful smile.

"So you'll stay."

Portia looked again at the volleyball game, in time to see Jeremiah and Nelson, each reaching for the same high ball, crash into each other instead. Jeremiah's parents, it suddenly occured to her, must be here, somewhere. Their son was graduating from high school, and this day with him did not belong to her.

"No. Thank you," she told John. "I'd better keep going. My mother has never asked me for help in her life, but her phone calls are getting a little frantic. I don't think she really remembered how hard it was, having a baby in the house."

"It is hard," he agreed. "But worth it."

"Yes," Portia said carefully. "I'm sure that's true. And I would love to stay, but as you've so charmingly pointed out, I'm going to be close enough to drive a pig on a motorcycle. Or something like that. So another time, yes?"

"Yes." He nodded. "Absolutely, yes. I really am sorry, but I think I need to get back to my post. We have a few end-of-year meetings next week, and then I'm free. Can I call you?"

"Can you ride your heifer over the mountain?" She smiled.

"Yes, exactly."

"I don't see why not. But when you meet my mom, I'd maybe lose the gentleman farmer getup. You know what snobs radical women can be."

"I'll come with my copy of *I'm OK—You're OK.*" He grinned. "I know how to get on her good side."

He didn't seem surprised to be swatted in response to this.

"You don't want to just say hello to Jeremiah?"

Portia turned. She looked for him again and saw that the game was over. Nelson already had drifted off, rubbing an elbow. Jeremiah and another boy were taking down the net, pulling up the stakes. His black hair lifted in the breeze. He seemed to be laughing at something. She wondered what he was laughing about but understood that she could live with not knowing. For today, it was enough that she loved him. Merely loving him—that felt miraculous.

Portia opened her car door. "Another time," she told John. "But congratulate him for me, would you? You're right, it wasn't a straightforward thing, but I don't think I've ever admitted anyone I felt so confident about. He's going to be amazing. He's already amazing. You should be really proud."

John shrugged. "Just a little nurture. He already had the nature, wherever it came from."

He said this in a distracted way, as he was simultaneously pulling her against him, in farewell or in greeting, she wasn't sure. Portia closed her eyes. A number of surprisingly cheerful things occurred to her in rapid succession, but she said none of them out loud. Instead, she hugged him back and said, "Come see me soon."

He laughed. He said: "I'm on my way."

ACKNOWLEDGMENTS

Admission is a work of fiction. With the exception of the Princeton loca-tion, all of the events, people, and stories depicted in this novel are wholly products of my imagination. Apart from the not insignificant qualities of integrity, capability, and dedication to the very complex and difficult work they do, none of the admissions officers in the novel have counterparts at the real Princeton. Any similarities, therefore, are entirely coincidental and not to be considered real.

I would like to thank, in particular, the admissions officers I worked with at Princeton, in my capacity as outside reader, during the 2006 and 2007 admissions seasons. Former Director of Admission Chris Watson (now Dean of Undergraduate Admission at Northwestern) answered my many questions with openness and humor and once told me that everyone who leaves admissions writes a book about it—why shouldn't mine be a novel? Keith Light (Associate Dean of Admission at Princeton and now Associate Director of Admission at Brown) and Assistant Dean of Admis-sion Chris Burkmar were great supervisors. My fellow outside reader Suzanne Buchsbaum thoughtfully read the manuscript. Former Dean of Admission Fred Hargadon provided a historical perspective and was so generous with his time. Finally, I am very grateful to Dean Janet Rapelye for hiring me; I truly loved the work and regard her as the embodiment of grace under pressure.

Others across the admissions landscape gave me their time and insights. I thank Bob Claggett (Dean of Admissions at Middlebury College), Maria Laskaris (Dean of Admissions at Dartmouth College), Holly Burks Becker (Director of College Counseling at the Lawrenceville School), Maggie Favretti (history teacher, Scarsdale High School), and Eli Bromberg (Assis-tant Dean of Admission, Amherst College) for their time and perspectives.

Lisa Eckstrom donated her close reading, great friendship, and add-a-pearl tales of life with a philosopher. Gideon Rosen, professor of philosophy at Princeton, cheerfully supplied nearly everything in this novel that implies a knowledge of matters philosophical. (Who knew that zombies had anything at all to do with philosophy? Not I.) I can never adequately thank Debbie Michel, the Florence Nightingale of plot, for getting me out of tight places and being such a spectacular reader, writer, and all around individual. Suzanne Gluck, the best of all possible agents, and ably supported by assistants past (Georgia Cool) and present (Sarah Ceglarski), has beautifully represented this book. I am incredibly lucky to be in her orbit. I have waited precisely twenty-one years to work with Deb Futter. What can I say? It was worth the wait. (Thanks, too, to her great assistant, Dianne Choie.)

Of the many books on college admissions I have read over the past several years, I particularly admired and made use of two: Jacques Steinberg's *The Gatekeepers: Inside the Admissions Process of a Premiere College* (still the best available depiction of how the process currently works) and Jerome Karabel's *The Chosen: The Hidden History of Admission and Exclusion at Harvard, Yale, and Princeton* (an exhaustive and fascinating history).

Anyone who manages to get their hands on a copy of the 1928 Harvard Yearbook will find a class poem very like the one referred to on page 192. The poet was Charles Cortez Abbott (1906–1986), who would go on to write several books on finance and found the Darden School of Business at the University of Virginia, but not—alas—to publish his poetry. His poem has resonated for me since I first read it, thirty years ago, and I still find it terribly current.

Finally, as the dedication reflects, my greatest thanks must go to my parents, Ann and Burt Korelitz, who have waited far too long to have a book dedicated to them, and who—as they would be the first to tell you—could not have cared less where I went to college.